C000282966

THE
CAPTIVE
WIFE

FIONA KIDMAN

National Library of New Zealand Cataloguing-in-Publication Data

Kidman, Fiona, 1940-
The captive wife / Fiona Kidman.
ISBN 1-86941-686-4
l. Title.
NZ823.2—dc 22

A VINTAGE BOOK
published by
Random House New Zealand
18 Poland Road, Glenfield, Auckland, New Zealand
www.randomhouse.co.nz

First published 2005

© 2005 Fiona Kidman

The moral rights of the author have been asserted

ISBN 1 86941 686 4

Text design: Elin Bruhn Termannsen
Cover illustration: gettyimages
Cover design: Matthew Trbuhovic
Author photograph: Rob Kitchin, *Dominion Post*
Printed in Australia by Griffin Press

Fiona Kidman has written more than 20 books, mainly novels and short stories. Her novel *The Book of Secrets* won the Fiction category of the New Zealand Book Awards, and several others have been short-listed. She has been awarded a number of prizes and fellowships, including the Mobil Short Story Award, the Victoria Writers Fellowship, and the OBE for services to literature. She is a Dame Commander of the New Zealand Order of Merit.

Fiona Kidman lives in Wellington.

For Ian Kidman
and
Niyaz Martin Wilson

AUTHOR'S NOTE

This is a work of fiction based on real events and people.
Their characters are reflected insofar as surviving documents
and accounts can be relied upon. Some of the characters,
both Maori and European, are fictitious.

Contents

BETTY GUARD'S NEW ZEALAND 1830s

Bay of Islands

Mt Taranaki

Cook Strait

Chatham Islands

Moturoa Is.

●Mt Taranaki

Te Namu Pa

Orangituapeka Pa

Waimate Pa

Stephens Is.

Kapiti Is.

Mana Is.

Tory Channel

Arapawa Is.

Port Underwood

Kakapo Bay

Cloudy Bay

Port Nicholson

COOK STRAIT

Before Sydney existed it was a narrow shelf of land along the western bank of a little stream that lost itself in mudflats at the head of a cove. Naked Aborigines speared fish in the tidal waters below and, when they rested, carved shapes of fish on the sandstone rocks above.

When the white men came, the boots of convicts and their guards beat out the first track on Australian soil along that shelf of land. The advance guard of the First Fleet sailed round from the swamps in Botany Bay, edging into Sydney Cove on the evening of 25 January 1788.

This site in the sand was where the first merchants would build their wharves and storehouses, the future main street a shell of roughly level ground between the oyster-covered rocks on the western beach and the high crags above. Next morning, Governor Phillip hoisted his flag near the mouth of the newly found run of fresh water that stole silently through a very thick wood.

Then he looked about for a place to plant his detachment of Marines and a thousand sick, sullen and iron-galled felons.

On the east side of the cove were pitched the tents of the Governor, the Judge-Advocate, the Provost, the Surveyor and some of the Better Class convicts. Across Tank Stream, on the western slope, were placed the main tent rows of the male and female convicts, storehouses and the barrack lines of the Marines.

Near here was the site of the first hospital, its history a litany of how people fail one another, a sight no more terrible than when the three ships of the Second Fleet dropped anchor, foul and stinking from their six months' voyage.

Some died as the ships came up the harbour; for a month after the tides rolled their naked bodies up on the beaches from the Heads to Dawes Point. As each fly-blown wretch fell dead, his companions fell on him like wolves, stripping and dividing the clothing, prising open the stiffening jaws to snatch the half-chewed plug of Brazil tobacco from the dead man's cheek.

More fell dead in their chains and rags, rowed on their last ride ashore. Somewhere close to the running tide lie the bones of the unknown hare-poachers and pickpockets, shovelled into Sydney's first burying ground.

The settlement changed, from a camp to a town, the western shore lined by timber wharves, launching slips and cottages of brick or stone plastered with pipeclay and roofed with shingles or thatch. On the eastern side, mansions rose with domed ballrooms, plate and silverware, and music by night.

Sydney grew up as a garrison town, the barrack walls ten feet in height and two feet thick, built of honey-gold blocks of squared stone pierced by four gates, one on each side of the rectangle. The redcoats moved in and the gallows rose, the brazen notes of trumpets sounded reveille and retreat.

based on found text by GEOFFREY SCOTT

Part 1

The Oystercatchers

Chapter 1

New South Wales, 1826

Today I took the young girl Betsy Parker to collect oysters. She is a beautiful girl. Her hair shines and her teeth can split an apple in one bite. She is just on 12 years, the niece of Charlotte Pugh. I had a great need to get out of my house for there are children underfoot everywhere and I am the father of none of them.

I got myself a house of my own in Cambridge Street, that part of Sydney known as the Rocks. It is down near the sea and close to some good alehouses. I bought it for peace and quiet when I am laying up off the ships which are very crowded and leave a man no time to think. I took on Charlotte Pugh thinking she wd do for me in a useful way. I pay her enough but she is always off with men of 1 kind or another, there are children bawling all over the place. She's a good-looking woman, is Charlotte, or she was when I took her on. I fancied her appearance, tell the truth, even though she had a man who also got work from me, name of Samuel Garside. Well, I could tell he was not up to much. Garside left her with a girl and a boy, and took off to marry another woman. Not that it did him much good for now he's up and died and neither woman got aught but grief. She could have done worse than me. All I ask her to do is keep the house clean and have a hot dinner or 2, and on both counts she does well. She has blue eyes and light red curls and when first I knew her she had a lively way with her. I'll guarantee what she keeps in her little box down there is very nice but it is a crowded house with all that have visited.

When I am off at sea I have only loose women to lay my poker in. I come back looking for a warm hearth, and some good company, but I find the woman who keeps house for me has yet another man under the roof I have paid for, and so she no longer takes my fancy. That is what I tell myself. Her last man was also called Samuel and she has another boy with him, she has called him Samuel too. I guess my name is not right. I am no Samuel, I am just John Guard, and there are times I think I might put the wench out on the street. She should know better. She is a free woman. Her mother and father were government people come in irons, although they have been free people many a year and who am I to talk for I am no better. But she is a currency lass born free, not confined to work for me. Charlotte may go where she pleases and I do not know why she stays here with me.

For the last year or 2 there has been an improvement, except for all these noisy children. So I was coming round to saying well what's done is past and perhaps it's time to settle down, but last week I come in from a long journey round the coast of New Zealand and the ship laden up with seal skins, and I am thinking of what the future might hold, and perhaps I will come across a place in New Zealand to settle down, and what do I find but she has another girl in the house. This is my niece Mr Guard she says, in a voice that tells me she is wheedling again. Other times she will call me Jacky, which is her fond name for me, the 1 she uses when she has made a good stew and there is money in the pot and all is well between us. When she calls me this silly name I sometimes wonder if she wishes she had laid in better store with me. Well I have come close to it time and again. Get in the bed I am going to say and then something holds me back.

At the end of the last trip to sea it had been on my mind again, because I am sick of the bachelor life and afraid to catch the pox but who's to say I won't find it here, and I do not want to cause more Samuels, least not with her. But she is the 1 that warms my hearth, and it might as well be her. And then here is this girl and I change my mind again.

This is Betsy. She is my sister Harriott's girl, Charlotte said, soon as I'm in the door. I knew this for I had seen her once or twice. I went to fetch Charlotte's mother, Granny Pugh, when Charlotte was down with the last baby and it wdn't come. That is where Betsy lives, with Granny Pugh. My mother will know what to do Charlotte said, between her screams and crying and shaking, she can deliver a baby, so I fetched Granny who fished young Samuel out feet first, and all the time Charlotte calling her an old witch and other bad names no woman should know. I saw the girl once or twice after that but I don't let on I know her. At 1st I was very cool towards her.

Your sister, that Harriott, what's she done now, I said to Charlotte, for these Pugh sisters get up to pretty much the same old larks, and Betsy's mother Harriott is known about town for taking off and leaving Stephen Parker alone with the children and then him up and drowning and nobody left to look after the children, except poor old Granny who is past caring for the 3 Parker snot-noses. While Harriott has more and more children with the sawyer John Deaves.

My mother is dead Charlotte said and I should have seen it right away, the way she was dressed head to foot in black and her hair hidden away.

There are 3 children in this house already I told her, sharp as a razor and it's true I'd have ripped the bitch's throat out on the spot for I can see what is coming next. I don't want another 3. I know I should tell her that I am sorry about Granny Pugh for it's true, she was a good woman in old age, though given to fighting and spitting when she were young, from all accounts. She had more than her fair share of trouble and I am sorry to hear that she is gone.

I do not want Harriott's children in this house I said. There is not enough room for all of us here now. We have gone over this before.

It is just this 1. Betsy.

Where are the other ones? I said, although I knew the answer.

They are in the orphanage where Granny put them.

Well that is where they will have to stay I said.

She did not put Betsy in the orphanage, she is too old, she is 12 already.

All this time Betsy Parker was looking at me with a bold stare, the way those Pugh women have, a look that says come here and I think I can not have seen it right, remembering she is a girl. Her dark hair falls in waves about her shoulders and I'd have put her at older than her years, already she is growing tits.

Harriott is sorting things out said Charlotte. John Deaves has told her he will put a ring on her finger and make an honest woman out of her and they will bring the children back to their place. He is finding a bigger place to live. Meantime Betsy is helping with the little ones. She is a good girl, very capable.

I had to agree the children were quieter and not so much snot around their noses as I'm used to seeing. Still they huddled in a mass like ants around the jam, which I cannot stand.

I looked at Betsy and saw the girl is not so much bold as sad and frightened, willing me not to turn her away. I recalled this one was Granny Pugh's favourite. I guessed she was fretting. Tears filled her eyes that are handsome and large with heavy lashes. Her tears did not fall.

You can stay the week I said. But remember my brother is coming here to stay soon and there will not be much room. My brother Charles is a sevener too, like I was, my little brother who I reckon had himself sent to Australia so he could be near to me, not that there is much I can do for him until he's done his time, but that is nearly here. He did not take to convict life easy. He looked one sick canary when first I saw him. The yellow uniform that is for the bad convicts did not flatter his complexion, reflected the whites of his eyes. He was flogged more than once or twice, 150 lashes once. I wished he could see, as I did early on, that it's better to be agreeable to the guvs. It's the quickest way to freedom. Already when he came I was on my way to better things because I did what I was told and planned the day when I wd be free and got out sooner than my time. It pays to lick an arse or 2, they taste better than maggots in a stew. But Charley has had to serve his full 7 years. He has been an assigned convict servant to a Mrs Harris for some time and does not have to wear uniforms any more so things is getting better and soon they will let him off, but he has made things harder for himself than he need have done.

I told Betsy you better come with me.

Where are you taking her Charlotte said.

To find some peace and quiet.

You're a grown man, don't go friggin' with her.

I'll frig who I like I told her. I was about to add that I wd have frigged with her long ago if she had kept herself to herself but she wants to hear nothing from me.

Jacky, Charlotte said. I know she's serious, taking a risk with me when I'm in a mood because by now I was. She is a good girl.

I can see that, I said, come on Betsy. I grabbed the girl by the wrist. We're going for a walk you and me.

As we walked towards Sydney Cove beyond the port my spirits lifted. The sky was a dark blue and the sea serene. I saw 2 ships unfurling their sails as they set out on an ocean voyage, making white splashes on the ocean. Behind us the town lay peaceful the spires of the churches lifting near as high as the big Norfolk pines that stood on guard along the shore.

You want oysters that are plump I said to Betsy when we was at the mudflats. You want them big just when they're ready to spawn nice fat oysters. There's some think them too rich when they're fat but I like 'em creamy and moist. How do you like your oysters Betsy?

Fat she said, turning over what I had said. I always gave the fat ones to Granny and David to make them strong. Sophia didn't like them, I think she's too young. I don't know what they give them to eat in the orphanage Mister Guard. I am afraid David will die there, he's just a little boy.

I felt sorry for her then because I know what it is like to be worried on account of a brother. She was kneeling on the rocks looking out for oysters. I could not help myself. I put my hand on her head. It felt like an egg shell and as if it wd break as easy. She sat very still, not moving, as if she was expecting something. As if she knew I could do what ever I want with her. I took my hand away and she stayed sitting like that.

Aren't you worried for your sister too I asked her.

She is a girl and they will not hurt her the way they do the boys she said in a low voice that I could hardly hear. Besides she is like me, she is quick to go about what she is told. When she said that I thought clever girl, this 1 thinks like me. But David is slower she went on he is very small for his years and he had the measles not long ago. I thought he wd die. I don't know whether Granny told them that.

Perhaps your mother can.

My mother. She straightened herself up and surprised me with a knowing look. She pulled a face, her tongue pushing out her lips. I saw she knows what's what.

Your mother will take you all home. I said this to comfort her but she pretended she had not heard.

We looked around the mudflats and down below there was lazy oysters, a gang of them all together, which is what oysters like to do. You will not find an oyster on its own. You can hear oysters whistle to each other. I've heard some argue this is nonsense but it is true, oysters sing when they are together.

The girl looked at me intent not as if I am a crazy old man.

I am old enough to be her father twice over but when I thought about her little snatch I felt myself stiffen up. I told myself stern as I could, keep your pricker down John or it'll be on its way to harm.

Instead I showed her how to open the oysters even though I suppose she must have done it before for who else wd have opened them for Granny Pugh. We now had a couple of buckets full. I took my knife from my belt and rested an oyster on a shelf, flat side up. I showed her how to push the knife through the shell and lever up the hinge. Push, push down on the knife I said. She has a lot of strength and did it in a trice.

I slid the knife beneath the oyster, cutting through the muscle and lifting it on to the frilly cup that is the top shell.

You must eat them off the shell I told her. They are best eaten without rinsing I say quite soft for I want her to have the 1st one.

The sea was coming up in little waves and the air turned cool for this time of year for we are in November now when the days are long and the temperature stays up here in Sydney. I watched the way Betsy opened her red mouth and put the oyster on her tongue, letting it sit there a moment with her lips parted. Then she closed them round the fish and swallowed swift but still I thought I saw the path of the fish in her throat as it travelled down. We opened oyster after oyster and I fed them to her 1 after another.

When she had eaten a dozen or more and I had had my fill we took the rest home.

We shall have an oyster stew tonight I said. It is my favourite. Charlotte banged about a bit because it takes more than 1 pan to make her best stew. But she is out to please me. When the stew was ready the kitchen filled with a warm muggy smell. Soon we were content and fed for the night. Betsy cleaned the pans and then took herself off to bed, top and tailing with Charlotte's oldest boy.

When the children were settled I said to Charlotte, that girl has been through hard times.

Happen she has. Charlotte does not give much away.

Her mother should know better.

I'll not have you talking about my family like that said Charlotte snappy like.

Ah the pot calling the kettle black.

You don't need to talk like that.

You women lie down too easy I said.

My children are all with me.

Because I put a roof over their heads.

She did not answer that. Charlotte is 26 years old. Her face has become puffy and pale, the eyes once like blue lightning are often dull.

I am afraid for the girl I said, turning her argument against her. Afraid you'll put her to some young stud before she's ready.

Oh don't tell me John Guard she says, don't you tell me you never took advantage. What is in your head with this girl. *Fair maid is a lily o*.

I heard her mother's voice then. Granny Pugh was always full of old sayings, she had a rhyme for everything. But this is 1 I know for it is said also by men with a laugh in their voices not to mention hope. It is about a girl who says yes to everything a man puts to her. A woman who says yes too easily. *Gently Johnny my jingalo*.

I did not say these words, did not give her the satisfaction of knowing whether they are familiar to me or not. Instead I turned a dark look on her that silenced her.

I am putting out to sea again next week I said after a bit. Leaving that to hang in the air.

You're hardly back said Charlotte, like she is unsettled by me coming and going.

Perhaps it is me she wants after all, but the moment was over long ago. I do not want to hold Charlotte, not even to cool me down. I wd see to that business down the street when I had done talking with her. Even though I am tired of hooers and their tricks but what is a man to do.

I said to her, I will take the girl with me.

You cannot.

I can I said. She will be all right with me.

I am not myself. I am a man who likes my own company well enough, that is all. It is said of me that I'm a loner but that is because men who are in charge of things do not go about telling the world their thoughts. Although there are things I need from a woman, I have never taken a woman to sea. Now I found some idea stirring in me that is strange to me.

She is my daughter's girl said Charlotte. You cannot take her.

I could. We both knew that. I could have put down 20 pound on the table and the girl wd be mine.

Something made me stop.

I put down 12 sovereigns on the table. She is to go to school I said.

Charlotte looked at the money. That is not enough to keep her. She has gone and got herself a job. She is going to work for the Jews who have opened for trade up George Street.

All right I said, putting 10 pounds on the table and making sure to take the sovereigns back. There is Ragged School at the end of the week. See she learns to read and write and do some sums.

Charlotte sniffed and twisted her shoulders. I could tell she was jealous.

I put some sovereigns back, 3 or 4. That is for you.

All right she said brightening up.

And then I said here is another tenner. It is for Harriott to get her children back from that orphanage. Though why I'm putting money in John Deaves' pocket which is where it will end up is more than I can tell.

Charlotte looked at me as if I'm peculiar which perhaps I am.

Chapter 2

Sydney, 1829

From behind the pages of her book, an account of the fall of
Rome, Miss Adie Malcolm watches the girl in the third row
of desks. Although it is autumn, it is not the season as the teacher
knows it. She sighs noisily, not just because a hot breath of wind
is torching everything in its path, and the schoolroom is like a
furnace, but because she knows her task is thankless. Why speak
of classical Rome or the miracles of Greek architecture to
children who will never experience these glorious creations,
never see the Sistine Chapel or the Parthenon? It seems only
yesterday that Miss Malcolm had travelled to Athens, accompanied by her brother, visiting the great Temple of Poseidon before
setting forth for the Greek countryside. It was at the temple that
she had had her first intimation of how scandalously the young
could behave. In recent months, it had been discovered that a
certain Lord Byron had etched his name upon one of the sacred
bricks, as if he were a common thug, a vandal with no respect for
the work of the masters. Better that he is dead, Miss Malcolm

thinks, as she watches her charges laboriously write their essays. His much praised verses were downright immoral. Romantic and sentimental, the way the girls among her charges would be, given half a chance.

When she thinks of her brother, Miss Malcolm trembles; it was in his hands she had trusted herself to come to this distant country, far away from home. 'Adie,' said Percy, 'now that our parents have died, we're free to go to the new world, to make a brave, fresh start. Just you and me. We've seen enough of the old world — why don't we strike out for Australia?'

Sailing across the world — it was not what Miss Malcolm had imagined might happen to her. She would have been happy to remain in the house in Lincoln where she grew up, but Percy was always a boy with a heart set on adventure, and she couldn't, for the life of her, see herself being left alone. But of course, that is exactly what has happened. He'd stepped ashore in Sydney and in the space of a month had been discovered by Miss Maude Hatherley, a spinster of even more indeterminate age than Adie Malcolm herself, who didn't seem to mind a man who was plain in his appearance, provided he had means. Although, as it turns out, Maude is not quite past child-bearing age. Adie shudders to think of it. And so much for her new life; she is a governess again, exactly as when she left the shores of England, and the nearness of all she considered beautiful and worthwhile. Although, for now, until something better comes up, she supervises a class of ragged children in what passes for a school. The school meets for three days a week, designed to serve the needs of children who work for the rest of the week.

'Please Miss,' says a girl in the third row of desks. That girl.

'Yes, Betsy.' Miss Malcolm's stays are troubling her, much too tight for the Sydney climate, and for a moment she can hardly breathe. A river of perspiration runs between her buttocks. She hopes that the girl will not ask for anything that will require her to move from behind her desk.

'I need more ink, Miss.'

'Ink? Well, I dare say you do, Betsy, given that from where I'm sitting you appear to have more ink than words spread around your page. I told you to fill your inkwells before class began. Did you not do that?'

'I forgot.'

'You forgot. Yes, Betsy Deaves, you forget a great deal of what I say to you. What goes on in that head of yours when I'm talking?'

The girl stares back at Miss Malcolm as if she is her jailer. 'My name's Elizabeth Parker.'

'I have you here as Betsy Deaves. I don't think you know who you are.' She feels inclined to slap the girl, give her a smart knock with her pointer, only Betsy, or Elizabeth, call her who you will, suddenly looks larger and stronger than Miss Malcolm had realised. The wild notion that she could be attacked, here in Sydney, in this pit of iniquity, is not beyond the imagination. Betsy, for that is the name that has been given to Miss Malcolm by Mr Spyer, who is the girl's sponsor for a position in this school, has dark eyes that roam the room when she is being spoken to, as if she is a captive bird looking for an open window, or just a ray of sunshine, despite the shutters that cover the glass halfway up. Betsy wears a brown cotton shift that fits too snugly over her well-developed breasts. Miss Malcolm worries that the girl will come too close to her, that she might brush against her with her ripe young body. Miss Malcolm has not seen her own body unclothed from top to bottom for twenty years and there is something too immediate and intimate about Betsy's physical presence that alarms her.

If she had had her way, Betsy wouldn't have been allowed to come to class in the first place. But her supervisor, the principal of the Church of England's School for Convicts' children, had said she believed the girl not beyond redemption, and that Mr Spyer's intervention was an admirable thing, given his own background. Betsy came from an unusually troubled home, even in this troubled place, and her mother no better than she should be. Still, the supervisor had reminded Miss Malcolm, in a voice that allowed no room for argument, there was room for rehabilitation among the souls of convicts, especially the children, so that they might not go on and offend as their parents had; it was up to them to do their best. Betsy, she said, had demonstrated a great aptitude for figures that should be encouraged before it was too late.

But it was already too late, Miss Malcolm might have said, only she dared not. She is stout, with short teeth and long gums, not a naturally prepossessing woman but one whose strength is measured by her willingness to impart knowledge and her ability to keep discipline. There are more than enough unemployed governesses in the colonies, and she does not wish to join their ranks. All the same, she feels it her duty to point out that, at fourteen, Betsy is a head taller than most of the other miscreants in the class, and that disciplining her is quite a different matter from six cuts of the cane on an outstretched palm, or the bent over bottom of the younger malcontents.

All the supervisor says, by way of response, is that she is sure Miss Malcolm will find the girl a fair sponge for knowledge. And this is what bothers Miss Malcolm most, that Betsy Deaves does soak up knowledge, and when there is not enough of it, she gets bored and makes trouble.

Her hand is up again. 'Yes, Elizabeth,' she hears herself say, as if in a dream, knowing the girl has won a round.

'Could we do more sums, Miss? I can't make no sense of this.'

'Any sense. You must say, any sense, not no sense.'

'Yes, Miss.' Is it possible that a grin trembles at the corners of the girl's red mouth? And, in the same moment, it occurs to her that Elizabeth, or whoever she is, might pinch her lips to make them look like that.

'Your enthusiasm for calculation is admirable, young lady, but you must complete one task at a time.'

'I don't see what this has got to do with me.'

Ah yes, Elizabeth, Miss Malcolm thinks inwardly, you have

put your finger on it. We are of an accord. 'It is important that you learn about the great civilisations of the old world,' she says stiffly, 'in order to understand the moral dilemmas of the new.'

'Where is this Acropolis?' the girl asks, trying to stifle a yawn but not quite covering her strong white teeth. She pronounces the word with an emphasis that makes it sound like Acropole-is, and Miss Malcolm thinks this is done on purpose. How frightening to think that the girl might really be clever.

'A*crop*olis,' she corrects. 'It is in Athens in Greece. Far across the sea, a great journey from here. It is one of the temples that form the sacred triangle, with Poseidon at Cape Sounias and Athena on the island of Aegina, built for the gods.'

'That's not what I've heard about God.'

'Different,' says Miss Malcolm, 'and I'd thank you to remember that.' Even as she speaks, the spectre of unemployment rears itself anew. She can see that it has been an error to discuss her passion for classical mythology in this place. Unless there is some swift divine intervention she will find herself branded an heretic. She, who has prayed nightly and painfully on her knees, since her own girlhood. An ink bomb explodes on the floor beside her. As she looks frantically around to find the source, she sees there is no way of telling where it comes from. One of the O'Leary boys no doubt, longing for expulsion, so he can run free and make mischief. There is no place for children with names like theirs in a school for Protestant children, but everything is upside down in this part of the world. If she sees Elizabeth smile again, she may not be able to refrain from striking her across the cheek, slapping that look off her face. She might even be able to convince the principal that the girl is inciting the younger children to wickedness, especially the boys, who are bent on impressing her.

Betsy, or Elizabeth, stares straight at Miss Malcolm and says: 'I'm about to make a journey across the sea.'

'And where do you think you might be going?' Miss

Malcolm asks, hoping that sarcasm will quell the ripple of unrest that threatens chaos in the room.

'I'm going to New Zealand. Today is my last day.' At last, the tension is broken, the children turning their full attention to their classmate.

'Really, but you should have told me. I had no idea.' Relief is making Miss Malcolm voluble. 'And what will your parents be doing in New Zealand?'

'My father, as you know, is dead,' says Betsy steadily, 'and my mother is not coming with me.'

'You have a position to go to? A maid perhaps?'

'No, I might have a maid of my own. I'm to be wed in the morning. Don't you wish you were me, Miss Malcolm?'

'I do not believe you, you wicked creature. You're a lying girl as well as a blasphemous one.'

'I did not blaspheme Miss, not at all, I take the word of God very serious, and as God is my witness, I will be wed in the church in the morning. My husband-to-be is a man I have known for some years, for he was an acquaintance of my father, and a friend of my aunt who also works for him. He has been what you might call my gentleman caller, though he doesn't have to call to see me, for nearly three years. Jacky is a man any girl would be proud to marry, quite tall, or at least tall enough, for already I'm taller than most men I know. His beard is black, and his voice like thunder when he is angry, though he never is with me. He has his own station in New Zealand where whales are trapped and boiled down — he tells me all about it when he sets me on his knee. I am going to keep the records for him and enter his ledgers with the coming and going of the money he gathers. And so, Miss, I am taking my leave.'

Chapter 3

4 June 1829

My dear and esteemed brother

I believe it is time that I gave you news of myself, and what is happening in Sydney.

I continue to live in this boarding house, respectable enough in its way, run as it is by a Mrs Watson. The meals are regular and the rooms kept clean and so far we have had no rascals allowed past the door, although you would not believe how the town is overflowing with them these days. Certainly, you were wise to leave Sydney and move to a more salubrious place. I have a picture of you in my mind at this very moment, seated on the verandah of the lovely house that you and Maude have been so fortunate to acquire. You will be looking across green fields and the spring blossom in flower, just like dear old England. Yes, you are far better out of it, especially now that a blessed event is coming your way, and indeed, I do understand what a great surprise it must have been to you and my dear sister-in-law when you learned this news. There are fights here that make the hair on my head stand up of its own accord, and is not something that the young should ever be exposed to. The last few nights some entrepreneurial fellow has been charging three shillings a half hour to watch Aboriginals doing club fights with one another.

One of the Aboriginals was seriously wounded the other evening, which has been the cause of much conversation. I dined with Mrs Roddick one night, whose husband is Lieutenant Gerald Roddick of the 50th Dragoons. I first met her at a church meeting. She, poor soul, was frightened out of her wits, as she had had to go and fetch a doctor for little Austen who has been taken ill with a bad chest cold, and on her way home she came upon this frightful spectacle, which has left her in a state of shock. It is hard for the women when their husbands are away, as is Lieutenant Roddick, who has been at Norfolk Island. A lady at dinner, overhearing this conversation, did mention that it was one way to get rid of these savages from the streets, if they are all killing each other off. But I am of the opinion that these are souls that might be saved, and we should not write them off to oblivion so easily. Still, I am in no mind to go about the task of saving them myself, it is difficult enough looking after my charges at this wretched school where I am landed up at the moment. There are girls taller and stronger than me, and one of them challenged me just a few days ago in a way that quite took my breath away. Her name is Betsy Deaves (she calls herself Elizabeth Parker in moments of high-mindedness), the daughter of a slattern from the Rocks and a man now dead in Sydney Harbour, some say he drowned himself out of grief when she left him. Yet the way she looked at me, you would think she saw herself as superior. Then she told me she was getting married. I hope for her sake there is a marriage band at the end of it. If she is anything like her mother, I would not be surprised if she is simply running off with the man. It is very unsettling to be *so close* to God knows what awfulness.

I do the best I can to stay cheerful. Governor Darling has assured Mrs Roddick's husband and his regiment that he will not allow the emancipist sympathisers to gain the upper hand. All the same, it is troubling that people should want the ex-convicts, the ticket of leave men, to have the same rights as free people here. It's even been suggested that they should sit on juries. What is the world coming to? I wonder, did that possibility occur to you when we set out for Australia?

My dear brother, forgive me, I should tear this up and start all over again, for that sounds like a reproach, but just think of it as the musing of your Big Sister, Addled Adie, as you used to call me when you were a wee boy, all for a jape. I could never be cross with you for a moment. All the same, it is a dangerous town, and I feel that, not only might I have some respite from it, but I might also be of great assistance to Maude, when her time comes. I learned many little nursing skills when I attended our mother, during the last years of her life. No, no, there I go again, I know that a lying in is not a deathbed, but Maude will need someone to bring her cool drinks and change her sheets regularly, and I would like to think that it was done by none other than,

Your own and always loving

Sister Adie.

PS Mrs Roddick has suggested I might call her Emmeline when we are alone together. I am glad to have one good friend.

LETTER FROM MR PERCEVAL MALCOLM, PARRAMATTA, NEW SOUTH WALES TO HIS SISTER, MISS ADELINE MALCOLM, ROSEWOOD BOARDING HOUSE FOR LADIES, CASTLEREAGH STREET, SYDNEY

12 October 1829

Dear Adeline

I cannot keep silent on the subject of your last visit here, which pained my wife greatly.

It grieves me that I must write to you in this manner; it is not what our parents would have wished. I have always deferred to you as my older sibling, and I do not ignore the consideration that you have shown me in the past. However, as a married man with a child, I must now assume the role of Head of the Family, and observe the duties that go hand in hand with that responsibility. My dear Maude had made great preparation for her lying in, and everything was put in its proper place when you arrived and took over our household. But nothing was to your liking. You shifted every little thing about our house, so that the servants were unable to find anything. You criticised and carped about so many of our domestic arrangements, that I swear you turned the milk sour more than once. It is no thanks to you that our son was born in good health, for my dear lady was in such a state of agitation when the hour came, that she might have died. I am not accustomed to the sounds of such anguish.

I spoke to her gently after you had left, and said, dearest, what did my sister say to you to make you carry on in such a way, with such coarse and dreadful language? What provoked it?

She turned away from me and said it was nothing, I should not take too much from it, which I thought very loyal and discreet, not wanting to offend our once tender relationship.

I have said to her that you must not, I will not allow you, to come to the house again, or not for a very long time, until you see fit to make amends and she has gratefully accepted this assurance.

As for your own situation, I beg you to take stock of your life. There are plenty of opportunities for women out here. I am sure you can better your position if you put your mind to it. Marriage may be out of the question, but you mentioned earlier that you had made some friends. Seek out their society, I beg of you, and leave well alone. Avoid the emancipists and those who would perform useless tasks in the service of the Aboriginals and the criminal elements. It is all in vain. They must learn their place.

Thank you for your inquiry about our son. Young Herbert is doing very well.

Yours respectfully,

Your brother, Percy Malcolm

Chapter 4

JOURNAL OF JOHN GUARD

At sea, August 1826

I was born in the Parish of St Marylebone 1792. I remember Mother, she had a face that was pale and decent, and hands that held me kindly and there was food on the table when she was there. I still see the way her wedding ring cut into her finger. Father kept a strict house, he believed it is the duty of a man to set a good example, and the wife to do as her husband tells her. My mother was such a woman. But that is about all I can tell of her for she died when my brother was born, the 1 time she disobeyed Father for he pleaded something dreadful that she would not go and leave him. I never saw my father so unhappy. Father's sister, she was a hard woman, stayed in the house after Mother was gone. She cooked us gruel and meat and veg., but it was never the same again. Father made us learn to read and write though my brother young Charles took to it more easily than I did. And then Father died and that was that and we found he had no money left. I have wondered what my aunt knew of it but what is gone is gone. Before he died he gave me a book he said was as good as the Good Book itself and had much in it that I could learn from, it is all I have of the old life. The book is called *The Whole Duty of Man* and lays out all the things a man should do in life. I took to looking after Charles who I call Charley. We had not much stuff, no blankets to speak of for they had gone to the bed of my aunt who had left by then and good riddance. I took a quilt from a house that was open 1 day, meaning to give it to my brother for he felt the cold, that boy. That is 1 thing I will say about him coming to Australia, his chest is strong now, the heat has done him good.

That was when I was arrested and put on charge. 7 yrs transportation for a bloody quilt, and not much of a 1 at that. 1st I stayed aboard a hulk moored in the Thames for 2 yrs before they took me to Australia.

I was stripped of all my clothes. We was issued with slop clothing, very coarse upon the skin, grey and marked with broad arrows, hemp shirt, jacket and breeches and a cap, double irons on our legs. You is felons now they reminded us, as if we needed reminding. Then we got sent to our deck. Things were not so bad on the upper and middle decks. This was where they sent you if you did their bidding. But at the beginning all of us men and women together were sent to the bottom of the hulks where there were no portholes so it was dark and the air smelt foul. The hammocks was slung close together, elbow to elbow, in rows each side of the deck. At the head of the lower deck was a black hole, a punishment cell where prisoners were kept in solitary if they broke the rules. It is hard not to break the rules when you cannot move for the press of bodies. People broke down and cried for where they were and that was enough to go to the hole. I swore I wd never get put inside the black hole. I learnt to please the masters. Some of the other prisoners I beg your pardon felons said you are a crawling bastard Guard but when I got more rations for them they stopped their name calling and gave thanks to have me speak on their behalf.

I will get out of this malarkey early on I said to myself. And that is what I did.

I got ready to put to sea as soon as I was a free man. I planned to go to India, to pick up spices and all that trade, but that was when I get word that my brother was coming to do his 7 yrs. Keep it in the family. I thought I cannot go to sea until I have seen my brother. 7 yrs had passed too since I last set eyes on him. Charley was not happy but there was naught I could do for him and at least I had seen him.

It was the girl who made me think of writing things down. The day I took Betsy to pick oysters, the day I said she had to go to school, I wrote down what had happened. It is the kind of thing my Father wd have had me do. He was never a man of greatness but he worked in the city and he read books. When I think of him, I think it should not just end here with me dead, which could happen any time, the life I lead. I could be left behind on some Godforsaken island along with the circling birds and the seals and my bones picked clean and nobody wd know who I was but perhaps this book wd remain. Somebody needs to know something of us, my bro. and me, and where we come from.

Perhaps my brother will have children, it is not too late.

I wd have liked to have a son but as I have not found a woman who pleases me, it might be that it will never happen. In my Father's book, the 1 he gave to me, it says women should have quietness about them, for all the ill fruits of a wife's unquietness are notorious and few neighbourhoods free of them. By that I suppose it means men are driven to drink and other women by their noise. All of this was written 100 yrs or more ago by a man who wd not have known that Australia was in the world. What wd he know of the noise of a forward wife if he had not seen the things I have and heard the things I have heard? No it is better left. The book has no advice strong enough for the wives of the Rocks and I am a man who likes silence more than company.

The girl is naught but a child. Still I tell her you must learn to read and write. Perhaps it will change something in her and things that might befall her.

Meanwhile I write as if I am telling her this story that is mine. What follows is an account of where I have been and what I have done since they set me free from my captivity.

After I waited for Charley to arrive, I had to give away the idea of sailing to India and find another ship. This I did. I sailed with Captain Siddins on a sealing expedition aboard the *Lynx*. We headed for Deception Island which is in the South Shetland Islands south of Cape Horn. Word had got out of a giant seal ground there. We took ourselves there for the season which is very short with high hopes for a rich catch and not too long at sea. But dangerous. Mountains of sea all about. Gale force winds continuous. Deception Island is a mountain, about 9 miles across with a harbour which is landlocked but for a narrow entrance. At least it offers shelter if you make it without running aground, as many do. This is where we put down anchor. We got there in December when a blood red sun come up out of the dark which is as close to summer as it gets. The harbour was filled up with ships come from Nantucket and Britain and none of the crews too friendly towards each other. Think on it. All of us thinking we would be the 1st.

Blood is all about and precious little else. Each 1 of us takes a thick wooden stave studded with nails. We go to the rookery and there we club the fur seals and sea lions till they die. Birds above scream and whirl. The creatures bark and roar. There is a stink that no man can describe of the rotten carcasses of 1s clubbed and skinned in the days before. But a man gets skill at this. You learn quick how to kill with 1 blow.

That year we come back with 5000 sealskins worth a guinea a piece. Sounds v. good. We expected more. At least I know then how to kill a seal.

Life at sea suits me. I can stand the waves without a sickness in my stomach and the masters told me straight up that I am quick to learn. That is the difference between me and my bro. Charley is good at reading and talking but he wd be no good at sea. I have always had a quickness about me. A man at sea needs to read the way weather will turn in the blink of an eye, and which way the fish and animals of the sea will run. Or when a man will turn ugly. These are things you do not find in books, not even the good book Father gave to me. They are what a man knows. Next I tried out whaling for I heard there is good money to be made, there being high demand for oil for lighting and bone for corsets. I set off aboard the *Woodlark*.

The mastheads at sea are manned from sunrise to sunset. Every seaman takes a turn of 2 hours standing on the cross-trees. Some days in the tropics it is a good feeling, 100 ft above the water in the balmy air. I feel closer to the Lord, and far above the muck of men who live like pigs in the straw below. In winter it is colder than a frog's tit.

The 1st day we caught a whale was about midday. It was a good day, fine and sunny. I was on the top gallant cross-trees. About a mile leeward I saw the spouting of many whales. Thar she blows I shouted, the whalers' cry. A pod of sperm whales heaved before us.

The captain ordered the lookouts down to the deck to help launch 3 boats from their davits. Then the Captain told 1st mate to take over the ship while he went headsman for 1 of the whaleboats. I was ordered into it to take an oar with a man called Rangi. He was a savage from New Zealand. I found it strange for though he was strong and a good sailor he was not the same colour as me and at first I was afraid to touch his skin, but there are worse things under Heaven, and aboard that ship, and I grew used to him. Everyone kept a very civil tongue when talking to him for he was considered the best harpooneer.

We hit the water hard, and rowed towards the whales. Within striking distance we laid up our oars and turned on the brute. Rangi stood up steady against the thwart a lance in his hand. He raised his arm above his head and thrust it deep in the whale's shiny black side. The whale lashed the sea with its tail. Its huge head came up out of the water as high as Tower Bridge. It was frenzy and madness out there. We stood in danger of being sucked beneath the waves. The Captain ordered Stern All and gave the harpoon line 2 turns around the loggerhead. The line rushed out. The Captain and Rangi changed places, the Captain in the bow holding another lance. That whale took us all near to damnation. The Captain lunged with the lance. The whale dived deep and we went racing along holding fast on the line. I thought we would be taken to the bottom of the sea.

So it went. The whale came up over and again, another lance. If I was a soft man I might have wept. For when it comes close I look for a moment that seems like eternity into the whale's eye, it is big and plummy and soft like a cow's and full of agony I cannot describe. It is animal and human at the same time. I am a little lad again and I seen my Mother's face flash before me and I silence a cry inside me.

But I was there to kill a whale not cry about it. Next thing the creature rose beneath the 3rd boat, smashed it to pieces, and while we were busy getting ready to finish off this bastard, the other boats were picking up the men. The whale was done for, blood and froth coming out of its blowhole. The Captain put it out of its misery.

It was left to Rangi then to put the blubber hook in its side so the whale could be winched up on the deck. The weight of the whale was very great. The ship heeled over as it was lifted on board.

And that was my first whale. We cut the head off while it was still in the sea, and brought this on board on its own, the jaw and teeth taken out. A whale has 42 teeth. And inside the head there is the most valuable oil which is spermaceti, it is v. fine oil. We lowered our buckets over and again into the head and casked it before we tried the blubber. After the excitement of the chase it is dirty work, stripping the blubber. It is like peeling an orange. We collected the bits from the Mincer, wielding his long and dangerous knife, and passed them to the try-pots. The try-works is between the foremast and main mast, a brick kiln that heats 2 pots that are near the height of a man. The furnace is underneath the pots.

We used wood to start the fires but after the 1st oil had been boiled out we used some of it as fritters to keep the fires going. Darkness had come upon us by then and it took us all the whole night long of cutting and passing the whale and stoking the fires. The sky was lit up by the roaring fires and some of us kept watch lest the sails should catch alight. It must be like that in hell. The noise went on and on until it was morning. Some men were complaining of their backs and asking for rations of rum. They were slackers and I could not be bothered with them. I said you may take your rest but I want my pockets full of gold when I put into port and the master will not pay us if you put yourselves to bed. After awhile they came around and kept on working. When the day broke we decanted the warm oil into casks, then closed them up for sealing and storing in the hold. The filth of what we had done was everywhere. There was no getting away from sweat and blood and the whole ship covered in soot which we must clean before we could rest.

Afterwards we had double rations of rum and I give Rangi a cuff about the head as meant for a comrade. And now I look back and see the look that passed through his eyes. I am a chief he says to me, I am related to Te Rauparaha.

And who may he be when he is at home I said.

You are fortunate he said that we are at sea and you do not know any better but I am a chief among Maoris and you do not touch the head of a chief. He sounded like a missionary the way he talked. As if he was an Englishman. Not surprising, for he had lived some while with the Reverend Samuel Marsden in Sydney who is a pious kind of bastard though it is not for me to use profane words when speaking of men of the cloth.

And why is that I asked not taking him in a serious way.

His head is tapu he said, not to be touched by other men. It is a sacred place. If you was to do that when you was among my people it would be an insult that would carry death and those with you would be killed as well.

But I would not know this I protested.

That is no excuse said this savage and I was close to felling him for this was silly talk but there was a look in his eye that told me it would be just as well to hold my wrath. I did not say that I had seen the head of many a Maori chief or otherwise dried up like old leather and bartered for souvenirs in Sydney streets. There is a move to stop this trade. I have never thought to buy 1 for myself, not finding in them the kind of decoration I fancy. Instead I asked him who is this Robulla or whatever his name is.

He told me that I must not say his name like that. Te Rauparaha he said. You say it. And he wd tell me nothing more until I said it to his liking and then he spelled it for me too. Te Rauparaha is the big chief, the biggest of them all, a fighting man who has beaten all the other tribes around him in war. You should meet him Rangi said for he wants to do trade and barter with English ships. He told me how Te Rauparaha had made his headquarters on Kapiti Island (which I have heard sailors speak of, I think it the same one they call Entree Island). This island is near Cook Strait that runs between the 2 big islands of New Zealand. Te Rauparaha has food and flax to barter for white man's goods and muskets in particular. I am making a note of all of this because I know there is a big demand for flax in Sydney right now for making sails and coarse cloth to dress the convicts in their uniforms and the best rope that money can buy with which to hang them. Well business is business and I want to make my fortune quick. I like the sound of this place New Zealand. I think I will have a look at it before too long.

Which happened soon after when I went aboard another sealing ship this time as master. The ship was the *Harriet*, a barque of 240 ton owned by a ship builder name of Captain Underwood back in Sydney. He was once a convict like me. He come up to me one day and said I hear you are a man with a talent for the sea and know how to read and write a log book. I said, yes mister, for I am not giving any credit to another convict until he proves his worth.

You can keep your head and do not take to drink at sea Underwood said.

That is so I said for I place a value on my skin.

I have heard that men will take orders from you.

Is that right now I said for I had not heard that said in my presence.

I will make you a ship's captain.

Well you are talking now sir I said. And good day to you and thanks Captain.

Thus I went sailing in the deep south in what is known as New Zealand waters, so all the time I was coming closer to that country. On our way north the ship was laden with 4200 seal skins and 2 ton of oil. We stopped off in the port at Kororareka, a grog town in the Bay of Islands so my feet was finally on New Zealand soil. There we took our rest and everything else on offer. I smoked a pipe or 2 of opium brought in on a ship from the East and my head was filled with dreams of girls and then there were brown girls theirselves that twined around my body 2 at a time. When I woke my body was full of sweet ease and my pockets empty. 1 of my men came to tell me there was a ship anchored in the Bay and that it was taken over by convicts on board being transported to Norfolk Island. A mutiny no less. Well who am I who was a convict to ask questions and I am not here to tame my fellow men unless they should be working for me. But they looked a bunch of rascals.

Some Maoris in their war canoe had tried to help the captured crew and the convicts had shot them up very bad and a missionary asked me wd we help to sort this matter out. It will do me no harm I thought to see if this matter can be settled. Call me a turncoat if you will but a man has to do what is best for his self. If I had turned a blind eye they might say I was as bad as them. A man always has to be on the lookout if he is not to end up back inside. We opened fire and shot up all the sails and then the hull of the pirate ship and the whole lot of them surrendered and that was that.

By now I was getting rich enough and somewhat tired of all the sailing around so I set up house in Cambridge Street in the Rocks district of Sydney and arranged to deal in goods coming off the ships. I had 2 servants. There was the woman Charlotte Pugh who does for me and every now and then I return to the idea of setting up together but she had other thoughts. You wd think she wd have taken up a good offer as she has the 2 children by Samuel Garside who done her wrong. I had too a manservant, the convict called Samuel Browne who helped with unloading when the ships were in port. Samuels must be her undoing for I found them in the alleyway one night her with her skirt around her waist and him up to the hilt.

Well I said don't stop for me for neither seemed too keen to carry on and him not knowing where to look. So they was stuck there in the alleyway and I thought I might as well get to see what he has on offer for her. I said come now Samuel and took him by the shoulder so that he must step back and what I saw was nothing much but perhaps it had had a fright.

Charlotte covered herself up quick though I saw she had a fine head of hair peeking out. I laughed then and said it doesn't take much to satisfy you Charlotte Pugh. I could give you twice as much but I won't. It makes a man thirsty seeing another man in the drink but I did not want to mix good seed with bad. Be sure to wipe it clean I said to Samuel.

But it was enough to send a man off to sea again what with her brats at her heels and the smell of her ripe cunt in the kitchen. Enough to put a man off his tucker. And then she was in the family way again.

I'm ready to go to sea again I told Captain Underwood for I had heard he was hoping to send the *Harriet* to sea for sealing in the Auckland Islands. Not that I knew much about them.

They is far away Underwood told me in the half-light of the

Antarctic sea. The cold winds come in off the ice. You need to keep warm and look sharp.

At least I knew the *Harriet*. This was a ship I was coming to know as if she was my own. She turned this way and that at my command. I wished that I knew a woman like her. What happened down south is something I must set down here and put to rights although there is some does not have a good word to say for me on the subject.

Today we hit heavy weather worse than usual. I see that day clearly in my mind. Heavy NW gales with extreme squally wind and rain driven by heavy gusts is what I wrote in my log book that day. We took shelter in the North Arm beneath Mt Raynal, a high peak on that empty land which is bare in the way of the desert I have seen in Australia, but grey and barren like a virgin spinster. The trees, what there are of them, are bent towards the earth. We dropped anchor and it held fast and that was lucky for us. The wind died off although the rain kept falling. Alongside of us comes a boat with 2 men aboard.

We come off the *Sally* says the older of the 2, a man I come to know as John Wilson.

I know a bit about the *Sally*, it is a schooner that usually trades in timber and coal, but had put out to sea with the idea of quick money without knowing what they was letting themselves in for down there in the south. I know the *Sally* is sealing in the nearby Western Arm of Carnley Harbour under a Captain Lovatt. He is a good enough man but I do not think he has done much sealing.

Things is not too good over there said the other man who I find out soon is Mark Shaw.

You'd best come aboard I said and the 2 men come on board the *Harriet*.

So what is the trouble then.

They tell me the rum rations are cut and the food is bad because they have not put in enough provision. To make matters worse the master was running scared against the wind and they had got no seals to speak of and all they wanted to do was get some work and go home. I was thinking it wd be trouble getting their boat back to the *Sally* which I wd have to do or my name will be mud but I am glad enough to have the extra hands.

Well I said to them you're welcome to stay as I've got a man down sick who should never have put to sea and another who doesn't know how to work. Let's see what you're made of, the pair of you.

So it was not just Lovatt's boat I had to worry about but now his runaways as well. I began to see myself back inside again and I am a man who must go free.

Next day part fine weather fresh SSE wind and 5 boats made land. There we found a very promising rookery of seals, as good as any I have seen and not another ship in sight. We clubbed 500 in a very short space of time. I was watching Shaw and Wilson all the time. I could see they did not know how to skin a seal. They stood about looking gormless. I wished I had never clapped eyes on either of them. I wd have done them a favour if I had knocked them off then.

It came to me then that I wd leave them here. And that is what I did. I took them on board and fed them one more time. I took the ship round by Port Ross which is to the north of the main island and told them they are on their own now. May God have mercy on their souls and I hope as how another ship will pick the pair of them up in which case they wd do well to keep their secrets to themselves another time.

They should have died there and Wilson did but Shaw got picked up 6 month later, all skin and bone and crawling on hands and knees. That is how the story got around that I am a murderer. Well it would be better that I had done them in. Shaw was all for telling where the new rookery was in exchange for his life and blacked my name.

Murderer they say when I walk down George Street. Wet behind yon ears I say.

People say I am a hard man and wicked with it. But hard men get things done. Next thing when I am back in Sydney I got a message to see Mr Robert Campbell. I am not 1 to get excited but I must say my heart beat fast upon reading his letter. Campbell is the King of the Wharf, the man with the biggest shipping business in all of Sydney, the merchant prince some do call him. This is the man who stopped the redcoat gentry in their tracks, those what made handsome profits from other men's work in the early days. What they done, these thieving rascals, was go aboard each merchant ship that come to Sydney and buy up all the cargo. Then they sold it for 500 times more to the local people. It took a man like Campbell to bust them. He bought a strip of land that is called Campbell's Cove and I daresay will be that for all time and built ships that he alone owned. So he could say who could come and go aboard them and it was not redcoats. He has built there his house, a wharf and stores, and he deals in seal skins whale oil and timber not to mention cattle from India sugar tea coffee rice and muslins.

His message said he wd like me to come to lunch and talk over a business proposition. I told Charlotte she must iron my best shirt with special care. And then she went and burnt it, a triangle like burnt toffee on the right side beneath the collar because she has her mind on other things. Betsy who was there to visit said don't worry Uncle Jack, for that is what she has taken to calling me ever since the day she and I went out for picking oysters, though she says it with a funny little smile as if she knows something I don't. I will get you another 1 real quick from Mr Spyer. And she was down the street, lickety split, and back again in less than 1/2 an hour while I walked up and down. It will never fit I said to Charlotte, she did not wait to ask what size, she will not know. The shirt was perfect, the best I ever put upon my shoulders, and though I was mighty upset and not myself, the girl had made me calm. I went off to see Mr Campbell wondering which knife and fork I should pick up when I sat down to lunch. Which is not the most important thing I know but all of a sudden I was like a lad and shy. My Father wd have known what to do. But there is nothing in the book of words he gave to me that tells you the difference between the fish knife and the 1 for butter.

Not that Campbell seemed to notice that I was nervous. He took me by the arm as if we was the best of friends and we strolled through his garden and looked at his peacocks. I have heard much about you Guard he said.

I said who has been talking about me for I am careful who knows my business and he says why Captain Underwood has spoken with high regard for you.

I said that is all right then and he showed me into his parlour where we partook of a good lunch such as an English gentleman might eat and drank some wine and I watched what he did and it all came to me easily enough.

I could not at first believe my ears when Campbell said what was on his mind but it was correct, he offered me a partnership with him in a ship called the *Waterloo*.

Underwood says you should have enough money for a ½ share he said, which troubled me a little because I do not like people to speculate on what I am worth but I let it pass.

The ship is a 70 ton schooner, the *Waterloo*, carrying kangaroo skins, wheat and seal skins between Sydney, Van Diemen's Land and New Zealand.

I said thank you sir, I can oblige you there. And I added that I had heard of the demand for flax and that I knew where I might do some good deals and at that he was very pleased.

Well he said, it might be that the sailing can be shared around, and you might like to work ashore from time to time. Have you got a good lady?

I said I am not a married man.

That is a pity he said. A wife is an asset to any man. What has kept you from the goodly estate?

I said then that I had not met a woman I fancy well enough at which he shook his head and said well that is up to you but a man in your position should be able to pick and choose.

In my head I knew I had not told him all the truth.

After this something happened so big and strange I knew it to be an omen of my future. I was sailing the *Waterloo* in New Zealand waters. It has turned out to be a tidy ship and much to my liking although it is not the *Harriet*. Again we carried seal skins from the south, not planning to go ashore, when up comes a strong NW gale near Cook Strait. The waves were green mountains like nothing I had ever seen, they curled and smashed, beat and flayed us, they were big as God's wrath, and at evening we were driven harder and ever more relentless towards a rocky headland. I had been warned of this place and never thought of seas as fierce and without forgiveness and I thought I was a fool that I had not heeded more the warnings. The *Waterloo* was carried forward on the crest of a mighty wave. Suddenly we found ourselves in smooth water near the shore of an island.

It was hard to believe that in the midst of all this wind we should come across a place so calm and still. But it was so. We had found fair haven.

Later I heard the island is called Arapawa and the place where we had come is Te Awaiti which means The Little River.

But not for me. It is the place of my deliverance. I will call it always Fair Haven, the name I have bestowed.

This is the word of the Lord. God Almighty. I was saved.

In the morning, the storm passed over and I was able to look around me, as a man who discovers a new land might do. We were in a small bay with a wide beach of stones. Over the beach fast flowed a stream of clear water. Up above were trees of many kinds, hard knotted and close together. We climbed the hill. To the south we saw a range of mountains covered with snow like flowing milk. All around us the birds were crying out.

What I saw then fair blew the breath out of my mouth. In the waters of the bay a pod of southern right whales played near the shore. These are black animals and carry great quantities of oil. I had heard of the right whales coming north from the Antarctic to calve in quiet waters but this was something I never thought to see and it was here right before my eyes.

I had an idea of how I might go on for the next little while. And in my mind I was seeing the girl.

She has been in my mind a long time. She comes to me most often on the watch between midnight and 4, when the dawn is just about to break. Sometimes as daylight comes there is a moment I cannot explain, a moment so fast that I never believe I've seen it after it has passed. It is like a green flash, a flicker in the sky. I have asked a sailor or 2 if they ever seen it but they tell me no and now I dare not ask anyone except they think me strange. But it is in times like this I think of the girl and that she is growing older. Somewhere someone may be entering her, they will ride her, tearing her apart like a woman ripping open a seam or a man the canvas of a sail. It will happen and she will be lost to me.

And I know I do not want that to happen. I want to put her on a promise to me. I need to take her away from John Deaves and her mother and Charlotte and her men and all the women who take bad fortune as their due.

Perhaps there is a name for what I feel. I want a girl who is mine and nobody but me has had her.

I will teach her with what kindness there is in me.

I do not want anyone but her.

Chapter 5

LETTER TO PERCEVAL MALCOLM ESQUIRE,
PARRAMATTA, NEW SOUTH WALES
FROM HIS SISTER, MISS ADELINE MALCOLM,
c/- THE RODDICK HOME, MACQUARIE STREET, SYDNEY

December 1832

My dear brother Percy

It is now some years since you have seen fit to reply to my letters, but it is my duty as ever, each month, to write you an account of my life here in Sydney. It has been a difficult few weeks, and I am sure you will have it in your heart to take pity on me, for I have lost my dear good friend Mrs Emmeline Roddick, whom I loved as my life. As you know, I have lived in the Roddick home for close to three years, as the governess of Mathilde and little Austen. Emmeline became weaker and weaker with the chest complaint for which there is no cure, an evil scourge that respects neither gentle folk nor criminals, though no doubt a great deal of it has been carried here on the convict transport ships. She had become as a sister to me, albeit a younger sister, for there was a difference of several years in our ages. Lieutenant Roddick remarked on it when he was home, which is not often of course, because of his military duties which take him away for so much of the time. The poor fellow, he's always been a devilish sort of man, if I may use such coarse language, but he has a merry way with him when he is happy. I do not wish to sound improper, but I would describe him as a handsome man. His dark moustache, sadly, is now tinged with grey, but it is a full moustache, indicating a sturdy constitution, and he is such a big man, at least six foot four in his stockinged feet. Which I admit to having seen, for he took off his shoes and tiptoed around Emmeline's bed so as not to disturb her in those last terrible days, when she slept fitfully, only to wake gasping for breath that was beyond her reach. I sat and read gently to her each day, and pressed cold flannels hourly against her forehead, but to no avail, she was gone to us.

The question of what is to happen to me has not been broached, but I fear that before long I will have to return to Rosewood. What will the servants think, me living here in the same quarters that are occupied from time to time by Lieutenant Roddick? I could, of course, take a room down by the cook's; it is a bare little space, but perhaps I can make it homely. Besides, Hettie is a coarse creature, a ticket of leave woman. We will just have to see, with poor Emmeline not cool in her grave, it's too soon to enquire about the arrangements. Someone has to see to the children.

Your silence suggests that you continue to hold some grievance against me, real or imagined. All the same, your lack of interest in my welfare will not go unremarked for long. Indeed, it has reached my ears that you have not been received at the Governor's second residence at Parramatta for some time. I do have a number of friends here, through the kind offices of dear Emmeline in the past, and I am frequently received at Government House, although the new Governor Bourke, like dear Lieutenant Roddick, is recently widowed, so he is in mourning. No doubt you will have heard about this; it happened soon after his arrival. His daughter is standing in as his hostess but their receptions are confined to a small circle among whom I count myself one of the privileged few.

I am aware that you have been petitioning for more acres of grassland, and I can only say, your conduct could rebound unfavourably on you. I would never volunteer information against someone whom I have held so dear all my life, but do not think that questions have not been asked. If I am forced back into lodgings, I am sure that the quality of our familial ties will soon be under scrutiny.

It is worth noting, perhaps, that the new Governor, Sir Richard Bourke, has greater sympathy with the emancipists than his predecessor. At first I was scandalised, but I am beginning to think his attitude may lead to greater harmony in the Colony than in recent years. No doubt, you will have heard that Governor Darling's departure was fêted by those who support convicts' rights, with feasting and celebrations. A brass band played 'Over the hills and far away' and a huge sign on the newspaper building crowed HE'S OFF, while a fireworks display spelled out the words Down With the Tyrant. I felt myself quite borne away with the excitement of it all and I believe I may have the stirring of a liberal conscience in my breast. But that is what happens when people are dispossessed. How could this ever have come upon me? Of course, I have not shared these thoughts with the Lieutenant, who is a man under orders.

When Sir Richard arrived, the frenzy was as great, but on so much happier a note; bonfires were lit and the streets illuminated in greeting. You, with your hundreds of convicts working on the farm, cannot hope to go unnoticed. Do not come to me in great remorse when it is all too late, brother.

Your ever affectionate sister,
Adie Malcolm

Part 2

The Governess

Chapter 6

We are happy in noticing the arrival of His Majesty's Ship Alligator, *once more in our harbour, especially after the successful termination of the enterprise in which she has been engaged; the particulars of which, we are now enabled to present to our numerous and respectable Readers.*

It will be remembered that His Majesty's Ship left this Port on the 31st August, with the Colonial schooner Isabella, *having on board a detachment of the 50th Regiment, under her convoy, for the purpose of rescuing from the savage inhabitants of New Zealand, the wife and children of Captain Guard, and the remainder of the crew of the ship* Harriet.

Mrs Guard states that when the New Zealanders first took her prisoner she was nearly exhausted with the loss of blood, which was flowing from the wounds she received in her head with their toma-hawks. They voraciously licked the blood, and, when it ceased to flow, attempted to make an incision in her throat for that purpose, with part of an iron hoop. They then stripped her and her children naked, dragged her to their huts, and would have killed her, had not a chief's wife kindly interfered in her behalf, and when the bludgeon was raised with that intention, threw a rug over her person and saved her life. The savages took the two children from under her arms and threw them onto the ground; and while they were dividing the property they had stolen from the crew of the Harriet, *kept running backwards and forwards over the children as they lay upon the ground — one of which, the youngest still retains the marks of this brutal operation. They afterwards delivered the youngest child to the mother, and took the other one away into the bush, and Mrs Guard did not see it for some months after.*

Account of Betty Guard as reported to the Sydney Morning Herald, *November 1834.*

So, it is another day for scandal on the streets, broad and narrow, of Sydney Town. Three weeks have passed since the story of Betty Guard was first aired in the press. I am the talk of the town. Crowds queue for the newspapers in order to get another instalment of the details, something to mull over dinner parties at Government House and between dances at Mrs Manning's balls, and cause a stir here at the Rocks, where ticket of leave men and women huddle in their cottages on the brown sandstone that edges the shoreline. When I walk down the street, a way opens up for me to pass through, as if I were not of them any more, but rather, as if my deep and dark past puts me in a class all of my own. Down here among yesterday's canaries, who have done all manner of things, you would think I was the devil.

Look, I might say, I am innocent. I am just a woman unclothed by savages. What would you have done? Don't you understand? I am a heroine. All the newspapers will tell you that.

I might say, my Granny and Granddad were on the First Fleet and who do you think you are when you're at home.

Instead I say nothing. I keep walking, not looking to the left nor to the right.

Last week a skit was performed at the Theatre Royale, a prelude to the main play, featuring a pale maiden with fair tousled ringlets falling this way and that as she leans back, her head almost touching the stage. A bottle of red ink drips over her snow-white tunic, and an actor smeared head to toe with coal dust and only a loincloth to cover his manly parts, swoons upon her throat. A bearded sailor wrings his hands in anguish in the wings. Cock-a-doodle-do, squawks a dancer clad in a swirling ostrich-feather cloak, flapping his arms as if he were a rooster. He dances on tiptoes across the reclining pair, holding his arms outstretched. 'Thereby hangs a tail,' the rooster cackles, and the lights dim to thunderous applause.

It lasted only a night or so, for there are those who protest my virtue and are incensed on my account; it has been said that even the Governor stepped in to have it stopped. Two nights or three, it was long enough for men from Cambridge Street to take themselves up town for a look and so it is known about, word for word, around this way. My husband Jacky Guard stayed home. But of course he has heard about it. Even if he speaks to no one, my aunt Charlotte Pugh speaks to everyone.

I do not have fair ringlets anyway. I am tall and dark, handsome some say, though my Aunt Charlotte thinks I have a strong chin for a woman. It is your eyes, she would say, back in the days when she was not displeased with me; they are scorching eyes that men might die for. When I was a girl she would twine my hair round the stems of clay pipes after a wash, so that it came out curly, but now it falls in waves down my back when it is free. People watch me for signs and messages I will not give them.

All the same, I've been in no mood to go out upon the town, for at the Rocks it is possible to bear the curious stares, the hushed voices. These are my own people and soon something else will come up to take their interest. Someone will come along with a circus. Last year there was a Bengal tiger in a cage. Or somebody will drop dead with drink.

Up in town, though, along George Street where the smart

people stroll, it will be another matter. They will want to prod and poke, in a manner of speaking, and make excuses to hold a conversation. These are the same people who will spend a shilling to watch the Aboriginals fight. The fights are supposed to be banned but who can resist the spectacle of one black man on another, tearing each other to pieces. It's cheaper than the circus.

But neither can I stay in, day after day, because Jacky will not speak with me. He has a dark and brooding stare that he keeps corked up in the corner of the room near the hearth where my aunt, Charlotte Pugh, prepares our dinner. I would help her but she will not let me. As if I am an interfering guest. The heat is rising outside, soon it might rise to ninety-five in the shade, but still he sits near the flames, and I am afraid of him. He has an old water-stained book in his hands that he turns over and over. It was his father's book and his father's before that. This book is not the Bible, it is worse than that. I need to get away from Jacky and the book, and whatever it is telling him he must do, for that is something I do not know, what lies between its covers.

Besides, it will be Christmas soon and I have decided that John and Louisa will have presents this year, even though we have fallen on hard times. They have spent a winter in the bush among the Maoris, and now that is all behind us, and we are here in Sydney, safe and sound, and I am a mother who does the best she can. I would like to remind my husband of that.

In the room next door, Louisa begins to cry again, the forlorn wail of a child who cannot be comforted. My mother will soon be here, I tell Charlotte. She is coming and she will care for Louisa. Charlotte looks at me with a dislike that makes me want to weep. Charlotte was always well disposed towards me; she took me in when my mother went off with Deaves the sawyer, and my grandmother had died. It was Charlotte who rescued me, gave me a roof over my head. Without her, I might never have met up with Jacky again, never gone off to New Zealand, never been shipwrecked.

Never? I say that as if I wouldn't have missed the experience.

Perhaps that is so. But what does it matter, when everyone has their own salt to put on the meat.

I have dressed modestly today in a dress of grey linen. I wear no jewellery. My bonnet is without feathers and the light scarf I wrap around my neck is plain wool, even though the day is warm. For that is where their eyes slide, those of the people who stare at me, straight to the base of my throat, to see the wounds of which I have complained, and which the newspaper has taken up with such enthusiasm, the spot where they tried to open my vein and drink my blood.

It was only a little cut, I might say, all healed over, and no teeth marks at all. Their thirst went unquenched. Oh, so much that I might say. Even if I did, they would want to see.

I won't be long, I tell Charlotte. Already I hear my mother's approaching footsteps, heralded by the chattering of young John, who has become a handful since he lived among the Maoris. They told him he would be a chief and let him run wild, and now he won't do anything I tell him. I don't want to see my mother, I have little to thank her for, but she's about all I have at the moment.

Goodbye, Jacky, I say. I'm going no further than George Street, I'll look up the old shop and see what treats I can find for the little ones, I'm sure they'll let me have a little favour or two up there, you know how kind they were.

He doesn't speak a word. I take the back door so I won't have to walk past him, out through the gate that leads across the ditch, where sewers drain. In town they have men who come with their buckets when the lights are out and nobody can see.

So I make my escape, heading towards George Street where I hope to find my employers of some years back, when I was still a girl, not taken, though I was promised. Their names are Mister Spyer and Mister Cohen, two Jewish gentlemen dealers who came from England free men, not convicts like my grandparents, and my father and my stepfather, and my husband — not men in chains, just fortune seekers. I was their maid of all works who measured out rum for sailors, kept brass things shiny and dresses sorted. I loved the feel of silk and satin running through my fingers when I lifted bolts of material. I held them to my face and breathed in their faint spicy smell, ran my fingers over the rich brocades.

Along the lower end of George Street are to be found open markets filled with bustle and noise and colour. Parrots and cockatoos swing in cages before the doors of shops crowded with sailors jingling Spanish dollars they have earned at sea. Down the left-hand side are stalls where maize and wheat are sold; on the right, green vegetables, turkeys, ducks, geese and sucking pigs. I compare the best prices, in order to buy something to put Charlotte in a better mood on my way back. A shilling for a basket of peaches and nicely ripened cheese at fourpence a pound, which I can afford, just so long as I don't have to touch the peaches, for I am like my grandmother in this respect: I cannot bear the feel of a peach, which puts my teeth on edge, or worse, feels like my fingernails are bending back on themselves. I would like to linger over the booths of drapery for, as you'll have gathered, I'm partial to quality and, from the beginning, Jacky has spared nothing on me. All that is changed now; he has neither the mood nor the money to indulge me, for all our ships are lost at sea. In spite of myself, my eyes roam over hoop petticoats and some fine lawn camisoles; it's hard to explain but it's as if I'm looking down into the lives of women and girls who are like the person I was once, and cannot be again.

I hurry on, not looking left or right now, past a myriad creaking signs over the inns — the Crooked Billet, Three Jolly Sailors, Rose of Australia and World Turn'd Upside Down. Well, that last one would do me, though it was meant for sailors who believe that when they put to sea and sail over the horizon they are hanging on by their toes to the opposite side of the world. Though how it works I can't tell either, for all the world round here looks flat to me — you couldn't get flatter than Australia. But out on the ocean with Jacky, I've seen the way the sky curls over on itself, and I've worked out that there is some solution to the riddle of the world and how you get from one side of it to another without falling off.

I find myself glancing over my shoulder, as if I am being followed by something or someone, a shadow as large as a whale on the horizon, and I know that though he is not there — or, at least, I don't think he is following me — that it is the shadow of my husband.

When I reach the shop, I see it has fallen on hard times. The grog barrels drip into their saucers as ever, but there is not much else but a collection of dusty pewter mugs on a shelf, some cheap fabric stacked any old how, and a few odds and ends collected in tubs. The tobacco is tenpence a pound, which is daylight robbery, and available much cheaper at the port. Gone are the hats and hat boxes, which were almost as pretty as the hats themselves, not to mention the gentlemen's hats with stovepipe crowns and ribbon round the brims, and fine kid gloves, and gold watches in locked glass cabinets, and a range of the best china money can buy. Once, when I was over from New Zealand, I bought a beautiful meat dish here, pale green and white, my favourite colours. My Granny said people who prefer green are cold by nature but that I do not believe, though she was right about most things. The centrepiece has pattern of thistles and roses and shamrocks, not that I have seen a shamrock. The platter has channels down the sides so the meat juices run down to a hollow; I pour them off to make the gravy. Well, I never expect to see that again. Ngai Tahu tribesmen have burnt down our house again, that I do know. Not for the first time, over these past months, I have thought that Jacky may not have chosen his friends wisely. Te Rauparaha and his Ngati Toa warriors served him well at first, but we have been in the middle of a war between the tribes of the north and south for years now. Not so bad when Te Rauparaha was on the winning side, but the tides have turned against him, and we are the enemy of those at war with him. I cannot say I blame them, that they do not like us.

As for whether we will ever return, I have no way of

knowing. For I'm not sure that I mean aught to Jacky now. I don't care for the way his eyes follow me around the room at nights when I'm turning back the covers on the bed. I am filled with sorrow when he turns away once I'm in the bed, and goes back to the kitchen. I hear him and my aunt Charlotte Pugh talking in low voices. I wonder sometimes, will I get out of this alive. But perhaps it's just that I got into the habit of thinking like this when I was in captivity. I've seen Jacky in a mood before, and he has got over it. But never as black as this. I tell myself that Jacky came back for me, to the wild Taranaki coast, to rescue me away from Oaoiti, the chief who held me as his own. And that he will recover from all of this. If he would listen to me, I would say, forget about it. Forgetting is everything, and all we have.

But I don't know how much I will forget. Or what I will remember.

You do what you must.

'Well, ma'am, I didn't expect to see you here,' says Mr Spyer in his timid little chirp. He sits behind the counter, his curly black hair trying to make its escape from beneath his skull cap. I always found him the friendlier of the partners, though an anxious man. Mr Cohen was more on the make, eager to please the administrators and military people. More than once, I wondered if he did not like the people of the Rocks shopping in his store, as if they gave off a bad odour that might affect his more elegant clientele. One thing for us to work for him, another to serve us. Many are surprised that convicts and their families have money in their purses. There is work for all who want it, and sealers and whalers bring money into the port that those on military rations can only dream about, for all their airs and graces, especially now their rackets on the poor have been stopped. Not that I will be buying much today, and Mr Spyer senses that as soon as he sets eyes on me.

He shakes his head in a mournful way, knowing I've come down in the world. Of course he reads the newspapers. He offers his regrets for all that has befallen me, and speaks of his relief that I and my children at least, *at least*, dear Mrs Guard, have been spared. All the same, he is holding back.

I tell him what I have come for: perhaps a marked down toy for John, a doll of some kind or another, or perhaps a little bracelet for Louisa, who won't know whether it's Christmas or not. It is not just her age I'm thinking about, for some days she looks so pale and weak I wonder if I'll ever get the roses back in her cheeks. She was a bonny girl, gaining weight, before we were stranded on a rocky shore. A girl of my own is what I always wanted, and I might as well be dead as lose her, yet I saw her treated rough and trampled on, and that is not an easy thing for a mother to get over.

Mr Spyer shakes his head again, a refusal in his eyes.

'What is the matter?' I ask. 'Are you afraid Mr Cohen will catch you giving discounts?'

'It is not that,' he mutters, and I swear that he blushes. Then I know what it is: I am an embarrassment to him. And yet his eyes hold their old sympathetic kindness which has always drawn me to him. 'People are saying how remarkably brave you are.'

'It *is* Mr Cohen, isn't it?' I ask. For there was a man who wanted to go up in the world. And too serious for his own good.

When he doesn't answer, I remind him with as much dignity as I can muster, of the times he has helped out poor souls down on their luck, which at the moment I certainly am, but the words die in my throat. 'It is not as if I am asking for money,' I say.

He gives me a quizzical look.

I lower my eyes and slip from my finger the ring that Jacky Guard gave me when I left Australia that first time. It has not left me, not even when I lived in the bush.

Of course, the toys were an excuse. I did want them, but I want money even more.

Mr Spyer looks long and hard at the ring.

'I can lend you a little,' he says, 'but I do not want the ring.'

He reaches into the drawer where he keep the money and extracts five pounds.

'You must take the ring,' I say, and my eyes are hot with tears and wounded pride.

'No,' he says. 'That will do you no good at all, to be seen around Sydney without your ring. What would your husband say? Now, please choose a toy or two for the little ones.'

'I'll pay you back,' I say. I am in two minds as to whether to leave there and then. But I hear a rustle of taffeta behind me and a woman comes towards me, a puzzled frown on her face. She is a woman close to fifty.

'Why, it's Betsy Deaves,' the woman says.

Nobody has called me that since I worked here at Spyer and Cohen's, for that is what I was known in those days. Momentarily, I think she must be one of the customers, but there is something more familiar than that about her, and then it comes back to me. My teacher at the Ragged School.

Before I can say her name, Mr Spyer says, too heartily, 'Well, yes, fancy you remembering our Betsy, Miss Malcolm.' He has snatched a wooden horse with wheels out of a tub, a cheap pull-along toy, and thrusts it into my hands. 'From me, Betsy.'

I take the toy, for I would be cutting off my nose to spite my face if I were to turn it down, and place it in my bag. All the while, I consider the woman before me. She looks in better shape than when I last saw her, her portly thighs well strapped in. Her skin is clear and rosy, even if folded a little round the chin. And her hair, which I used to think the colour of mouse fur, straggling out of its bun, is caught up now and coiled around her head in a fashionable way. Altogether, she looks like a woman who pays attention to her looks.

'Thank you so much,' I say, endeavouring to recover my wits, 'but most people call me Mrs Guard these days.'

Miss Malcolm's hand flies to her mouth. 'Oh my goodness Betsy, you are not her, not *the* Mrs Guard?'

I inform my old teacher that I am indeed Mrs Guard.

'I did not recognise the name,' she says.

'I was never Betsy Deaves,' I say. 'Don't you remember, I did not take my stepfather's name?'

'Neither you did,' she says. 'But you were Betsy.'

'And now I am Betty,' I say impatiently, for all this seems trivial. I show her the ring on my finger, the one that only a moment before I had tried to pawn to Mr Spyer, the gold band with its curving rim, studded with seed pearls. 'I told you the day I left school that I was going to get married to a whaler.'

'You were always a forward girl,' she says in a sharp tone.

This is a bad turn in the conversation for I have often thought of Miss Malcolm in the years since our paths last crossed, and more kindly than she might have expected. She believed in the gods, something I've had reason to ponder over. She had an ear for magic. I am about to say something to improve her opinion of me, but nothing comes out. She too can read a newspaper, better than most. She will have formed her own opinion of me, and I imagine she will see me as having brought it all upon myself.

I can't explain what happens then, but I find myself weeping, and the next thing I am being led away from the store by Miss Malcolm, before Mr Spyer's astonished gaze.

Chapter 7

Of course the whole affair of Betty Guard and her rescue has been talked about in every salon in the town. Government House is not immune to speculation as to whether the rescued captive is a true heroine, or a woman no better than she should be. Only two nights earlier, Miss Malcolm had dined with the Governor and his guests when it was the subject on every tongue.

'It does seem that something went on, wouldn't you say, something out of the ordinary?' This from Mrs Deas Thomson who is married to Clerk of the Council, and is also the daughter of the Governor. 'Is Mrs Guard telling us the whole truth about what happened during her captivity?'

She puts these shocking questions to the assembled party while red wine is being poured to accompany the meat course. The crystal glitters under the chandeliers, like a small river of flame that makes Adie Malcolm remember candles snaking their way through the great churches of Italy. She closes her eyes and for a moment she is under the high dome of the Duomo. This was a passing illusion for, despite the exalted company, the fine table settings and the undoubtedly superior furnishings, Government House in Sydney is little more than a rambling shack, draughty in winter and overheated in summer. Each new Governor has demanded in vain that a new one be built. None of this really matters to the governess: she is enchanted to be sitting between Mr Deas Thomson and Mr William Barrett Marshall, the surgeon who had been on board the *Alligator*, the ship that had led the expedition to rescue Betty Guard and her children from the cannibals of New Zealand. Anne Deas Thomson had been a friend of Emmeline Roddick and she remains true to her promise that she would continue to include Miss Malcolm in social gatherings when her patroness was with them no longer. Since Mrs Deas Thomson's mother died within months of Governor Bourke's arrival in the colony, she is now her father's official hostess — and the most powerful woman in Sydney. Miss Malcolm considers her hostess a woman without affectation, very merry and bright, and a wonderful singer, which makes her popular with both the ladies and gentlemen, even when she says quite outrageous things. Right now, it is clear from the expressions on the faces of some of the ladies, such as young Mrs Bowman, that the topic raised is not comfortable dinner conversation.

Miss Malcolm reminds herself that Mrs Bowman comes from a grazier's family, like her dear brother Percy's, where the emancipation of convicts is considered abominable (whether Percy has come to this by his own deductions or those of his wife Maude, his sister is unable to discern, but Percy was a boy who did not believe in harming snails). The view will prevail that Betty Guard would have been best left where she was.

All the same, she is surprised that Mrs Deas Thomson has raised the topic of Mrs Guard in this manner, for it is her father, the Governor, who has been so sympathetic to Mr Guard and the fate of his family. Perhaps Mrs Deas Thomson is not entirely at ease with what has taken place and wishes to signal her concern.

'Well,' Mrs Bowman begins, with a nervous clearing of her throat, 'it has been said that she was wearing the very best of the New Zealanders' clothes, a feather mat, and her hair down and all over the place.'

'Surely you're not suggesting she took to their ways?' says one of the gentlemen present. He is a fellowman of Gerald Roddick, the lately widowed husband of Emmeline, who is not present tonight, though from time to time he and Miss Malcolm do end up in each other's company in society, by accident rather than design. She wishes he was here, for if called on to give her views she might say something out of turn. The delicate matter of Mrs Guard has been raised in their household, and the lieutenant has been surprisingly dismissive of the captive wife, despite his enthusiasm for the rescue mission. Not that he had gone on it, for his health was indifferent at the time the expedition left. But he has heard a great deal about it from his comrades who retrieved the unfortunate family.

Miss Malcolm had been scandalised, reduced almost to tears, when she read the newspaper accounts. That poor woman, she had said repeatedly. To which the lieutenant had simply replied that it was a good thing to teach the New Zealanders a thing or two, and if a few of them had been shot it would remind them that British people were to be respected. Not a word about Mrs Guard.

Without thinking, Miss Malcolm exclaims to the assembled guests, 'Surely not. Not a brown man with a white woman.'

A sudden hush falls around the table, and at once she knows she has spoken so far out of turn that she may never recover her position. Such lewd thoughts are not common to her, but even as she speaks she knows others have thought the same, by the way they glance at each other and away, and down at their plates. 'I mean,' she hurries on, 'she would have had no choice. If it were true at all. If, well, if anything untoward had happened.' She wishes she could stop herself from talking.

'I agree,' says Mrs Deas Thomson evenly, as a waiter delivers portions of roast lamb, carved and ready for serving, on a huge platter. 'Sad as it is, the evidence suggests that some white men will mix with dark-skinned women. But it would be against the natural inclination of brown or black men to associate with white women. Pass the vegetables and do begin or the food will get cold. I think someone should consider starting a collection for this family as they have had the greatest misfortune.'

The Governor has been deep in conversation with Mr Bowman, who is both a surgeon and a grazier, trying to convince him that if democracy is truly to exist in the colony, emancipated convicts should be entitled to serve on juries. His face is rather flushed as if the exertion of convincing the younger man is almost too much for him. 'Perhaps,' says the Governor, anxious for diversion, 'we should ask Mr Barrett Marshall for his opinion, since he was present during the rescue. Sir, what do you make of the matter? Surely, you can tell us how much Captain Guard has suffered?'

'Sir, John Guard is naught but a murderer.' The surgeon's face is very pale. A line of sweat beads his upper lip as he spits these words. 'You will know that there was a massacre of Maoris on the beach, after the boy, the last hostage, was retaken.'

'I see,' says Governor Bourke. He reaches for his napkin and wipes his face, then folds it very carefully, placing it beside his plate, though his dinner is hardly touched.

'Mr Barrett Marshall, is it possible that you have been led astray by the natives of New Zealand?'

'I beg your pardon? I have been led astray?' The surgeon chooses his words with care, but the implication is there, that it is the other man who is at odds with truth.

Bourke's face darkens with dislike. 'It happens, you know. Several missionaries have met their downfall in New Zealand. It's a seductive place for some men.'

'What exactly is your point, sir?' The surgeon has earnest brown eyes. When Miss Malcolm had first been introduced to him, she had thought him charming, even a trifle impish, but now she believes she detects a certain coldness about him.

But the Governor will not be drawn as the discussion threatens to spiral still further out of control. 'Ladies and gentlemen,' he says, raising his glass, 'a toast to the successful completion of the 50th's mission, and the restoration of Mr Guard's family to him, safe and well.'

The surgeon does not raise his glass, a fact that is noticed by most present, the men in particular, but goes unremarked. As the dinner is resumed, Miss Malcolm realises that if she does not talk to Barrett Marshall, nobody else will. Even Mrs Deas Thomson is looking chastened.

'The poor man must surely have been out of his mind,' she says tentatively.

'He was out of his mind with rage and jealousy. He would have murdered the chief who kept her safe, had he not been stopped. But plenty of others were killed on the same account.' The surgeon keeps his voice low and insistently soft, as if to make his points without being overheard.

'By Captain Guard himself?'

The surgeon shrugs his shoulders and looks weary, as if all of this is academic.

'I have met Captain Guard. Here, at this table,' says Miss Malcolm. 'While his wife was still being held captive.'

'Well, then, surely you understand what I am talking about.'

'He looked merely sad. And he had little to say for himself.'

'Well, I would have imagined you a good judge of character,' says Barrett Marshall. 'Surely you saw him for what he was.'

'If what you say is true, shouldn't he be brought to justice?'

'It was his men,' says Barrett Marshall, with a sudden unease. 'It was his men who shot the Maoris. Guard was back on board the ship.'

'Then how can you say that it was him?'

'They sought revenge on his behalf. His brother was among the murderers.'

'You seem very sure in your judgments.'

'The military were no better. They burnt and pillaged the homes of those humble savages. Not for nothing is the 50th Regiment known as the Dirty Half Hundred.'

'Oh really sir, I must object — your language is unseemly.'

'You're familiar with the works of Erasmus?' asks the surgeon, for they have discussed Miss Malcolm's classical interests over the fish soup and found common ground.

'A little, yes,' says Miss Malcolm, aware that they are beginning to attract attention from others at the table.

'They who deem it a trifling loss and injury when the poor and low are robbed, afflicted, banished, burnt out, oppressed, or put to death,' Mr Barrett Marshall quotes, in his persistent voice, 'do in truth accuse Jesus Christ — the wisdom of the Father — of folly, for shedding his blood to save such wretches as these.'

'I see,' says Miss Malcolm, who fears she may have a sliver of mutton bone stuck in her throat. She covers her mouth with her napkin, hoping not to attract attention. Mr Barrett Marshall is observing her intently. 'I wouldn't have thought, from what Lieutenant Roddick has said . . .' But what the lieutenant had said goes unuttered, for Miss Malcolm thinks she is choking to death, the prickle in her throat grown to the size of a spear.

'You're in trouble; let me take you to the drawing room. Don't panic, Miss Malcolm, just breathe quietly through your nose and follow me. I'll take care of you.'

The walk past the astonished faces of the assembled dinner party guests seems the longest Miss Malcolm has ever made. She remembers the children she has banished from her classes in years past, and feels very much as they must have — in as much as she can feel anything except the burning pain when she tries to swallow.

In the empty drawing room, the surgeon instructs her to lie back on a chaise longue beautifully covered with surf-green velvet, a tender and caressing colour which Miss Malcolm thinks she might shortly be sick on.

'Please open your mouth,' says Mr Barrett Marshall. 'You must be very calm. If I have to send for my instruments, then it becomes a matter of life and death that you remain composed so that your air passages remain open.' He peers into her mouth, and gives a triumphant little cry. 'Why Miss Malcolm, all is well.' He reaches inside her mouth and grasps an object within, pulling it away. 'See,' he says, holding the filament of bone to the lit candelabra, 'it was stuck between your back teeth. Not a problem after all.'

Miss Malcolm lies back for a moment longer, in a state of confusion at the nearness of the man leaning over her. He does not draw away as quickly as she would have expected. Her hand flutters to her breast. He must be twenty years younger than she is.

'All is well,' she is able to murmur at last.

'Indeed.' The surgeon's white hand clasps hers for an instant, and then he withdraws it, sitting up straighter.

'What must you think of me? I cannot go back into that room,' says Adie Malcolm. Her voice is husky and does not sound as if it belongs to her.

'The soup was ample,' the surgeon says. 'I am happy to sit here while we recover ourselves. Besides, I do not think the gentlemen at dinner are very pleased with me.'

'You really believe Captain Guard is as bad as you described him in there?'

'My dear lady, I tell you solemnly, that man has blood on his hands. He was a common felon. A man who has done very well for himself in these parts, even though he's crying poverty now. Have you not heard how, when he was on a sealing expedition, he abandoned two men to die on the Auckland Islands in the Antarctic winter without provisions? One of them survived to tell his story. Now if that is not murder, what is?'

'Perhaps he had his reasons.'

'Reasons. There are always reasons for Guard. He is a violent man. Doesn't what I have just said persuade you of that?'

'It's hard to know what to believe,' Miss Malcolm says. Her head is swimming. 'There's a growing view that convicts have rights too. The Governor is of that opinion.'

The surgeon lowers his eyes. His fingers look round and spongy. She shudders inwardly, that they have entered her mouth, as if she has tasted soft dough. The unkind cut about the lieutenant's regiment returns to her. 'It was you who quoted Erasmus to me: are we not all wretches in the eyes of God?'

'I shall find a servant to bring some brandy,' he says, 'and then I think I will leave.' She understands the subject is closed between them.

'Tell me then,' Miss Malcolm says, after some time has passed and they have drinks in their hands, 'what then do you make of the woman, Mrs Guard?' She feels as if she owes her life to the surgeon, despite his stubbornness and the unattractive hands, and that she should make amends. Nor is she certain of her ground, which seems to shift even as they speak. Here is a man who professes to love the poor and wretched, and yet speaks so badly of others, especially of convicts.

And the truth is, she is constantly torn between one point of view and another. She would like to extend Christian charity but her expectations are so often failed when she encounters what she thinks of as the convict class (she has only to consider the lieutenant's cook and her surly rule in the kitchen). In her heart, she understands there is little point in asking the lieutenant in whose house she lives what he believes to be for the best. His target is always of the moment, chosen by his superiors. One day it will be the convicts (and soldiers have little use for them, for what are they but a natural enemy, the reason for the soldiers' existence in Sydney); the next day it will be the Maoris across the Tasman; another day it could be the Aboriginals.

But just thinking of the lieutenant makes her heart ache with tenderness. He has had so much to bear, is so unhappy that his life is hardly worth living. She must try as best she can to see all points of view, to consider the matter from every angle.

'The woman? Oh,' says the surgeon, a trifle airily for her liking, as he swallows brandy, 'she had some interesting observations to make about the way the New Zealanders live.'

'Is that all?'

'All? What is all? She was captured and she was rescued.'

'Was she glad of her release?' The brandy's trail of fire is doing its work, and restoring her voice.

'Well, one assumes so. She was returned to her husband.'

Miss Malcolm wrinkles her forehead. 'Forgive me, but if this man is as evil as you say, would she truly have been pleased to return? Might she not have been happier with the savages?'

The surgeon finishes the remains of his brandy with a noisy suck. 'She belongs to her husband, of course.' He stands up, straightening his waistcoat. 'Forgive me, madam, I will take my leave now. Would you please give my excuses to our host? I am returning to England in the morning and I'm due to embark soon after dawn. I can promise you, I will be taking this matter further.'

'In what way?' Miss Malcolm asks, startled.

'I will write a book about it. I assure you, it is a story that will shake England when it is all said and done.'

He pauses in the doorway and turns back. 'She changed her story,' he says. 'Mrs Guard *changed* her story.'

Chapter 8

And here is Betsy Deaves, or Mrs Guard as she is now, sitting in Miss Adie Malcolm's sitting room, in the house of Lieutenant Roddick and his late wife Emmeline, for whom Miss Malcolm remains in mourning, though she no longer wears black.

Though Mrs Roddick has been dead for three years, Miss Malcolm has still no sign of a respectable place to which she can move. Besides, nobody expects her to go. She has spoken from time to time with her employer, asking him what he would like her to do, but he is always so busy, so distracted in his grief, that the matter has been allowed to drop. The children are so fond of her, he murmurs absent-mindedly, and this is true, though it is difficult to see how he knows this for he sees them not twice a week, and then only for a half hour at a time.

Besides, the governess does not want to leave a house so full of memories of happier times. The rooms are ample and cool, with a verandah where one can sit and catch a trace of sea breezes when the summer is in full heat, and there is a jacaranda in the garden that blooms in the summer and an apple tree that fruits in autumn. There is Indian cane matting on the floors, and cedar furniture, softly shining tables and sideboards, while the walls are hung with delicate watercolours painted by the late Mrs Roddick, and her mother before her. There is a piano on which Miss Malcolm teaches Mathilde and Austen to play, and she is pleased with their progress. The cook, who is named Hettie, is steady and does not drink, even though her nature is disagreeable. Not quite the same can be said of the lieutenant, who keeps a couple of dozen imported wines in the house, which, even though his visits are infrequent, need regular replenishment. His gout troubles him on and off. Miss Malcolm cannot, in all conscience, approve of the circumstances that have led to this condition, but she was nonetheless relieved to see him confined to barracks when the *Alligator* and the *Isabella* set off to the wild New Zealand coast to rescue Mrs Guard. The thought of any ill befalling him is too terrible to contemplate. On account of the children, of course.

Mrs Guard is hunched down on a pink velvet sofa, twisting her handkerchief through her fingers like a child. An empty lemonade glass stands on the occasional table beside her, a half-eaten sandwich rests on a plate that she has pushed away. She dabs at her face, but the piece of muslin is wet through and Miss Malcolm hands her another of her own.

'Surely,' she says, 'after all that you have been through, your husband would not abandon you?'

'He keeps me on for the sake of the children,' says her visitor sullenly.

'Surely, Betty — you don't mind if I call you that, do you? — you have endured such a terrible ordeal that you are not yourself. You're imagining all this.' Miss Malcolm is anxious not to prolong this visit because the children will soon be back.

'I thought you'd understand,' says Betty, 'not that I ever thought of seeing you again, but I did think of you when I was out there in the night, in the pa, which is the village where the

Maoris live, with the sky and the sea stretching all around me, and I was a different person. I thought some nights that I might fly to the stars, like your gods.'

'My gods?' says Miss Malcolm, startled. 'I have only one God.'

'No, you haven't, Miss, your head was always full of yarns that no reasonable person would have listened to, but it passed the time, and I was entertained, and perhaps I took in more than you thought.'

'They were only stories.'

'Don't tell me they weren't true?'

'Why don't you tell me what happened?' says Miss Malcolm, casting around for inspiration, anything to deflect these unexpected questions. She has long tried to put Europe behind her.

'Now why would I tell you that?' counters Betty.

'Perhaps it would help.'

'Oh, help me, you want to help me, is that it?'

'I think you have had a hard life,' says Miss Malcolm faintly. 'That is what I understood.'

'I should be getting back home.'

'Another glass of lemonade?' Betty hesitates and Miss Malcolm senses she will stay. At the back of her mind anxiety about the children persists, but Mathilde and Austen have been collected by carriage earlier in the day for a picnic at the park, with friends of the Roddicks. There is to be a cricket match and, though Miss Malcolm has been invited, she has been glad to have a little peace. She has become as much nanny as governess to these children, and she wonders whether her age is against her, and how long she will be able to take care of these precious charges.

'It would take longer than the time I have today to tell you what happened to me. If I was to tell it from the beginning,' says Betty.

'Well, the beginning is a good place to start.'

'Will you be my friend, Miss Malcolm?'

'Well, yes,' says her hostess, flustered. 'I will do what I can.'

'No, I mean, my *friend*. You know, it is one thing to tell the newspapers the things they want to hear, but it is only that. It is only half a story, or no story at all. And it is, of course, the story my husband will have me tell them.'

'You have told your husband another story?'

'Not at all. I have told him nothing except what you have seen in print.' She raises her hand to the shawl that she has kept drawn round her throat during the conversation. 'Would you like to see the place where the savages sucked my blood? They cut me with an iron hoop, and placed their mouths at my throat, and sucked, drew my life blood, straining it up through their teeth. Come, look at me, Miss Malcolm.'

In spite of herself, and all her instincts to withdraw from this hideous image, Miss Malcolm leans close. The shawl has dropped away to reveal the young woman's long throat that, at first glance, appears only to be marked by a fading sun tan. But then Miss Malcolm sees a small crescent-shaped scar. Betty arches her neck, the better for the mark to be seen. 'It is healed now,' she says. 'You can see that it is only half a story. The evidence is less reliable than the truth, don't you think?'

'You've become very worldly.'

'Now, come, you can touch my head,' says Betty, as if the other woman hadn't spoken. 'Give me your hand, and feel this place on my scalp. You'll note that, under the place where I have my hair arranged to cover it, there is a bald spot. Perhaps it will be like that all my life, but whatever the case, it's still quite painful. That is where my tortoise-shell comb, the beautiful creamy-gold and brown piece that my grandmother gave to me when I was ten, because it was hers, and she said I must keep it and wear it in remembrance of her when I was grown, was struck by the Maori tomahawk. Naught but the comb saved me. Come, touch the spot, feel how raised it is, like a rib of knitting. Those are the teeth of the comb which have been pushed into my skull and there is no getting them out though Lord knows I've tried.

Harder, run your finger back and forth over them. It relieves the itch, my scalp is still very tender there.'

Miss Malcolm pulls her hand back as if it has been burnt.

'Seeing that you have offered, I would like you to know, to bear witness.'

'You want me to cover something up, something you have held back?' A vision is forming in the governess's mind of having to lie on oath, or of betraying the lieutenant in some grievous way that might bring discredit on his household. Miss Malcolm has begun to tremble. She feels herself straining in her stays, hears the harsh rustle of the light purple fabric of her dress and knows that all of this is too much for her. 'I did meet your husband last year,' she says. 'I sat beside him at dinner at Government House when he came to seek help from the Governor to secure your release.'

'You move in high society these days, Miss Malcom.'

'My circumstances have changed since we first . . . met.' Her voice falters. Does teaching this girl count as having met her? she wonders.

'And you told him what a bad girl I was at school, did you?'

'I did no such thing,' says the governess firmly, endeavouring to reassert herself. 'I did not know of the connection.'

'So what *did* you talk about then?'

'I found your husband quiet, withdrawn, as if he were suffering greatly. We had little to say to each other.'

Betty sighs and turns away from her.

'Is it true,' asks Miss Malcom, feeling faint, 'what they say about you?' As soon as these words are spoken she wishes she could take them back, but it is too late.

'What do they say about me?' A goading note has crept into Betty Guard's voice, despite her young and still tear-stained face. A wet patch is gathering on her dress where the shawl has fallen away and Miss Malcolm sees the outline of a nipple.

'You want to know what I did at night with the Maori savages, don't you? You want to know how far I have fallen. I don't know that you're the right person for me to tell this story to. You're afraid of what you'll hear, even before I've begun telling it.'

'What are you suggesting?'

'I see it written on your face. What have you touched? Am I infectious? When you tuck the children into bed tonight, will your hands give them bad dreams? Oh, I could tell you about bad dreams, I have them every night. Tell me, Miss Malcolm, have you ever lain down beside a man?'

'I beg your pardon?'

'It doesn't matter. I shouldn't have said that. It is not what happens under the covers between a man and a woman that gives me bad dreams. There can be worse things than that.'

Miss Malcolm looks at her guest and trembles afresh. 'But if you are taken against your will . . .' she says, a note of entreaty entering her voice.

Betty draws herself up, appearing to recover herself. 'Yes, if you are,' she says, 'that is bad indeed.' She touches the growing wet spot on her dress; now the other breast has begun to leak as well. 'I should go home to my little girl, there's nobody else can feed her there at the moment.'

'I think perhaps you should,' says Miss Malcolm, averting her eyes.

'So you don't want me to tell you my story now?'

'You will tell me half the story and then I will never know the end,' says Miss Malcolm peevishly.

'But you are my friend now,' says Betty, with a small artful smile, rearranging her shawl. 'What I cannot tell you today, I can tell another day.'

'You're planning another visit?'

'Before this one has ended? That is for you to decide, Miss Malcolm.'

'So when will you come next?'

'Perhaps tomorrow. At about this time. Do you have other plans?'

'I — there are the children, you understand.'

Betty glances around the room. 'What tidy children they must be. Never mind. You're their governess?'

Miss Malcolm nods. 'I'd like you to come. I'll be free tomorrow. At this time.'

'Well, we shall see. I must put my thoughts in order.'

With that, Betty Guard collects her bag, and the little wooden horse given to her by Mr Spyer, and Miss Malcolm is astonished at the way she appears to glide out of the room, as if she were on smoothly rolling wheels herself.

Chapter 9

Te Awaiti, 1827

Back from Sydney. Much has been settled with Mr Campbell who is a true gentleman. I reckon sir, I said to him, that Te Awaiti is as good a site for a whaling station as any.

He looked puzzled. You have learnt their lingo Guard?

Not really sir, I try to make a note of what they say, so that when the rascals change their minds and tell you 1 thing is something else, and a place is not where it was yesterday, I have a record.

Very good Guard. I could see he was impressed.

The sailors call the place Tar White I said.

Well that is good enough for me.

Anyway I said, the island is much covered with bush. There is excellent timber that grows above the bays, on its high hills and in the deep valleys. There are many coves and inlets, with fresh water streams, some areas of flat land near the beach where we can build houses and fishing works. The whales come about the beginning of April and have their calves somewhere near by, and stay until the middle of September.

I persuaded him that a whaling station wd be a better way to harvest these whales than at sea, for we can have many try-pots on the beach, all going at once if we catch several whales in a short space of time. Besides I told him, we wd get a bigger return on the *Waterloo* if I stayed on land to collect goods for trade when there were no whales about. I wd work hand in hand with the chief Te Rauparaha.

He warmed to my plan and spoke of employing a master to sail the ship while I was ashore.

This was good news to my ears but I had not finished yet. I am now doing well enough that I can afford to buy a ½ share in the *Harriet* from Captain Underwood, for it is a ship I have always wanted for my own. I asked if Campbell was willing to be my partner. And to my pleasure he agreed straight away.

Why we will have a regular little fleet of ships he said, and poured another tot. Have you thought again of marriage says Campbell, when we was finishing our cigars.

I am not sure that it is for me sir.

He looked across at me. I heard you had a daughter.

I have no daughter I said.

Well then, who is Betsy who lives with John Deaves, for I have heard she is not his.

I am her patron I said, and Deaves is her stepfather. She works for Spyer and Cohen, who are 2 Jewish dealers who know naught about business but are good to her. On Saturdays she goes to school.

He wrinkled his brow. She is young he says.

That is all there is to it I said, rather short, though I do not like to be short with such a man. She is just a girl.

A girl she may be, but Betsy is about as tall as me already. Last time I seen her, she could look me in the eye. She is shaping up to be a handsome woman. Not that I tell her this for handsome is as handsome does.

When I ask the dealers how she is doing, they say she is a quick girl. And we hear she is doing well at school.

As I had instructed Charlotte, Betsy has gone to live with her mother and so have her brother and sister. She has taken the name Betsy Deaves. She is not partial to it but I told her it is all for the best. Harriott and Deaves have tied the knot and you have to make the most of things I tell her.

But that house feels like it is full of monkeys with all the Deaves children and David and Sophia back from the orphanage. It pleases Betsy that they are there, esp. David the one she likes so much though for my money he is a snivelling brat. You would think he would be glad to be rescued from that orphanage. He is a boy not happy about anything as he quivers and cowers in a corner.

Now when I want to see Betsy I do not call, I tell Charlotte to bring her to my house in Cambridge Street.

But lately it seems to me that Betsy thinks more of school than work. The way she talks has changed. She is on about Greece and the gods. I tell her if it's gods she wants she need only go to New Zealand. The natives there have gods for everything.

So now I have built a house in New Zealand. Men from Sydney come to work for me. The women from hereabouts are happy to be their wives. The try-pots stand on the beach at Tar White. Every morning at daylight the boats are sent out. When we are fortunate enough to kill a whale we tow it ashore, flinch and boil it up on the beach. If the creature is tried out when it is fresh, the oil is more pure and does not smell bad like Greenland oil.

The easy part is killing the whale, it is towing it inshore that is the worst. The water in the bays is from 14 to 20 fathoms. If the whale should slip away, that is a long way to fall. A long way for our boats to be pulled to the bottom of the sea. All the same, we bring in many. We get 10 tuns, may be 13 tuns of oil for a good 'un and 300 weight bone. The cows are best. They give more oil than bulls. It is a shame about the calves. We fasten up the calf first, in order to draw the cow. The cow will always follow its young. The younger we can get the calf the better because the cow gets thin towards the end of the season from feeding its calf. They are big brutes.

Even when times are lean with the whales there is good trade to be had. I collect perhaps 20 or 25 tuns flax, go down south and get some seals, as much whale bone as I can lay hands on, some pigs and potatoes and I have good loads to take to Sydney. I do not encourage my men in the trade of dried native heads which is illegal in Sydney these days.

Besides I keep in mind the word of my friend Rangi, the 1 I met when I first went after whales, that it is not safe to touch the heads of the Maoris. I do not want to offend the Maoris esp. now I know Te Rauparaha the head chief here. It is better to be his friend than his enemy. It is easy to make a mistake with their taboos but they will not take that as an excuse.

So far I am on the right side of Te Rauparaha. He is keen to trade. Robulla my men call him or just the Old Serpent. For he is a tricky lot. I wd not trust him if my back was turned. He is a man about 50, not tall in height but then I am not either and it makes no difference. He could be taken for younger, he is hale and stout, only his hair moving backwards. To meet him you wd think him striking at first his eyes like that of a prowling animal. His manner is meant to hide his ferocious nature but soon it shows.

He is after all manner of things: tomahawks pipes fish-hooks clasp knives baccy rum cotton handkerchiefs which seem to his liking as are red blankets. Also cartridge paper bullets cartouche boxes bayonets cutlasses bullet moulds and leather belts. But most of all it is the muskets.

They are like a drug he cannot have enough. Mind, the New Zealander will not take any old gun nowadays, they know a good musket just as well as white men. Before they buy them they take off the locks and have a damn close look at them. They like best those with a Tower stamp with stocks dark in colour and lots of brass.

What Te Rauparaha does with his muskets is none of my business. He rules Cook Strait from his island of Kapiti. He can have his island and I will have mine and as long as we keep that in mind we can be friends.

1 time I was at sea on a short trip and the house burnt down. I built another 1. I do not know where Te Rauparaha was at this time but nobody has seen him about. They wd tell me if it was him. The men's wives know these things. This is not to say he does not do his work in darkness.

I thought of shifting for I have found another port I like even more than that at Arapawa Island. I did not know it was there at the beginning. I come across it by accident when bearing across Cook Strait in the *Waterloo*. The day was bright and very clear. I spied a low-lying neck of land on the farther shore I had not seen before. I changed course to go and explore. If I thought Te Awaiti a fair place it was nothing to what I came to now — bay after bay lying against a shining sea, amazing calm and gentle in the air. We came across a wide-necked bay facing out to the islands in the strait. It being close to evening I ordered the anchor dropped to shelter there for the night.

In the night the ship began to shake. There was a fierce rumbling sound. My 1st thought, we was on the rocks. I went up on the deck and all was quiet and we were riding high in the water and no sign of trouble. I dropped the lead-line over and found 7 fathoms deep beneath us.

I took myself down below and there it was again. I think perhaps it's an earthquake, of which the natives have told me, when all the earth rolls from side to side and mighty mountains shift their seats and tumble into the sea. I believe none of this but what am I to think on hearing this harsh and grating sound so close beneath me. I think the ship is about to capsize.

Again I went on deck and cast the lead-line, finding the same depth as before. Then for'ard it started like a living thing. In the moonlight I saw the cause of all the fuss, it was a whale and her calf rubbing against the anchor chain, as if to get the barnacles off their backs. Dawn was coming up fast and the last of the moon hurried away, and I saw 7 whales and their calves making their way out of the bay, taking their time.

I knew then, this was where they come to have their calves, that when they pass through the strait they are on their way in and out of here. I had a vision before my eyes of a huge port filled with whaling ships the biggest the world has ever seen. As we sailed out a cloud came down across the sea and we sailed through it, the damp like quiet rain upon our faces, and I called it Cloudy Bay.

About the house burning down. Mine is not the only 1. Some of the others have gone up in smoke. I heard the trouble was over 1 of the whalers' wives, for she already had a husband when she come to live with him. The trouble is often about women. Not that it is anything to do with me. They think I am the chief which is true but not in the same way that the Maori chiefs rule. They expect me to put a stop to it. I have had a word with the men, told them to be careful who they take up with or they will get us all killed.

After that, I think the trouble will pass and it is easier to stay at Te Awaiti than shift camp. In the back of my mind, I put away the idea that Cloudy Bay is there for the taking, but first I need to turn a profit for Mr Campbell on this station. I decide that I will tell nobody about Cloudy Bay.

About this time I begin to think that if the girl wd come over with me and settle it might be a good thing. Perhaps it wd be better for her than in Sydney and I wd stay more often at Te Awaiti. On my own, it is much like an animal's life, living on whale meat which is not good to the taste and wild turnips. I need someone to put in a garden and cook my dinners and wash the clothes.

Was this when I began thinking of bringing Betsy over?

No.

I have been thinking of her night and day for going on 2 years.

She has flashing eyes.

Her smell is that of the sweet untouched.

My balls ache but I do not want to put my poker in other women the way I did. When I do it is never what I want.

Part 3

Golden Brooches

Chapter 10

In her heart, Adie Malcolm does not believe that Betty Guard will return. After the first day, when she has failed to keep their appointment, she tells herself she must contain her disappointment.

And yet each day at three o'clock, she finds herself waiting. The house is empty, except for Hettie the cook, for in this past week she has found reasons for the children to visit the homes of others. She knows this has to stop. This morning at breakfast, the lieutenant had called in, and drawn up a place at the nursery table. This is so unusual that Adie's hands had shaken and spilled tea on the linen cloth, long ago embroidered with love knots and daisies by her friend Emmeline for her hope chest. Pale golden daisies spiral out from the centre towards the edge of the cloth and then suddenly stop near the edge. She sees Emmeline's beautiful fingers with their translucent fingernails tracing a path on the linen as she explained why the daisies did not, as intended, cover every inch of the cloth. Emmeline had first set eyes on Gerald on her sixteenth birthday. Straight away she had known she was in love. Her mother has been coaxing her to persist at her embroidery: all the other girls were doing petit point and tapestry while she was still on lazy daisy. She had sworn to her sister that day, *sworn* she had breathed in a whisper, that she would go on making daisies until the day he proposed marriage to her, and then she would learn to crochet. She was sure this would happen the very next time he saw her, for she had dropped her handkerchief and he had picked it up and put it to his cheek. So she knew that this sudden stinging attack of love was mutual. Only, unbeknown to her, he was about to leave the very next day for Prussia with his regiment. So for a year and two months she had sewed on and on, often, it seemed, in vain, until one day he appeared again, and as soon as he saw her fell to his knees, beseeching her to marry him. The hand she held out to him was worn from the thimble, and the daisies had spread across the cloth as if a thousand bees had pollinated it, but at least she was able to stop. And at that point in the recital she would say, with her small laugh that Adie had so loved, 'It's nothing but a rag, something I would never use for more than serving the children their breakfast on.' Adie tried to keep it fresh for all but the one day of the week when she instructed the girl who came to clean in its washing and ironing. Every morning she encouraged the children to count the daisies, which Austen still did, though Mathilde was getting bored with the game. And the lieutenant must have forgotten for the moment, the way he put his elbows on the table when he sat down, although a slight frown flickered over his brow when the tea was spilt, and Adie could have cried with vexation at her clumsiness, and the pain her carelessness would have caused.

'Forgive me,' she had said, as the stain spread among the little marguerites, wandering between the toast and the empty shells of boiled eggs.

He had shaken his head, as if uncertain of what she was talking about, watching his children. Mathilde is seven, a sturdy girl with dark braids and a full raspberry-coloured mouth;

Austen is a frail little boy of four with wispy blond hair, his complexion the colour of skim milk.

'Eat up, old chap,' said the lieutenant, picking up a discarded crust dipped in egg yolk and thrusting it in the boy's direction. The child squirmed away, his eyes pale and yet hot at his father's words. 'You'll never make a soldier at this rate,' said the man, and for a moment Adie thought him about to weep. His heavy moustache needed a trim; it was curling over his still full upper lip, redder than that of most men. This is where Mathilde gets her rosy smile. Adie had a swift impure vision of his mouth pressing down on Emmeline's throat which caused her to utter a small inarticulate squawk. She half rose to her feet as if choking on what she had just seen in her mind's eye. If it had not been for that woman and her talk, this would not have occurred to her. But at that moment his proximity jolted her senses, so she almost felt the ripple of hair on his wrists, lying on the table beside her, could smell his rank breath, like hay that had been out too long, or digestion in need of a good cleanout. She could taste that smell, as if his tongue were in her mouth. She had closed her eyes, holding onto the edge of the table.

'The children,' he had said, as she lowered herself back into the chair. 'Are you finding them too much, Miss Malcolm?'

'No. Why ever would you think that, Lieutenant?'

'Mrs Bowman says they have spent a lot of time at her place just lately.'

'Oh really,' she had cried out. 'Mrs Bowman has asked Mathilde and Austen to call so often since they lost their mother, I thought she would be insulted if I did not allow them to join her children more often. She has told me they are good company for each other.'

'I beg your pardon, Ma'am,' the lieutenant said, though with a touch of insolence.

'I am insulted,' Adie had replied. 'Yes, that is what I am.' Of course, racing through her mind, was the conversation last week at the Governor's dinner party. She might have known there would be repercussions. She wondered, then, if she should talk to the lieutenant about what had happened, her random comments, her disappearance with Mr Barrett Marshall that others would have noted, and perhaps repeated. But a voice within told her that that would be reckless, might complicate matters still further. It had even been on the tip of her tongue to tell him about the visit of Betty Guard. And yet, she found she could not.

'Well, never mind,' Roddick had said, as if their difference was already in the past. 'Perhaps if you could keep them home for a day or so, it would be all to the good.'

'Really,' Adie said, this time with a touch of steel in her own voice, 'an arrangement has been made for today, and if I am to be in charge of the children, then I can't simply cancel things at a few minutes' notice. I will keep them home tomorrow.'

'That seems to be settled,' he said. 'The headaches are all right?' he asked, apparently as an afterthought, and looked away, as a gentleman should when such matters are raised.

A flush travelled from Adie's collarbone and up her throat. For a moment, she felt betrayed by the late Emmeline. The headaches of her middle age are a secret she had shared with no one else. Besides, in the years since she has had the children to herself she has not had much time to think about the headaches and they have all but disappeared.

She felt her mettle firming, even as her cheeks flamed. 'I will speak with Mrs Bowman's governess this afternoon about future arrangements for the children. I am sure they will be disappointed if they are not to see each other again.'

At five minutes past three on that Tuesday afternoon, the last one that Adie Malcolm will be free for some little while, there is a soft insistent rap at the door, and Betty Guard is back.

Chapter 11

I have come dressed with care for I want to make a good impression on Miss Malcolm. My dress is navy blue, with ivory buttons fastening the front. I wear turquoise faïence beads around my neck, and my grandmother's best brooch for luck, not the mourning brooch that is shared by all the family, but the one she held onto after the fall, when my grandfather lost his money and land.

The brooch is made of gold filigree and cloisonné enamelling. My mother and my aunt both eye it as if it should belong to one of them (though, goodness knows, they would have fought over it) but Granny gave it to me and I will always hold it fast. By good fortune, I left it behind on my last voyage to Sydney, otherwise it would be lost in the bush that lines the coast of Taranaki. My capture took place, not on the way to Sydney, as many have supposed, but when the ship went aground on our way home to New Zealand. I have always kept a good wardrobe at our Sydney house so that I don't have to carry my town clothes back and forth across the Tasman. There is little call for fancy clothes in New Zealand, not on a whaling station. All the same, I hadn't meant to leave Granny's brooch behind me when I was here for Louisa's christening. I was in a panic when I first discovered it left behind, for Charlotte cannot be trusted to keep her fingers out of my belongings. But as I often wear it, I suppose she never thought to look.

I feel dashing today, my outfit finished off with the silk scarf and bonnet I bought last year.

I have brought Miss Malcolm a gift of a paua shell, shaped like a small dish. The outside is rough but the inside is like luminous blue and green mother of pearl, streaked in swirling lines of pink and silver.

'It is so beautiful,' she exclaims. 'This is a jewel of a shell. I hope it didn't cost you a great deal.'

I laugh. 'There are thousands of them to be had around the coast of New Zealand,' I say. 'The flesh of the shellfish is black and like a steak. It leaves the strong taste of the sea upon your breath.'

She continues to sit and wonder over the shell. 'Such blue. A *passionate* blue,' she murmurs, her voice quivering. After a further exchange of pleasantries, and discussions about the weather, she uncovers a prepared tea tray and goes to fetch some hot water. I hear her voice down the passage, low and insistent, as if she is having words with someone.

I have time to look around the pretty room, which I couldn't take in at all on my first visit. Though it is nicely decorated, it is a little shabby as if it hasn't had much attention beside cleaning for a long time. A portrait of a lady hangs above the mantelpiece. The woman is very fine-boned with one of those big straight noses, Roman I think they're called, and a look of pathos. She reminds me of Mrs Ivy Kentish who came to stay at our whaling station once and spent her whole stay with us in tears. So she had been shipwrecked and it was all a misery, but you learn to make do with what you've got, and at least she was alive. I could see this woman in the picture carrying on just the same, fainting and fluttering her eyelids when she came around, and jumping horses without falling off. They're tougher than they make out, women like that, not my kind at all.

Miss Malcolm follows my eyes to the painting. 'My dear friend Emmeline,' she says, as she pours water into the teapot. 'We are out of mourning here, officially that is, but all of us still mourn her in our hearts.'

I wonder if Emmeline would still be mourning Miss Malcolm if things were the other way round but I do not say this of course. This explains the run-down front room, the rubbed fabric of the chairs. No point in giving her the name of a good upholsterer; Miss Malcolm is simply a servant in this house, even if she appears to have the running of it.

As I sit there, I'm aware that she is waiting for me to make some startling revelation. She too, has dressed carefully, as if for company. Her gown is of dull oyster satin, the neckline filled by a lace collar that frills about her throat.

But I have nothing to say to Miss Malcolm. She is old and foolish and I don't really know why I've come to see her. Well, that's not exactly true, I do have an idea, but it's not one I can tell her straight away.

'I've been having bad dreams,' I say. But I cannot go on.

'What have you been dreaming about?' she asks, as if this will get me going, like the reluctant child she once knew, and no doubt still sees.

Now that I'm here my whole plan seems mad even to me, and I'm madness itself. It's just this — since my last unrehearsed visit, I've remembered something my grandmother told me about fixing trouble. And Lord knows, I've enough of that. I've lain awake at nights, mostly alone, and pretending that I'm asleep when Jacky finally collapses beside me, and thought about Granny's advice. Find a virgin, her touch can heal — only the touch must come from the right thumb. Well, I suppose any virgin would do though I don't know a lot except those who are children at the Rocks. I want a grown-up one, and Miss Malcolm seems ideal.

But I can't see how I will get Miss Malcolm to touch me ever again. I could have offered to shake her hand when I arrived, but she would have thought that is what men do, and found it odd. Perhaps I could seem to faint and she would have to take my pulse to see whether I was still breathing.

But all this is nonsense, and so I think I will tell her about my dreams, as she has asked. Only, there are so many, and some I do not want to tell her.

'I've been dreaming about my Granny,' I say, which is the truth for I dream of her almost every night. She is like a small dark sparrow hopping on the edge of sleep, admonishing me sometimes, but mostly praising me, for Granny believed in me. I was her special child.

I can tell that Miss Malcolm is disappointed. 'Granny is where it all begins,' I say. 'There is no story without Granny. She is the person who has loved me most truly and asked nothing in return, and now she is gone. She speaks to me from the grave and without her I would not be alive now. Granny Pugh is at the centre of everything I have to tell about my life before I married Jacky Guard.'

'What have you dreamt of her?' asks Miss Malcolm, as if by humouring me I will move on to something more interesting.

But I cannot tell her. Granny comes to me in many forms, and you know how it is, it's easy to forget dreams when you wake, and there are so many in my head, I cannot sort one out from another today. Sometimes she comes in the form of an old black spider, spinning her web, for even when she was old her eyes were dark coals and her skin tawny. Some say spiders mean money, others say they're a sign of death, and Granny herself was served death too often.

'I will tell you about my grandmother, and perhaps that will help me understand all this trouble in my head,' I tell the governess.

Miss Malcolm has no choice but to sit and hear me out.

My grandmother was born Hannah Smith, in the old country from where you are from, near Winchester. I believe her parents died when she was still young and she was left alone. I have wondered whether she might have come from gypsies. At any rate, she became a servant girl, which is where she fell in with a bad lad called Daniel Gordon.

Perhaps she was set to marry Daniel and wanted to look smart at the church, who can blame her, I like to look nice myself. At any rate, he was with her when she took some clothes from the house in Upham where she worked and Daniel was a groom. The mistress said to Daniel, tell Hannah to go and help herself to some of those old clothes that have been put out for pedlars. Or that is what he told Granny.

But the mistress must have changed her mind, or perhaps it was never true in the first place. Granny did say that there might have been confusion as to which pile she intended to throw away, but that was never clear to her. She took a red cloak, and it was not until later that she remembered that red was an unlucky colour, as well as two pairs of shoes and a pair of stockings.

Next thing, she is arrested for stealing, and finds herself in the dock at Winchester Quarter Sessions. She was sentenced to seven years' transportation beyond the seas. No word of what happened to that rascal Daniel Gordon. He'd vanished. What he did leave for Granny to remember him by was a little boy, and this lad was only three months when she was ordered onto one of the hulks. This is fifty years ago, around 1785, before the First Fleet set out for Botany Bay.

You will know of the hulks, Miss Malcolm, although perhaps you never saw one. I hope for your sake that it is so, for they are wicked places. Not that I have seen them either, for I was born free in Australia, so I can only go by what I've been told. As well as my grandmother and the man she later married, my grandfather Edward Pugh, my family are all from convicts, including my husband John Guard.

They put Granny and her baby in the black hole at the

bottom of the ship because she screamed and cried to be let out so she could find Daniel. Well, to hell with him, don't mind my language, Miss, but she was better off without him. Granny was locked up in that place with her little baby, all in the dark, and all alone, and nothing but muck to eat, but she must so she could keep her son, her little William, alive. She wept and pleaded to be let out into the light, for she feared the baby would go blind, and all the time she had an iron around her leg so that she could not leap at her gaolers and kill them as she would have if she could. When I remember Granny, I wish for nothing more than I could have been there to help her do the job. But I was still to come, a long way off, and far down in her history.

When Granny got to Sydney a long time had passed. By then little William, my Sweet William as she called him, as if he was a flower, was going on two years of age. On the way to Sydney she was taken on and off three ships altogether, which may have been because she kicked up such a fuss. She told me she would fight other women on the ships for scraps of food for William, even if it was something you or I would think twice about feeding to a dog.

First, she was put aboard a ship called the *Charlotte*, the name she gave my aunt. I've lived with Charlotte on and off since I was a girl. At Rio de Janeiro they took her off that ship and put her on another called the *Friendship*, and on board that one was my grandfather. At that time he was the lover of a woman called Elizabeth Parker and they had a child called Nancy.

I see how that surprises you, Miss Malcolm, for Elizabeth Parker was my name, my true name, when first you knew me, and now you are wondering if I've simply made you up a ghost story. Hear me out.

I don't think there were many rules for transporting convicts, for later on they separated them out, the men from the women. My grandfather had been ordered to go to America for stealing a greatcoat, but at the last minute, due to a war over there, he got sent to Australia too, along with Elizabeth and their baby. I remember him as a small man with a pockmarked face and a leathery skin. He seems to have had a way with women.

I did ask my grandmother, was it because of Elizabeth Parker that they put you off the *Friendship*, because it occurs to me that my grandmother might already have had eyes for Edward Pugh, who would become my grandfather. And I wonder, did the two women come to fighting.

She would not give me a straight answer over this, but as I was a child I can see why. The reason she gave was she had smuggled eggs aboard for Sweet William. But on the journey she was found out, and eggs on board a ship are said to cause contrary winds, and there are sailors who will not allow them on a ship. They will not even say the name of an egg and are more likely to call it a roundabout. So all the roundabouts were tipped overboard, and at the next stop, which was the Cape of Good Hope, she was taken off and put on to a third ship which was called the *Lady Penrhyn*, and it was by this means she eventually got to Sydney.

Meanwhile, the *Friendship* carried on to Sydney and within a month of its arrival Elizabeth Parker was dead, but that is the way it is, there are always the dead when the convict ships sail, and this happened right at the beginning when more died than arrived alive. On the other hand, it could have been that my grandfather had turned away from Elizabeth, having met my devilish Granny, and Elizabeth died of a broken heart, but who's to know?

There were more deaths to follow.

By this time Granny's ship had arrived in Sydney, and she too had come ashore to join the people living in tent city. Soon she and Edward Pugh met up again. She must have given him a good deal of comfort. It would have made sense for them to set up a new life together, especially as she had Sweet William to consider, and he had little Nancy. They would have seen at very close quarters how short life could be, and how pointless it was to wait.

The authorities gave permission for the marriage to take place. Granny always remembered her wedding anniversary, even if my grandfather did not. What is the date Edward, she used to say, and jab him in the ribs with her elbow. When he looked blank, as he always did, she would say, it is the fifteenth of June you old fool, the date I wed thee, and count back the years to 1788, when this wedding took place.

To my grandmother, it seemed some good was coming out of all her trials. She looked forward in great excitement to her wedding day. A little wattle-and-daub church had been set up along what is now George Street. The weather was crisp and clear in the days leading up.

Nine days before the wedding, her Sweet William died. He fidgeted and cried in the evening but he didn't have a fever, and she settled him down to sleep, and then herself. When she woke, William was still and cold beneath the blanket, and she cried, 'God have mercy on me, what have I done?' My grandfather took her in his arms and said, 'It is nothing you have done. It is this place, and it is too far away for God to hear us.' When she told me this she wept, and that is the only time I saw my grandmother crying, though she did say that the following week, she cried all the way through the wedding service. As well as her grief over little William who had come so far, and suffered so much, only to be snatched away from her in a moment of happiness, I think deep down my grandmother felt guilt over Elizabeth because it was her my grandfather should have been wedding. She may have wondered if it was an eye for an eye. My grandmother said she should have known better than to agree to marry on a Friday, but perhaps she didn't have much choice. Do you know how the old rhyme goes, Miss Malcolm?

No I do not, says the governess.

Monday for health
Tuesday for wealth
Wednesday best day of all

Thursday for losses
Friday for crosses
Saturday no luck at all.

For, as if that were not enough, Nancy died a month later, the girl who had been Elizabeth and Edward's. I should have known she was sick, my grandmother said, for her fingers were blue like the claws of birds when she curled them around mine.

My grandmother believed she had brought bad luck on my grandfather, though I think she was hard on herself, for he was a man who brought a fair bit of bad luck on himself. Later when he'd served his time, he was given some land out Parramatta way, although it was not the pick of what was on offer. That went to the military and those who arrived free. I've heard you have a brother out that way, Miss Malcolm?

I see that the governess is very pale.

Well, it's none of my business. Still, perhaps your brother was able to buy some acres of good land but a ticket of leave man took what he was given. He wasn't much of a farmer, for he'd been a carpenter by trade; it was Granny who had green fingers. She could grow almost anything, and milk a cow as fast as hot rain on the roof, and raise chickens, so there was always food on the table. That is how I came to be born out that way at Parramatta, where I was baptised at St John's, for at the time my mother and father were living with them.

My grandparents eventually had five children of their own, which my grandmother said were blessings, though some more than others. The first one was David, born just nine months, give or take a few days, after the wedding. My grandfather had work in those times, for he was a carpenter and they were in short supply and there were many houses to be built. There was not much work for the women convicts except to keep body and soul together and Granny was carrying the new baby. All the same, she helped other women with their laundry, for there were many worse off than her. They gave her what they could in return.

Their husbands gave her their convict hats, which they hated, and she sewed a quilt made of nine of them she had unpicked, which was to cover the new baby in his cot.

But David did not live long and so the grief continued.

David was the son who was to have filled the place in her heart where Sweet William had been. My grandfather suggested they call him by the same name but at the time she was against same-naming that many people believed in. She saw it as a bad omen, though later she changed her mind about this.

This naming of people is important, I tell Miss Malcolm. It is worth asking yourself how you came by your name, for often there is a story behind it. What of you? I do not know your first name, but perhaps it is one you were called for your grand-mother?

That is just an idle thought on my part, but Miss Malcolm says in a strangled voice, You are right, my name is Adeline and, indeed, I was named for my grandmother. It is a saintly name, a name that was given to the daughter of kings.

I feel that she wants me to know that she is better than the women of my family. I say a little quickly, perhaps unkindly, Well, well, saintly, Miss Malcolm. If you ask me, names are all tied in to the omens and tidings such as my grandmother saw at every turn.

The woman half rises from her seat and I think she is about to send me on my way. All this talk of the dead is unsettling her. Or perhaps she finds me too forward. She says in a low voice, My friends call me Adie. I can't tell her whether it's an invitation to call me by that name or not.

Well, either way, it did Granny no good when it came to naming David, for he perished with the runs, if you understand what I mean, and no offence intended. But the next two, who are my uncles Simon and Edward, did survive, although they took off for city life when they were young and we haven't seen hide nor hair of them since, though I believe they are working on farms out towards the Blue Mountains. My mother, Harriott, was born next and last my Aunt Charlotte.

I am the first of Granny's daughter's children, the first grand-child that is known of, though my uncles may have other children. I should say something here of my father, Stephen Parker. He was a convict who came some years after the First Fleet. By then my grandfather was on the farm at Parramatta and entitled to convict labour of his own, assigned servants as you will know them. Not that he trusted convicts, which is funny when you come to think of it, but then he and my grandmother had a bad experience once, when a man called Michael Dennison stole a pound of flour from their house one Christmas Day, not long after they'd arrived in Australia. At any rate, Stephen Parker came to work on his land, and that is how he met my mother Harriott.

My father and grandfather got on very well, and soon he had his feet under the kitchen table, not taking his meals with the other hands. Granny was not so keen on him. That man has a weak chin, she said, and he doesn't work hard enough on the farm.

My mother was seventeen at the time. She is a woman who has always pined for town life, even when she was a girl, for the family had been down to Sydney twice in the ferry and seen George Street lit up with lanterns at night. And my father was a man who liked a drink, and he promised her that as soon as he was free they would come to Sydney. So that did it for the two of them, they felt theirs was a match made in heaven, no matter what Granny Pugh said. For her wedding, my mother wore a trailing white lace cape and held a bouquet of mignonette and ferns in her hands. This was the beginning of the end on the farm. All of us finished up moving to the Rocks, but not before I and my brother David were born. Yes, my brother was named after the lost baby, but how I came by my name is another matter.

When I say David's name, I feel I've said enough and fall silent, the tears like bruises behind my eyes. But I am like Granny, and I would not let a stranger see me crying and so I pull myself together.

My grandfather had asked Granny if she would call one of her girls Elizabeth, after the first one that he loved, Elizabeth Parker. She refused point blank and I can't say I blame her. My grandfather let the matter rest.

My mother nearly died giving birth to me. As Granny told it, my mother had brought forth the afterbirth without me inside. Granny knew that was a bad sign and that I might suffocate in my mother's womb. She spoke roughly to my mother and told her to stop her wailing. She called to Charlotte, who was in a fright with all the noise, to come in and sit on my mother's head. Placing one foot on the bed to give her balance, she thrust her hand inside my mother and grasped me by the shoulders. In my mother's story, Granny was panic-stricken too and perhaps she was, so many children had already slipped through her fingers, as it were. She tore me from my mother's body, and gave thanks that I was still breathing.

It was her pact with the devil, my mother said. Mostly I think she was bitter because my grandmother had not told her what it would be like and that babies came from parsley beds.

It was a long time before she would look at me. She lay in bed for days and days, not able to move, and slow to heal, ranting and raving at everyone who came near her. Granny stoked up fires, even though it was December, to boil water and cook broths. She left the naming of me until my mother was well enough to speak for herself, though my grandmother thought that childbirth had touched her in the head, a view she continued to hold forever after. That Harriott, she would say of my mother, she was never the same after her first-born. That woman developed a taste for men that is hardly decent, especially in one already married, which I think now is rich coming from Granny, who had had her own fine old fling. I heard her once say, you'd think she had the itches between her legs.

It was during those days when my mother hung between life and death, that my grandfather came into the room where she lay. My grandmother wasn't watching, simply worn out perhaps, and asleep in some moment when I stopped crying and gave her a rest.

My grandfather said, Harriott, what name are you giving this child? My mother said she did not know, because her husband Stephen Parker had been expecting a boy and they had not talked about it. Please then, will you call her Elizabeth he said. It is a name that I fancy. My mother did not know what had taken place when he was a young man, nor that he had had a lover before Granny, and said yes, she was happy to call me that.

When Granny came in, my mother told her that my grand-father had named me Elizabeth and it was all agreed. At that, Granny said, the candle on the table burnt blue, and as I expect you know, Miss Malcolm, that is a sign that there is a spirit in the room, an apparition which my grandmother saw. For my name was not just Elizabeth, but Elizabeth Parker.

You might have asked Stephen, Granny had said. Or so my mother told me. She must have remembered this, in particular, for as a rule my grandmother never had a good word to say for my father.

I think it was then Granny decided she wanted me for herself, that she must protect me, for she had been offered a second chance to make good to the woman who perhaps she'd wronged.

I believe that is why Granny kept me with her as long as she did, when she could no longer take care of my brother and sister, for my mother has not been inclined towards child rearing, for all that she has babies at the snap of her garters. I swear a man has only to lay his trousers across the end of the bed and my mother will give birth to another.

Miss Malcolm makes a whinnying noise and I know I have taken things too far.

I shouldn't go on in this fashion, I say, for you don't want to hear all of this, it is not about David, or what happened.

Please, I want you to go on, says Miss Malcolm, wiping her eyes with a lawn handkerchief.

I didn't want to make you upset, I tell her. And yet a part of me is not telling the truth. I am quite enjoying the triumph of seeing Miss Malcolm in such a state. My old school teacher.

It is not that, says Miss Malcolm, in an agitated way, it is just that you are making me see some things in an unexpected light.

I wish you no harm, I say, for she is again just a foolish ageing woman who is meddling where it is best she leaves things alone. I have given up all thought of being touched by her right thumb.

I didn't think you did, Miss Malcolm says in her prim and saintly voice, descended from kings. I can tell how truly shocked she is by the things I've told her.

It could be harmful to a lady in your position to come to know the people of the Rocks too well.

Miss Malcolm straightens herself up. I choose my friends. It is nothing to do with you. But soon the children will be here, so we should stop, for this conversation can go on another day.

I've told you enough, I say, and yet I have not. I have not begun to tell her about my brother David.

Somewhere, in the depths of the Roddick house, there is the distinct clatter of pots and pans. Not for the first time, Adie Malcolm stirs and looks edgily across her shoulder, as if she is half expecting someone to appear.

'It sounds as if dinner is on its way,' says Betty Guard.

'The children will be back soon,' says the governess, seeming uneasy, signalling that the conversation is over.

'What is your cook making for dinner?'

'Oyster pie, I believe.'

'Oysters, eh? My husband fed me oysters when I was a girl. I didn't know it then, but they make a woman keener to be with a man. Did you know that, Miss Malcolm?'

'An aphrodisiac,' says Adie, the words slipping from her mouth before she can prevent them. 'Aphrodite, the goddess of love,' she says by way of embarrassed explanation.

'Ah, those Greeks of yours. Well, now I couldn't look at an oyster if you offered it to me.'

Adie rises to her feet. 'I'd like you to come again next week,' she says.

'It is something about the smell,' Betty says, as if she hasn't heard the invitation. 'I used to make a grand oyster pie. My husband bought me a recipe book. Does your cook use recipes, or does she make it all from her head?'

'I don't know,' Adie says, walking towards the door. 'I'm not sure that she can read and write. I've asked her but she avoids an answer.'

'I can,' says Betty, 'because you taught me.'

'I remember.'

'It changed me. I could not have sat and had a conversation like this with you if I had not met you. I am grateful for that.' The smell of oysters wafting down the corridor has become pungent and strong. Betty covers her nose with the edge of her shawl.

'I think the oysters are not as fresh as they might be. You should speak to her.'

'About your visit.' Adie's dismissal is becoming urgent. 'It cannot be the day before, or the day after. It is this day one week hence or not at all. Do you understand?'

'Oh yes, I understand.' But Betty stands poised as if listening to some other voice, her nostrils flaring and quivering. 'Some say it smells like pork, tastes like pork, but the smell of an oyster that is not fresh gives me the same sensation, the same reminder. It is the paleness of the flesh that is similar.'

'What is that? What are you talking about?' asks Adie, her voice chill and afraid, even as she continues to move her visitor to the door.

'Nothing. I'm sorry, nothing I should mention. It's the dreams I've been having, the ones I told you about.'

A door bangs near by. Footsteps hurry along a corridor.

'Louisa, my little girl, has not been well,' Betty says. 'She has a cough that pains her, but it's not the whooping cough, which is different.'

Adie clutches the rail of the verandah, as if to keep herself from falling. 'But you do understand? About the day?' she says.

A sense of panic has gathered round the conversation. Both women seem suddenly afraid of something, or someone who might catch them in each other's company.

'I do, Miss Malcolm, but I cannot promise one way or another,' Betty says.

A carriage draws up in the driveway. The two Roddick children are being delivered home after their outing.

'You must leave now,' Adie says to Betty. 'At once.'

But Betty has had a moment to register the children, bustling Mathilde and little Austen, both clutching wilted bunches of flowers, as they climb down, assisted by the driver of the carriage. Betty cries out then covers her mouth again with her shawl. 'The little boy,' she says. 'He is like my brother. He reminds me of David.' She turns and flees without speaking again.

Chapter 12

Lieutenant Roddick unexpectedly dines at home. The children are excited but their father says they must not stay up late. Although Mathilde winds her arms around her father's neck, he is adamant that their tea will be served in the nursery. He has had cook make up their plates already. And he will thank Miss Malcolm to see that they eat what is put in front of them and that they go to bed on time. They need early beds, he pronounces, for tomorrow he expects them to resume lessons in the afternoon. I've heard you've been playing truant, naughty things, he chides.

As she supervises the children's meal, Adie Malcolm realises that Hettie, at least, had known the lieutenant would be home, for she has made several dishes. Adie eats modestly when she is alone; her digestion is not what it was. Today, when she calls at the kitchen for the children's supper, she sees that, as well as the oyster pie, there is roast beef with Yorkshire pudding and vegetables, and a pudding followed by a syllabub. Adie wonders aloud if there will be a number of guests, but Hettie says curtly that if there are, she hasn't heard about them. She is serving dinner for two.

Adie finds herself in a fresh state of agitation, wondering about the second person at dinner. She is unsure whether the lieutenant expects her to join him, or whether it is a friend, or perhaps another lady altogether.

Not for the first time, the unwelcome thought crosses Adie's mind that one day the lieutenant might remarry. Gerald Roddick does not suffer widowhood well. Thinking of this sends a shiver of despair through her. If he were to look for someone else, where would he begin? There is not a woman in the world who could match Emmeline. For the sake of the children, Adie tells herself, she must be alert to the kind of person who might seek to fill her friend's shoes. Her lips press themselves into a determined line.

'We'll dine at eight,' says the lieutenant, catching her in the passage as she returns the children's plates to the kitchen. So that is one worry off her mind. And now her heart flutters with anticipation.

When they are seated at the dining room table, the lit candles flickering over the silver, Gerald clears his throat. 'A little wine, Miss Malcolm?'

'Just a tiny drop then,' she says, not wanting him to drink alone. He pours a glass of clear white wine to accompany the oyster pie that Hettie has left on the dresser for their entrée. The hot food sits on platters, under gleaming silver covers.

'Perhaps you would be good enough to lift us each a slice,' he says. 'I have asked that we dine without interruption.'

Miss Malcolm touches her fingers to her lips. A thought, so improbable that she can only blush, has just occurred to her. But surely she is too old? And as soon as she thinks this, as quickly she asks herself, too old for what? But straight away the answers present themselves. Perhaps not, after all. And, that. Not too old for that. She knows that the idea has been lurking there all along.

'There's something I need to talk to you about.' His voice is a caress, as she serves up the pie. When she is seated, her fork trembles on the rim of her plate. She takes a slow mouthful of pie, waiting for him to speak.

'I understand you are seeing something of Mrs Guard,' he begins, his tone still soft.

Adie's heart falls like a cold stone. She had almost persuaded herself that nothing untoward had been taking place in her life that would be noticed by others. She can hardly credit that news has travelled so fast, for it has only been twice, and only this afternoon that Mrs Guard has come in any planned fashion. After a pause, she says, 'That is so.'

'I've heard that woman is not as good as she might be.'

'I do beg your pardon? Mrs Guard has been through a terrible ordeal.'

'She has spoken to you about it?'

'Well, no. Not really.' She realises as she speaks that Betty Guard has talked to her a great deal and told her very little of consequence, so far as her rescue is concerned. 'She speaks of her family. I think she feels alone in the world. Not that she has said so. But I sense something quite tragic about her.'

'I wonder, from what's been said, if her captivity was as harsh as it sounded. She hasn't mentioned the native chief?'

Adie puts the cymbal of her noisy fork down. Her rapid breathing seems to fill the room. 'I know nothing of this. Mr Barrett Marshall's gossip, I presume.'

'The surgeon? He's left the colony.'

'He was determined to make mischief,' Adie replies.

'What he says can't be dismissed. He was a witness to what took place. Besides, there are others around who knew her in the Bay of Islands. People were shocked by her behaviour there.'

'What did they say about her?'

'I fear that I cannot repeat what I heard. Not to a lady. Let's just say that some things took place between her and a native man for which she appears to have no regret. And that her husband behaved abominably. There is a view that the woman is possessed.'

'Possessed?'

'As if by the devil. For how else could one account for a white woman having no shame about her dealings with the native tribes?'

'Perhaps she does.'

'Well, perhaps you could enlighten me. You know a public appeal was got up for the family?'

'Yes, indeed, by the Kentishes, whom I understand were rendered the greatest of assistance by Mrs Guard and her establishment in New Zealand, when they were shipwrecked in that country.'

'People are anxious about the Guards. They don't want to be taken for fools.'

Miss Malcolm thinks that Betty was right, that the oysters are a little off. The pastry is sticking to the roof of her dry mouth. She takes a gulp of wine. A bubble of wind rises in her stomach and she wonders why, whenever she is close to a man, her body lets her down in this remorseless way. 'Are you asking me to make enquiries?'

'Oh, it's neither here nor there to me,' Roddick says. 'Have you had enough of that? We should try the roast beef.'

'I don't think I could.' She doesn't know which she is refusing, the business of Betty Guard, or the meat that is to follow. 'The Governor has been a great support to the Guards.'

'He would be, of course — he has stood up for Guard. It is very political, and not everyone supports the Governor's views.'

'Like the Bowmans?' she says, with a touch of bitterness.

'I think it more than simple prejudice against the emancipists. Or the woman's reputation. The word is that Guard did not act well to the natives in Taranaki, and there could be a court of inquiry.'

'And none of this was the fault of the military? I thought they were there to keep order.'

The lieutenant wipes perspiration from his brow. 'More wine, Miss Malcolm? You must at least try the beef? Oh, nothing to do with the soldiers. Guard and his men simply went berserk on their own account.'

'Mrs Guard has told me nothing of her rescue. She seems easily distraught.'

'Well, of course some unpleasant things happened. I would not like to see cannibals at their feast. Nobody should see that, let alone a woman,' says Roddick, wiping his moustache with his napkin. 'Perhaps these things altered the state of her mind. All the same, it seems to me that Mrs Guard is not the kind of visitor we should encourage. There are the children to consider.'

She sees how black his moustache is against the white linen of the napkin, how crisp and manly he is. She cannot think of other words for it. Her throat clenches round the rising bubble of gas as she excuses herself from the table. What else to say, but another headache.

At the same time, she feels a stubbornness overtaking her. It was something her mother warned her about, and Percy had been all too keen to remind her of, in the past. But what difference has it made, when it has came to her brother, whether she was meek and mild, as opposed to wilful?

Then the lieutenant does something surprising. He catches her free hand and presses his lips to the back of it, before turning it over, and repeating the gesture in the palm of her hand. She sees it as a sign of his forgiveness, and something more. They have been aroused, she feels, by the open nature of their discussion. She is flooded with longing, to be touched more, and everywhere.

She feels his eyes follow her up the stairs.

When first light breaks Adie Malcolm gets up and brushes her hair before the mirror. Although it is deeply flecked with grey, it is still silky fine. She holds it in her hand, twisting it like a rope before releasing it again over her plump shoulders and is surprised by the effect. She does not entirely recognise the woman looking back at her — still plain, in need of better teeth and with too many folds under her chin, but someone with brighter eyes and a better complexion than the last time she looked at herself. She dabs lavender water at the base of her throat and in the crooks of her elbows.

Adie goes to the window and pulls back the curtain. A tree in the garden is covered with what appear to be dense white magnolias, though she hasn't known magnolias to bloom in this part of the world. Surely she must be imagining those huge petals, about to unfold. In a moment, perhaps hearing the sound of the window latch, or because it is time for them to wake, the petals move and stretch, begin to flutter. A cloud of white cockatoos rises in unison with a whirr of wings and the tree is left bare. She lies down on the bed and sinks into a brief sleep.

Chapter 13

10 January 1835

Dear Sir

I thank you for your esteemed correspondence and the concern you express for the welfare of my sister. As you say, she is a woman in middle life and has had her share of disappointments, for which I have to confess some responsibility. Perhaps I should have allowed her to remain back home, in the old country, for she does not seem to have settled well in the Colony. I had hoped that her longing for a family of her own might be tamed and subdued by her work amongst the poor when she arrived here, but that did not happen.

Unfortunately, she believed when we came here that I would remain at the centre of her life. You understand, for I am speaking very frankly, that she considered her life's work as caring for me, and ironing my shirts and cleaning my shoes while I did business in the new town of Sydney. I should have disillusioned her of these plans, for that was never my intention. Nor, I believe, could she have imagined the place she would find, for her head has always been in a make-believe world of gods and heroes from the ancient times. I have been troubled, on seeing these preoccupations of hers, that she might lose sight of the very God of very Gods, the great Creator who made us all, and to Whom I have been drawn ever closer since my marriage to my dear Maude and the birth of our two sons, Herbert and Nathaniel. Nathaniel is a very recent arrival, a joy beyond our wildest hopes. Truly, my wife is a miracle.

I hope my sister is not foolish enough to think that you might take the place of a brother to her. I am sure someone as estimable as you will attend to any such aspirations with firmness and gentle courtesy. [Here the letter has been partly scratched out, and started again, as if the writer has considered a number of ways to address the problem he sees.]

As to your children, my dear sir, I am convinced that my sister will bring no harm to them. I believe that if you hold your ground, she will soon see the error of her ways.

If the worst comes to the very worst, I will of course take her in, until such time as a suitable berth can be arranged for her return to England, and I am able to work out a settlement to keep her in comfort. I have had a little cottage built near the river bank, our household staff having now expanded with the arrival of Nathaniel. I might be able to accommodate my sister there. But let us hope that it does not come to that.

Thank you for your patience, may the good Lord succour you in the sorrows you currently endure.

My wife sends you her kind regards.

Yours faithfully

Percy Malcolm

PS Mrs Malcolm says, and I am in agreement with her, that a firm line should be taken. My sister suffers from too good an opinion of herself. I hope you will not see that as unChristian, but it is best to be aware of her true nature. My wife is a practical woman. I feel bound to deliver her opinion along with my own.

Chapter 14

I am not sure that Miss Malcolm is giving me her full attention today. There is something different about her, both excited and watchful. I have liked the attention she has given me in all our conversations, for the rest of my life feels bereft. Jacky has stayed so distant towards me I cannot bear it. All the last week he has slept in the big chair in the kitchen. I have been thinking of taking the children to my mother's place, but there is no room for the children and me to be comfortable. Louisa is little better, though I try to tell myself it is not so. Her eyes implore me to give her comfort I do not have. I should be with her, but I will go mad if I do not get away from the Rocks and the glare in my husband's eyes. In this spacious airy house, I can think of myself as some other person not weighted with the burden of the past. I imagine myself in this parlour, receiving visitors with an inclination of my head and a small smile, pouring out tea and offering a scone and a slice of fruitcake. I would, of course, have done something about the upholstery.

What I see in the governess is a kind of happiness which

cannot be explained, and she is not going to tell me. I have brought her a gift of some enamelled buttons. They are quite fragile, painted with tiny blue cornflowers against a white background. I have cut them from an old dress of mine that was stored in the bottom of the wardrobe at the Cambridge Street house. I tell her that they will look nice on the dress she had worn last week, which was nice enough but plain.

Her face had lit with pleasure. You shouldn't bring me these gifts, she'd exclaimed, but I could tell she was pleased. Nothing in this house will belong to her.

As if reading my mind, she said simply: Everything of my mother's that was brought from England is at my brother Percy's place. Percy and Maude's.

After inspecting the buttons and exclaiming some more over them, she assumes again an attitude of listening, as if for someone in the house. This is cook's day off, she says. I'm sure she will have gone to town.

This explains her fidgeting. I ask if we should leave it for another day.

No, not at all, Betty, for I find your story riveting. There is so much I want to ask you.

It is my story, I say, and you must not ask me things.

I am sorry, she says. I did not know there were rules.

Well, of course there are. If you ask things I cannot tell you about, you are no better than my husband and my aunt. Without meaning to, I put my hands around my ears.

Betty, says Miss Malcolm, I am sorry to have upset you. If you would like to leave it for today you have only to say.

So we are going around in circles, she and I.

We sit in silence for a minute or two. The mantel clock ticks very loudly *dud dud dud*.

With an effort, she says, I would like you to call me by my Christian name.

Adie? I cannot hide my astonishment.

It is how friends address each other.

Thank you, I say. I know what this must have cost her. I'll stay a little while, I say, because something tells me I may not see her for some time. I don't know what it is, a premonition or a warning, my Granny would say.

I cannot stop thinking of David, I tell Adie. She shifts uneasily, and I remember I had alarmed her with likening the little boy Roddick to my brother.

Still, it is true. I think of him more, now that I am living back here at the Rocks, than I did in New Zealand, for I keep expecting to see him when I turn a corner. David. Beloved boy, I might add, but it sounds fancy. Instead, I say, he was like an angel, that boy. I remember first seeing him, even though I was only two when he was born. He was wrapped tightly in a sheet, and very still, which frightened me. I wondered if I'd imagined that for most children can't tell you clearly about their early memories; usually what you think you have seen is what has been described to you by others. But I asked Granny when I was older if I had seen this right. She gave me a sharp look and said yes, this was exactly as it had been, and I must be a child with second sight. I don't think this is so, for if I had been able to look ahead I don't know that I would have followed Jacky Guard the way I did. Perhaps it would have been better if I had known what to expect.

Or perhaps it was simply that when Granny left us for the afterlife, I stopped seeing things so clearly.

My uncles had disappointed their parents by moving away from the farm, so there was nobody to take it over when the family decided to move to Sydney. In my mind, I hold a picture of Granny, on the last day at the farm, walking beneath the trees she had planted, the fruit of which she had gathered and made into sweet jams and preserves, the trees where her children had swung and built houses of their own. Though I was very young at the time, I still hear the melody she was singing, the convicts' song which she did often sing, only usually more heartily as if it were a bit of a joke. Not that day.

> *Singing too-rall-li-oo-rall, liad-di-ty,*
> *singing too-rall, li-oo-rall-li-ay*
> *singing too-rall-li-oo-rall, li-ad-di-ty*
> *oh we are bound for Botany Bay.*

My mother liked all the people around us in Sydney, but Granny said it was the worst day's work she ever did, packing up and leaving the farm.

She looked around her and saw terrible sights at the Rocks and wished her grandchildren elsewhere. It was not just the public hangings and the drinking, it was the way we all lived cheek by jowl with the next person in the narrow cramped alleyways, and having to walk through the streets to the standpipes for water. It was the smell of rotting meat and rubbish we couldn't get rid of, and cesspits in the garden. The smell of your own — well, I beg your pardon — is bad enough but that of a dozen other families on a hot day gets you down. But on the good side of the ledger, when we first left the farm we had money in our pockets, and there were many things to buy. We bought cups and saucers, enough for everyone, and matching china dishes in blue and white, a kettle and a tea caddy, we bought linen and nice clothes, umbrellas for the rain and lamps that cast a pretty glow at night. It is not all bad at the Rocks, whatever people might think, looking in on us from the outside.

But my grandfather who had moaned about the farm now wished he was back there, and in a short while he was dead, and by that time there wasn't much money left at all, though Granny had managed to save a little.

Before long, my mother gave birth to my sister Sophia. At least as far as I know, she was my father's child, for by that time my mother had begun to act differently, singing and dancing around the house and staying out late. My grandmother's face would grow black with rage. Sophia was born without trouble. She slipped and fell from my mother onto the kitchen floor before Granny had time to catch her, and no damage done.

I don't know what my father thought about all this. Of course it was a man who had brought about this change in my mother. He was a convict, a sawyer by trade, called John Deaves, Deaves being the name you first knew me by. His skills were in demand and he was wealthier than my father. He lived at Lane Cove and before you could say three farthings, my mother had gone there to live, and was in the family way again with the first of my three half-brothers. I don't believe Granny ever saw any of these boys. She told my mother she didn't want to set eyes on them. She was left with all three of us on her hands, David and Sophia and myself, not to mention my father Stephen Parker moping around the house and drinking himself to death.

I became Granny's right hand from the time I was old enough to do my first errand. She was soft on David too. Anyone would have been, he was more like a girl than a boy. He had yellow curls, not like the rest of us who are mostly dark and take after Granny Pugh. His red lips puckered up like a girl's, so that ladies always wanted to kiss him. Some people treated him as if he was odd. That is, until the day he tried to save our father's life.

After his daily round of the Cat and Fiddle and the Currency Lass when my father came home his face was red, and he stumbled about breaking things. Granny was taking in laundry, and she had had enough of this. The copper was always on the boil and our house smelt like clothing stew. As in Parramatta, she grew a garden too, but it was just a little pocket square of land, not enough to feed five mouths. My mother dropped by from time to time, wearing silks and a shawl with a beaded fringe, and left some coins for Granny. My Aunt Charlotte had taken up with a man called Garside; the two of them were servants for John Guard, my husband as he became. I've heard from my aunt, when she's in a nasty frame of mind, that he fancied her but she fell with her first baby when he was away at sea, and that was that. But at least she was employed and now and then she would leave a shilling for Granny, not because of us, but because Granny was her mother too.

Granny hid these little takings but my father usually found out where they were, even though she changed the place every time. One day she told him he should go and leave her to bring us children up on her own.

His eyes filled up with tears and there was an embarrassing quaver in his voice when he spoke.

I'll change my ways, he told Granny, I'll go to sea with Jacky Guard.

He won't take you, she said. He's a hard man, you have to work for people like him.

I had met Jacky Guard a time or two when we visited Charlotte and was afraid of him. He hadn't long been at sea since his discharge, but already there were some cruel stories around him.

You don't know, my father said.

I do, because I've already asked him.

Bugger you, you old hag, he yelled at her then. You'd send me away from my children? First their mother deserts them, and whose frog spawn is she? Now you want to send me away. They will have no parents at all.

I understood from the way he spoke that my father had a sore heart over my mother.

At that, Granny sighed. Look Stephen, she said, I don't like what has happened any better than you, but I cannot feed these children and your drinking as well.

My father took his coat then and went out. Perhaps Granny thought that was the last she would see of him, but that night he came home sober, his hands red and raw from hanging on the end of a pick, breaking rocks all day. He gave her five shillings and she was pleased with him. This kept on all week, and on Sunday, my father said he would take David for a ride around the harbour and they would perhaps pull in a fish or two.

David was a wee boy, only six at the time, and you could see him glow with excitement. It was as if his father had seen him for the first time ever, and perhaps that he was in need of a father's attention, for the boys in our street gave him grief, called him names and threw stones if he went near to join in any games. I was the one who taught him how to play hopscotch, and roll his marbles. It was me who taught him how to swim and hold his breath when he dived beneath the surface of the water in the bay.

When my father suggested this treat David swelled up with joy. For a moment I felt the green-eyed monster at my shoulder for I too would have liked to go out in a rowboat. But then I tried to take pleasure in the way David smiled and skipped.

It will be your turn next Betsy, said my father, and this was the first time he had ever called me this name. I've wondered since if this was his rebellion against the way my grandfather and my mother had joined forces to give me a name without consulting him.

The boat had been lent to my father by one of the men he worked alongside. It was a solid-looking craft. The day was perfect, the harbour aglitter in the sun and as settled as cream in a jug. And yet, in Cockle Bay, the boat overturned, perhaps a sudden wave. I've seen it happen more than once in New Zealand, a surge like a spirit that changes the shape of things in a moment. Whatever it was, my father was not strong enough to contain the boat in its larrikin skip and jump, and he and David were both in the water.

A passing boat stopped and picked them out of the drink within a few minutes, but my father had already gone and drowned, and might have dropped straight to the deep had not David been holding onto his hair trying to keep his face out of the water, his little feet dog paddling as fast as they could on the spot.

That is how they found them.

People brought food and money for the funeral. John Deaves gave a sizeable amount. Is it blood money, my grandmother asked, with scorn. She took it anyway. It would be a respectable funeral, she said. Even my mother wore black mourning dress and jet beads.

My father was laid out in his coffin in our parlour, wearing my grandfather's second best suit (of course, grandfather had been buried in his best one) and though it was very short on my father's long body you couldn't see that when the sheets were in place. Afterwards, a carriage was hired to take him to the cemetery.

A year or so passed and people forgot we were poor. There was always someone else who was in need. I saw Granny was finding it hard to breathe some mornings. Her face went a nasty spotty red as she gasped for air. Sometimes she acted strangely and I heard her talking to herself, though what she muttered I couldn't tell. She often sang the old songs. One day I found her sitting in the kitchen with the fire out, and she was singing in a rickety old voice.

> *By hopeless love I was once betrayed*
> *And now I am, alas a convict maid . . .*
> *For seven long years I toil in pain and grief,*
> *And curse the day when I became a thief*
> *I ne'er had been, alas, a convict maid.*

This is a song often sung at the Rocks, but never with such pain as I heard in Granny's voice that day.

I look up, and see tears in Adie's eyes. One rolls down her round cheek, and she dabs at it with a handkerchief.

Another time, Granny stood backside out to the street and lifted her skirts at the world for all to see. I pretended I hadn't noticed and chased after Sophia to stop her falling in the well, doing what I could.

David had begun to help as well. He was more confident now, and less tormented, though at night he had bad dreams.

Often I took him into my bed and held him beside me. In the night, I would wake to find his hands knotted through my hair, and his face wet with crying which must have been what woke him. I did not tell Granny about these things that happened at night, for she would have said it was not right, a boy of his age having to climb into bed with his sister and weep. I did not mind though and I think part of me thought of him as if I was his mother. It went through my head that my hair was our father's hair that he still held fast in his hand.

Then there was a lull, and Granny seemed more herself. I don't know if she talked to my mother about what was to become of all of us. If she did, my mother must have refused us, or whether she simply could not bring herself to see how old Granny was. One morning Granny got up, looking older and sadder than I had ever seen. At breakfast, she said, Well David and Sophia, today is a great day for you. You will have a new life and many more friends than you have ever had before. We will pack your bags and take you to a new home.

In this way I learnt that David and Sophia would go to live in orphanages. David was being sent to the male orphan school and Sophia to the one for girls. At that time David was seven and a half and Sophia was five.

When I heard this I begged Granny. Do not send him away I said, meaning David. I did not want Sophia to go away either, but already she seemed better able to look after herself than David. She has always been more like my mother as a person.

It will be all right child, Granny said. You will stay here with me. But it was not for myself that I was so unhappy. Nobody would know at orphan school that David was a hero and I was afraid he would be hurt all over again.

Hoping to console me, she said that she was preparing a special meal that we would eat at lunchtime. We would pick fresh peas and she would cook them with a roast of mutton and potatoes, and perhaps there would be some griddle scones and apricot jam.

The four of us sat on the back step that faced the garden and shelled the peas into a pot, as if nothing bad was going to happen. Granny held up a large fat pea to the light before opening it with a cry of satisfaction. You must remember girls, she said, though Sophia wasn't listening, being too busy stuffing her mouth with raw peas, a pod that holds five peas or nine is lucky. If you place it above the door the next dark man who comes through will be the one you marry. Come Betsy, she said. She had taken to calling me this name my father had bestowed, that last day before he met his maker, perhaps out of respect for him. Here is a pod with nine, let's see what lad comes passing by.

To please her, because I knew she was hiding sorrow, I took the pea and climbed on a chair so that I could reach to put it on top of the door. I had hardly pushed the chair back under the table when a shadow fell across the path, and around the back of the house came Jacky Guard.

Jacky is not a tall man but he has shoulders like an ox. His black hair reminds me of a crow's wing, though these days it is streaked with gray, and so is his beard. He is a fair-skinned man, which shows up this darkness. His eyes are not exactly brown, but lighter with flashes of green in their depths. The colour changes when he is angry, the green glowing almost with a yellow light that is hard to describe. I was scared stiff. And then I started to laugh. My grandmother gave a reluctant chuckle when she saw what I was thinking, but he was not in a mood to be amused, and her smile faded.

Charlotte has told me of your plans for these children, said Jacky. I must ask you to reconsider. If it is a matter of money, I would be glad to help out.

It has been decided, it is done, Granny said. I have had a letter written to the Colonial Secretary, and the children have been accepted. There is no turning back. I am too old for it.

I see, he said. He did not like what he heard.

I think it will be the best chance for them, she went on. They will learn some reading and writing which is useful in this colony.

Their mother was taught a little but she has never made use of it, and now she only has time for Deaves's brats. Looking over her shoulder at David and Sophia, she said, They'll have food and shelter and someone to watch over them.

He shrugged, taking her point. My own house is already crowded out, he said.

I know all of that, Granny told him. Charlotte's hands are full too.

She sighed and turned away from him, not wanting to talk about it any more. It has been decided, she said again.

And what of you, Granny Pugh?

The girl will look after me, my grandmother said, her gaze falling on me.

Betsy is just a child said Jacky, glancing at me. He stood with his thumbs hooked through his braces. He was wearing a straw hat with a flat brim and a blue cotton shirt, and didn't look as threatening as I had first thought.

She is ten, Granny said, and wiser than you think. I don't want anyone else but her.

After Jacky Guard was gone, I said Granny, he is an old man, I cannot marry him.

He is not that old, she said, thirty or thereabouts.

I looked at her to see if she was serious but she never said another thing. Soon we would eat and then the children would be taken to the orphanage. A woman was coming to collect them. For them, it was like a great adventure, they did not understand that they were leaving us.

But I did. I stood and waved and waved to David, trying to look happy for him, because I did not want to frighten him before he had even left us. Just as they rounded the corner of the lane, he looked back. Betsy, he called, I want to come home.

After that, I did not see my brother and sister for two years. My grandmother never saw them again.

There is not much more to tell of Granny Pugh. I was with her to the end. Death never comes the same for any two people and I have seen my share, although I am still twenty years of age. One minute, Granny was talking to me, the next she was not. I think she had found some peace in herself, for she talked not of old England, but of the farm at Parramatta where her children grew up. Look, she said, look out there, old Daisy is ready to be milked. Fetch me the bucket, child. And while my eye followed whatever it was she saw, she grew silent.

Shortly after this, I took myself over to my Aunt Charlotte's house and said, Granny has passed on.

When Charlotte had seen for herself, she said, You had better come and stay here for now. I tried to say that I could look after myself in the house, because I had been looking after two of us for more than a year, but I was overruled, and anyway, the house hadn't belonged to Granny; it was rented.

That is how I came to stay for a short time with my Aunt Charlotte and her children, who had various fathers all with the first name of Samuel, which I thought strange.

Later on, I went to live with my mother and her new husband, and after awhile they sent for David and Sophia. We were told that we must take the name of Deaves, which my brother and sister did without complaint, but it did not feel right to me. I wore the name like a hair shirt and every time I was thus addressed I felt a prickle of anger. Nor did I care for living with John Deaves for he was a forceful man and given to rage when there was too much noise, which there often was on account of so many children. He did not mind it so much from his own boys, but the three of us Parker children learnt that we must creep around and not give him bother. My little brother was white as whey from living in the orphanage, and sometimes he was so quiet I thought he had simply melted away in the distance of Sydney Harbour. Our mother did not seem to notice, but then she never had. She sang and shrieked, as if she must entertain Deaves whenever he was around, and sailed down the street with him, dressed from head to toe in her finery. At night, when we were abed, I would whisper to David in the dark. I would say the old nursery rhymes that Granny taught us, even though he was growing to be a big boy now.

Humpty Dumpty sat on a hill
Humpty Dumpty had a great fall
And all the king's horses
And all the king's men
Couldn't put Humpty together again.

But why, David asked me, why couldn't they put him together again, and I could tell that he was crying in the dark. Would he never get better?

I don't know, I said, perhaps he will some day.

I'll never sit on a hill, he said.

Sometimes we have no choice, I told him. We have to do the hardest thing.

I have done the hardest thing.

When he said that I felt as if my heart was breaking. He seemed much younger in his years than me, or our little sister Sophia, who though she stole quietly about the place when Deaves was in, could cast aside her silence and be as merry as any children in the street.

Tell me the one about the little nut tree, he whispered. And so I said it for him, for it was gentler by far, the one that begins:

I had a little nut tree, nothing would it bear
But a silver nutmeg and a golden pear.

So then he said I would like a nut tree, and I could tell by the sigh in his voice that he did not think he would ever have one.

I will look after you David, I said. If I have a real regret in my life so far, it is that I didn't keep David by my side when Jacky came for me. But I don't think I had a choice. Like the children going to the orphanage, some things are decided before you have had much say. My mother thought she had chosen her own way, because she had broken away from her mother, and had more than one man. But it is hard to tell if it was what she chose, or whether it was just her way of saying that she wouldn't be told by others what to do. My grandmother had chosen constancy, so far as I could tell, or had done after she was married to my grandfather. I have sought to be like Granny, whatever people say of me.

In the springtime, that year that I lived in the Deaves household, blue wrens nested in a bush beneath the window of the room where David and Sophia and I slept. Sophia did not wake until late, but in the mornings, when the sun was rising, David and I would look out the window and watch the mother wren rising and preparing to feed her young. She flitted hither and yon, like a blue dart, her feathers shining in the new morning light.

But I didn't look after David. I left it too late.

Chapter 15

At sea, Sydney to Te Awaiti, 1828

The next time I was in Sydney, I asked Charlotte to let Betsy come over for a visit.

Sydney Town is changing all the time. I am just one of many whalers who come and go. Last time I was in port there were 70 sailing ships, half of them whalers. There is talk that money coming in here can be measured in millions not thousands of pounds though who is counting I do not know for I was told when a boy that in order to count to a million a man wd have to count day and night for 5 yrs of his life without stopping to sleep. There is foreigners everywhere, you cannot understand a word they say, they come from France and Spain and Italy not to mention America and men with pigtails from China land. There is a library and a museum and streetlights placed at 50 yds apart that look like old London at night. It is very smart. But then too there are wild dogs roaming the streets not to mention whooping cough and smallpox going the rounds. What with 1 thing and another and the girl growing up so fast, too fast, the time was on me to make a move. I was in a panic as if I were coming down with a fever of my own.

I think Charlotte knew what was up for when Betsy and I sat down in front of the fire she said well, I will leave you 2 to have a talk and she shoos her boys out too.

I took Betsy on my knee. She did not seem surprised. Close up I saw tiny veins in the lids of her eyes. Those lids are like the shells of tiny birds. I thought about the first time I had placed my hand on her head and though she has grown big and sturdy and has some cheek there is also something about her that I am afraid of breaking.

Soon Betsy I tell her it will be time for you to come away with me. She sat still but again did not appear surprised. We will have a wedding. At this she nodded.

Well then if that is decided I said I must tell you some duties for a wife that perhaps you have not learnt at school. The first is for obedience. That should not be hard for I will not ask more of you than I should. Besides it is a lawful command that wives render obedience to their husband in the Lord. In the good book St Peter says likewise — ye wives, be in subjection to your own husbands. The first task I give you is to work hard at arithmetic for I will want you to count my money and keep my ledger books. When I take you with me I expect you to be good at that.

Next a wife must be faithful to the bed. Not that I think you will be tempted. There are rough sailors in New Zealand who have become landlubbers and work on the whaling station. They live with native women as their wives. They drink much rum. I am not a man given to too much drink. I drink a tot at the end of a hard day's work but you will not see me in my cups. Then there are natives who are called Maoris and they wd not be a temptation to a girl.

At that Betsy laughed, which is music to my ears. I wd not lie down with a black fella she said, as if it was a great joke.

The third I said, Betsy, is that you will owe me love. This is wrote big in my book that you will give me this whatever happens whether in health or sickness, wealth or poverty. You owe me comfort and support. Round this place I see women who are harsh and sullen towards their husbands, as your mother was to your father. They are a burden and a plague but you are not like them. I like your cheerful nature. I saw how you looked after your grandmother when she was alive. I think you are a girl with love. With love will come babies. I thought perhaps I wd not have a son but now I have decided it is not too late. Put your hand here Betsy. That is my red hot poker that I keep for you. I see that you know what I am about. I pull her closer so that she is sitting right on the mountain I am making beneath her. I put my hand carefully on her little box and I feel it all aquiver.

I said Betsy I wd sore like to put this poker where it belongs but we will wait until we have left Charlotte behind us. I will not do this now though it is not easy to wait. It is good that you are not afraid. We will do this thing and make a son between us.

Then I groaned in the pit of her shoulder. I have never wanted any woman like I want this girl who will be my wife. I hold on to her until the heaving stops. It is all right, I said, it is all right, there is nothing wrong with me that a good lie down in a bed together will not fix. It is how a man is when his poker is on fire. I took her hand in mine and put my mouth to each little finger tip.

You old dog she said and laughed and pulled her hand away. I looked at her face and I could not read what was there, something dark and a mystery for me. I am not your Uncle Jacky any more.

She gave a little undecided laugh. Jacky she said.

I will come for you soon I told her then. I cannot wait for you much longer.

Now I go to make all ready for her arrival.

Chapter 16

Hettie delivers a tray to the dining room where Adie Malcolm sits alone. On the tray is a small mutton pie and three slices of bread still with their crusts on. Hettie is a sallow woman with the hint of a moustache and heavy brows. Her eyes give the impression of looking over the shoulders of the person to whom she is speaking.

'Did you enjoy your day out, Hettie?' Adie asks.

'Until it came on to rain, Miss,' replies Hettie, 'then I came back and stayed in my room and put my feet up.'

'But the rain cleared at lunchtime, before the children went out,' Adie exclaims. She has been happy all day and now she feels menace in the air.

'So it did now.' Hettie closes the door behind her, and it seems only moments later that Lieutenant Roddick's footfall lands in the hallway. When he enters the dining room, his face is dark with anger, though Adie does not see this right away.

'Lieutenant, we were not expecting you,' she says. 'I am sure that cook can find something in the larder.' She pushes her plate away from her, as if to share her meal.

'I have told you, I do not want that woman near the house.'

'Mrs Guard?' The words hanging in the air like a noose.

'I thought that was clear.'

'Lieutenant, you don't understand,' she begins, and falls silent, as she absorbs the full extent of his rage. Suddenly, she is very hungry. Her stomach has had its first whiff of mutton and is groaning for more. She presses her hands over her stomach to contain its rumbling.

'You don't want to her to come here. Yes, I see.'

'Who cares what they do, they are riff-raff from the Rocks. But not in my house, I will not have the likes of them here. There is gossip about her condition.'

'Her condition?' cries Adie. 'I have seen her this afternoon.'

'I do know that.'

'And so I am reduced to eating bread and water, Lieutenant? Let me remind you, I am an adult, not a child to be punished.' Her hands, pressed into her stomach, are white-knuckled. 'Mrs Guard is not about to have a baby. Or certainly not one that has been hiding itself since the time of her rescue. That is nearly five months ago.'

Roddick's look grows darker still. 'How would you know? A woman can hide such things.'

'I am sorry, but you are mistaken,' she says.

The nearness of him is overwhelming, his smell ripe and musky, like leather and whisky on the breath.

'So she told you more this afternoon of her sojourn in New Zealand?'

'No,' she says, in a low voice. The room feels cold.

'The mistress of evasion.' She hears his contempt, but this is such an apt description of the conversations Adie has had with Betty Guard that she can only shrug her shoulders in reluctant assent.

'You must never let her come here again. If she does, I will have you removed.'

'Removed? You cannot mean that.'

'Oh yes,' says Roddick, walking towards the door. He casts her a look of pity and dismissal. 'Your brother has said he will take you in.'

Chapter 17

Adie

Adie Malcolm picks her way through the streets of the Rocks district, seeing the houses hewn from brown-gold rock, solid-looking dwellings though the walls are knobbly and irregular, the closely cropped roofs made of hardwood shingles. In the back yards grow small gardens, filled wall to wall with vegetables, among the remnants of native shrubs and trees. Here and there, dandelions and clover spill through the cracks on the street, their seeds imported with peas and beans, radishes and turnips. All of it suggests disorder. And yet, Adie thinks, there must be a pattern to it, for she finds herself more quickly than she had expected at Cambridge Street.

She is on foot and alone. She wears a hat with a vestige of a veil, though it does not cover her face for that would draw more attention than she desires. At the end of the street she hesitates, still composing in her head what she will say to Betty Guard.

Then she sees a large group of men and women walk from one of the houses. The group is headed by a man with squat shoulders and a thick neck, yet he has an air about him — a presence, she will say to herself afterwards. For at first she does not recognise John Guard, so altered is he since their last meeting. There is something sombre about the tread of these people. Miss Malcolm looks for an awning or a verandah to draw behind but, finding none, she stands with her hands folded. The group moves towards her, and in the midst of them she sees the figure of Betty Guard, shrouded, like all the women, in black mourning garb. Her collar is drawn up around her throat, and a black hat is drawn over her left eye, so that it takes the governess a few moments to recognise her. Her face, or that which is exposed, is very pale in the harsh sunlight, her lips set. Two youths come out of the house carrying a diminutive coffin between them.

Betty

I stop in front of Adie Malcolm. I want to spit in her meddlesome ugly old face. I want to tell her to get out of here and go to hell. I cannot understand what she is saying to me, she is babbling away about not wishing to see me again. Well, the feeling is mutual. Feeling? I am numb and do not feel much, it takes me all my time to put one foot in front of the other. I am sorry about what happened to your brother, she raves, standing in front of me and barring my way.

My brother. I don't know what she is talking about. What do you know of my brother? But that is unfair, for I have spoken more of him to her than anyone else. That is why I do not shove her away, send her flying across the cobbles.

As I stand in silence, I see Jacky turning with his eyes full of yellow fire. I say, in a quiet manner, That is behind me now, Miss. This is what is happening now. That coffin that you see carried by my half-brothers is Louisa's coffin. That is the body of my daughter, Louisa.

Jacky

My wife was not there when our daughter died. It was late in the

144

afternoon and I could see the child was sinking. I took her in my arms beside the fire and I rocked her and I sing to her. I sing 'lavender's blue diddle diddle, lavender's green' and just for a moment I see something I had not seen in a long time, which is the face of my mother who I think is gone forever, but here she is and here is her voice in my ear and her look in my daughter's face. I seen a shadow of the woman she might have grown into, one I might have looked at and said to Betsy that was my mother's eyes. But that will never be for now the baby's eyes was closing. I did not think they wd open again. And where is my wife? She stays away and stays away. I have heard she is hanging out with the nobs but I do not ask her. What good will they do the likes of her and me. I have lost everything, 2 ships at sea, and there is nothing left but what is in this house.

Perhaps it is not her to blame. I cannot bring myself to touch the woman now. When she asks me what is wrong, I says you know what is wrong. She says, I bring your babies safely home to you. That was the best I could do for you.

When she comes in, I says, now is you satisfied? You have been and left your baby and now she is dead.

She gives me a look that could pierce my heart if I let it. She says I knew she would die. I could not bear to see.

She has stayed rock silent, 24 hrs now. She has not slept nor moved nor made any cry. Her mother and her aunt come and dress the little one in her christening gown that was made for her last year and it fit her still. Then they take Betty and push her arms inside her mourning dress and she lets them do it. They place jet-black beads around her neck and on her breast they place the mourning brooch her grandmother wore when old Pugh died. Inside of it is a lock of hair. I do not know whose hair it is now, it is a brooch that does much service.

The next thing I know there is a woman standing in the middle of the street stopping my wife in her path. I remember this woman from long ago, the fat daft old teacher I sent Betsy to, to learn her sums. I have seen her before and not let on that

I knew who she was. Why should I? Betty wd have been better off if they had never set eyes on each other. She put ideas in her head that she did not need. She looks like a mad woman as if she has been out in the sun too long. She is waving her hands and beating them on her breast and I see Betty clench her fists. I think she is going to hit the teacher but she stands there in the street and the snot comes out of her nose and spills and her mouth is stretched back in a terrible way and I hear her howl as a wild dog might do.

I move to pull her back inside, for by now there is a crowd gathered from out of ev'ry house. I take her elbow, and she pulls herself away.

Do not touch me.

She puts her arms up to fend me off and knocks her hat off in the street. She covers her face with her fists but does not stop this noise of an animal that makes me want to put her down. If I had a musket in my hand I wd do her that kindness.

You better go missus, I say to the school teacher. You better get out of here. I see she does not recognise me in all the crying and shouting that is going on. As she turns to leave, I see a redcoat standing at the end of the street, looking at her. I can tell she does not need me to make any more trouble than she has already got. I know the redcoat. His name is Roddick, the one who drinks and did not come to New Zealand with his brothers-in-arms.

The teacher walks away from my wife who is quieter now she has had her yell. Her shoulders droop, her arms hang at her sides. The redcoat walks towards the teacher. Another time I might have stopped to watch but I do not.

I pick up my baby girl's coffin myself and walk down the street not looking to see who will follow me.

Part 4

A True Love of Mine

Chapter 18

Te Awaiti, 1829

As I was taking a wife to Te Awaiti I laid in good stores so that we could go for a long stay and not lack in comfort. Before the journey I brought aboard:

57 bags of salt

45 casks of flour

14 casks pork

23 casks sugar

6 ½ chests tea

1 bag of pepper

1 bag of canvas

2 puncheons of rum

2 cases of gin

6 baskets of tobacco.

In all the rush to get everything on board there was no time for me to wed Betsy. I could tell she was disappointed but she is a good girl and said naught. By this time she knew the duties of love a wife must show for her husband. I took her to the ship the night before we sailed and showed her what was what. She tried hard not to cry. It came as a surprise to her even though she had flirted and carried on. Well there is no way a woman can know what it is like until it's done. But she was a snug fit down there and I told her she was a good girl. I think she is all right about it now. I cannot get enough of her.

When we got to Te Awaiti, Ngai Tahu the Maori tribe to the south had burned down our huts, up to their tricks again. So we dropped anchor off shore the first several nights and I kept Betsy on board while we ran up some more huts. Our houses are built out of supplejack plastered with clay and the roofs thatched with reeds. When our new home was watertight I took the girl ashore and we set up house. I must learn to say wife. Perhaps we will find a minister to put a seal on it. Not that there are any round here. There are missionaries in the north but they are not men to my liking. My men give me sidelong looks. I know they are thinking May (or perhaps April) and December. I have taken to calling her Mrs Guard when they are near.

Te Awaiti, 1830

I look back on what I have wrote this past year. Nothing much but the weather and the tides and the whales we have caught and the stores brought. But my life is not the same. It is better now the girl is here. I have not thought to write down so much for she has filled my head instead with her talk and carry-on. But still I do not have a son. Lately I have been wondering if she does not like me well enough for my seed to take hold in her. She gives no sign of this and I tell myself there is no fool like an old one, worrying over these matters.

During the whaling seasons, on my ship the *Waterloo* (½ my ship, for the other ½ is still owned by Mr Campbell), we employ a sea captain by the name of Richard Hall to carry our cargo to Sydney. Between seasons I go on with the arrangement to captain the ship, sailing south to pick up flax and sealskins. Often I take the girl to sea with me because I worry that the

Maoris might take her. A good thing she is not seasick. Some of the men don't like a woman on board. When they think I cannot hear they say that the ship is a hen-frigate. But I am the master and I say what goes. When one of them speaks out of turn I smash his face with my fist and when they have nursed a sore jaw for a day or 2 the message gets through to them.

One thing I have not writ about is my brother Charley who has come with us for the whaling. My brother and I are not alike in many ways. When he 1st came to Sydney I wondered if he was my brother after all and not some man with a likeness who had taken his name. Or some other Charles Guard, no relation to me at all. But 1 time when we were swimming in Sydney harbour I saw the birthmark on his spine, 3 stars in a triangle, and I knew it was him all right.

What is different about him? He is thin and bony for a start and given to reading books. I think our father saw more promise in him than he did in me which has stayed a sore point to tell the truth. After he done his time and got his ticket of leave he was a bit of a dandy round Sydney. I saw him come down to the wharves 1 day dressed like a gentleman in a blue suit and white waistcoat. I was loading stores at the time. I said to him Charley you'll never make a living unless you do an honest day's work.

Work he said. There are other ways to work besides muck and tar. When was the last time you took a bath?

I took no notice of him for a few years after that. I heard he'd tried his hand as a salesman and for a short time teaching school. But he is a fool if he thought he could get away with that for Charley has had no education to speak of. Reading, writing and a little arithmetic do not a teacher make. My Betsy knows as much as he does. Anyway, when he was broke, which happened as surely as night follows day, he come to me and asked what jobs can you offer. I looked him up and down and thought he will be an albatross around my neck, but he is my brother and what is a man to do. I said well you'd better put to sea with me. He went green around the gills for he was sick all the way from the old country to Sydney. He told me once before how he wd never set foot on a ship again.

You can be my storeman I said and when you have your sea legs I will teach you the art of catching whales.

This is how I came to have my brother Charley with me. I can tell he will not settle long, will come and go, and stay in Sydney whenever he's got money in his pockets. For the time being he is with us and does his share. My wife can do with help and I see they get on well enough.

For it is a hard life on my wife. She has to live as rough as any man with long hours of work and to live like a woman as well. The washing is the worst especially when it's winter in the Sounds. There is always wet clothes, a case of running out at 1st sign of rain, bring in the wash, run out with it when the shower passes. There is whole days when there is nothing much else, but still there is the cooking to do.

I've told my brother Charley to keep an eye on her when he can.

Some days Betsy is very quiet. When we are abed she whispers to me in the winter air Jacky you will not let the Maoris get me.

I will break them before that happens. I do not allow the Maoris to take liberties. You should know that.

For it is true I take no nonsense and punish those who give me trouble. Like an unruly seaman I give them a tap and it brings them to their senses and if they do not mend their ways I will not employ them any more. I think the Maoris know where they stand with me.

I came in 1 day and found Betsy standing in the hut with a bowl of flour untouched on the bench before her and the fire gone out. She was looking into space.

What is it Betsy?

I cannot hear the birds she said.

But there are birds everywhere. And so there are, birds full of song, the air filled with the beat of their wings. Parrots and wood pigeons, hawks and saddleback, huia and kokako, and birds that sing all night.

There are no cockies she said. And I see then what she means. The birds here are dark of plume and sing more sweetly, not full of noisy shouts like parakeets and cockatoos.

But I told her listen hard and you will hear the birds. They sing a different song.

Yes she said and put her head on one side. I do not know if it is just to please me or what. After a while the fire was lit and things back to normal. That night she made her own music. It was a cold night and still, there were fires on the beach. She sang for us several songs for she has grown up with the music of the Rocks people. She finished with the old 1 about the cambric shirt, about the king who promises to marry a maid if she can make him a shirt out of a piece of linen 3 inches square.

> *Come buy me, come buy me a cambric shirt*
> *Without any seam and good needlework*
> *Savoury sage, rosemary and thyme*
> *Then you shall be a true love of mine.*
>
> *Come hang it all out on yonder thorn*
> *That never has blew blossom since Adam was born.*
>
> *And now you have asked me questions three,*
> *And now I will ask as many of thee.*
>
> *Come buy me, come buy me, an acre of land*
> *Between the sea water and the sea sand.*

She sang each 1 of the verses that number 12 and the men on the beach sang the chorus to each 1 and clapped, wiping their eyes on the cuffs of their shirts and all the time the sea roared, and far away heading towards Port Nick we saw the slow moving lights of a ship like fireflies. Betsy did a little dance and a curtsy. I ordered another ration of rum all round.

She is not bad for a girl said one of the men, in his cups. His mate laughed and tipped a wink in my direction. Then the wives of the men, who had been listening too, began singing back in great harmony. It was the most peaceful a scene I have seen here and the sweetness of all their Maori voices was soothing on my mind. I think then we are in for better times.

It is time to set down some of what Te Rauparaha has been up to. Nobody should think they know what he will do next. You can only take him minute by minute. He might think he is a general but he is what soldiers might call a mercenary for he makes war for profit. I don't know much about him except that when he was young he came down from the north and joined up with Ngati Toa. They are a tribe driven south from the western coast by Waikato tribes. Te Rauparaha led them in fighting all down the Taranaki coastline, defeating everyone in his path until he reached Cook Strait.

He acts like a king, and white men who come to New Zealand find it best to treat him like one. Early on he learnt that if he traded with pakea he would get rich. He calls us pakea, or somesuch. I have heard it means a flea. He has got rich through trade and it goes without saying that if pakea want to prosper they must be on his good side. On Kapiti Island he boasts 2000 slaves preparing flax for trade and as many muskets.

But he takes things too far. He has long been set on war with Ngai Tahu, the big tribe of the South Island. He finds many reasons to quarrel. Above all he wants more land and the green-stone jade that is to be found in Ngai Tahu country. Along the way has come plenty of battles. They are filled with bad blood. For each there must be revenge. Utu. So it is hard to follow what each battle is over. Te Rauparaha's men go into the battle with a chant that shakes the sun. Ka mate, ka mate they cry. They stamp their feet in time and twirl their spears.

Ngai Tahu was weak from having fought among themselves.

They made easy pickings for Te Rauparaha. But now Ngai Tahu have recovered and are fighting back so we are piggy in the middle here. Their warriors come in waves from the south, wanting to push Ngati Toa back to where they come from.

I have made it my business to make a friend of Te Rauparaha, thanks to young Rangi who showed me how to catch a whale. He made the path easier for me. This did not happen overnight and Te Rauparaha and I do not always see eye to eye. Things can fall apart when you least expect it.

Late one afternoon, on his way north after a raid on the south, he came by with a war party of 500 men and decided he wanted to see me. He sent most of his troops in their canoes ahead to Kapiti. It soon came out, he was after more muskets. I told him I need more flax for my next trip to Sydney and I wd see what I could do for him.

At this moment Betsy chose to come after me with some story about the sheep running away with her shoe. She was laughing and giggling like a silly girl, hopping round with 1 shoe on and 1 shoe off.

Go away I said, can't you see I am doing important business.

Oh business she said and put her hand to her mouth. She looked Te Rauparaha up and down. He had no clothes on except a string belt round his waist. His old brown flesh was battered and scarred and filthy with the blood of others.

You get yourself inside I said.

Te Rauparaha was looking sore put out.

She is young I said by way of an apology.

You have a sheep he asked.

Yes I have 10 I said which is true for I have got them from a man who is farming them on Mana Island, another island in Cook Strait.

Throw in a sheep with the muskets he said.

Not likely I said. For I was planning on cooking lamb for a treat for Betsy. I was feeling pleased with Betsy for she had been 2 months without blood and I was very hopeful.

Te Rauparaha's eyes blazed black with anger. You will give the girl the sheep before me he said, or that is what I took him to say.

I shrugged and walked away, not wanting to argue in a language I cannot get my tongue around. Betsy was prancing ahead and I didn't want to growl at her. All the same I said to her, you cannot make a fool of me Betsy. That man is not to be played with.

Near dusk we heard a great commotion at the water's edge. I saw Te Rauparaha struggling with 1 of my sheep, trying to load it in his canoe. I picked up my 2 good pistols and a cutlass, and took off. The sheep was part way in the canoe and Te Rauparaha could not get away from me for the animal had its back feet trailing in the water and going baa baa for its life. The chief was very unhappy at being caught like this.

You is a thief Te Rauparaha I said.

He picked up his tomahawk and came at me. I stood stock-still and drew a line in the sand with my cutlass.

Cross that line and you are a dead man Te Rauparaha, old fool.

He rushed on towards me but when I my cocked my pistol he stopped at the line. He ran back to his canoe and then back at me, his teeth bared in a snarl, spit upon his chin. I did not blink.

I will kill you I said.

Inside me I was thinking he wd not give up. He is famous for that. I looked deep in his eyes to read his intention all the time hoping he could not see inside of me. I thought if he did I wd have to kill him in cold blood. I did not much care to do that, for he is more trouble dead than a sheep. But he is an old sheep stealer and men have swung for less. Out to sea a canoe full of his warriors was looking on. It wd be him or me. I tightened my finger round the trigger and then I saw him blink.

He turned and walked away and I felt the bile of disappointment ride up inside me. I had wanted to kill the old bastard. And something more. I wanted a fight.

The sheep struggled free of the canoe. Te Rauparaha got in in its place. He pushed out to sea and was gone into the dark night of the Strait. I heard his oars swish and paddle and then I went back to the house where Betsy had my dinner waiting.

I thought that some time I might pay for that.

Chapter 19

Te Awaiti, 1831

The truth is I need Te Rauparaha.

I see now that Te Awaiti is not the best place for a station and Cloudy Bay is in my mind. This area is away from the prevailing winds that sweep across the Cook Strait, the deep torrent of water between the 2 big islands of this country. In my head, I see the spot I want for my own, a sheltered bay full of kakapo, 1 of many bays and inlets that wd make a site for a port. I cannot do this unless I have Te Rauparaha on my side. He thinks he owns Cloudy Bay.

I went to see Mr Campbell on my next trip to Sydney. Mr Campbell I said it is time to build another station. I have just the place for you.

Oh yes and how much will that cost me.

4000 pounds I said. You will get the money back in short order.

At which he seemed happy enough for he has had good returns on all his investments with me. I showed him my books that are very neat thanks to Betsy's hand. I saw he was impressed.

I made a deal with Te Rauparaha. I thought I wd keep it to myself because Betsy does not like the man. I set up another book that I filled in in my own hand and kept it with my pistols which Betsy is not allowed to touch. If the Maoris come for you do not try to fight I have told her. You will come off worst. Go with them and I will come and get you back.

So I built a base at the bay I have chosen. I was taking things a step at a time. I did not want to squander Mr Campbell's money. But I reckon I am right about the place for it is so much easier to nab the whales here. We set up a lookout on a hill above the bay and watched for them to come. We called the lookout Hungry Hill for it is a way to go should you run out of tucker. Soon as we saw a whale down we go and launch the boats.

As I have related the mother will not leave her calf so we tether it and then she is handed to us, easy as that, no fuss about it.

The male is smarter. He does not often come in shore.

So now I have 2 whaling stations working at the same time and 2 ships and more men are coming here to work.

I did not find it easy to take to my brother and his fancy ways. He had brought books to read. Sometimes, back at Te Awaiti, I came across him and Betsy sitting and laughing like there was no work to be done. They made me not at ease. Charley is more fair of complexion than me, his hair light brown and wavy, his beard soft and fluffy like a puppy dog's tail. I said Charley I think it is time you looked to find yourself a woman. There are women round here who will live with you.

He shook his head and smiled to his self. I wanted to shake him.

Charley I said have you had a good look at any of those darky women.

I can't say that I have. Not looking me straight in the eye.

Well then I said, that is a mighty strange thing for a man your age not thinking about what to do with his poker. Not unless you have been putting it in the backsides of men which is useful when there is no women to be had but buggering around is not the same as putting it in a woman.

You would know about that he asked with a bit of a smirk.

I have spent more time at sea than you have Charley boy I said without raising my voice. I know what some men is like when they have been without the necessaries for some time.

So what is this about he said and I hear his insolent tone. Is this because you're afraid Betsy might fancy me more than you.

I felt my heart grow still and cold. This is my brother and I cannot kill him the same way I could Te Rauparaha but I wondered if I might have to do this yet.

Betsy is going to have a baby I said. You will treat her with respect.

Then Betsy asked me why doesn't Charley talk to me any more.

Why do you think.

When she doesn't answer I said because I have told him not to. You are too friendly with him by far. You belong to me Betsy.

But I have done nothing she cried out.

I want to believe this is true. But yesterday I walked up from the beach. We had caught a whale and the men were trying the blubber on the shore, the sky was dark with smoke and steam. I saw that Charley was not there and we needed all hands.

He was standing outside our house and why does this not surprise me. When he saw me he tried to move away but I was too fast. I grabbed him by the back of his collar and threw him down the bank.

Inside Betsy was sitting at the table. It is a table I have built myself. She held her head in her hands.

So Charley is your darlin' I said and yanked her to her feet.

She flung my arm from her.

What have you been doing with Charley?

Nothing she said. As God is my keeper. Her face was red like rhubarb. I could not tell whether this be from anger or guilt. Why are you so cruel when all I do is what you tell me.

She is lonely my brother said. He had picked his self up and walked back to the hut. He was leaning against the door as if he owned the place and it was all I could do not to break his neck. If he had not been my bro. that is what I wd have done. She worries after her little brother he told me. Can't you tell that she misses her mother and her aunty he says to me.

Then she can go back to them, you tell her that.

Tell her yourself Charley said.

You are talking about me as if I'm not here Betsy yelled.

Be quiet I said grabbing her by the arm.

She is young my brother said, not much more than a child.

She is 16 years. And I could not help myself I touch the swelling apple of her belly the pip-squeak container of my own flesh and blood.

At that my bro. turned towards the beach, his eyes narrow against the smoke. I can tell that he does not like the work and he does not much like me but these are troubles I cannot fix.

I dropped Betsy's arm without so much as a word for what was there to say.

Chapter 20

Te Awaiti, 1831

That was a month ago and as I take up my pen to write I think that I should speak to my wife for silence is a habit hard to break. She has hung on my arm and pleaded for a word from me but I have not been in my right mind for words. My tongue seems to have become frozen around words. All around me are the sounds of Maori lingo and yet they take on English words at the same time as if they are laying claim to my mother tongue. At the same time I hear Betsy and Charley and the men of Te Awaiti using the words of Maori so there is no telling where I begins and the other leaves off. But I cannot make head nor tail of much of it and so I become more alone in my self.

It is like the thoughts I have about who is God. Who is God that would shackle men in irons, starving in their manacles, worked like oxen and worse from dawn till dark. That thrashes them and beats them and turns their souls upside down until there is no good left in the cup. Around me are men who have been to hell and back. They will stand by me these men. I treat them well. But what have we made here at the end of the earth but another place of toil and dirt and grog. For that is all they know. Their women are like mine, big with children, but they will be a different race, not one thing nor another. The Maoris will go on fighting and burning us if we do not make a place of order.

But there is no order in my head. I know I cannot stay silent long for soon Betsy's time will come and there must be a woman at her side. I have no knowledge of how to help her and we have stayed silent for so long that I do not know how to begin again.

You are a surly bastard my brother said 1 morning. We had not had a whale for a week and for once the air is clean and clear of smoke as a May morning in the English countryside.

You never knew our mother I said as if he had said nothing.

Your privilege he said with a sneer in his voice.

I was fortunate I said. Although it is hard for me to recall her exact look. But sometimes I think that I see a look of her in Betsy.

He looked at me surprised then. You have never said anything of that.

I have not always thought of that I said. It has come to me that that is why I chose her, for a look that is familiar. A way of walking as if she is proud but obedient with it. Not pretty not plain but not caring one way or another. Perhaps I said, for this thought had come to me in a flash, she has a way of holding herself that I saw in my mother before she gave birth to you.

And then said Charley in a quiet voice you never saw her again.

That is so.

I cannot carry that blame on me forever.

No. I do not ask you to. I am thinking I should get Betsy back to Sydney for the birth of this baby.

I think perhaps it is too late for that he said.

That is for me to decide. I am her husband. Charley is getting away with too much.

Dan Hatton's woman will look after Betsy he said. My brother was ignoring me as perhaps I deserve. Dan Hatton's wife is a woman of the Rangitane tribe who has been all but wiped out by Te Rauparaha. The women, what is left of them, have been eager for the protection of the whalers.

Her mother lives here in the bush he said. She is an old kuia and knows what to do.

I heard how he was slipping into their way of talking. Does Betsy know this I asked.

They have spoken with her about it. Or that is what Dan has told me. But how should I know for I have not spoken to Betsy. You should ask her yourself.

It is the 1st day of the month of October. My wife has been often with the women in the week that is past. The women do not call my wife by any of her given names. There is no b sound in the Maori lingo nor any s. Peti they call her, dropping these foreign sounds. I have heard them call to her at the river and seen her raise her head in answer.

Betsy I said when I go to the hut for my dinner.

She did not turn around. I thought her sullen but that is not in her nature. Rather, that is the beast in me.

Betty I tried again and she turned as if in a dream.

When you has had this baby I said we will go to Sydney and bring your brother David back here.

Thank you Jacky she said whispering as if there was someone else in the room. These are the first words we had spoken in a long time.

Elizabeth.

Betsy.

Peti.

She has been reborn in this place.

Her hands were cupped beneath her belly. It is like rods of fire in here she said. Fetch someone Jacky. Help me.

This was how I came to find myself at the door of Dan

Hatton's hut. An old woman without teeth and her daughter who I know as Hine were wrapped in shawls beside a fire. The kuia wore a round cap of black feathers. When they saw me they stood up as if they had been waiting for my signal. They rose and followed me across the cleared ground between our huts.

When my wife saw that they had come she said Jacky I wish I did not have to do this.

I wish you did not have to do it either. There is no other way out.

They could cut me open she said piteously.

Then you would surely die.

Down at the beach my brother Charley stood looking out to sea smoking on his pipe. I know how women die giving birth and it could be he was thinking about this some more even though as we have agreed he is not to blame for our mother's death.

The women were waiting for Betty. I saw their brown hands reaching out to her and I thought that perhaps theirs wd be the last to touch her living flesh and I was very afraid.

There is no other way I said again.

She followed the women down a bush track to a new hut which had been built just for women to give birth. I thought I should not let her go.

I heard Betty's voice in pain and the women chanting.

I made to follow them. From the door of the hut I saw Betty naked from the waist down, kneeling in front of a pole running down the middle of the room. She seemed to be holding it and pressing against it. Hine's mother looked up and saw me and the 2 women waved me away their faces angry as if I should know better. I knew them to be right, a man should not be near his wife at this time.

I went to our hut and although there was work to be done about the place I could not settle to any thing. So I took down the book given to me by my father so many years ago. I thought that if there is a God now was the time to take notice of His word. It is springtime and the air is clear and the sea calm. In the stillness of the bay I heard screams that rose louder and louder.

I lit the lamp's wick and as the dark fell I read again the Husband's Duty as set out in my book, which forbids all harshness and roughness to the Wife: Men are to use them as Parts of themselves, to love them as their own Bodies, and therefore to do nothing that may be hurtful and grievous to them, no more than they would cut and gash their own flesh. Reading these words I saw I must do better by my wife and thought that I wd pray and if He answered me this one time I wd do better and be more kindly to Betty. I got down on my knees while the distant screams grew thin and asked that God spare my wife's life. I promised that if He did I wd work harder to believe.

I looked up from these prayers and saw Charley at the door again with that smile that makes a mockery of me.

Betty has been working hard while you were on your knees. You best get over to the whare he said, they have news for you.

In the doorway the old woman held up my son for me to see. Hine clasped a blood covered shell. Behind them Betty lay on a bed of bracken covered by a blanket from our bed. I wanted to go to her, but again my way was barred. This room is tapu Mister Haari says Hine. There is still work to be done.

So I stood humble at the door and thanked God that my son was alive and squealing like a little pig and my wife was mopping her face with the back of her hand, and I heard her say, tell him that John is born, tell him it is all right. I turned back and looked at the night sky and saw it full of stars. My son will have a good life I thought. I will see to it. Nothing will harm him. He is why I have been put on earth.

Charley was sitting on a bank near the path as I made my way back to our house.

She is well I said. I have a son.

He nodded. I am pleased for you. His voice sounded young and lost.

I have been too harsh I said. It will not happen again. You are my brother and my wife is a good woman.

I saw a smart reply on his lip and then he thought better of it.

We will take a cup of grog I said. So we went inside and for a moment I put my arm about his shoulder.

There is new trouble among the Maoris. I have said nothing to my wife but the men know all about it. So does Charley I suppose but I say nothing to him either. We are friends again him and me but I have always kept myself to myself and nothing has changed that. Besides I do not want to spread alarm around our camp by making too much of this trouble though it is known by every ship's master sailing in and out of Cook Strait. Te Rauparaha has pulled off one of his craftiest tricks and things have taken a turn for the worse. Te Rauparaha has been after a chief called Tamaiharanui at Akaroa for a long time in revenge for the death of his wife's father at the hands of Ngai Tahu.

Now he has made his raid with the help of a white man called Stewart, master of the brig *Elizabeth*. Te Rauparaha offered good trade if he wd hide them in the ship's hold rather than take their war canoes down the coast and warn their enemies of their coming.

Stewart had with him a man by the name of Cowall who thought nothing of how he came by flax and other cargo, he talked Stewart into saying yes. Stewart is an ignorant man. White men do not mix their trade with native wars. But Stewart wanted favours of Te Rauparaha and said yes. He took Te Rauparaha's war party to Akaroa. When he got there he did not let on what cargo he had aboard.

Stewart tricked Tamaiharanui on board the ship. Then his wife. Then his children. And they were all captured. The crew had become afraid and begged Stewart that he sail away. But the war party was now in charge, through sheer weight of numbers and Stewart could not control what he wd do next.

In the night Te Rauparaha and his men took the ship's skiff and whaleboat and landed ashore. They set about killing every last person at Akaroa. It's said Akaroa's hills were that night lit by the fires of burning whares, the creeks dyed with the blood of those slaughtered. A feast of bodies was held upon the beaches and the next day the remains of what had not been eaten stowed upon the *Elizabeth*. The ship sailed for Kapiti still with the chief and his family on board.

Tamaiharanui killed his daughter on the voyage north rather than let her die by Te Rauparaha's hand. Back at Kapiti, Stewart handed over Tamaiharanui to Te Rauparaha, turning his back on what was to follow. Te Rauparaha killed and ate the chief, eyes first.

But it was there at Kapiti that trouble rose for Stewart. Another ship was at anchor there, the *Dragon*. The master of the ship, Captain Briggs, took the story back to Sydney and reported Stewart. But Governor Darling did not act quickly enough to bring Stewart to justice and he has got clean away.

Well where wd we be without the flax trade. Te Rauparaha is very helpful if you get on the right side of him.

But this is not the way to do it. Soon there will be more fighting and worse, of that I am certain. And the pakea is in for dangerous times.

Part 5

The Dispossessed

Chapter 21

Mrs Perceval Malcolm lives in an ample house on the plain beneath the foothills of the sheep station her husband has established at Parramatta. She is a shrewd woman who, following her recovery from the difficult business of providing heirs, has learnt to keep the most excellent account of all the ingoings and outgoings on the property. She sees herself as her husband's saviour, for though the man has money, he is not accustomed to using it wisely.

Those who meet Maude are surprised. They expect to find a large firm woman, with her hands firmly on her husband's purse strings (it has been rumoured that she once turned up at an auction and forbade her husband to bid another penny on sheep she considered inferior in quality). What they find is a small woman, not more than five foot one, with a smooth complexion that makes her age difficult to guess, dressed in flowing pale muslin gowns. She never goes out of doors without a hat and veil, so that there is about her an air of misty uncertainty, a fragility that is beguiling.

Her house is a long brick dwelling, built with convict labour. There are six rooms, an elegant central hall, a well-stocked cellar and a verandah. The main room is decorated in different shades of blue which Maude feels are cool and soothing in the harsh Australian climate. The garden is ordered in an English style; in spring, almond, apricot, pear and apple trees blossom while wistaria festoons the columns of the verandah. Roses bloom all summer and now, as the season progresses, dahlias and gladioli are making their appearance. A jacaranda tree is the only sign within the garden that the bush landscape was ever there, although the servants' quarters are down the path through an avenue of rustling blue gum trees that form a natural screen from the house.

These quarters consist of two-roomed cottages, each with a porch, one for the cook and one for the nanny, and a row of lean-tos containing hammocks beneath one long roof, for the gardeners. The farm labourers are far away, though once a week Maude rides side-saddle on a tall, sprightly roan along the fence-line of the paddock where they are quartered, just to satisfy herself that there is not mutiny in the air. The green lands are covered with fine grass; the farm is stocked with hogs, fifty head of cattle, more than a dozen horses and two thousand sheep. Percy has a dozen greyhounds for hunting and there is always a plentiful supply of wild ducks and kangaroo for the table.

Maude thinks of the house as her own, though of course it is hers and Percy's, but without her it would be all a disaster, as she once said in an unguarded moment when her husband talked of some new and flighty plan. Sometimes she cannot believe that he can be so undisciplined in his thinking, though she believes she is getting him in hand. His sister is a case in point; she does not know how many times she has had to stand over him when he has sat down to write to her.

'You know I will not have that woman in my house ever again,' she has said more than once.

But exactly what was it that Adie had done, Percy blustered

the first time she said this. She only came to help. You were so ill at the time.

To which she had said in a cryptic way that nobody could find a thing in the cupboards after she left, and nothing would surprise her, and she cannot tell to this day whether she has all the silver Percy bought her on their marriage (though she has been known to tell people that her silver was her mother's, brought all the way from England). You know what those spinsters who go to stay with relatives are like, she had told him. They fill their trunks with the family jewels, because they think the world owes them a living.

Besides, as Herbert and Nathaniel grew up that woman would fill their heads with nonsense about travel and ancient ruins, when all they need is an understanding of farming and an appreciation of a gentleman's life in the colonies. Maude Malcolm has entertained governors at the house more than once. She was especially fond of Governor Darling, though she has heard that his successor Governor Bourke is a man not to be trusted and too liberal by far with the convict stock. She has yet to meet him but he has been described to her as a man with large dark eyes and full deep lips. The thought makes her skin crawl, she says to Percy over breakfast. As for sending gunboats to New Zealand on behalf of lawless ruffians, she cannot imagine what the world is coming to. She says this, on reading the newspapers that describe the infamous expedition to rescue the convict's wife.

'But surely, Mrs Guard is not a convict,' Percy murmurs distractedly.

'Are you not listening to a word I say?' Maude demands, pulling the bell for more tea.

Percy is holding a note in his hand, his eyes blank, his gaze as if locked on some space behind her ear. She glances over her shoulder as if half expecting to see dust on the china cabinet. 'What have you got there?' she demands, for nobody will have gone to collect the post this early in the morning.

'A message brought from Sydney. It was delivered while

you were dressing. Did you not hear the horse?'

'Well then, is it good news or bad?'

'It depends on how you see it. My sister is on her way for a visit.'

'On her way? Percy, this cannot be.' When she sees he is serious, she uses what she hopes is a suitably firm voice. 'You must put a stop to it. She is nothing but a troublemaker.' Maude gets to her feet in a state of agitation, beginning to clear dishes, before remembering that she is no longer the serving woman she was in England.

'She is already on her way, on the river ferry. The messenger came on ahead.'

'Outrageous. How dare she come uninvited?'

'It seems she has nowhere to go. Lieutenant Roddick has asked her to leave.' Percy looks despairingly at the letter, as if willing it not to be true. 'I cannot keep this from you, Maude,' he says. 'It seems that she has been visited at the house by Mrs Guard. Roddick has asked my sister to desist in her invitations to her, but she will not keep away from the woman. The lieutenant is concerned for the welfare of his children.' Percy says this all in a rush, for he knows that in a moment she will snatch the letter from his hand, and he must be seen to have told her before she finds out for herself.

'This is disgraceful,' Maude says, after a pause that seems never-ending. In one of the rapidly growing poplar trees at the edge of the garden, a kookaburra shouts with laughter. A young man with a manacle round his leg limps past with another bucket of water from the river to pour on the garden. Maude puts her hands to her ears. 'We shall be ruined. I have a party of ladies coming to visit this afternoon.'

'It will give them something to talk about,' Percy says daringly. Her look confirms that he has gone too far. 'I cannot send her away. If it is disgrace you are considering, then you will only make it worse if she is at large on the streets of Sydney with nowhere to go.'

'What do you suggest that we do?' she asks, her expression signifying a momentary defeat.

'Make a room ready for her. I'll explain to her that you have guests and that it would be better for all of us to discuss her difficulty after their visit. Let's make her as comfortable as we can, and perhaps she will listen to reason.'

'I have a better idea,' says Maude. 'Let's clear the nanny's quarters, and give her the cottage to herself. I'm sure she would rather be alone at a time like this.'

'And what will you do with nanny?'

'Why, I've been thinking for some time that it would be better for her to sleep closer to the children. Herbert is really too active for me to manage on my own in the evenings, I'm sure you've noticed. It will work out well,' she says smoothly, patting her softly greying hair. Now she rises purposefully, unable to resist the urge to organise all that needs to be done. Adeline (Maude refuses to call her Adie) will be here within the hour, and Maude will have everything in order before her arrival. This way, she can be whisked immediately to the cottage down the lane.

But it as not as easy as that. She should have known better, Maude tells herself bitterly, in days to come. Adeline arrives, drawn round the mouth, her eyes red from weeping behind the swathed veil of her hat. There is more to this than meets the eye, Maude thinks, but she cannot put her finger on what it is.

Percy goes to the cottage and remains closeted with his sister. When he returns to the house he tells Maude he has nothing more to tell her than what she already knows. Adie has befriended Mrs Guard, an old school pupil of hers who has thrown herself upon her mercy. But, he insists, there is nothing more to be known of the *Harriet* affair than there is already. The Governor may yet be embarrassed by his actions in dispatching the military convoy to New Zealand, but if that is the case, his sister is none the wiser as to the reasons than when she first met Mrs Guard in the markets. She is, he says, quite distraught at the loss of her employer's favour.

'Ah,' says Maude. 'So that's what it's all about.'

'What is what all about?'

Maude has observed that Percy's light blue eyes have faded this last year or so. His face is tanned like a razor strop and as shiny, his mouth appears sharp and hard beneath his moustache, but his eyes give him away. He is, thinks his wife, like an old man already, though he is barely fifty. 'Why,' she says, 'she's in love with Lieutenant Roddick.'

'That's preposterous,' he splutters.

'Pre-*pos*-terous, is it?' She laughs, a guffaw far removed from refinement.

Days stretch into weeks. Percy lurks around the lane when he thinks Maude is not looking, hovering anxiously between his wife and sister. They do not discuss the visitor at the end of the garden. Maude arranges the meals with the cook and has them sent down the path three times a day.

Eventually, a letter is delivered to the post office, addressed to Adie. The seal is that of Lieutenant Roddick.

'Ha,' says Maude, holding it up to the light. 'Is it money?'

'My dear wife, I beg of you,' says Percy.

'Money to pay off her wages, do you think? Or perhaps he's feeling guilty about something. Now there's a thought, Percy, your sister may not be as virtuous as you make her out.'

'It may simply be a letter between friends.'

'I think I'll deliver it to your sister myself,' says Maude.

'That would be very unkind,' Percy says stiffly.

'Well, are you likely to tell me its contents?' says his wife, using the silver butter dish to hold the letter firmly on the table-cloth. Not until she has extracted a promise from him, is she willing to release the missive. He wonders at the steeliness of such milky fingers, the backs of her hands threaded with a blue lace of veins, the way they hold a horse in check, and how he once saw her crack the neck of a chicken, not long after they came to the farm.

Adie sits in the cottage like one dispossessed. She had arrived with a large portmanteau of clothes, though she said some of her belongings were still at Roddick's house. Whatever she has brought with her, it is clearly not enough, for every bit of the room where she sits is festooned with her private garments, her stays and petticoats (Percy cannot help but notice that they are fine white lawn) drying out of sight of the passing servants.

'I hope it is good news,' Percy says, awkwardly handing her the letter.

Adie turns it over, studying the seal. 'Maude's been playing with it, to see if she can open it, hasn't she? Are you going to let me read it in peace?'

When he doesn't move, she says, 'You're afraid of her, aren't you?'

'No,' he says, 'but I am not as strong as either of you. I never imagined myself between two women with equal will.'

Adie sighs then. 'You're mistaken,' she says, drawing the letter from its envelope. 'I have less resolve than I gave myself credit for.' She gestures around the cottage. It is furnished with an iron bed, covered with a patchwork quilt, a small table, a wash bowl and jug and the two raw cane chairs they sit in. She returns her reluctant gaze to the letter. Then a flash of delight illuminates her face, such as Percy has not seen on her face for years. Not since she first saw Michelangelo's *David* in Florence on their first Mediterranean tour. It must have been twenty years ago. Long before all this. Before Australia.

'Lieutenant Roddick wants me to return,' she says. 'The children are missing me. I knew they would, of course. Mathilde will manage, but Austen, well that's another matter. He is the kind of child who pines.'

'You'll go then,' says Percy, more a statement than a question, hoping to hide the eagerness in his voice.

But she hears it. She has always read him too well. That is at the heart of his problems these days, the inability to have a secret inner life. He didn't know he needed one, until it was too late, for it had never troubled him that Adie knew him through and through.

'Not just yet,' she says. The lively expression has vanished, leaving her face a mask.

'But why?' he says.

'It's not enough. That he should use the children as an excuse.'

'So really, you are hoping that he will ask you to go back?'

Immediately, he wishes he had put this another way, as he sees her rising colour. It is one thing to expose his own thoughts to his sister; he does not want to know more about her than he would wish. He cannot bear to think of what she wants, and must surely be unattainable.

'Don't misunderstand me,' says Adie, 'it's simply beneath my dignity to be summoned like a servant. I was his wife's friend, you know. Her very best friend in the world, who closed the lids of her lovely eyes that one last time.' She gulps, trying to hide sudden tears that slide down her cheeks. 'It is the bright light here,' she says, 'it is affecting me, the same as it does you. My eyes cannot bear so much light.'

Chapter 22

The February heat is intense, and March is slow to turn to autumn, ushered in with heavy skies but no rain. In the second week of the month, after a night that is suddenly and mercifully cool, a second visitor arrives at Malcolm Downs without announcement.

Betty Guard is hatless when she knocks at the Malcolms' front door, her hair loose and wild about her shoulders, as if she has departed in a hurry. Her dress is a soft cinnamon colour, the bodice laced with ribbon between her breasts, giving the impression of nakedness and darkness, for she has come without a shawl. Later, Maude will recall that the woman looked *native*, as if she had no shame.

There is not a servant in sight, and the rapping is so insistent, that Maude opens the door herself. 'The servants are not allowed to use this entrance,' she says on seeing this apparition.

'I've come to see Miss Malcolm — Miss Adie Malcolm,' Betty says.

'And who may you be?' Maude's heart is lifting at the

prospect of someone coming to take Adie away. For days there has been an intolerable atmosphere in the house, and she knows that sooner or later she must relent and allow her sister-in-law to take up residence with them. Percy has killed a snake along the path that leads to the cottage. Things cannot go on like this. Maude knows that the servants will soon become aware of the true situation in their household, and begin to behave insolently towards her. She feels her strength deserting her.

'I'm Mrs Guard,' says the young visitor, and extends her hand, as if she had not heard the other woman's rebuff and they are equals. 'Betty Guard. My grandfather used to farm these parts. You've got things looking very nice.'

For a moment, Maude thinks she is going to faint. She clutches the hat stand behind her, nearly pulling it over. Of course, she should have realised at once.

'You are not welcome here.'

'Is Miss Malcolm here?' says her visitor, in an insistent way.

'No.' Maude recovers herself, considering how best she might be rid of this new intruder.

'I've heard from some soldiers in town that she's here.'

'She is not in the house.'

This is the moment Percy chooses to emerge between the trees. He is wearing breeches tied close above his boots and carries a spade.

'Oh, down there, along the path,' Maude cries, exasperated. 'Am I to have my whole house taken over by madwomen?'

At first, I tell Adie, I thought of Te Awaiti as paradise, even though there were times when I was scared. But it was exciting to have a place that was mine and to own things.

The house Jacky built for us was plain and square, with four rooms, but it was solid and kept the rain out. The kitchen had a fireplace with an iron pot and a copper for the washing. There was a room where we laid out food — the dining room I suppose you'd call it — we called it the outer room; it was not at all luxurious, still it was separate from the cooking smoke. Then there were the inner rooms, the room where we kept our bed, and another room that Jacky said would be for our babies when they came. We walked on dirt at first, though later, in the winter, Jacky laid a timber floor, and I could put down a pretty rug. Each house we had was built like this. I say each one, since it was not long before it was burnt to the ground when we were gone to Sydney.

This happened not once, but several times. Somewhere in the dark bush that pressed close against our house were people who did not like us being there. The trees of New Zealand are different from the ones here in Australia. The foliage is dark and swirling green, with not so many flowers, but it is peaceful and mysterious. At the beginning, I was not afraid. It was pleasing to know that there were no snakes.

But when I understood that the bush provided shelter for our enemies I did get scared. What have we done to deserve this, I asked Jacky. The first time the house was burnt I cried, for we had furnished it like a real house, with a mirror and chairs in the dining room. Oh, it was very nice. All of this was gone when we returned.

Around this time, I had met my husband's friend Te Rauparaha, who came and went as if he owned the place. He was all swagger, a small man with the reputation of a giant killer. He has a hooked nose and a forehead that slopes back, deep-set eyes. I think he fancies himself as handsome, but I did not take to him, though Jacky said I should be polite. I didn't trust him. Jacky thought he had his measure, but I thought he was fooling himself. As it happens, I wasn't wrong.

Before John was born, I crossed the Tasman and back three times, and each time we went back to New Zealand, the house was gone. We got used to taking our belongings with us, so every time we set sail, we would load our furniture, our spoons and china and the mirror that I could not do without, not to mention our bed and blankets, onto the ship. Jacky didn't like this much because it took up room that could be filled by flax and timber and baleen, but there was nothing for it.

We never stayed long in Sydney. Our visits were simply for trade. I stayed with Charlotte sometimes, and other times with my mother and John Deaves, but I did not care for it. I was treated differently, as if I was simply a visitor who did not do enough work, no matter how much I tried to help. My brother David had grown tall, but he was still too pale and very thin, like he would snap and break. I wished I could take him with me and fatten him up a bit, but whenever I thought about this, I couldn't imagine what he'd do with himself in New Zealand. I knew he couldn't hold his own with the men, and Jacky wouldn't want a big lad like him doing nothing round the place. He had already made work for his own brother, and that had led to trouble of all sorts.

I wished sometimes we could have the wedding Jacky had promised, but we were always busy when we went to Sydney and there were still no missionaries in our part of New Zealand. Besides, we were thought of as man and wife. And Jacky let me shop to my heart's content when we were in Australia, and sometimes he bought me things himself. He gave me a charm string button that I lost when I was taken captive. It was so elegant, a brown glass ball set in a gold claw. I wore it on a thread of leather round my neck, along with my necklaces of gold and moonstone. He said I looked like his gypsy woman. I did wonder if I reminded him of Granny Pugh, but I didn't ask. But I could tell he liked the way I walked down George Street, turning heads. There is something to be said for being tall. You know I'm just a fraction taller than Jacky, though you wouldn't tell it at a glance, the way he stands. He bought me combs, too, although I preferred the one that had belonged to Granny. He has always liked my hair and often draws his fingers through it. Or so he did, in the days when I could do no wrong in his eyes.

And here I think I must tell the governess a little of the misunderstanding over Charley.

Betty and Adie have eaten lunch together, freshly made bread and some sliced apples washed down with tea. Adie eats a little stew as well, but Betty rejects the plate offered by the serving girl. 'It's kangaroo,' she says after the fork has touched her lips. 'I don't fancy wild game.'

'Why, it's a delicacy,' Adie says. 'The flavour is so piquant, and it's very fresh. I understand my brother shot it yesterday.'

Betty wrinkles her nose. 'We left shooting rabbits and the like to poor people and poachers in England. We prefer to eat beef and lamb now we can buy it.'

'I'm surprised,' says Adie, 'you make it sound superior.'

'To be honest, I'm not inclined to eat much at all right now,' says Betty, breaking open the skin of a banana and peeling it.

After the first rush of astonishment, Adie has welcomed Betty. For a moment, she had thought to demur, for Betty is the cause of all her troubles, and yet she has become enamoured of the young woman's presence. Besides, her solitude is turning her in on herself. Some afternoons, in the heat of the past month, she has thought of walking outside and sitting there until the sun burnt her up. She knew it could happen, that if you did not seek shade you would die, and this time in the cottage has become a purgatory of loneliness. When she closes her eyes she sees violent orange colour behind her lids, as if the sun's rays have reached inside her already. On other days, she has woken full of determination to find a way out of her troubles, but by the end of the morning it has ebbed away. The sensible thing would be to demand that her brother give her her fare on a ship returning to England, and to leave without delay. But none of this is as simple as it seems. Percy holds the key to her own modest fortune, which she understands Maude now sees as her own. Returning to England penniless is not a prospect that appeals to her. Besides, there is the question of Lieutenant Roddick and her own reckless ageing heart that has tricked itself into an affection she is sure will never be returned, but cannot be denied.

I became more afraid. It's true Adie, I'm unschooled, except for what you taught me (which means you know exactly how much I do and do not know), but I'm not silly. I began to see that the Maoris had much to complain about. We killed many whales. But whales are rangatira, chiefs of the sea. They stand for riches and plenty in the Maori world, but only when they are cast up on the shores of the ocean. True, some Maoris had begun to work with us at killing whales; they wanted our trinkets and treasures. The first Maori my husband ever met was on board a whaling ship. But what they got was nothing but the stench of dead animals and smoking fires like glimpses of like hell on earth.

Then there were the women, leaving their tribes to live with the whalers. We had a bad spell for some months, when few ships came to Port Nicholson, and the same mountainous seas that prevented them from coming in stopped us from going out. We ran short of food, and ate roast kiore — and if I tell you that these are rats, you may understand why I don't fancy game — and wild turnips. Some of the women tried to go back to their tribes but they were not wanted, unclean from the white men. You could see they were broken-hearted and repented of their mistake.

It was round then my husband began the whaling operation over at Cloudy Bay. We were back on our feet again. Jacky took me to see the new station. When I saw it, I knew it was where I wanted to live. Not yet, Jacky said, it's too soon.

Our son was nearly two, and another baby was on the way, and I was impatient.

But, because of the baby, I agreed to stay near Hine and her mother at Te Awaiti until it came. I think I would have died when John was born, if they had not been there. And Hine made me laugh, and taught me how to weave patterns with string threaded through my fingers. Her little boy Manu was a year older than John, beautiful in a way my children can't be, the colour of China tea.

I would like a baby that colour, I said to Hine once, when we were watching the children at the water's edge.

She gave me an odd look. I don't think you would, she replied.

Perhaps it was on account of these women who had helped me that my way of looking at things began to change. Not that I mentioned this to Jacky, for I knew he wouldn't understand. In particular, I didn't like the way the whales were killed, nor did I feel easy about the way Jacky kept on the good side of Te Rauparaha, when all about me I saw how much damage he was doing to my friends. Jacky and I had fallen out for a while, and then he made it up to me, and was nicer to me than he had ever been before. He called me his little treasure, his finest possession and all manner of things like that. He's my husband and there is much between us and I did not wish to hold a grudge in my heart. But there were times when I found myself strangely unmoved, as if I could not quite trust him again. Charley was right when he said that I was lonely, though that was not so much the case, now that Hine and her family were my friends. When I was not doing my tasks, young John and I spent much of our time with them. John was a merry baby and he spoke with the Maori children as he played, seeming to know their language better than ours. He reminded me of his father, for he was always the one who suggested mischief to the others, in the way of a little leader.

But Jacky had not trusted me when I needed him most, and now I found myself more critical of him than at the beginning. His friendship with Te Rauparaha was something I couldn't speak of, for I knew he would brush me aside. But I knew that trouble was brewing, for the women told me what was going on around the Strait.

Then I didn't see Hine for a little while.

The whare she shared with her husband Dan had been moved several times, once because of flooding, another time because it was in the way of some storehouses that were being built. Later, Dan had gone to sea and not come back.

I asked Jacky where he had gone, because I knew how badly

Hine wanted to know. Then Jacky told me Dan'd picked up with a ship in Port Nick, and I wasn't to tell Hine. The ship was heading for South America. That is probably the last she will see of him, he said. The girls in South America are prettier.

I didn't like that. I knew he could be wrong about things. Mind you, he could still make me feel guilty. I often wished I could have seen what was coming with Charley; sometimes I felt as if it had all been my fault. Because Jacky was older, and so much in charge, you understand.

But it was on account of what he had told me about Dan that, for some time, I had been unable to bring myself to look for Hine. I was just a couple of months gone with Louisa when I took John on my hip for a walk to the next bay in search of her. I wanted to tell her about the new baby. But I couldn't find her.

What I did find round in the next bay stays with me still. Lying on the beach were some sixty half-cooked bodies of men and women, along with the body of a young child spitted over the remains of an open fire. You're very pale, Adie. Don't flinch. Remember, it was you who unlocked my tongue.

Let me tell you how humans are cooked. A hole is dug in the earth, some two feet deep. A fire is lit with dry wood, and a quantity of round stones are added which are made red hot. These are removed, except for a few at the bottom, but by now the whole pit is like a furnace. Over the stones that are left, layers of leaves and flesh are built up, one after another, until there is as much above ground as below. Then water is thrown over this mixture, perhaps a bucketful, or two, in our measurements. All of this is covered with old mats and earth, so that the steam is trapped underneath and the cooking begins. By this method, the flesh is cooked very quickly.

As well as the child on the spit, there was evidence of this cooking method all about me, on the beach and beyond.

Straight away, I guessed this was again the work of Te Rauparaha. Later, I learnt that his men had taken a war party to Kaiapoi. After a victory, they captured hundreds of prisoners and brought them by canoe up to our island. They had been camped for nine days.

I discovered Hine, cowering in bushes with Manu beside her. I would never have found her, except that she called out to me in a little voice.

I turned to her, holding my hands palm up to the sky.

Who has done this? I said. Was it him?

Te Rauparaha had ordered an oven to be built on the beach, she told me, before sending off slaves to collect firewood. When they arrived back, he killed them with his tomahawk, while the rest were ordered to cook the bodies of their friends. They served their joints in flax baskets.

I screamed so loud it's a wonder they didn't hear me in Sydney. John began to cry too. I turned away from the scene, and quieted myself, hoping he was too young to understand what he had seen.

Why didn't you stop them? I asked Hine.

She just looked at me as if I was daft in the head, which I suppose I was.

When I told Jacky, he said that he knew about it.

But you did not tell me, I said.

I saw no need for it. I did not know you were going to go prowling around.

Prowling around, I said. Forgive me but I only live here and I wish I did not.

You don't mean that, he said.

I am in a good mind to stay in Sydney the next time we go back.

Well then, I shall leave you here, he rejoined.

And then I will be cooked and eaten too, and so will your son.

At that, he gave me a long hard look. Even though he and I had been so careful with each other since the quarrel over Charley, I saw that deep down he, too, had misgivings about me. After the birth of John, Charley went to sea, and I hadn't seen him in a long while. The silly part of it was, I had never had a fancy for Charley, only his conversation. From the beginning, it was Jacky I hungered for. Don't look alarmed, Adie — however I tease you, I won't embarrass you by explaining it all. There are some women who do what they must for duty and others who do it because their bodies will not allow them to do otherwise. My mother is one of the second kind, and I am somewhere in between. Or so I thought. I did not wish to sample others when I went with Jacky. Not that whalers are romantic. Their hands are meaty and raw from the cold water, and their clothes stink, always stiff with salt and oil. The smell of whale oil is almost impossible to describe, a cross between vinegar and vomit that seems to leave a stain on the skin. I could never produce enough hot water to keep Jacky clean and scrubbed. But that was the way of it. You didn't think about it after a while.

I have said too much, forgive me. Much has happened to me, much that is hard to forget. Jacky craved me, his eyes always following where I went, and his manner seemingly very kind. And when it was night I made him truly happy. That was enough.

I didn't want us to fall to quarrelling again. His silent rage was something I feared then, and still do. So I turned away without speaking further about what I had seen.

I did not mean for you to find out about the bodies on the beach, he said more kindly. It is not something a woman should know about.

But these things cannot be hidden from me, Jacky.

What do you want me to do about it then?

I want us to go and live at Cloudy Bay, as soon as we can. It feels safer than here.

To my surprise, he agreed straight away. He had named the whole area Port Underwood, out of respect for Mr Underwood in Sydney who had given him his start. I wondered if he shouldn't have called it after his benefactor, Mr Campbell, but as usual it was all decided before I was told. And I wasn't going to argue with him then.

I understood then how deeply concerned he was. Not only did he agree to us leaving Te Awaiti, he said he would go ahead and build us a house there and then, and that he would send for Charley to stay with me.

I was very surprised by this. But you know what they say, blood is thicker than water, and when you think about it, who else could he trust? Going through his mind, perhaps, was the thought that if he didn't send for Charley it would look as if he had not got over what was supposed to be mended.

At first I said, that is not what I want.

He looked quite distracted, as if for once he didn't know what to do. You are in the family way, Betty. There is John to consider.

I could camp out, I said.

You need a roof over your head and a bed at night and it will only be for a week or so.

So I said yes. It occurred to me that this might actually put matters to rest for once and for all.

This was how I got to know Charley well, and to live more or less in virtue alongside a man who was not my husband. I found myself laughing often at things he said. We would walk light-hearted along the beaches, skipping stones on the water with John, and racing each other to see who could pop the beads of seaweed on the crunchy sand first. Once, of an evening, he took some clothes out of his canvas bag, a cravat, a silk shirt and a little waistcoat, and dressed up as a dandy. I don't know why he had these clothes with him, it was not as if we were about to go to a ball. But we laughed so hard, I thought I would break in two. I did a little curtsy and pretended to dance. Other evenings, we read his books together by candlelight. One night we pleasured each other, just for curiosity's sake, but it did not feel like a sin. There had been a storm in Cook Strait all day, the sea lashed up into a frenzy, and he slipped in and out of me like an eel, gentle and not at all like his brother, who batters me with his body. Because I was already five months gone, I knew I could not catch a baby. In the morning, it was as if it hadn't happened. The bay was humming with white spume, a reminder of the storm that had passed.

'You have not asked me why I'm here,' Betty says, after a silence.

Adie is cooling herself with a silk fan that had belonged until yesterday to Charlotte Pugh (who is possibly still unaware that it has changed hands). Betty has brought it as a gift. It is hand painted in the design of a peacock tail, so that it ripples with tunnels of blue light. Like the paua shell, the governess had exclaimed.

'A passionate blue,' Betty had murmured.

The gift, of course, had been a perfect choice, both beautiful and practical. How could Adie not have been seduced by it?

Now Adie feels overwrought, as if she is in some kind of slow swelling pain. 'I'm sure you'll tell me,' she says. She feels her face burning and hopes that it is not obvious to the other woman. She is very shocked by what she has heard, and knows, at the same time, that she could sit listening to more all night. The pain is pleasurable; she cannot describe anything like it. Yes. Yes, if she thinks about it, it is like the pain she has felt when the lieutenant is very near to her.

'It isn't true,' says Betty. 'About Charley. Of course I didn't do that. Jacky trusted me.'

'Then why did you tell me it was so?'

'To see what you would do. Whether you would throw me out.'

'What do you want of me?' asks Adie, agitated and angry. She does not know whether she has been tricked, and dare not press the question. Worse, she would like it to be true. For a moment, she has believed it. Perhaps it is.

'I thought you would have worked that out. I need somewhere to stay until Jacky is no longer angry with me.'

'Why is he angry with you?'

'It's too hard to explain.'

'Has he found out about Charley?'

Betty's brow puckers. 'Charley? This is not about Charley.'

'I think you're not in your right state of mind. You've recently lost your child for which I am most truly sorry and would have paid my respects had you allowed me.'

Betty rests her head wearily on one hand. 'Sometimes I think he is grieving for Louisa, as indeed I am. Other times it is as if I have died. In his eyes.'

'And have you?'

'Died? I don't know. A part of me, perhaps, gone the way of the patupaiarehe. My head is away with the fairies.'

'You may stay here tonight. It's too late for you to return.'

'And then what? I go back to his silence.'

'How long has he been like this?'

'Since the rescue. When the ships came to Taranaki and he took me back from Oaoiti, who is the chief who protected me while I was held by the Maoris.'

'I see,' says Adie. And somewhere, she thinks she does begin to see, that some key to the mystery has been turned. His name may be Charley. Or not.

'I cannot bear silence,' Betty says. 'It is like a blunt axe and just as painful.'

The cook has arrived with the evening meal on a tray, boiled fowl, cooled and sliced and served with a celery sauce, and small heads of broccoli; slices of rich fruitcake for dessert.

'Tell Mr Malcolm that I will need a bed and some blankets for Mrs Guard.'

'Well,' says the cook, whose name is Susan, a woman with an oily forehead and quick eyes. Sometimes Adie thinks the world is ruled by cooks. 'I don't know what Mrs Malcolm will say about that for she has taken to her bed with a sick headache. She put off this afternoon's guests.'

'If she is in bed she need not know about it,' says Adie, over-taken by a new reserve of energy. 'Now do as I ask, or I will come up and tell your master myself.'

'Why have you allowed them to put you here?' says Betty, when Susan has gone.

'I thought *you* would never ask me,' says Adie, attacking the fowl. She lifts the meat looking for the slick of jelly that gathers under cooled poultry, and scoops what she finds onto her fork, letting it slowly dissolve on her tongue.

'Well, tell me,' Betty says.

'I like it here. I like to listen to the gum trees.'

'I used to listen to them too when I was a girl.'

'They are like papyrus whispering together, leaf on leaf. Like the ancient scrolls.'

'But you have not told me. Was it to do with me?'

'It is no matter. My position in Lieutenant Roddick's house has ended. I will shortly return to England.'

'You must tell me if I have harmed you in some way. I was not myself when you last saw me.'

'My dear child, I understand that.'

'I am not your dear child. You don't know what it is to have a dear child.'

Adie is silent then.

'I'm sorry, Adie,' says Betty, 'I didn't mean to give offence. My husband so wanted his son. My daughter, well, I had learnt what it was like to be lonely. I wanted a little girl in my image. I cherished her more than my mother or sister or aunt. All of them have shown indifference towards me.'

'Like my sister-in-law,' says Adie, with a rueful smile.

'Just so. But to have a daughter, that's different. Louisa was my little flower from the moment Hine gave her into my arms. I touched the tip of her perfect nose, and stroked back the surprisingly pale hair, for we are given to darkness in our family, though Jacky said he remembered his mother as being light in colouring, and Charley is fairer than him, and I said, Darling girl, my precious little pea pod, I will love you forever with every inch of my breath. And now she's dead and I have both love and hate for those who held us in New Zealand. For in spite of being shown many kindnesses, I believe Louisa would yet have been here, had it not been for our capture.'

'I am so sorry,' Adie murmurs. She thinks of young Austen who is probably wondering now why he has not had a bedtime story, and of Mathilde, who will be settling down in a matter of fact way, making the best of things, but missing her all the same. It does not seem the moment to speak of them.

'It's true,' she says at last, 'that I've become drawn to your story. And that a woman of my age who has lived her life on the fringe of experience is wont to behave extravagantly when she thinks she has come across the real thing at last.'

'I suppose that's not so bad,' says Betty, 'though it tells me how I'm seen by others. The world isn't judging me very kindly. Nor is my husband.'

'He has no right,' says the governess hotly.

'Right. What is right? It's almost impossible to tell. I'm a practical woman, Adie. I've had no choice to be anything else. My husband would say that he, too, is a man who knows how to make the best of a bad job.'

Chapter 23

I never went back to Te Awaiti. When I stood in front of our house at Kakapo Bay, I believed I was home. The bay is a small sheltered haven. A hill rises in a gentle slope up a narrow valley towards easy rolling hills. Jacky had built me the best house yet. It was much like those that had gone before, only longer and the rooms more nicely in proportion with each other. It looked like a real house, like one of the houses in the top end of George Street, only the water was lapping just beneath my feet. I find it hard to describe the colours of the sea and the sky in that place. Some days when the sky is angry, the light will be green, and the sea boiling. Other days it will be so blue that you cannot tell where heaven and the sea leave off from one another, much like a man and a woman when they have been together. In the Maori world it is said that Rangi is the sky father and Papa, the mother, is the earth, and they were separated only so that light could enter the world, and so people would have space to move around. They are never really apart. On other days, I would stand at the water's edge and pinpricks of fog would appear like blue sand flung in the air, and when it passed the sky might have darkened, or it might simply melt away, leaving the air clear again.

It is ours for all time, Jacky said, placing his arms around my waist, a gesture that was not like him. I placed my hands over his, so that we were joined together, his hands and mine, over Louisa, soon to be born.

All of a sudden, I was so happy, as if we really had made a new beginning.

Hine had agreed to come with us, for the time being, and it felt as if she was part of our family too, and soon my brother David would be here, for Jacky had made the arrangements with him the last time we were in Sydney, that he would come and do carpentry for us, rather than put to sea. He had been doing some work for John Deaves and was becoming handy with wood and tools.

I have bought this bay from Te Rauparaha, Jacky said.

I felt something in me grow cold. From Te Rauparaha? But he is a murderer.

He knows a good bargain when he sees it, Jacky said, and laughed. I did not like what I heard. He said: I have paid him with a large cask of tobacco worth one hundred pounds, five bolts of cloth, ten oxen, eight iron pots and twenty blankets.

That is a great sum, I said, still doubtful.

Better than that, he will leave us in peace, for we have struck a deal.

So he is our friend now?

That's about it, Jacky said.

I got over it after awhile, because what else could I do. Jacky had sold Te Awaiti to a couple of whalers called Dicky Barrett and Jack Love, from Port Nick, so now we were free of the place and the dark deeds that had taken place there. John and Louisa were doing well, though Louisa had been born with the same difficulty and pain that accompanied John's arrival. A settlement quickly began to appear; there were more ships calling in and it all felt more sociable. Te Rauparaha's brother Nohoroa, who was a more kindly and open man, lived in the bay and was our neighbour.

The year before last, 1833, started out then as a good year.

But things can turn bad very fast. Friends of ours on board the *Dragon* were attacked by Maoris while bringing in a whale and killed. Killing, cooking, feasting, that was the order of the day again.

And so many battles had been fought between Te Rauparaha's warriors, and Ngai Tahu in the south, so much treachery committed, that the tribes would not let things rest. A war party led by Taiaroa from the far south came up, seeking revenge for those who had died at Akaroa and Kaiapoi. Only now we were not just in the path of returning war parties, we were in the direct line of fighting. Te Rauparaha must have known this when he sold us the bay. Why would he need to own a battleground, when a white man would pay him so handsomely for taking it off his hands? And perhaps be eaten, instead of him.

The warriors got closer and Te Rauparaha ever more treacherous, to his own people as well as to his sworn enemies.

'It's surprising that his people continued to support him,' says Adie. The night has drawn in around them. Outside there is the mutter of night things. Moths flatten themselves against the windowpanes, drawn by the lamp's glow.

'Well, I think he would have turned on them too had they not.'

'They hate him and yet they long to have him amongst them. They cannot do without him. It reminds me of Alcibiades.'

'And who might he be?'

'A statesman of Athens, a soldier turned killer. There was a saying, Better not bring up a lion inside your city, but if you must, then humour all his moods.'

'You and your Greeks. But you're right. That's how it is with Te Rauparaha. And humour him is what Jacky did. Te Rauparaha had become our protector, when it suited him. But with that came the full fury of his enemies.'

You might wonder what all these battles had to do with our shipwreck and what became of us, but what had gone before was all of a piece. It's late, but I'll tell you how we came to be shipwrecked. Who knows, we might go our separate ways tomorrow, and I may never see you again. You've been very kind. I see that things aren't good for you and that my being here is not helping you.

In September, a ship called the *Sarah* was forced to put in to Port Underwood. The ship had left Sydney, heading towards England, via Valparaiso, but it had developed a leak that couldn't be contained by the pumps. The captain was a surly man who simply wanted to patch it up and keep going. There were four ships at anchor in the bay when the *Sarah* limped in. All the masters came and inspected the ship and told this captain that it was not safe to go on. On board the ship were a Mr and Mrs Kentish, Robert and Ivy, and their children.

I see from your expression that you know them. And yes, it is Mrs Kentish who very kindly organised a collection of money for our family.

It would be uncharitable of me to say anything but the best of them. They are well-connected people who came to Australia as free settlers, like you and Mr Malcolm, but not cut out for farming. It can happen. My grandfather wasn't a free man when he came, but he got to take up land, and look what came of it: we ended up in the Rocks with naught. The Kentishes are of the same cut, for all their airs, though lately Mr Kentish has turned his hand to shopkeeping, and I hear that they're prospering.

The captain of the *Sarah* was not impressed with the idea of caulking the topsides of the vessel and returning to Sydney. He swore to keep on towards Valparaiso.

My advice to you, Jacky said to the Kentishes, is to stay here and wait for another ship to take you back to Sydney. My own ship, the *Waterloo*, is on its way from Sydney, and when it has dropped off some supplies, it will head back there. I wouldn't take my children on that leaky tub if I was you.

So that was settled and the Kentishes moved in with us, and I can tell you I was glad we had a more spacious house, for Ivy Kentish was not an easy guest. You might have noticed, despite that porcelain skin and those dolly curls of hers, she can be fretful. At the time it was made worse by her nursing her baby, as I was Louisa. Her milk wouldn't come in whenever she was upset, which was most of the time. Or perhaps it was because of the shape of her nipples, like flat raspberry stains on her chest, that the baby couldn't get a hold on. She didn't want to stay with us, and she didn't want to go on the *Sarah* but she had no choice but to settle down until the *Waterloo* arrived. Which it never did.

Where had it gone? Well you might ask.

Our ship had gone aground on the rocks near Kapiti, and although the crew were spared, the ship was stripped of all its stores by Te Rauparaha. It was late in the year before we discovered this, when the crew managed to make their way to Kakapo Bay. By now the bay was deserted, and of course, back in Sydney, Campbell and Company, who are, or I should say, were Jacky's business partners, did not know what had happened to the ship, nor of the need to send more supplies.

Soon we ran out of salted meat and sugar and tea and all those things we depended on, and what we had left were potatoes and fish, which is not a bad diet, though Ivy Kentish swore she couldn't look at another crayfish if it killed her, which I thought sad because they are a great delicacy. We were running out of potatoes, and had got down to eating cabbage tree hearts. Nohoroa had predicted to Jacky that Taiaroa and his troops would attack when the potatoes began to ripen.

We were now under siege. Jacky issued muskets and six rounds of ammunition to all the men, and they took it in turns to sit up at night. Mr Kentish didn't seem to know what to do with his musket at first. Perhaps he thought he was supposed to cut the wood with it, I don't know. Well, you couldn't tell with those two, they were altogether useless at almost everything. No wonder they were going back to England. But once he understood that the Maoris might really invade us, he sat up all and every night with a sabre at his side and a loaded musket on the table. I kept out of his way and didn't come out to the kitchen until it was morning, lest he made a false move. He slept most of the day, waking only to fret over his wife not getting enough to eat.

I said to him, Mr Kentish, we are doing the best we can. I know it's not the best hospitality in the world, but it's all we have to offer.

It cannot be helped, he said, attempting a brave face, but my Ivy is used to the finer things in life. I doubt you would understand.

Well, I said, I may not have seen the Elgin Marbles and I only know of the Acropolis from afar, but I have heard of the world beyond.

At that he looked very surprised, and I thought then of you, Adie, and was grateful. Mr Kentish made the common mistake of believing that people from the Rocks are simpletons. He didn't understand that, although we were short of food, Jacky could buy him twice over. Oh well, that is not entirely true, for by that stage of course we knew that the *Waterloo* had gone, and this ship was vital to us. I was thankful we still had our interest in the *Harriet*.

A ship came at last and delivered provisions to tide us over. Charley was on board, on the lookout for a job again. By now fresh stories arrived every day that Taiaroa was about to attack Cloudy Bay. The men wanted to get away, and the season being all but over, there was no reason to hold them back. And it was decided that, when the ship left, our family should leave with the Kentishes. I could tell Jacky didn't want to go but neither did he want us to sail alone. I was in two minds about it. It's one thing to stay and keep a brave face when you just have yourself to look after, but now I had two babies it seemed reckless to stay. I might have insisted on staying if Ivy Kentish hadn't got me so worked up. She screamed at every little thing and had hysterics from top to bottom when a friendly canoe pulled up on the beach one afternoon. I'd become jumpy too, not sleeping well at nights.

I think we should go, Betty, Jacky said to me the night before the ship was due to sail.

What of Te Rauparaha? I thought he would protect us?

He is more on the run than not these days. He'll look after his self first. And who is to know who did for the *Waterloo*? He said this with a deep and bitter anger as if he could taste arsenic in his mouth.

So much for our friend, Te Rauparaha, I said to myself.

We should have Louisa baptised, Jacky said, it will be a good chance to have that done. I was pleased to hear him say that, for though she was thriving, you cannot be sure how long a soul can survive, can you, Adie, and it would grieve me to think of my little girl waking up in the afterlife and the gates of heaven not open to her.

If we went, it meant leaving our belongings, for there was no room on the ship and not enough time to pack before it must leave. Then Charley told Jacky that he would stay and watch over things while we went to Sydney, and another seaman agreed that he would stay too, and we were grateful.

I was to see Charley again sooner than expected. Within days of our leaving, Taiaroa did attack, and Charley and the other man were taken captive. The Maoris at the settlement were killed. For some reason the two pakea were spared — perhaps they were saving them for last — but a schooner arrived in the bay and they were rescued.

We had made it in safety to Sydney, and the Kentishes bade us farewell without so much as a backward glance. A week or so later, Charley appeared at the Rocks, and I learned that our house had been burnt again.

Also, that Hine was among the dead.

You may think it strange that I was willing to return. Yet so much of our lives had become tied up with Kakapo Bay that when Jacky said let us go back, it seemed like the most natural thing in the world. The whaling season was almost upon us again, and if we were to go back, the time was right. Jacky arranged to take the *Harriet* back to New Zealand, with Richard Hall on board. Captain Hall would sail her back to Australia with a load of flax and timber. And we would take up as we had before, if somewhat the poorer.

Charley did have news about the fighting that gave us hope. Taiaroa had declared himself tired of battle. He and his warriors were going back south to settle in for winter. Perhaps they felt that they had taught Te Rauparaha a lesson.

Charley was coming back with us. He and Jacky seemed at ease with one another, as if something between them was settled.

And David was finally coming to live with us. When I knew it was decided, and nobody was looking, I put my arms around him and said, Don't be afraid, you will like it well, living with us. He was half a head taller than me, and he went red in the face. Don't be silly he said, pushing me away.

I said, Cross my fingers and make a wish and hope to die if it don't come true. Which we did when we were children.

All right, he said.

What did you wish for?

I'm not telling you.

Did you wish to have a girl? There are girls in New Zealand who would like you.

Don't, he said, as if he was going to cry.

I felt unkind then. Besides, I hadn't worked out a wish for myself. My heart was still sore over Hine, but nothing could bring her back, and now with David coming over to us, I had got most of the wishes I had asked for in the past.

Part 6

Separations

Chapter 24

So we were off to New Zealand again.

Jacky rounded up a whaling gang while I gathered warm clothes. It would be winter. I bought long flannel underpants for Jacky and David at Spyer and Cohen's. I noticed their stocks were low.

We'll have you back any day, Mr Spyer said. You brought a smile to people's faces.

I'll teach *you* to smile, I said, which was one of our favourite jokes, for he had a solemn little face. People often behaved around him as if they were at a religious ceremony. Smile please, Mr Spyer, I'd say to him, as if he was having his portrait painted.

It is you who is the oil painting, he would say.

But though I felt concerned for him, whereas once I would have added a little extra to the bill, I knew now I must be careful with our money. That was another of our games: I would give him extra and he would give me a little refund when Mr Cohen wasn't looking, so the rubber was more or less squared, but usually in my favour. This time I settled the account down to the last penny; it was all business.

We left in late April. I dressed in a blue dress of heavy cotton for I knew that we would be in warmer weather for a day or so, but I had a plaid dress in my cabin portmanteau for when we sailed further south.

The *Harriet* had now done several voyages across the Tasman and a number to South America. Going aboard her was like stepping in a carriage with sturdy horses and a safe driver. All told, there was thirty-two of us aboard, no other women. Charley and David were there, but apart from them, the men were a rough lot, those who hadn't been able to find work. Jacky didn't have much to choose from, as the season was almost upon us, and most of the ships had their crews signed up well before-hand.

Nothing went amiss for the first few days at sea.

David was seasick for the first day or two. He had never been on board a boat before except the rowboat when our father drowned. After he recovered I had to tell him to keep out of the sun. He was inclined to sit towards the bow of the ship with his face raised to the breeze, a dreamy expression in his eyes. It was difficult to describe to him how different New Zealand was from Australia, though I did try. I told him about the Maori people who lived there, and also that there were certain ways he must behave, if we were stay on good terms with them.

Will they eat me, he asked in mock horror. That they might do so was beyond his understanding. I think about David now, and wonder if he really was slower than other children, if that was why life was so hard for him. But it was more that he had a different way of seeing some things. He had trouble learning to read and write at the orphanage. When he looked at words he seemed to see them backwards from the way I did. And yet he had an amazing memory, and he knew every street and lane in Sydney, as if he was a navigator.

On that last day of our journey he said, We are nearing land now.

I saw gulls wheeling above us, and knew I should have seen them first. He had only my description of a voyage to go by, but he had remembered that we would see the birds first, before we saw land.

It was a beautiful day. Later, as the sun dropped, the sea looked like it was fire. As night fell, we began the run down the Taranaki coastline, heading south for home. In the morning we would be there. The word home tripped off my tongue so easily now. I felt the old familiar excitement that I always did when returning to New Zealand, even though I knew I would find only the ruins of our house. I regretted, in particular, the loss of my beautiful green-and-white meat-dish that I'd bought when we were in the money. Funny the things you hanker after.

But the bay would be the same, and the islands that lay in the harbour mouth. I had come to love the country as if I had been born to it. As dark closed in we saw the green-black bush pressing towards the shore, and here and there the glow of a fire and smoke on the horizon. On our right were the Sugar Loaf Islands, their shape as the name suggests, though the Maori name for them is Moturoa. On their black crags stood the remains of a small whaling station. A pakea man by the name of John Oliver lived there. Jacky knew him. We saw, too, the peak of Taranaki. It is a most beautiful mountain that rises gradually and evenly to a spire above a wide surrounding plain of land. This is the area from where Te Rauparaha had been driven years before.

But then, as we seemed to be gliding through the dusk, there was a sudden shift in the weather. A south-westerly came out of nowhere, a smudge of fog across the ocean, and then the wind hit us, catching us full on, and we were driven towards shore. The ship turned about, and we headed back to sea, for it is a rocky and uninviting stretch of land that would have holed us in a trice. Before the fog closed in, I had glimpsed the high faraway firelight of two great pa that stand on sentinel sites at the lower reaches of the Taranaki. A small beach of gravelly sand lies beneath high cliffs; deep ravines run between the two sites. I always looked out for them when we were passing, trying to imagine what it must be like to live so high up there, and see so far out to sea.

But now the shroud of mist had fallen, and there was nothing there, just the air like damp flannel against our cheeks, and the cold turned biting and cruel.

Get below and make the children secure, Jacky said, as if I needed to be told. There was such a pitching and rolling in our cabin, I could scarcely stand, let alone hold on to the children. I called out for David, who had followed me below, and between us we got John into a bunk. I crawled into mine and held onto Louisa.

This weather will pass I said to David, who was a nasty green. Go on, get yourself out of here. I did not want him being sick in the cabin, I had enough on my hands with the children.

And the weather did die down, though the ship heeled in the water several times, as if we might roll over, but I told myself, this ship had seen worse weather than this. Gradually the sea settled, and whoever was at the wheel must have been lulled into thinking it would be all plain sailing ahead.

The children and I were asleep when the hull was ripped open. It happened so quickly: one moment we were peaceful, the next, on the floor, rocks slicing through the side of the ship as if it were a sugar crust. It was around four in the morning; we were five miles south of the cape of Taranaki.

Jacky waded through the cabin in his thigh boots. I hadn't changed out of my blue dress and it was sodden and trailing in the water. Jacky scooped one of the children under each arm.

There is no time to be lost, he said, as I looked in vain for my portmanteau, which was now sailing around in a sea of its own beneath the bunks.

Getting ashore was easier than I expected. We were so low in the water, I was able to step out onto the rocks. Jacky saw every last man got off the ship. The weather had worsened. The seas were furious and huge, sheets of white water bucketing down one after another. All we could do was huddle against the cliffs, hoping none of these immense waves would catch us and sweep us away.

As morning broke, we saw a desolate landscape behind us. At least we discovered a small break in the rocky cliffs. We were able to follow this gully a little way in, away from the worst of the roaring water. But if our scratched and filthy band had hoped for salvation, there was little to be had. The earth was naught but a thin skin on the rocks and what vegetation there was, low and scrubby. A streamer of blue sky appeared beneath cushiony clouds, as if taunting us with fair weather to come, but the sea was still running high.

The men went back to ship, holding onto each other as they inched across the rocks in an effort to rescue as many of our belongings as possible. I saw David struggling for a foot-hold on the rocks, spiky as devil's teeth. I wanted to call him back, but if he was to become a man among men, he must work with them.

The results of this expedition were laid out on the shore to dry: ten muskets, a small quantity of sails, a whaleboat, some food and a baling pail. As soon as the sails were dry, the men went about turning them into rough tents. Later in the day, another two of the ship's boats were brought ashore, but every-thing else was whipped away, bobbing and sailing in the boiling surf, while the shattered hull of the *Harriet* was cast up, further along the rocks. This was the second ship we had lost in a few months. It will be the ruin of us, I thought. All the toil and hardship of these last five years come to nothing.

At least, Jacky said, we might be able to patch up one of these boats enough to sail down the coast to Cloudy Bay. It wasn't a happy prospect, but it offered hope. The weather had changed yet again. Torrents of rain began to fall. Jacky and I shared out rations of salted pork, and the men washed it down with rainwater collected in the pail. The rain collapsed the sail tents against us.

I asked Jacky if he knew where we were, and if there were any Maoris nearby and what we might expect if they turned up.

He believed that we were just north of the pa of Te Namu. The head chief was Te Matakatea of the Taranaki tribe, famous for holding off Waikato invaders, the previous year. His name meant 'clear-eyed' and he was considered a crack shot with the musket. About twenty miles south were the twin pa of Waimate and Orangituapeka, and these too were strongholds of Te Matakatea.

These were the great fortresses I had seen the night before. Taranaki and Ngati Ruanui, who lived at the twin pa, had banded together to fight off their enemies.

And us? What will they do to us?

We will just have to wait and see, Jacky said, and I did not like the way his mouth tightened around the words. They don't have many muskets, but what they have they will use well. On the other hand, he said, Te Matakatea had had good dealings with white men, and perhaps he would spare us.

It was on the tip of my tongue to ask whether these tribes were enemies of Te Rauparaha, but in my heart I already knew the answer.

David was blue and shivering, his breathing shallow. I brought him in under the tent with us. I'm sorry David, I whispered, so that the others would not hear, you would have been better off in Sydney.

I would rather be with you he said, which I thought brave of him. I would have liked to pull him close to me for warmth, but could not do so without bringing shame on him. I could hardly understand what he was saying. I thought him delirious, but after awhile I recognised an old prayer of Granny's, one she had learned from a ship's chaplain on one of those several ships that brought her from one side of the world to the other. I said the words with him because remembering Granny gave me strength.

I bind unto myself this day
The virtues of the starlit heaven
The glorious sun's life-giving ray
The whiteness of the moon at even
The flashing of the lightning free
The swirling of the wind's tempestuous shocks
The stable earth, the deep salt sea
Around the eternal rocks.

After that, I thought he had stopped breathing, but then he began again, more easily, as if rested in himself. I fell into another patchy sleep, praying the weather might clear so that work could begin on the boats.

I was rewarded at least by clear skies, but it was too late. The news of our shipwreck had travelled.

The hour is late and the governess dozes. Perhaps she's not as old as I thought. Fifty at least, but that is not truly old. My husband Jacky is already in his forties. I never thought of him as old, but now I'm twenty and he has moved into middle-age, a man full of brooding thoughts, I've begun to see him in a different light. I think back just the space of eight years when Granny foresaw him as my husband, and of the girl I was then. I believed he would take care of me, but he could have been my father, and a father was what I lacked. I am all but penniless now, but I have a rich and desirable body, something I didn't know when I married him, and I yearn for a touch that I might return. Sitting here in the Australian dark beside my teacher, I believe I have learnt more than she can ever know, in spite of all her gods.

The fan I gave Adie has slipped from her fingers. All evening she has waved it back and forth but all it has done is stir the heavy air. Her upper lip is beaded with sweat like rainwater on the edge of a drain, her mouth twitching open, allowing tiny snores to escape. She stirs and seems to smile. Perhaps a dream drifts by, passionate blue and silver, like the gifts I bring her. She wakes and shakes her head, as if to clear her thoughts, but her eyes are heavy. I don't know what she hears, but I talk on quietly anyway, for now I've begun I can't stop.

I talk of how we fell out on that rocky shore, as raiders from the pa fell upon us, demanding whatever they could lay hands on, and when we didn't give it up, taking it from us. Of the impudent way they laughed in Jacky's face. E, Haari, they mocked, who is in charge now?

Where is Te Matakatea? Jacky asked.

He is at Waimate, they said.

Does he know we have been wrecked?

The men from Te Namu laughed in his face. You are a big man, Haari, why do you need protecting? You have always had your own way.

The crew were divided, wanting to save their own skins first. This should have come as no surprise, some of them being violent thieves and murderers to begin with. When Jacky's back was turned two crewmen, Thomas Mossman and James Johnson, gave away some of our provisions and much of our gunpowder to Te Matakatea's men. They did this behind our backs. We could not understand why Mossman and Johnson and several other men began walking off with the tribesmen.

It will be all right, Haari, said one of the Maoris. We will treat them well. And he laughed.

That will be the last we see of them, Jacky said, and then their theft was revealed.

I will go after them and kill them, Jacky shouted. He was breathing heavily, his chest rising and falling as if his heart would burst.

There is nothing to be done, I said. I was afraid he would go off and leave us here without protection. The mood of the men left behind was very sour.

We will take a whaleboat to sea, Thomas White said, within my hearing. He was a man I had taken against from the first, his dark jowls set as if with an inner fury.

Even though it's holed, I asked, for I was not going to let him get away with this. Perhaps he thought a woman couldn't understand the King's English.

We can bail fast enough to keep it afloat, he said. We can bring back a rescue boat.

A likely story, Jacky said, when I told him. Mind you, the plan is not entirely foolish but these men cannot handle a boat holed like this. And who's to say they will come back, once they've saved themselves?

You're not going yourself, I said. Or begged. I knew that if anybody could do it, it would be him, but I was terrified of being left alone.

Perhaps, he said.

Would you take us?

Never, he said firmly.

Then you cannot leave us. I heard my voice piteous and weak.

He did not answer. That evening, I saw him and Charley and Captain Hall deep in conversation.

David, after seeming to rally, was ill again. Young John had stopped eating altogether. I wondered if we too should make approaches to the tribe, like the deserters. They were, no doubt, having a more comfortable life than ours — unless they'd been eaten. But though the people of Taranaki were not well disposed towards us, they might consider a deal if Jacky offered something in return for our shelter. By now, I was willing to risk it. My hair was matted thick, my throat and nostrils raw from salt spray. The children were failing, my milk had all but dried up. I had offered John my breast, big boy though he was, but there was nothing there.

We had now been on the beach for more than a week. It was the seventh of May. Two things happened that day.

First, three of the deserting crewmen arrived back at the beach.

What has happened? Don't your friends at the pa want you

any more? I asked, in what I hoped was my most sarcastic tone.

They didn't look at me. I knew they had done something wrong. Though they wouldn't talk to me, I guessed from their appearance that it was something very bad, and that we were now in greater danger.

Later, the women at the pa would tell me what had happened. All had seemed well for some days, and the men had been well fed, in return for their gifts from the *Harriet*'s stores. Then three young girls, not yet twelve, had had their bodies torn open and tossed aside by the men. Afterwards, the men took their place beside the fire, picking fernroot from their teeth, with the virgin blood of the girls on their hands, as if what they had done was of no account.

No wonder they had taken flight. Their wits had not completely deserted them, for soon they sensed the mood around them after the tearful girls were discovered. They escaped the fury of their hosts by running back to us.

It was late in the afternoon when the second thing happened.

Two hundred warriors advanced upon us. There was no question of a fight, we were outnumbered on every side. All that remained of our belongings was taken. The warriors took with them such items as soap, though God knows, we were past washing or bathing, sugar and a sack of flour, which at least I could have made a paste from. When they left, we looked at each other, gaunt and hollow-eyed, the bones in our cheeks standing out like those of the skeletons on the beaches of Te Awaiti.

Days passed, which I remember as if in a dream. I am not sure whether it really happened or not, but I seem to recall Charley coming to me in the night and kneeling beside me. It will be all right, darling, he said, I'll take care of you. Another time I might have been shocked by his endearment.

I sat bolt upright and Jacky was not there beside me on the hollowed out sea-grass that was our bed. Has he put to sea? I cried.

I knew by the look in Charley's eyes that it was so.

But in the morning Jacky was there. Again the seas ran high. I thought perhaps he had tried and failed to launch the boat.

What will become of us? I asked myself many times.

David seemed to decide this for himself. He was now truly delirious and spoke like a madman. Tell Mama she was the best mother in the world, he said, holding onto my hand. His eyes were heavy, the lids swollen so that he could hardly see.

I thought those were powerful words of forgiveness but I did not let them move me. She is all right, I said. Our mother is our mother. You can tell her these things yourself, for soon we will be rescued. I was willing him to stay with me, for John and Louisa to stay. If just one of them were to slip beyond my grasp, then I would know God had forsaken us altogether.

On the tenth of May, we were taken by the Maoris.

The first raid happened soon after dawn. Thomas White was killed before our eyes.

Around midday, musket fire hit our party. Our group returned the fire. I saw, in part, the manoeuvre Jacky and Charley and Captain Hall had been planning: what were left of our muskets were being fired from positions on the beach where they were most likely to hit a party descending from the hilltops. More than twenty Maoris fell before this onslaught, but in all, we lost fourteen men. Richard Hall was the first to go. The beach rang with the men's dying shouts, some bitter at their fate, others muttering prayers, and words of love for people far away.

David staggered to his feet.

I tried to pull him back with us. I cried out, David, for God's sake, stay with me. You cannot fight.

I don't think he heard me, or if he did, my words made no sense to him. He walked upright, the first steps he had taken in days, putting his shoulders back. He walked out into the line of fire that came from above. I ran out to stop him, and felt a blow like a tree trunk falling on me. Above me stood a man with a raised tomahawk. A look of astonishment crossed his face. He glanced at his weapon as if there was something wrong with it. I touched my head, and felt a burning pain. My head was split, but not shattered as it might have been. Instead, the tortoise-shell comb in my wild and tangled hair had shielded my skull from the violence of the blow. Blood ran from a wound in my throat where the axe had grazed as it slipped off my shell, as if I was the tortoise.

Then I saw David fall, watched his blood running across the sand.

Mama, I am truly sorry, I said, whether in my head or out loud, I am not sure. Please forgive me, Mama.

His blue eyes stared blank at the sky. My brother was just eighteen years of age. Among the tangle of limbs, brown and white, strewn across the beach, I saw the tribe, too, had lost boys who were little more than children. So they lay together.

I touched the sticky blood seeping down my chest, but I felt nothing, as if the blood belonged to another person. I heard a voice rising in a wail. It was my own. I heard Jacky say: Do not take on like this, it will not make things better.

But strong and sinewy hands were pulling me.

Run, Jacky shouted, but there was nowhere I could run. Charley, and other men who had survived, were in retreat along the beach, and suddenly the tribe seemed to lose interest in them. They still held onto Jacky, his arms pinned to his side as he looked on from across the beach.

A man with smouldering eyes, not unlike those of Thomas White in their hatred, stepped forward. I would later learn he was the father of one of the girls taken by the sailors. His was the first hand to tear my clothes, the blue dress peeled away. Others followed him in undressing me, my corset stripped off, so that my breasts sprang free. In a few minutes I stood naked, and there was nowhere to hide myself. Voices rose in sighs and ahs and I prepared myself for death or the sharp spear of the men's bodies between my thighs. The children were crying. I could not comfort them. I raised my ashamed eyes and saw Jacky's face, full of anguish, as he struggled in vain against those who held him.

My first tormentor reached over with his lips puckered. He brushed the nipple of my right breast as he leant into my throat where the blood still trickled and fell on my shoulders. With one hand he pushed my hair away and with the other he held me still. I felt his mouth close over the wound in my neck and begin to suck.

He stood back, as if offering others the chance to follow, but he must have swallowed all the blood, because the flow had stopped. He seized an iron hoop, which I believe had come from the wreck of the *Harriet*, digging it into my neck in an effort to open up a fresh wound.

As the frenzy of excitement continued, the men holding Jacky were perhaps distracted, looking towards their turn with me, for when I looked again, he was gone and I knew he had slipped their grasp. A musket shot rang out, but he was lost to them.

Now the mood turned uglier still, as I struggled to cover my nakedness, my hands in front of the bush of hair covering that last forbidden place. But death was on their minds and the man lifted his spear.

Only, at that moment, more people arrived. One of them was Te Matakatea, and with him was a woman. She saw what was happening and stepped forward. There is something to be said for the kindness of women to one another at the worst possible hour. The woman threw a cloak over my body, and in that instant I was saved.

The woman was the wife of Te Matakatea.

Instead of execution, we were told to follow.

But it was as I feared, the children and I were alone. I carried Louisa in my arms. A lithe dark man I had not seen before carried John in his arms. I guessed that he must have come from Waimate with Te Matakatea. I could barely keep up with him. Perhaps I imagined it, but he seemed to throw a look of sympathy towards me. He did not speak to the men who had taunted me on the beach. In this way we came to the pa of Te

Namu, high above the sea. We climbed to it by a rope ladder that could be drawn up as quickly as it was dropped.

We found ourselves in an open space before a meeting house.

That night the chief's wife asked her husband if my life might be spared. He listened intently, nodding his head as if in sympathy with her arguments. It was to these two people of the Taranaki tribe that I owed my life.

The slim young man who had carried John also spoke with Te Matakatea. I learnt that his name was Oaoiti and that he was a chief of Ngati Ruanui. In this manner, it was decided that I would live there at Te Namu pa, as part of the tribe.

Before this could begin, we had to submit ourselves to a ritual stampede, in which we were trampled underfoot, while the people of the pa shouted I know not what. But I took it to mean that we were no longer pakea, stripped of our whiteness, and must now consider ourselves Maori. I saw the pain Louisa was in, even as she was torn from my hands and hurled beneath the running trampling feet. I saw a foot descend on her chest and believe I heard her rib snap.

My little girl.

I saw then that I was bleeding, not from my wounds, but from that time of the month, the first since Louisa's birth. A man looked down at me, with utter disgust, as if he had trampled on shit. But at least the trampling stopped.

I was placed in a hut surrounded by stakes at the edge of the pa. A woman was sent to mind me. I never learnt her name. It is considered rude to ask a person's name directly, and after awhile it became too late for me to find out, though perhaps they thought I knew. It may have been Ruiha, or perhaps it was simply that she was a ruahine, a woman who knows spells. I think of her as Ruiha. I knew I had been sent to the hut because I was unclean, and that I could not leave until I was finished bleeding. But then something else happened that I could not have imagined. I had thought that in sparing me, my children would be allowed to stay with me. Louisa was given to me, though later that night she was taken away, cradled in the arms of one of the women of the tribe, who said she would care for her, and I did not mind that.

But John was taken away from the pa, riding off on the shoulders of a stranger. I ran to the door because I heard him calling me. He wanted to get down but he was grasped by his ankles, on either side of the man's neck, so that he couldn't move.

Please, I cried. I turned to the woman who I thought was my friend, but this time she shrugged as if there was nothing she could do. He is going to be a rangatira, she said. He will get the very best care, or words to that effect. As if I should be proud.

No, I said, that cannot be.

Mama. Mama, John called. I will be a good boy. Don't let them take me away.

Stop, I shouted with all the voice I could muster, and that language I had spoken with my friends in Cloudy Bay. Kati. Ko taku tama tena. Stop. That is my boy. *My* boy.

Nobody appeared to listen as I fell to the ground. I remember it flashing through my mind, as my cheek rested on the beaten earth of Te Namu pa, that I had failed every person I loved.

I did not see John again for several months.

I rest my forehead on the cold glass of the windowpane. Outside in the thin light of the new day, Australian birds stir and shout with their bold mocking voices among a garden that Adie has told me looks as if it is straight from the English countryside. Barefoot I step outside. The scent of late honeysuckle rises from beneath the dew, sharp and sweet. I see the tousled dahlias in the wispy dawn, a line of gladioli at attention like soldiers, and wonder where the next line of musket fire might come from.

I have an odd premonition that the most important part of my life, that for which I will be remembered, has already passed.

Chapter 25

LETTER FROM LIEUTENANT GERALD RODDICK, SYDNEY
TO MISS ADELINE MALCOLM AT PARRAMATTA

2 March 1835

My dear Miss Malcolm

I enclose some drawings the children have made for you. How can I prevail upon you? Your presence in my house is essential. Every day, Austen cries and asks for Nanny Adie. I did not know he called you this. He is inconsolable. I have a woman come every day, but although I think her kind enough and she does not beat the children hard, it seems she does not truly understand their needs.

At first, after you left, I thought that children should accept their lot and not question the arrangements made by their elders. But as I see my son growing more despondent every day, I wonder how I will ever make a man of him. Shoulders up, boy, I say. I ask the cook if he has eaten everything put in front of him, but she reports that the plate returned on his tray is hardly touched. Of course she is not a good cook. Do you think she should be replaced with a better one? Miss Malcolm — Adeline, if I may be so forward — I would allow you to find a better cook if you returned to my household.

I know that in the past you have encouraged me to seek an education for Mathilde at one of the better schools for young ladies. I see she is sorely in need of some lessons in deportment, for her manner has become quite rough and rude, like that of the convict children of the Rocks. She still has the language of a lady, but there is a certain insolence about her that I cannot tolerate. But I will do whatever you suggest to improve her attitude.

I am quite at a loss as to how these children should be brought up without you here to help me.

If I have done anything to offend you, I do ask your forgiveness. You have nothing to fear from me. As far as the matter on which we have disagreed is concerned, for all I know Mrs Guard may be more sinned against than sinful, and perhaps I have been too quick to judge. Your friendship towards her is as a trifle to me, if you will just come back.

Yours,

Gerald Roddick

'The cheek of it,' says Adie, her hands trembling, as she reads this over her breakfast tray. She and Betty sit in the shaded porch in front of the cottage, the small table before them.

'He is very condescending in his manner,' Betty says. She is pale and drawn, with dark circles beneath her eyes from lack of sleep.

'*You have nothing to fear.*' Adie quotes the letter with a spit of contempt in her voice.

'Oh, I thought you were referring to his words about me. *Perhaps I have been too quick to judge.*'

'That? Well, yes, I do see that that might be wounding to you. Rumour without substance is always unkind.'

'Well,' says Betty with some vehemence, 'he's just offering a general view of my character, isn't he? Nothing you can put your finger on, nothing that I can go and say to your lieutenant, what is it exactly that you mean? What sin have you heard about of mine? For he would say in answer, but I have said nothing of you, I have only spoken in the kindest terms. I'm taking your side.'

Adie looks at her friend carefully.

'I don't think you've told me everything, Betty.'

'Why on earth would I do that?' Betty says, with the semblance of a laugh. And then, as if to turn away her sharpness, she adds, 'You mightn't always hear me, Adie. Or perhaps I don't put into words some of my darkest reflections.'

'I'm sorry. I was very tired last night,' Adie says, after another silence. 'I can't imagine what I'd have done, in your circumstances.'

'You'd have done whatever you must, whatever you had to do to save your children's lives. You'd have pretended to yourself that nothing existed except the place you were in. Until you came to believe it.'

'So you think I should go back to Lieutenant Roddick's house?' says Adie, as if she has hardly been listening.

'Roddick?' Betty is glad of a diversion from scrutiny of herself. 'Well, like me, I suppose you have the children to consider too. But these aren't your children,' she says, with the appearance of a frown. 'Surely that's different.'

'In what way?' The teacher's voice is querulous.

'They'll grow up and grow away, and then you'll be on your own again. What cause will the lieutenant have for you remaining in his household when they are gone?'

'I don't want to think about that, Betty.'

'You love him, don't you?'

The governess fans her burning cheeks, her damp eyes.

'Why,' says Betty, 'you're a late bloomer, aren't you?'

'Am I? Do you think so?'

'Well, yes,' says Betty, without irony. 'But of course, if it's the lieutenant you're after, the whole thing changes. Either it's the children you're worried about, or the lieutenant.'

'Couldn't it be both?' asks Adie, her voice humble.

'It would be worse for the children if you returned and then left again. I expect they'll get used to someone new if they have to.'

'You can't know that,' Miss Malcolm cries.

'Well, I know a lot. It's different with every child. My daughter is dead. But my son has had plenty of mothers and does very well.'

'Are you thinking of leaving Captain Guard?'

'For the moment, that is exactly what I've done.' Betty appears light-headed and giddy when she voices this admission.

Miss Malcolm lets out a wail like a child. 'I don't know what to do.'

'About me, or yourself?' Betty feels like another person, older and wiser than the woman before her, whose shaky hand mops up her poached egg with a piece of bread. She looks into Adie's eyes watering in bright sunlight, so that the rims of her pupils seem to dissolve. 'What do you really want? If it's the lieutenant, you must weigh up the possibilities. Can you bear to bring up his children while you sleep in an iron bed in the maid's quarters, or do you have any chance of bringing him to bed yourself?'

Adie looks away from Betty, her eyes narrowed against the morning sun. 'Will you go back to Captain Guard?'

'Before I can decide that, I'll have to see if he asks me,' says Betty. 'You could say, Adie, that our misfortunes have something in common.'

Chapter 26

JOURNAL OF JOHN GUARD

Cambridge Street, the Rocks, August 1834

Musket shot thudded behind me. My head feels like it is exploding when I think back on what happened. I cannot bear to remember, but I cannot forget. As I left Betty and the children at Te Namu, I reached out to her but she didn't see me, and she could not have got away.

My poor wife.

Her eyes were like those of the cow whale that cannot save its calf once the chase has begun. In my pocket I touched a piece of broken tortoise-shell. I couldn't remember catching it but I must have put out my hand in an effort to save Betty as she was struck with a tomahawk. I knew the comb's familiar shape beneath my hand.

I was leaving her and the children behind. The truth of this hit me like a hammer blow beneath my heart. I should not have listened when she pleaded with me to stay. I should have taken the boat and run for it down the coast.

What happened should not have come as a surprise. Things

had things turned from bad to worse from the time we ran aground. Our sacking was muru, a plundering in revenge for wrongs done. The men who deserted us and came back are dead now and good riddance. I heard them have a laugh about what they done to the girls at the pa but they were scared all the same. No good will come of this I said to myself. I couldn't figure out why they let them come back but I see it now. They wanted all of us at once. They wanted us to know what had happened and what we were being punished for. It has to be said many Maoris do not like whalers. I have heard this said often enough and sometimes with fair reason. But whalers have done good turns as well as bad. In the end it usually comes down to women.

I caught up soon with my bro. Charley who had held back for me and not long after that we came across the other crew members who had escaped.

We travelled north during the night, for by now I had a plan in my head. About 40 mile to the north-west is Moturoa, where I'd done good trade in flax earlier on. These are Ati Awa people, known for their fierceness. But my friends Dicky Barrett and John Love, the ones who took Te Awaiti off of my hands, gave good help to these people when they were attacked by tribes from the north. It was thanks to the cannons they gave the Ati Awa that they had a victory. I saw nothing else for it but to push north and see if they wd help us.

Well, some hope that was. In the morning we had not got very far before we came across 100 savages waiting in ambush. They had been going south hoping to get their share of the *Harriet* booty.

Too late too bloody late I told them which did nothing much to help.

That was our lot. We seemed to have no friends. They took us captive and took our clothes. It's hard for a man to run when he has no threads.

I thought we were done for. They circled round us

tomahawks held high. After hours while which they talked and argued among themselves they decided to take us to Moturoa. I couldn't follow much of what was said. Betty wd have known what they were on about. This tribe understand English because of Dicky Barrett and Jack Love and the man Oliver who has lived at their pa. But they wd not speak to us, except in their tongue.

It was getting cold again and our spirits very low. Charley said well this is a nice mess brother. I spent 7 years a captive and now here I am a prisoner again.

I said at least you are alive which is more than can be said for Betty's bro and our mates.

For the time being he said. Anyway they were no mates of mine.

I didn't feel like arguing with him. I was sore inside about young David and also the loss of Captain Hall, not to mention all else that had befallen us. I could not bring myself to think on Betty and what the Maoris might have done to her. I recalled the chief Tamaiharanui who had put his daughter to death rather than let him fall into the hands of Te Rauparaha. Perhaps that is what I should have done for Betty, put her out of her misery. But now it was too late for that as well.

At Moturoa they put us in a pen and fed us potatoes. Of the man Oliver there was no sign. We heard he had left. We were offered meat. I said no for who is to know but that is human flesh. 1 of our men says I have heard it is no different to eating a bit of pork if you close your eyes. I said I will kill you with my bare hands if you touch it.

I will die anyway I expect he said. He was a poor wretch transported for attacking his master in England with a boot last. I made his boots too tight he told me. When he told me this we was looking at the stars and wondering what wd happen next and whether we are being fattened up.

So did you I asked him as much to pass the time as anything,

Not at all. He took them away and then he brought me back a different pair altogether and said as how they were the same shoes.

I should like some shoes I said. Any shoes.

Where wd you go if you had some Charley asked from my other side.

Out of here and fetch my son.

And what of Betty.

Oh Betty too I said.

I did not say that I had decided it best to think of Betty as already dead. If she was not she wd be made dirty by the savages. The blood boiled between my ears. Betty belongs to me.

Some days passed. It was easy to lose track of how many days and nights. But then news did come. My wife and daughter were living at Te Namu pa.

My son I said. What of my son?

He was safe too they told me. But at another pa.

I felt uplifted with hope. Well then I said to our captors, in that case you wd do better if you let us go so that we can bring a ransom.

We wd not be the ones to receive a ransom for your wife and children.

I heard their logic so I said, Well what about if we give you a reward for letting us go.

At 1st they laughed but the matter did not end there. That evening there was long talk on the marae. Speaker after speaker got up and waved their sticks and harangued the tribe. In the end we went to sleep while they were still talking.

In the morning I got a proposition. Their English had improved. What if I was to leave some of our men here for a ransom. This included my brother Charley.

How much do you want I said not liking what they were putting on the table but seeing no other way.

Surely they are worth a cask of gunpowder.

To this I agreed. But I was not letting them have it all their own way. I said, If I am to be sure my brother and my men will be safe then I must take some of your chiefs with me. Who is willing to come.

3 chiefs said they wd come with us.

You must allow me to go and get the ransom. If you will let me repair my whaleboat then I can leave.

They looked round at 1 another. We don't know if you tell the truth.

And I think it is all some game. We will go on and on like this.

Captain Guard tells the truth said the bootmaker, an acquaintance I was coming to like.

We will bring the boat here they said and you can fix it as you can.

I will need men to help me.

So they allowed some of the men to help me but the rest had to be their slaves. They gave back some of our clothes and what they didn't give back they wore themselves. I got back my shirt and a pair of trousers. I don't know whether they were mine to start with but at any rate, it was something to cover me. Then they chose their slaves of which Charley was 1.

Another month passed while we worked on the boat. We had at our disposal just a pocketknife, a few nails and a hammer. The bootmaker was useful in this respect, being used to fine work on his last and finding small holes I might have missed.

On June 20, we left. 5 of my men were allowed to go, but not Charley. I thought if he was an obedient slave he might win himself favour but they liked him too well.

Goodbye brother I said.

Well that is not the first time I heard you say that.

I hope I see you this side of the great divide I said.

You watch out for Betty he said.

I cuffed him around the ears but not hard. He is a different kettle of fish to me, for I saw tears in his eyes which I would never show no man.

Counting the 3 chiefs, 9 of us put out to sea.

For days we were hit by heavy seas. A strong N.W. gale tossed us about. We spent a night ashore but the boat sprung a leak and when we started out again we had to bail the water threatening to engulf us.

June 25 the weather was coming good. We found ourselves at Stephens Island where there were fat mussels on the rocks. We dried ourselves out and ate our fill. Feeling more cheerful by far we kept on going until we came to Cloudy Bay. It was as Charley told me no buildings left standing, no sign of any 1 thing that we owned.

A ship was lying at anchor in the bay, the barque *Mary Ann,* that had been taking on fresh water.

I cannot tell you how pleased I am to see you sir I said to Captain Sinclair. He is a man I have across many times in Sydney and from time to time there in the bay.

You look like castaways he said.

We are all of that sir I says. I told him our troubles, pausing only to swallow the rum he'd poured for me.

He listened with great sympathy. I will do all I can to help you he said.

Well I said suddenly weary, I am grateful but I do not know what is to be done next.

Why Jacky Guard that is not like you. He poured me another tot of rum which started a fire in my belly. The first 1 had hardly touched the sides on its way down.

There is much to be done he said. I will give you a good supply of provisions to use for a ransom, enough for your crew and Mrs Guard as well. That is the least I can do for a man deprived of the comfort of a fine young wife and children. Captain Morris is in Port Nick with the *Joseph Weller.* He is planning to go back to Sydney any day now. It should be no trouble for him to drop you off at Moturoa.

My spirits picked up a little at this prospect.

Sinclair dropped us in Port Nick and I went aboard the *Joseph Weller.* I knew Morris too of old. A short tubby man with ginger hair and sideburns known for his short temper. But he and I always got along. Sure enough he was sorry to hear of my plight and said it wd be not trouble to put us ashore at Moturoa.

But then it turned out we had to turn round and go back to Cloudy Bay to collect potatoes and baleen. This rubbed me up the wrong way because all I wanted was to get the whole thing over. Now started one of the darkest times I ever remember of my life. Whereas I had been relieved to make landfall and find the *Mary Ann* now coming back I was hard hit by seeing where my home had been and my wife and children content. To see it all empty from the deck of another man's boat was too much to bear. As if nothing had ever been. I have often seen dark shapes in my mind. It is not something a man tells other men about. I fear Betty has seen them peer out of my eyes. The shapes seem to dance before me. I see half a man or half a woman in outline, dancing and waving at me. I see cats that have been skinned standing on their hind legs. I see a creature that may have risen out of the deep, like a whale perhaps, only it is above me and threatening to bear its full weight down upon me. And I have nowhere to go. That is how it was in my head as I waited for the *Joseph Weller* to set sail. And always I asked myself what if this rescue should go wrong. I took a bottle of rum down to my hammock in the cabin. I drank all of it at one go. I buried my head under a blanket and woke when it was dark and the ship was under way. It was now July 14, the heart of winter, and storm clouds brewing.

Rain started again, the N.W. came up once more and the *Joseph Weller* could not make land. My worst fears had come true. Because of the storm it was impossible for the ship to drop anchor and set me ashore. I saw the outline of Taranaki alongside and then we left it behind. My heart were fair breaking. I wanted to call out. I wished to call my son by his name. John. And my wife. Wd she ever belong to me again? Betty. My mouth shaped the word but I could not say it.

I heard the Maori chiefs groan as the wake of the boat followed us steadily away from land, their adventure gone wrong too.

It was too late to have been a better man. At that moment I was ready to jump over the rail and swim. If I never reached shore it wd be all to the good.

We sailed on towards Australia, arriving here in early August. Nearly 4 month has been and gone since the *Harriet* ran aground.

Near as long since I saw my children and my wife Betty.

I cannot forget her try as I might. Betty and Jacky, the words echoing in my head. Peti and Haari. We were meant to be together, her and me for all time.

Part 7

The Captive Wife

Chapter 27

The pa at Te Namu was very small, but also secure. It sat on a plateau, like the top of a very high table, on a rocky outcrop of the coast, almost surrounded by vertical cliffs. Around this, runs hollowed out land, some sixty yards wide, separating it from the mainland.

Like a moat?

Yes Adie, perhaps that is how you'd describe it. Across the way is cleared space where the gardens grow: kumara, sweet potato, yams and gourds. From the top of the pa, which was like a sentry box, invading forces could be seen long before they arrived.

When I was placed in the enclosure at the edge of the pa, I felt great weariness. My head was painful from the blow I'd been struck, and I must have been weak from loss of blood. I thought I might be allowed to live but nothing was certain, and a part of me was ready to let go, to simply sink into that other sleep from which there is no waking. Louisa lay in my arms, bruised and sad. Like me, she seemed ready to give up the ghost. I saw by her eyes that she was in great pain, but past crying. She held my finger with the frailest of grasps. And all of this time I didn't know where John was.

Jacky, I said in my head, as if I was preparing a speech for him, to explain myself. They wouldn't let me keep him. I tried, but they took him away, our precious boy, and my heart is broken. As these thoughts followed each other round, I began inventing wild schemes of breaking free and going into the bush to look for John. But I wouldn't have known where to begin and who knew how far away he was by now. In quiet moments, I strained my ears as if I might hear his voice blown on the wind but I only heard seabirds, the circling gulls, and the voices of the people in the pa, who were strangers to me.

The day after our arrival in the pa, the people began cooking provisions taken from the wreck of the *Harriet*. If they had asked me, I could have told them the mixture they were preparing was a mistake. They mixed together flour and sugar and soap, and when it was foaming in the heat of the fire, they tested it for taste, expecting a delicacy. Of course, they found it disgusting, and I saw angry looks cast in my direction, as if it was my fault. The mood about the place turned sour. I could see them thinking they had been cheated. The flour we had hoarded with such care was thrown over the clifftop. They said it was some kind of sand and should be returned to the beach.

There was still more cooking to be done. In the morning, from the place where I was confined, I saw flames in the direction of the river we had followed after we were wrecked. Flames shot in the air, and I smelt burning flesh, a smell I know all too well. But I was puzzled. I wondered if this tribe had a different way of preparing human flesh.

That night the women came to me, and passed a flax basket of meat through the entrance to the hut.

I shook my head, no. And no again. They pulled it back, their eyes resentful, as if I had done them another wrong.

Ruiha squatted down in the doorway. She told me I must eat

something. For my child. She was begging me to take the food.

That is my brother, I said, and began to weep tears that wouldn't stop.

No, it is not, she said. We have killed a pig in honour of your coming. At that I began to scream, and backed away into the corner of the whare. I don't believe you, I shouted.

You don't understand, she said. Te Matakatea has ordered that the dead be burnt. He has made a great fire. It was so that your dead would not be eaten. You are our family now.

She went away and brought me a basket of sweet potatoes, and these I did pick at, in spite of myself. I knew it was true that if I was to do anything to save my children, I must gather my strength for whatever was to happen next. The food was very good.

All the same, I could not bring myself to speak to them, and I did not know what to believe. The scorched smell of the distant fire lingered in the air. From the whare, I saw dinner being eaten. I saw the man Oaoiti who had carried John up the hill. He ate with delicacy, and I thought, if that is my brother, at least he has eaten him with respect, and for that I was grateful.

My uncleanness brought me a few days of grace. Nobody came near me, except the women, mostly Ruiha, who brought me baskets of food and water in gourds. I was given a mat, and I was warm and dry, and at nights I lay down to sleep, Louisa nestled by my side. I would have given much to know where John was. And yet I believed I would see him again. I don't know what made me so certain. Perhaps it was just that I was his mother.

After days of sleeping and eating, I began to feel stronger. I watched the life of the people as they moved around the pa. The houses were built around the marae. At Te Namu, the entire space was closed, divided into fourteen smaller spaces. Everyone had lines of smoked and dried fish, and their own potato plot, though there were more gardens outside the pa, to the east.

There were only two sides to the fortress that could be climbed without ladders. On the third side, raised stages sloped away from the summit, to stop people climbing it. Inside the stockade stood large piles of boulders for hurling down on the enemy as they advanced. The year before, the people of Te Namu had fought off an invasion from the north. Beneath the stockades still stood the remains of burnt huts, torched in the attack.

One morning, I saw Captain Hall's smoked head impaled on a stake. I supposed it must have been placed in such a way that I would see it. I don't know who had done this, but whatever thoughts I had had of escaping I put aside. Some weeks passed. I now slept in a whare with several other women, in very close quarters. There were some fifty whare at Te Namu, built with rushes and interwoven with fern, the top thatched with long grass. The doors to the sleeping houses were very small, with scarcely enough air to breathe, the walls so close together. These women whose house I shared were girls yet to be married. The girls who had been raped by the men of the *Harriet* slept there and I saw how they lay in a huddle together, their faces to the wall. I guessed that they were no longer wanted.

But what could I say to them, a white woman who was part of their trouble? At night the fleas bit, and our breaths were clammy. During the day, I was allowed to move around the pa. The women greeted me, but I didn't want their company. I felt misunderstood, because I wanted my son and they were tired of me asking, as if I was crazed. Louisa was now much better and I knew in my heart that this was thanks to them, though I would not tell them this. Of course this served me further ill.

This went on for some time, until eventually I had to go back to the hut on my own because I was bleeding again. When it had finished, I pretended it had not, and stayed on for a few more days. One day, I saw a man whom I recognised as the chief Oaoiti, standing in shadow. He may have thought I didn't see him, but I had the impression he was staring in my direction. I knew he had been gone from the pa for some time. I now understood that

Taranaki and Ngati Ruanui people were living here at Te Namu, and further south at the two big pa I have told you about, standing on the cliffs. The two tribes had banded together to help each other after the fighting of the previous year, and despite some differences of opinion, I gathered that they passed regularly between the pa as brothers in arms. They had differed, though, over Te Matakatea burning the bodies of the crewmen. If this was true. But as I still did not know who to believe, and I did not speak with anyone unless I had to, I would never know the truth. I did know, though, that I was pleased to see Oaoiti. Perhaps it was that look he had given me as we climbed together up the hill, him carrying my son. Whatever it was, I was drawn to him.

How can I describe Oaoiti to you? He was a singular-looking man. Though solid and muscular, his build was clean limbed and he held himself lightly. His face was like a carving, his hair pulled up in a top-knot decorated with white feathers, so that it was easy to examine his features. His face was tall, his cheekbones wide. I thought his eyes an unusual shape, large and yet deep set. Like other men of his tribe, he wore a short thin beard. I think of him as handsome. But then, many people of Taranaki possessed great beauty. You might feel quite the opposite, Adie, were you to see them. But would they be so different from your ancient Greeks? This is where you and I have different eyes. Who knows, you and I may have seen Oaoiti in the same light. One of the things I remember, in particular, were his hands; although his palms were broad, his fingers were long and slim.

On a night when the wind lay still, I pushed the door of the whare open, and found it untied, so that I could go outside. Nobody appeared to bar my way. The air was cold and clear. At least three hundred people lived at Te Namu, perhaps more. I walked along the top of the cliff, and heard nothing, as if the place was deserted. It crossed my mind that the whole encampment might simply have moved on under the cover of darkness. But I did not believe this.

The pa was surrounded by palisades of wooden stakes, with small lanes leading between, so they could be blocked off with trapdoors if enemies came. I slipped through one of these entrances to the outer world and still nobody stopped me.

Before me the sea flashed like cold steel, behind me was the darkness. I sat down at the edge of the rocks, and knew that one step would take me away from all of this, through dark empty space. If it had not been for Louisa, left sleeping alone behind me, it would have been so easy.

What would Granny have made of it all, I wondered?

I remembered the tale of my naming day, and how grandfather had tricked her, by having me called Elizabeth, the name of his first, perhaps best, love. And how she had set out to show that she loved me better than he ever loved any woman.

I remembered the stories of the hulks, the filth below decks in the ships, and the starving and the dying. Only the faint-hearted and the children died, she told me once. The rest of us hung on. You have to, or there is nothing left.

I began to sing quietly to myself: 'singing too-rall, li-oo-rall, li-ad-di-ti, singing too-rall, li-oo-rall, li-ay'. I turned, as if a breeze had touched me. I thought I saw her thin wiry old body sitting beside me.

Hullo Granny, I said. But of course it wasn't Granny. It was Oaoiti.

What are you doing here? I asked, wrapping my arms around my knees and burying my face in my lap.

Who were you singing to? Was it your son?

What difference would that make, I said, in a muffled voice. We were both speaking very quietly. I lifted my head. My grandmother.

Uh huh. One of the old ones.

Yes.

Was she wise?

I thought so.

A kuia. A wise old lady.

Something like that, I said. And, indeed, she could have been one of the old ladies here at the pa, small, wizened and dark. Just thinking of this gave me some comfort, as if at last I could recognise someone.

He was so close to me I felt the hairs of his arms brushing mine where my mat had fallen away. But he did not reach for me or try to touch me. This is no good for you, he said. So much sorrow.

I can't live if I don't see my son again. I know he's alive. You're hiding him from me.

He sighed then. It is not me who hides him from you.

But you know where he is, don't you? I see you watching me.

That's not why I watch you.

You're afraid I'm going to find him, aren't you?

There's nothing you can do, he said, even if you could find him. He stays with Ngati Ruanui and he is being well looked after. Would it help you if you were to see him?

Of course, I said hotly, my voice rising.

He hushed me, his fingers on my lips. I trembled at his touch, and felt the way my trembling passed through him as we were both shivering. If he had wanted to, he could have taken me then, and for a moment it was what I wanted.

Be patient, he said, it will happen. He was talking about John.

The following morning, I was moved to a whare that I understood was to be my own. Ruiha came to settle me into the new house.

I'll see you get a reward, I told her, if you keep me and my little girl safe. And if my son is safe, my husband will bring a great reward. As soon as I said this, I wished I could take back my words, in case I had offended her.

She only smiled, nodding in agreement. She was a round-hipped woman, with hair a halo of dark fish-oil. I knew she was well regarded by the clean scent of the oil, which was always kept fresh.

I will tell the people that, she said. They will be pleased.

When I crouched down on all fours to enter the whare, she took pity on me. Someone would come and make the door larger for me. Soon a man appeared, armed with an axe and an adze, and the door-frame was enlarged, and a window space made. Then several more servants arrived, and a fence was placed around the building, so that it was like a small private cottage.

I asked if might I have the soap that was left over from their cooking, for I had seen it tossed away in the corner of the whare where I had slept before, but had not dared to touch it lest they thought I was taking back what they now considered to be theirs. She looked at me and shook her head. The white man's poison, I could see her thinking. Perhaps this was how I would do away with myself. The soap was brought for me all the same.

All this time the women combed my hair with oil, taking care to avoid the injury to my head, which seemed to be healing, though I could still feel the comb's teeth beneath my skin when I touched it. Their touch comforted me, and I began to relax, to think that all would be well. I began to be like them. Round my anklet a bracelet of shells was placed, so that when I walked, a small tinkling sound accompanied me. There would be no more night wandering that didn't alert someone from sleep.

By now they knew which food I preferred. That night I ate with them, and cooked fish was placed before me, along with the sweet potatoes I so relished.

The women poked me in the ribs and laughed.

In the firelight, the chief Oaoiti stared at me, and I could tell by his gaze that I pleased him.

Whatever it was they had talked about, my fate had been decided.

It is some twenty miles or more down the coast to the twin pa of Waimate and Orangituapeka, home to Ngati Ruanui. The first time I walked there with Oaoiti, I thought we would never reach the other side of the bush. As I followed him, he kept a steady pace, pausing only now and then to let me gain my breath. To look at the bush you might think there were no paths but I soon realised that an occasional tree had its trunk smoothed, a twig broken and that the undergrowth varied in its thickness. Still, it would have been difficult for someone who did not know the way to follow what might be taken for a path.

Waimate and its twin pa were built on rocks that stood alone, not unlike Te Namu, but much higher. Each pa was built on the edge of cliffs dropping hundreds of feet to the black beach. Orangituapeka was the taller, and better fortified, which I believe is one of the reasons John Love stayed there. But it was at Waimate that I met my son again. Waimate was very crowded, with two hundred or so houses forming streets that made me think of the Rocks. Smaller buildings were cloaked with turnip and kumara growing over the gable ends of the roof, so that they formed a pretty leafy canopy. I walked around Waimate with Oaoiti's two sisters. They were handsome women, older than him, and I could see that he was something of a pet with them. The pair of them fussed over me and patted me, stroking my pale skin and smiling. All the while I was with them, I was desperate to see John, but I understood that he was being brought to Waimate, and I must wait. There was to be no haste. The two women showed me the meeting house; it was intricately carved and so beautiful I must describe it to you. The walls were woven with cane around the whole room, and divided horizontally into squares with strands of plaited grasses, crossing four smooth and polished poles at regular distances. All of these were supported by a framework of arches, which soared to a ridge-pole at the top, surrounded by three carved pillars. This is the most beautiful building I have ever seen, more beautiful than the churches in Sydney with steeples and spires, or the Governor's house. And in the end, it is thanks to me that it fell. But I will come to that.

My reunion with John was difficult. Two months had passed and that is a long time for a child as young as he was then. My son looked at me with mistrust when he first saw me. An elderly man called Mapiki presented him to me as if I were a visitor who must keep a respectful distance. John was dressed in a handsome cloak, as befitted the son of a chief. He glowed with good health, though I did wonder if he'd been over-fed.

I said, Darling, it is me, your Mama.

He nodded his head gravely. Kei te pehea koe, he said greeting me in Maori, as if he had never known English.

John, you haven't forgotten me, have you, I exclaimed.

This time he shook his head with impatience, as if I was asking silly questions.

Talk to him now, the old man said. Hone is due for his rest soon.

Surely that is for me to decide, I said. I am his mother.

Mapiki looked at me with regret, as if I had wilfully misunderstood.

John came over to me, and gave me a small kick on the shins. I was so shocked I raised my hand in chastisement. Mapiki caught my hand before I could deliver a well-deserved slap.

We stood glaring at each other. I let my hand drop.

I'll go now, I said dully. To John, I said, Mama will come and see you again soon. We can walk on the beach together and gather shells.

At that he gave a little grin, like the boy I knew. I gave him a wave, and he waved back to me. For some reason, I didn't kiss him.

Oaoiti was waiting for me outside. Can you walk back today?

I said that though it was a long way, I would like to make a start. I should be getting back to Louisa, I said, though I knew she was being looked after at Te Namu. He nodded his head, as if he understood my need to get away from Waimate. The night being fine, we could rest if need be.

Do you feel better? he asked after awhile.

Better and not better. I'm sad that he didn't want to come with me. But I'm happy that he's well and I know he'll be safe with the old man.

We had stopped for a moment and I leant against him, wanting the reassurance of human warmth. I felt him tremble violently, as he had the night we had talked on the edge of the cliff.

Before we had gone very far I knew my legs would carry me no further. Oaoiti took me to a sheltered place where we could lie down. He had brought a gourd of water, and some dried fish which we ate before he covered us over with mats. I then took my sweet ease in the comfort of his body.

How did I know that you were in love, Adie?

Because I know what it feels like, to fall in love. It had never happened to me before. I fell and fell and fell.

Chapter 28

We deplore the extreme indifference of the legislature in affording ample protection to British interests in New Zealand where they are hourly liable to savage violation. We implore the immediate attention of the legislature on behalf of our countrymen, thus surrounded by danger.

The plight of Mrs Guard and her children is dire. Citizens can do nothing else but insist that every effort is made to effect their rescue without delay.

Sydney Morning Herald

Journal of John Guard

Sydney, Port Jackson, 17 August

I swear all I wanted was to get a ransom so that I could rescue wife and children.

When we sailed past the Taranaki coast the men on board were good mates and gave me extra tots of rum and tobacco. They will get their comeuppance those natives, you need not worry yourself Captain Morris said to me. I knew there was naught he could have done to quell the storm that had prevented me from landing. Weather is weather. What has happened is a disgrace a terrible thing he said, and we will see it is put to rights.

But some things are never simple as everyone knows.

Soon after we arrived at Port Jackson a Captain Anglim off the *Lucy Ann* had come aboard and talked to Captain Morris. The *Lucy Ann* had been involved in a fray further south in New Zealand where 500 natives of Cloudy Bay had attacked a shore whaling station. They had done several assaults on the whalers broken open their boxes and stolen whatever took their fancy. 1 of the chief's children got sick and died, which was put down to the visit of the *Lucy Ann* bringing bad luck. A threat was made to destroy the ship and kill all the white men.

Captain Anglim had acted swiftly. He invited some chiefs to come on board the ship. Then he sent a message to say they wd only be returned if the lives of the white men at the whaling station were spared.

When he got no answer he sailed away. So here was a pretty pickle. The *Lucy Ann* had a hold full of Maori warriors while I was aboard the *Joseph Weller* seeking to set my family free.

The two captains called on me.

Guard said Morris, you are the man to help sort out all of this.

Me I said. I must get my family back. I can sort out nothing until that is done.

These outrages must stop said Morris. We need the military to step in and put a stop to all this nonsense.

Anglim was in agreement. I never got the full measure of Anglim a clean-shaven man with a blue-black look around his long chin and narrow eyes.

I do not see that the military will get my wife and children back I said. All I want is to take the ransom to the Taranaki tribe.

No said Anglim it needs more than that. You pay them a ransom and we will never hear the end of it. They will be looting our property and taking hostages left right and centre. Their claims will become more and more outrageous. It is up to you Guard to go and see the Governor.

I said I do not think the Guv being a gentleman wd want to see me. I reminded them that though I am a free man all the same I have been a convict.

You have a mistaken view of this matter said Anglim. Governor Bourke is all for emancipation. He looks kindly on those who have done well. Men like yourself.

And why is that I asked. Why wd he bother.

You know very well said Anglim in a dry voice that he was brought out here after Governor Darling was so harsh towards convicts and ticket of leave men, which led to so much trouble and rebellion.

I served my ticket of leave many years ago I said in an angry voice.

It is all right Guard said Morris. We know that. Darling did not acknowledge that men like you have done well and so he went in a cloud of hate. Bourke sees all men as equal when they have done their time. He believes in their rights.

More likely I said it is because we bring in the money.

Morris went bright red for he is not a man to hide things well. I wd not put it that way he said. Times change. You are a good skipper.

Then said Anglim in his smooth way, the British have put in their representative Mr Busby into the Bay of Islands. I dare say you have met him.

I had met the British Resident, a man lean of face and short of hair with bushy black eyebrows that he raises in a superior way.

Yes I told them, in my view he is a toothless bugger. This man was sent by the King a couple of years back to keep law and order in New Zealand. He lives in the Bay of Islands which is a long way from Cloudy Bay. He does nothing to keep the savages in check I said. He is more interested in missionaries than traders. Whenever I see him he is in conversation with Mr Williams the missionary who is printing Bibles and converting the heathens into Christians.

Well Morris said all reasonable, you know Busby is under

several instructions. He's supposed to guard the Maoris against Europeans as well.

That is all a load of cock I said. You cannot do both at the same time.

Anglim said that is why they call him Man-o'-War Without Guns.

I should have seen what was coming I suppose. But the fire raging in me had blinded me to sense.

At present New Zealand does not belong to anybody but the Maoris Anglim said, and someone needs to take a hand in bringing them under control. It is time Mother England taught them a lesson. The best thing you can do is go to the Governor and ask him for some ships that carry guns.

You mean the redcoats I said, my tongue feeling thick and stupid.

They nodded their heads.

There is nothing to lose Guard and everything to gain. What do you think they will have done to your wife by now?

I was told at Moturoa that she would be returned in exchange for a ransom.

But how can you be sure of that? She is held at a different pa by people of a different tribe.

Well that is what I was told I said. Although I knew what they said was true. Look I said I know the Maoris better than you.

Which is all I had to go on. That they wd want the reward.

The 2 men looked grave. I wanted to smash their heads full of tidy tongues and fair talking. What they had in their minds was as mucky as any seaman's thoughts, beneath their spit and polish.

And my head was full of the same thing.

I know they are using me for some other game. But today if it will get my wife and children back I am past caring.

18 August

Should have gone to the house in Cambridge Street last night, but instead slept aboard the *Lucy Ann*. You need a good night's sleep Anglim said. And you must rehearse what to say to the Governor.

I will just tell him straight I said.

There is more to it than that. You must make a statement. A bold statement.

I began to like all of this less and less. I woke up feeling groggy. A cloud was sitting on my shoulder. Whatever was coming there wd be no turning back. I could see that if I did not play along with them Anglim and Morris wd forsake me. I have no ship I have no money nor have I any way of getting back to Taranaki if I do not play along now.

I knew some time soon I must take myself down to the Rocks and tell Harriott Deaves that her daughter was taken captive and her son dead. But I did not have the balls for that yet.

The word captive spun in my head. And still I had to tell Mr Campbell another ship had gone down to Davy Jones' locker.

I have written a letter for the Governor said Anglim when we had ate our breakfast.

I looked at what he had put. The letter put a request in very civil terms that we should meet with the Governor for the good of our whole colony.

There he said, I have put your name and mine. Do you sign with a mark or your name?

I took the quill without a word and signed the letter. He knew full well I could write. How else could I be a sea captain and keep a ship's log. Equal be damned. His every action was meant to show that he was my superior. He is naught but a sealer just like me. A convict will always be that to men who arrived free in this country. But he will not get the better of me.

19 August

No word from the Guv. It is early days yet. But I think he will tear up the letter Anglim sent. I do not believe anyone will listen. I took myself this evening to the Rocks. It felt strange and rare to be walking amongst those small houses, after the open spaces of New Zealand, the sea and the bush.

I found Harriott looking prosperous. Deaves must be doing all right. Harriott had a new glass lamp with lustre hand-painted on the rim. Harriott's lamp is engraved with 2 words Remember Me. It gives a good light. Or it did of which more shortly.

I wd like to give Betty a lamp like that I said.

Well why don't you said Harriott. She looked in blooming health and the thought crossed my mind, perhaps she has another man. They are like that some of that family.

I stood and admired the lamp for a long time for I did not want to tell Harriott about Betty and David and the 2 children.

I walked to the other side of the room and leant my head against my arm and said what I had come for. Harriott aimed the lamp for my head but it hit the wall and shattered all about. The flame inside wd have leapt the wall and burnt the house down had I not stamped on it with my foot and crushed the glass into the rug.

She stood there screaming so loud I had to shake her to shut her up.

Then I went to Cambridge Street and told Charlotte Pugh.

She looked at me like I was a madman or wicked.

She said at the top of her voice so the whole street could hear, I didn't give her to you to have her raped and murdered.

Get out I said. You have lived long enough in my house. Take your brats and bugger off.

And she did. I suppose she has gone to the Deaves' house and they can all muck and shout together and good riddance to them.

You look like death warmed over she said as she left.

20 August

An invitation has come from Government House to take dinner with the Guv tonight. Anglim arrived on my doorstep this morning. I had slept late and badly again. When I heard him banging on the door I thought it was Charlotte come back to get her belongings.

Go away I yelled out but the noise did not stop.

I will kill you for sure I said and opened the door.

Anglim's face was full of disgust for the low life looking at him.

You best clean yourself up Guard he said and handed me the letter from the Guv. It was written in copperplate writing that shows the hand of quality driving the pen. The paper was thick and the crest gold.

We have right on our side Anglim said.

When he was gone, I put on clean clothes and combed my hair and beard. It was none too soon for there was another knock on the door. A man wearing a brown hat and a hairy brown jacket stood on the step.

Good morning Captain Guard he said, respect in his voice. My name is Ralph Wallace and I am a correspondent for the *Sydney Morning Herald*. I wd like to find out more about the awful things that have befallen your family.

That is my business I said.

No sir said this man, his foot firm on my doorstep. I have to disagree with you. Now that your story has reached the Guv'nor it is of interest to everyone.

I do not want my name in the newspapers I said.

Captain Guard it is too late. Your name will be printed today whatever you say. If you will but talk to me a little it will be the better for your cause. The public will have much sympathy for a reasonable man in his hour of distress. If the people are behind you it will strengthen the Guv'nor's arm.

You had better come in and sit down I said.

That was the beginning. I am now a famous man with a famous story to tell.

By the time I made my way to the Guv's house the first edition of the paper had come off the press. There was people lined along the street hoping to get a look at me.

As soon as I arrived at Government House I found Kentish and his wife, the ones we had given shelter to at Cloudy Bay. I could not take my eyes off Ivy Kentish for she looked nothing like the sad sack that had stayed with us just some months before. She was pink like a china doll in her muslin dress. A great contrast to her previous pitiful appearance. She clung to my arm and said in a little girl's voice Oh Jacky, as if we was the best friends in the world, this is such a terrible thing and my heart is simply breaking when I think of my poor friend Betty.

There were several important men at table. They were friendly enough and the talk all about horse racing at the park and the coming of spring while there was ladies present. We had potted pheasant and beef cooked with oysters and a rhubarb pie. It was some time since I had had a good meal and I felt as hungry as the devil so it was hard to eat as slow as everyone else.

I must tell you Ivy Kentish was babbling to the company round the table Captain and Mrs Guard were such willing hosts even though they were *down* to their last potato. Such kindness I will never forget.

Our hostess Mrs Deas Thomson looked at Ivy with a frown. As if she had spoken out of turn. Ivy blushed and cast her eyes down but then I saw she was looking at me sideways. I thought she is making eyes at me that is what she is doing and I became all fingers and thumbs at my dinner for it is some time since that has happened. Mrs Deas Thomson is the Guv's daughter a very lively lady. Her husband had struck some trouble for Governor Bourke had got rid of the old man who was the Clerk of Council before and put in his new son-in-law in his place. It does not matter to me. Deas Thomson seems a good fellow.

There was no other women you wd call handsome. The woman on my right picked at her dinner. She was a governess called Miss Adeline Malcolm on the wrong side of 40 perhaps 50 and she looked round with eyes hungrier than her appetite. Her name rang a bell in my memory and I thought this is the woman who taught my Betty to read and write but I could not bring myself to talk to her. You could tell she wd latch on to any little thing to find out more about you. What a commotion she wd make if she was to know her part in Betty's life. And I recall she and Betty did not always get along so well together so I could not be sure what she might have to say. As it was she went on and on saying I am so sorry Mr Guard. I am sure your poor wife will be safe though God only takes the best. She was trying not to weep. As I didn't know her particular line of sorrow I said nothing. I wanted to close my eyes again.

But there was to be none of that. Also at table was a Captain Lambert who commands a man-o'-war the *Alligator*, anchored in Port Jackson. I did not know what part he wd play but I thought that he was there for a reason.

Mrs Deas Thomson played the piano for a short while after we had completed our meal. After that she invited the ladies to retire. The port and the cigars were brought out.

Straight away the Guv said now we will get down to business Mr Guard. I nodded my head not wanting to seem too eager. Now that I was among these powerful men in this handsome room I found myself ready for action as if I was one of them.

Now I want to hear the story for myself said the Guv.

And so I had to tell it all again which was hard. The Guv closed his head and kept nodding. All present listened with great attention seeming to be excited by what I had to say. I think Anglim might have got his nose put out of joint because nobody paid much heed when it came his turn. Morris had not come because he was due to put to sea in the morning. Earlier in the day he had said I have done what I can for you Guard and now it is up to you.

When I had finished the Guv and Lambert of the *Alligator* exchanged looks I could not read.

Thank you Captain the Guv said. I see it is a dreadful situation and we must certainly do something to remedy matters. I will set down a time 2 days hence for the Executive Council of New South Wales to meet. We will decide what must be done.

Much was at stake today. As promised the special meeting was called together. At the head of it was the Guv and then Lieutenant-Colonel Snodgrass who is the Colonial Secretary. Deas Thomson was there of course and a man I had not met before by the name of Riddell who was listed as Colonial Treasurer. Riddell is a quiet cove although a good mate of Deas Thomson. I hear they hunt together in the countryside round Parramatta way.

It is hard to remember all that took place. Deas Thomson had helped me to write my statement and it was read out. It did not sound like me but it was my story that I had told so many times. About the murder of 12 of my seamen and what had happened to Betty, the way the inhuman savages had seized and stripped her and split her head with their tomahawk and the children taken away before my eyes. And how we believed the savages had eaten our friends.

I said that Captain Anglim and I were willing to help His Excellency should he send any military force. My statement finished with a plea to the Colonial Government to help me.

When Deas Thomson read it aloud I remember the hush in the air. You could hear nothing but a sigh here and there. And then I signed my name again. A copy was written out for me as a record of what had taken place.

I should say that there was no sign of Anglim and I heard he had cleared out the same morning so whatever I said on his behalf turned out to be of no account.

There were many questions asked as if I were in a courtroom as I have been before but this time I was spoken to with respect.

Why did the Maoris set upon you? Governor Bourke asked.

I had to think about that for a moment. They came to plunder us sir. They wanted to eat those of us they could kill.

But says the man Riddell I thought the Maoris only ate their enemies.

Well I said that is more or less the case.

Had you done something to upset them?

I did nothing I can think on I said. Speaking for myself.

Did any of the crew do something to upset them?

Not in my presence I said.

You did not hear of anything they might have done.

At this the Guv and Deas Thomson began to look uneasy as if Riddell had gone too far.

What wd it take to get your wife and children back? said Deas Thomson cutting across all this.

I think the nine men who are left at Moturoa could be got easily enough sir if a ship of war was to go there and a few soldiers landed.

Could they be got without a ransom?

I didn't like this turn of questioning. They could be got without ransom if there was soldiers I said. Not without.

The Guv said it is not a good practice to pay ransoms. What about your wife.

My wife is some 40 mile south of Moturoa I said.

But said Riddell who I am coming to think on as something of a nark, if a ransom was paid how much do you think they wd want?

Well I said I think the men could be got for a canister of powder, some fish-hooks, a few trifling articles of that nature. More wd be needed for the woman and children.

Tell me said Snodgrass who had not had much to say for himself but had been following closely, do you have any other strategies in mind? He has cool grey eyes and a bristling white moustache.

We have 3 chiefs to return I said for I had been thinking about this. I think that if we kept them on board until the prisoners was returned we wd get them without a ransom.

So we wd need someone to negotiate with 'em?

Yes sir I said I think that we wd.

How are your skills at speaking Maori, Guard.

I follow a little I said but I don't know that they are good enough to negotiate.

The man should not have to negotiate for his family said Snodgrass. We will find some interpreters to go on this expedition.

By now I was getting the hang of the proceedings. This was more than I thought wd happen for they were talking as if they wd send a man-o'-war. I will not rest I said if a force is not sent down to punish the Maoris. There has been many murders your honours but nothing done to avenge them. They will all go on as before if nothing is done.

How big a force are we confronting asked Snodgrass. I saw he is a man of much thought and I was warming up to him.

In all there are perhaps 100 natives at Moturoa. The 2 tribes of Ati Awa and Ngati Ruanui could not raise above 300 men in the whole and perhaps 200 muskets. I reckon I said that if a ship of war was to go down and threaten to destroy their huts they wd give up the prisoners. Their pa could easily be destroyed by fire.

That is what you are suggesting Guard, asked Riddell sharpish.

As a last resort I said. Look I said I have been trading with the New Zealanders since 1823 and have lived a great deal amongst them. It is my opinion that if once they received a check they wd never attack a white person again.

When it was all said and done the Guv spoke. It was like he was giving a verdict. I will take concerted measures with Captain Lambert he said and the *Alligator* wd go to New Zealand to demand the return of the captives. He wd see if Lieutenant Roddick a resident of Sydney could accompany him but others could be called upon. Lieutenant Gunton and 25 rank and file of the 50th wd sail with the ship. A 2nd ship the schooner *Isabella* wd carry 2 officers and 40 rank and file under Captain Lambert's command.

I could not believe how fast all this was happening. Not much more than a week ago I was aboard the *Joseph Weller* passing Taranaki in a storm and near hopeless enough to walk off the boat. Now I was about to return with troops and 2 war ships. I am more cheerful in myself.

Charlotte and her children came back last night looking as if nothing had happened. She sent the children straight to bed.

When the house was quiet she came and stood at the kitchen door her hands on her hips. There is some say you is a hero Jacky she said.

Well there is some who should mind their own business I replied.

How is it that you escaped, and she did not?

They had her and I could not get her back.

But what if you had stayed?

I wd have been killed. And that is no way to get help for your wife.

What if they have killed her?

Well then they have killed her and there is nothing I can do about it. But I do not think her dead. That is why the Governor is sending 2 ships.

What if they have done that other thing I spoke to you of?

They wd not do that.

Wd they not?

It wd not be her fault I said and that is that.

Charlotte gave me a smouldering look I knew of old. What is it that attracts women to trouble.

Get yourself to bed I said.

Will you come with me Jacky?

I will think on it I said. And I am still thinking on it.

It is as I feared. Riddell is a trouble maker.

Edward Deas Thomson called me into his office looking very worried.

I feel I must show you this Guard he said. I need your opinion.

Riddell it seemed had been twitching away ever since the hearing. He had written to the Governor that a ship stationed regularly in New Zealand waters might make the natives take some notice. But a ship appearing and then going away might only make things worse. He went on to say that by the sound of it the Maoris had had losses as great as the Europeans. They could hardly be blamed for attacking us.

That is untrue I said. We don't know how many Maoris was killed and we did nothing but protect ourselves.

I am afraid that's not all said Deas Thomson looking glum. He calls your character into question. It seems Mr Riddell has only just learnt that you were a convict.

Ah so that is it. I pushed away the papers I had been studying so that they spilt across the floor. Forget all of this I said. When it comes down to it a man will always be haunted by his past.

And that you have been cruel to natives on occasion.

Cruel I cried out fiercely. I have been like a father to them. I have done nothing more except keep discipline aboard my ships and at my whaling stations.

It was as if it were all about to be taken away from me. Do you believe all this I said. Do you not see through it. First the man says all the natives will rise up against the Europeans. Well that is a matter of opinion but he has not been to New Zealand and like I said sir I have been there on and off since 1823.

Deas Thomson said in a patient voice, he wd like you to consider again the question of a ransom.

Well I am a poor man now and I do not have ransoms to give every time some native takes it into his head to make off with my wife. And as for my character well — I had run out of words to defend myself.

It's all right Guard said Deas Thomson looking at me as if by now I was a good mate of his. Don't take on about it. Riddell is a good fellow. We all think very well of him but we do not always agree. I had to be sure of your views.

I am an honest trader I said and I confess I was still somewhat sullen. There are many who will vouch for me. Including Mister Campbell though I have lost 2 ships to the sea.

He was anxious to soothe me. The men of the Royal Navy

are readying themselves to sail. The 50th have received their orders. The 2nd platoon will travel under the command of Captain Johnstone on board the *Isabella*. We have a drummer and a surgeon. The expedition will lack for nothing.

And what of an interpreter?

Ah yes. An interpreter. Have you come across a Mr Battersby?

I know a fellow who was in the Bay of Islands some time ago. He ran a grog shop there.

He has offered his services said Deas Thomson and he seems to know what is what tho' I have no way of being certain. I've seen him in conversation with the Maori chiefs when Captain Anglim brought them ashore and they seemed to understand each other well enough.

It troubled me to hear this news. Thomas Battersby is a man as seems open in his ways on 1st acquaintance but his is a bland face with things to hide. I think he likes an easy life. I had met him once on a return journey from the Bay of Islands when the *Harriet* put in there to deliver goods. Battersby was entertaining Fred Maning an Irishman trading in the area (who has taken up with a Maori wife) and a stout fellow from the old country called Edward Markham. They were all swapping tall tales. Markham in particular has a very high opinion of his self and claims he is of the nobility. He has made himself popular with Busby and the missionaries, but also has Maori women. He is the kind of man who will make trouble for his self and perhaps for others too for he turns his face 2 ways at once. There is rumour that Markham might have had something to do with the disappearance of that scoundrel Stewart, helped him get away when he was on the run, after Te Rauparaha's massacre at Akaroa, from aboard the ship *Elizabeth*. I've heard he and Maning have had a falling out now. Over land. Always the same. Land or women. I wd not trust the word of any of them and Battersby least of all who will do aught for money. When I last saw Battersby with them he was hanging on their every word and chuckling to himself. I decided it better to say none of this to Deas Thomson and thought to myself who needs an interpreter when we have guns and troops.

Everything will be in order within the week. You sail on August 30.

Thank you I said. Thank you very much sir.

I took to the town that night knowing all was set to sail. I went to the Blue Lion tavern and the Cat and Fiddle and the Currency Lass for good measure and wherever I went my drinks were bought by those I met whether they knew me or not. It seemed like every man and his dog wanted to be my friend. We'll make short work of those savages I promised.

Then I took myself back to Cambridge Street and gave Charlotte what she was after. She had waited long enough. I'll set your sail I said. I grabbed 2 handfuls of her hair and held her head to the pillow so I could get a good look at her while I gave it to her. Then she jumped me like the Furies and tore my face and neck with her claws telling me to give it her more. And every night until the ships set off. We gave each other no mercy at all.

There'll be no tears over this I said.

Chapter 29

Poor Betty Guard, all she suffered in that pa. Well, you have heard what people say. I don't tell them any different. What would they think? It is true, I am a woman wronged. No doubt about that. But who wronged me?

Life was better at the pa than you might think, Adie. The worst thing about Te Namu is the sandflies, which is what te namu means. There was food and shelter, we were neither hungry nor cold, the children — Louisa with me and John at Orangituapeka — were well fed and playful.

Now that I was Oaoiti's wife, I became part of the tribe, a special woman with her own house. On the morning after our night in the forest, Oaoiti and I had walked into Te Namu together, and though we were not touching each other, all eyes were on us, and both of us stood up straighter. I knew that this was what they had been expecting. That Oaoiti had told them I would be his. They could not have known if I would take to this with happiness. But I looked at him in the way a white woman does when she is with the man of her affections and smiled and gazed at him. I wanted them to know that I belonged to him now.

Yes, I was happy in my perch at Te Namu. Perhaps it was like being at the Acropolis; I wish you could have seen it and told me. The brilliant land and sea stretched before and behind me. The coastline was harsher than down south, the beaches black rather than golden, but full of rock pools to explore. In winter, the brightest star that shines in the sky is called Takarua, a woman who brings winter. The Taranaki people said it must be so, for I had come, and my skin was cold in colour. On very cold nights Takarua shines more brightly to warn of ice coming. You are Hine-takarua, they said when we woke to the ground stiff, the grass crimped tight with frost, Winter Woman.

At other times they called me Peti, as my friends at the whaling stations had done.

If there was one thing that made me unhappy it was that my son did not live with me, and that when I saw him, he and I still seemed apart. There were times when I wanted to shake him. Once or twice I thought he needed his father to put him in order. Jacky would not have stood for the way he behaved.

Perhaps you are wondering if I had forgotten my other husband.

The answer is yes and no. When I thought of him, he remained exactly the same. I did not care for him more or less. I loved him, I suppose, but what had once seemed like love now dimmed alongside the love I felt for Oaoiti. This was different, not something I took for granted. Remember, Adie, that I had been given to Jacky by my family when I was a young girl. I had been proud he wanted me but I had never had this sensation of falling, each time he came near me. And when I was not with Oaoiti, when I was waiting for him to come to me, my flesh felt stripped as if I was not whole.

On one of my visits to Waimate, I was given two beautiful cloaks, woven by Oaoiti's sisters — a korowai and a parawai. The kŏrowai was for every day, for it was perfectly waterproof, woven from pale flax fibre and decorated with black hand-rolled cords.

But the parawai is woven of the finest, silky snow-white muka; it was the same as giving a ball gown to a young girl here in Sydney. These gifts were given because I was their brother's new wife.

He has never had a wife he likes as well as you, they said.

I felt a fire of jealousy burning inside me then, for I had not thought about his other wives. It occurred to me that on those days and nights when I waited for him, he was with one of them and his children. I knew I should have understood this all along and that it would do me no good to mention it. That I was his favourite wife must be enough, and I vowed to make him happier than the others.

I had a hole drilled through my ear, which was not painful, and from it now hung a greenstone pendant. See, look where the hole is. You may touch it if you wish, Adie.

No? Well, no matter. I took the pendant off when I came home because my family thinks it makes me look like a savage. Besides, it was a gift from Oaoiti.

I was overtaken with languor by day and sleeplessness by night. Special morsels were fed to me at meal times, and I began to put on weight. My skin developed an oily sheen, so that when I bathed, my skin reminded me of Mr Spyer's bolts of satin.

There was always someone to look after Louisa. She shared the breasts of other women. I realised that, in my stupor of the first days, she would have died had she not had a variety of wet nurses. When Louisa was feverish, they gave her medicines and poultices made from leaves and bark. After a month or so, she had begun to look stronger, though it troubled me that she coughed at nights. Another trunk was washed ashore from the wreck of the *Harriet*. Happily, it contained Louisa's clothes. After they had dried out, I was able to dress her much as I would at home, protecting her from the cold. Winds blew off the white mountain rearing its head above us, piercing the clouds on dull days, dazzling us like crystal at a dinner table on days when the sun shone.

In the trunk I found also a pair of pantaloons, a shirt and a little cap of John's. Oaoti now took me to see him every week or so, and on my next visit, I took the clothes with me. Mapiki viewed them with care and then rejected them. They were too small, he said. I had to agree that John had well outgrown them, though I knew that was not the reason he was not allowed to wear them.

At least wear the cap, I said with a laugh, as if it was a game.

But John tore the hat off his head and threw it at my feet.

And then I slapped him on his bare leg. This was something that had been coming for some time. He let out a shout of indignation and began to cry.

Mapiki looked at me as if I was a murderess. I left the room hurriedly. Mapiki followed me out and saw Oaoiti waiting for me.

Take her away, Mapiki said, and speaking rapidly.

I saw that Oaoiti was angry with me too. You can go back with Waiariari, he said. I am busy here tonight.

No, I said, beginning to cry. Come with me please.

But Waiariari, another chief at this pa, appeared and I had no choice but to accompany him. He was a man with a thin face and heavy eyebrows. I thought he had also wanted me for a wife, only Oaoiti had claimed me first. I saw him watching me and scowling; perhaps it was just that I was white. I thought of running to Oaoiti's sisters, but pride held me back. I did not want them to know that I was in disgrace.

Waiariari accompanied me in total silence, at great speed.

I waited at Te Namu for three days, before Oaoiti came back. They seemed like the longest days of my life. People looked at me, at first with pity, and then indifference, as if I was no longer of importance.

On the third night, he entered the whare and slipped beside me on our bed of ferns. I clenched my arms around him in a fierce embrace. He held me as tightly, and nothing more was said of our quarrel. But I knew now that John no longer belonged to me and that if I was to be happy, I must try to put aside thoughts of him as my son. I remembered my grandmother again, and how she had lost children, and managed to survive. I told myself that at least both my children were alive, and that I should be grateful, but there were moments when it seemed as if John had slipped into darkness like Granny's children.

For most of the time, I believed I was learning to accept things as they were. I knew that Jacky had left Moturoa, and that some of the *Harriet*'s crew were still there, but I didn't know who they were. They are white men, I was told, with shrugs, as if they all looked alike. Ruiha had heard that Jacky planned to return with a ransom. But months passed and there was no sign of him. He could have been dead, perhaps drowned in that leaky whaleboat he had put to sea. As the days passed, the life I had had before seemed less and less real. I found myself wondering what I had seen in it. Watching whales die is no sport for a young housewife. There is no good way to kill a whale. And the men who kill them are not great company. They curse because the work sours them, and most of them drink themselves to sleep, although I could not have said that of Jacky. It was around this time I began to have a nightmare that keeps coming back, of the mother whale circling the spot where her calf was taken.

I had not forgotten the death of my brother, and somehow this was mixed up in the confusion of these ugly dreams, as was the image of John. So it was make-believe that I had given him up, because he and his uncle were haunting me. One especially cold morning, I didn't want to get out of bed. I lay gazing up at the roof of the whare and all I wanted was to weep. Silent weeping is an affliction of mine. Oaoiti came in and, seeing me like this, asked what was troubling me. Was it something he had done, or had I been treated unkindly?

Go away, I said, but he crouched in the corner of the room, wrapped in a blanket against the cold, and said that I must tell him. I knew he didn't want to hear any more about John. And to be fair, he had done his best.

I have been thinking of my brother David, I said at last.

I saw him stiffen, as if this was something he would rather not discuss. But he had laid himself open to my complaints.

You killed him, I said.

He was killed in the fighting, Oaoiti said, after a silence.

He was not your enemy. He was nobody's enemy.

I think your brother was an enemy to himself, he said at last.

Well, that's true, I said, he didn't fit in with the world, and it's interesting that you saw that, even though you didn't know him. But that was not a reason to kill him.

It's a pity he was there. He wouldn't have survived, said Oaoiti finally.

So that's all it is? Just where you happen to be. I was never meant to be here either.

He became agitated then. This is where you belong, he said. When I did not answer him, he said, with finality, this is the life you have now.

And then he said, I cannot bring him back, Peti.

I had stopped praying that we would be rescued. Even had I wanted to be, I did not believe God would listen to me. Besides, the God I learnt about when I was a girl was different from those of the Maoris. From the beginning of my time at Te Namu, I learnt that one turned always to the ancestor gods. I liked the story of how the world began better than that of Adam and Eve, and her being one of his ribs, and the serpent in the garden, with the brothers killing each other. I think Jacky saw me as his rib, a part of himself that he took for granted, except for when Charley was around me, and then he saw the serpent. I don't suppose he thought that, but I see now that men often don't notice their wives until there is another man around. Perhaps there is a certain smell that one or other of them brings to the chase that warns the mate of danger. Do you think that's possible? No, I can see you don't know. I thought I was a good wife to Jacky, but if he noticed he never said so.

I will never know who all the Maori gods are. Not unless I

was to go back. That wouldn't be easy of course, and who knows whether they would have me.

Adie's scandalised voice cuts across mine. I had forgotten she was there. You would go back?

Why, I thought you were asleep.

But you were talking to me anyway.

Don't mind me. You've put up with me long enough. I have to think of what I'll do next.

You wouldn't really go back to the Maoris? Adie is insistent and fearful.

Why, if they would have me, I think I might.

That's heathen talk.

I laughed then, not kindly or with much amusement. I think you've heard more than enough.

You were saying — that you had become like your captors?

Yes, that's true.

And your rescuers your enemies?

That is just how it was.

When did I begin to understand this? Well, it was the morning when I looked out the window of my house and saw a man-o'-war standing off the coast. This was in September, and it was a busy time at the pa for the planting of kumara had begun a month earlier. The men dug the ground over, while the women prepared the tilled earth in rows of hillocks. Now I was part of the tribe I was expected to join in this work. The constant bending and toiling was back-breaking but I felt myself grow stronger each day. The soil between my hands made me think of Papa, the earth, and that I was part of her, fertile and full of life. Soon I was as fast as the other women, and they offered praise. The weather turned warmer in fits and spells, though some days were nicer than others. This morning I'm telling you about was showery and cool, the beginning of a stretch of bad weather that would come between me and rescue for some weeks to come. Not that I knew then what was planned.

There were people milling round, wondering whether to go to the gardens or not, what the weather would bring. I'm surprised I was the first to see the ship.

For a few minutes I looked out, not quite believing my eyes, as a squall of rain gusted across the horizon. But then I saw what I later learnt was the *Alligator*, and a minute or so later another one hove into view. Two ships. Had they sent the whole navy after me?

I called out, my voice filled with fright. They are coming after us, I shouted. We'll all be killed.

That was my first thought. All of us.

All of us in danger.

The enemy is coming.

So that is how I had come to think of my husband.

Chapter 30

6 March 1835

Dear Sir

It pains me that I must prevail upon you in this manner, but I understand that your sister Miss Adeline Malcolm is currently residing with you. I have written to her on a number of occasions without the honour of a reply. She is needed here to do her duty by my two children who are in great distress over her absence. I would be grateful if you could persuade her to return. Or, at very least, to give me an answer.

It is said, too, in Sydney, that you are currently harbouring Mrs Guard, the wife of the infamous whaler who has recently been at war with the natives of New Zealand. The pair of them are eliciting a great deal of sympathy and excitement around town, but there are two sides to every story, and I think Mrs Guard is not as good as she makes out. I must say I am surprised that you are giving shelter to this woman, for she is nought but a corrupting influence, one of the convict class. I understood sir, that you were of a more exclusive disposition, and while that may not sit so well with our current Governor, governors come and governors go, and for the future of our colony, it seems imperative that someone should take a stand in the interests of decency.

I have told Miss Malcolm that I do not hold her association with Mrs Guard against her, but I would expect you, as her brother, to deal more firmly with the matter.

I propose to travel by carriage to Parramatta, at a decent interval after you have received this letter, and had time to consider its contents, to try and put some order into this sorry affair.

I am, sir, yours very truly,

Gerald Roddick

'Good Lord, somebody wants her,' says Maude Malcolm. She drops a piece of bacon rind to her terrier beneath the breakfast table.

Her husband stands, his eyes watering as they do when he is agitated. 'I must go and warn her immediately.'

'Sit down, Percy,' says Maude. 'You're not warning her of anything. After breakfast, I'll send a maid down to pack her bag, and tell her she can wait on the verandah.' Maude is dressed in a blue morning gown with a broderie anglaise gusset exposing her cleavage. She prides herself that her breasts have withstood the vicissitudes of time. They rise like a girl's, pale and swelling, with a hint of freckles where skin meets lace.

'Maude, that is enough. You've gone too far,' Percy says, jabbing his knife in her direction, so that she ducks. They both pause, appalled at having come this close to violence. Maude quivers, puts her fingers to her heaving breast. Percy's eyes follow the gesture, the invitation to pierce the white flesh that he enjoys so regularly, even though the sound of her voice has so come to displease him. That is the problem between them, of course: he has never met a woman of his sister's sensibility, and his sister cannot be his wife though he loves her just as well. Often, it has come to him in the night, when he is resting from the paroxysms of the flesh, that no one woman can be all things to a man.

'Roddick will be received like a gentleman,' he says. 'What will people make of you, if you allow them to see how badly you have treated her? Don't you ever want to go to Government House again?'

'Well then,' says Maude, 'I, for one, will be pleased to see the back of her.'

'You may tell Lieutenant Roddick that I don't wish to see him,' says Adie, on receiving her brother's news. 'I have come to enjoy my sojourn in the bush.'

'It's not the bush,' says Percy, 'it's the cottage at the bottom of our garden. I wish we could discuss this in private.' Betty hasn't budged since his arrival, waving Roddick's letter in the air.

'Mrs Guard and I have had a good deal of time to share one another's confidences,' says Adie, her voice dry.

'You knew that Lieutenant Roddick wanted you to return. I've brought you letters from him without making any enquiry of you as to their contents. I've treated this as your business, but now that he's written to me, I can no longer be silent. And soon he'll be here.'

'Perhaps you should see him, Adie,' says Betty, 'it can do no harm. Indeed, it might strengthen your resolve.' She offers this with a secretive smile at her friend.

'I won't see him unless you are with me,' Adie replies.

Already, the sound of horses' hooves and carriage wheels are rattling up the driveway. 'Tell the gentleman to wait,' says Betty. 'You must see that your sister's upset.'

'But you have to come now,' cries Percy. 'There is no time to be lost.'

'He doesn't want Roddick to find you in the gardening shed,' says Betty.

'It is not,' Percy says. 'It is . . .'

'Yes?' says Betty. 'What is it, Mr Malcolm? Your nanny's cottage?'

'I don't think it would be proper for you to accompany my

sister. This is a family matter.'

'Oh family. Well then.' Betty picks up a ripe fig from a bowl on the table and bites into it, allowing the tip of her tongue to run over its flesh. This is not lost on Percy who winces and draws back as if to put a distance between himself and his visitor.

'Please, Mrs Guard.' Adie's voice is small, her tone more formal. 'I need you.'

'Perhaps it's best if you go on your own,' says Betty.

'But I haven't decided what to do.'

'Because you haven't had a proposal. Well, he's not likely to make one in my presence.'

'A proposal?' Percy's eyes water anew. 'Adie, you couldn't. I mean, you couldn't expect it.'

'A proposition,' says Adie, recovering her composure. 'That is all. I'll see what proposition Lieutenant Roddick has for the terms of my return to his employment. I will hear him out.' She adjusts a straying frond of hair, and straightens the collar of her dress. She is wearing a gown of pale grey voile, which could do with a press.

Gerald Roddick is standing with Maude on the verandah when she approaches. He is dressed in his scarlet uniform, his sword by his side. His moustache is waxed and his hair has recently been trimmed. He holds his hands together behind his back, and does not extend them as Adie approaches.

'Lieutenant Roddick.'

'Miss Malcolm.' He gives a slight bow from the waist.

A silence falls over them. 'I don't know what to say,' he begins and at the same moment, Adie says, 'I've been so worried.' Then because neither has heard what the other has said, they stop again.

'How are the children?' says Adie at last.

'They miss you. I apologise for what I have put you through. I was harsh.'

'You have judged my friend too harshly,' Adie says.

'I fear Mrs Guard's character is something we cannot agree over.'

'I don't understand,' says Adie. 'She has been through such troubles and all of Sydney is up in arms over what has happened to her.'

'But that is before word got around.'

'Word about what?'

'Mrs Guard is ruined. It is said that she was brought to bed with twins and they were rather dark.'

Maude Malcolm gives a stifled cry, and covers her mouth with the back of her hand.

'That is absurd,' Adie says, blinking in the fierce heat that has risen as the morning progressed.

'Why do you think she's here? What has she told you?'

'Believe me,' Adie falters and carries on, 'it's not possible since I met her after her rescue.'

'How can you be so sure? Have you been by her side all these past weeks?'

'I am sure I would know,' says Adie. 'She has not spoken of more children.'

'Why don't you ask me?' says Betty. She stands at the end of the garden, wearing the same dress that she arrived in some days before, bathed in the dappled stripes of shadows as the sun falls between the branches of a gum tree overhead. A parakeet gives a loud squawking cry. It is hard to tell whether it is that which has startled the tableau on the lawn, or the appearance of the woman.

'So it's true,' says Roddick, 'she is here. Shame on you,' he says, directing his gaze towards Adie, 'for keeping her company. As for your brother, by what pretension does he call himself a gentleman that he has harboured her?'

'I will not have you speak of us in that manner,' says Percy. Adie, remembering him as a child, hears the quiver that used to invade his voice when reproached by their father.

'Will you not?' says Roddick, in an extravagant tone. 'Well, I cannot imagine you will allow your family to be dishonoured in this way.'

'I don't understand,' says Percy, bewildered.

'I will come back two mornings hence, when you've had time to think it over,' says Roddick.

'No,' murmurs Adie, 'I beg of you. It doesn't matter, I'll come anyway.'

'I wish it were as simple as that,' Roddick says. 'I think a man should fight for honour.'

'No,' cries Adie wildly. 'My brother is not a fighter. Maude, tell him.'

Her sister-in-law has stood listening to this exchange, a small smile playing over her face. 'Surely, it is for the gentlemen to decide.'

'Will you come with me, Miss Malcolm?' says Roddick.

'Not now. No. A thousand times no.'

'I will leave,' says Betty, 'if it will change things. Adie, this difficulty is over me, not you. Your family doesn't accept me, and the lieutenant listens to rumour. They are all worried that I will harm their reputations.'

'I'm not leaving,' says Adie. 'And I beg you Mrs Guard, to stay here with me.'

'I will come back the day after tomorrow,' says Roddick. 'Let's hope the matter can be resolved in a sensible way.'

He casts a last contemptuous look at Betty and turns on his heel.

When he has gone, Percy says in a wan voice, 'What does he mean by fight? He doesn't really mean a proper fight, does he?'

'That's what soldiers do,' Betty says, as she vanishes down the shadowy blue gum track.

Chapter 31

30 August 1834

As it was decided to take extra men on the expedition, we were delayed another day while more bread was baked. There was much counting of provisions. But at last the *Alligator* and the *Isabella* were ready to sail for New Zealand. There are some queer bodies on board the *Alligator* with me. The Royal Navy surgeon whose name is Barrett Marshall is full of godliness and soupy talk about how we should not pass hasty judgments on the Maoris until we see what is what.

I know what is what I said and from my pocket I took a piece of comb. It was the ½ I picked up from the beach when Betty was felled. I have seen my wife's head cut open with an axe. Do not tell me what I should think of them.

Well then he said in the same smooth voice, how wd you civilise them?

How wd I civilise them I said. Shoot them to be sure. A musket ball for every New Zealander is the only way of civilising their country.

His face turned to whey then all moist and sticky white. You cannot say that he cried. Have you not thought of what missionaries might bring to them?

What is that?

A knowledge of God.

There is missionaries in the north I said.

I know that for I have been there.

Then you will know that the Maoris still make their own sweet way doing what suits them.

The surgeon did not like what he heard and I do not like him.

Then there is Miller who is a pilot. I could do as good a job as him for he does not have much experience of the New Zealand coast as I wd wish and he is to help Battersby the interpreter. I am worried about this cove. His Maori is what he learnt when he was in the grog shops in the Bay of Islands. He was drunk more often then than not. Although he speaks a kind of pidgin lingo I don't reckon he understands much more than I do. I have enough for whaling — which you have to get right or you'll be dead, but that is not enough for what we are going into. I am done with Maoris in my soul but I have respect for the tricks they can pull. I think they could put it across Battersby.

I have mentioned this to Captain Lambert but he said he is under orders to carry him. Perhaps I should speak with Captain Johnstone he said who is the Captain of the 50th Regiment and the men who will do the fighting.

So I said to Johnstone you wd do well to put me in charge of telling the Maoris what is what.

I cannot do that Guard he said for I am under strict orders that the military carry out this operation. You have had your say in Sydney and now it is up to the professional soldiers to do our duty. We have hand-picked men and you must behave as a civilian which is what you are.

I was being put in my place and I did not like it.

I said to myself perhaps we wd have done better to stick to a ransom and be done with it. My mind went back to Captain Anglim who led me down this path and I do not think well of him for it seems I am out of the action.

Also on board are the chiefs I took to Sydney aboard the *Joseph Weller*. I have no time for them. They are sorry for themselves even though they are being taken home. They do not like bread and they will not eat salted meat so who is to mind if they go hungry.

3 September

We have now been at sea 4 days. Lambert and Johnstone consult each other all the time and plan how they will land the troops. Nothing much else happens. I drum my heels on the decks and wish I was somewhere else. I have been thinking about Charlotte and that what passed between us was not wise. But what is done is done and who knows whether I will get my wife back. I read my book to pass the time, the 1 my father gave me about my duties as a man. There is a section on the faithfulness of husbands. 'For those who are not faithful, it said the breach of the vow is no less for a man than a woman. Besides the Uncleanness, it is a downright perjury.' I was glad then I had not made a formal vow to the girl. I need not think of her as my wife, which is relief. Conscience is a terrible thing and I do not want the burden of it. Perhaps I will make her a vow if I ever get her back. I think about my son who is missing, and she is his mother. I will be smote down if I do not have my boy back. Until I had a boy of my own I did not know how much that wd make me believe in myself as a man. Nothing else been or gone has made my life worthwhile. I will die for this boy if I must.

I think I am in the hands of fools.

11 September

Land at last. I see the coast of Taranaki, as I have seen it many times before.

Lambert tried to land at Moturoa in order to rescue the crew but the N.W. was up to its usual tricks.

So we came to the beach beneath Te Namu pa where I believe Betty is held. I said to the Captain, I will go ashore, I will talk with them.

Enough Guard he said. The interpreters will go ashore.

And what message will you send with them I said.

You know what's been decided. They are to communicate with the chiefs and explain to them that our Government will stay on friendly terms providing the missing crew members and your wife and children are restored at once.

Without ransom I asked.

We have been through this many times he said. There will be no ransom. It will be explained that if they attack His Majesty's subjects again they will be punished in a most severe way. And if they do not hand over the hostages we will smash them and all that belongs to them to pieces.

But the wind being what it was the chance of setting anyone on the beach was small. A group of New Zealanders came down to the beach. At this point Lambert said you may go in the whale boat Guard with the interpreters and Lieutenant Clarke who is in charge. But I will shoot you if you try to go ashore alone.

I saw a man on the shore. Even from this distance he seemed to be smiling his teeth white lanterns in his face.

Who are you? the interpreters called out.

I am Oaoiti. A chief.

Are you speaking for the tribe?

She is not here Haari he called ignoring this question. How did he know my name. I felt something bad in the air. My hair prickled under my cap.

I called out to him then. Where is she? Where is Betty?

I swear he laughed. I did not like the cocksure way he had about him. She and the girl have gone to Waimate.

My heart fell into my boots. I didn't believe we could take the fortress of Waimate. We went back aboard the *Alligator*.

Where is this place Waimate Lambert asked.

It is 1 of 2 pa 1 is Waimate and the other is Orangituapeka I told him and they are both on very high cliffs surrounded by ravines. They are some 20 miles south of here.

Then said Lambert in a cheerful voice we will have to send the interpreters to Waimate. 20 miles is no great distance he says to them, you can walk down there and have a talk to them. When you get back here I want you to light 2 fires on that hill and we will fetch you.

I tried to tell him it is not as easy as that. But he wd not listen.

There being a lull in the waves we set Battersby and Miller ashore a little south of Te Namu where it was hoped they wd not be seen by the Maoris. Neither of them looked too happy.

I could only stand and watch.

I wrapped myself in my greatcoat and said not a word to anyone again that day. I did not sleep at all that night. I kept seeing the chief standing on the beach. As if he was certain about himself. And then I knew what it was.

13 September

We stood off from the pa sites of Waimate and Orangituapeka so that the Captain could see for his self how the 2 places are like fortresses. I had been told by Oliver who was at Moturoa and had been to Waimate of a winding path about 2 parts up the S.W. face where it ends in a cliff face with a ladder. The ladder can be pulled up from the top.

Hundreds of Ngati Ruanui were now gathered on the beach and cliff tops, waving muskets and tomahawks. I had no doubt they would kill anyone who came near.

A gale came come upon us. We could do nothing but run before it. When we got to the top of the South Island, I offered to take the helm, which was accepted and I guided the ship into a safe cove I knew. Why this is a very pleasant place said Captain

Lambert. What is it called?

I don't rightly know I said.

Well then, I will name it for Gore who was the Vice Admiral of the East India Squadron. A fine chap. I'm sure he would like to have a port named after him. Port Gore it is.

The officers did a bit of shooting practice and found some good rock oysters and had sport trying to set fire to the bush. Just as well they failed at that for there is no point in telling the locals where we are hid.

17 September

The weather improved a bit, long enough to secure the interpreters before we had to head south again. I was impatient to hear what they had to tell us. They looked scared half to death and didn't want to give a straight answer as to what they had been up to.

Have you seen my wife? I asked them.

No.

My children?

No.

Are they alive? Did anyone say they were alive?

Yes they said sullen as they come. In the end they gave up their story and the 2 Captains were not happy as to what they heard. For the men had not been to Waimate. Miller and Battersby had got themselves as far as Te Namu in the opposite direction but the Taranaki people did not make them welcome. The interpreters gave the message hoping it would be taken to Waimate but they got laughed at. The Maoris showed them dried heads of white men and laughed and jeered and said soon all the pakea wd look the same. Under cover of darkness they escaped into the bush where they stayed a night or 2 living on their rations. In the bush they met another group of Maoris who told them they wd soon be killed and eaten.

They decided between themselves there was only 1 course of action. They went back to Te Namu. We have come back they said to tell you that the white man is willing to barter with you. They will give you a very good ransom. They will give you a whole barrel of gunpowder.

And if that were not enough it seems the interpreters told the Maoris the ships out there want whalebone. The 2 vessels will trade with you.

Well said Lambert that is a terrible tale you have told for what you have said is not true.

But said Battersby dogged-like they say they will bring the woman back to Te Namu and you can get her from there.

I do not believe a word you are telling me said Lambert. His face was dark with fury.

She will be back at Te Namu tomorrow said Battersby.

The whole expedition seems to be falling to pieces. Who is to know what is truth.

18 September

I piloted the ship to a 2nd harbour to the south and we let the anchor go in 15 fathoms. By now I can tell the officers have more time for me as it was I who got the ship from one safe harbour to another. After dinner they offered me cigars that were very fine. The meals are prepared with great style for one of the cooks is Italian and the other Maltese. They both play the fiddle so we have music though it is melancholy to my ear and not something we can have a rousing good sing to.

This is a very good bay too said Lambert. And so it was. The hills were covered with timber and there are many clear streams. I think I should give it a name he said. I shall name it for gallant Sir Thomas Hardy, Nelson's flag captain at Trafalgar. Port Hardy it is.

Do you not think, said Barrett Marshall who has had little to say for himself on this journey, that it might not be better to find out what the Maoris have called it and translate the names the better to understand them? Should we assume that we are making improvements by dotting the place with English names?

Where upon both the Captains stared at him in silence. He shrugged his shoulders and walked away. For a minute it occurred to me the surgeon might be right. None of these new names mean much to me. Once when I was an Englishman they might have done. But I am not any more. What has England done for me?

A memory came back of when I was no more than a lad and locked up in Newgate Prison. I was taken more than once to watch an execution and I heard again the Bellman reciting the words that went before the hanging of men:

> *All you that in the condemned hole do lie*
> *Prepare you, for tomorrow you shall die,*
> *Watch all and pray: the hour is drawing near.*

I remembered the terror and wondering whether I might be next. I was glad to get out of it alive. They can call these places whatever they like, it is neither here nor there to me. I spat at Barrett Marshall's feet the next time I passed him. He is a lily-livered piece of work full of cheap kindnesses for the Maoris we have on board. I do not know why he wants to win favour from them. They sit and weep like children when some of the soldiers have them on a bit and draw their fingers across their throats as if they are about to lose their heads. They do not understand a little humour.

What I want now is to be done with this waiting.

We have to get back to Te Namu.

21 September

Well, at last we have made progress. We took ourselves up to the coast. Why what are these islands called said Barrett Marshall, leaning against the rail as we drew close.

Moturoa I said, thinking to please him.

He wrinkled up his nose like a small animal, and said yes but is there some other name for them.

There is some as call them the Sugar Loaf Islands I said, which I think is the name that Captain Cook did call them.

Well he said in a jolly manner that is a good name, yes indeed that is what they look like and my goodness they are steep. How surprising that there is a pa on them. How do people hold to the sides of rocks like that?

And I think you are a hypocrite I said thinking of his speech about naming places.

I saw I had got him on the quick and he was smarting but he decided that he wd not show it. I am reminded of the work of Gray he said in his grand way. A fine English poet. He writes so well about nature and the sea. Are you familiar with his work Mr Guard? Or should I call you Haari he said with what was intended as a merry laugh.

My name is Guard I said and I do not know any poetry.

The chiefs were put ashore at Moturoa and given muskets and flints and powder and ammunition. In return the crew of the *Harriet* were given over to us. I thought this an interesting exchange for it amounted to the same as a ransom. Only as it was the chiefs that had been given the gifts Lambert said it was different. There were 8 of the crew and looking like sorry scarecrows. Some of the men had got away and tried to head north. I don't know what's become of them.

Among those picked up was my bro. Charley. Have you seen Betty? I said to him.

No he told me.

But she is still alive? They've told you she is alive.

Oh yes he said and I didn't like the look he gives me. Knowing. He always knew too much for his own good did Charley.

28 September

There was less surf this morning and Lambert declared this the day we wd land on the beach beneath Te Namu.

In all more than 100 men were picked for the boats' crews.

There was a Senior Lieutenant and 12 rank and file of the Royal Marines 1 Cptn 1 subaltern 1 sergeant and 60 rank and file of the 50th all to go ashore under the command of Captain Johnstone. I was given a whale boat in my charge with my men rescued from the *Harriet*. We collected our rations thinking we might be ashore 3 days. We each took 3 pounds of biscuit 2 and 1/4 of salt pork 3 gills rum 70 rounds of ammunition. Lambert thought at the last moment the men wd not need their haversacks and great-coats because of the fine weather. I did not know this until we were about to go and I said this is ridiculous. You do not know how cold it is within sight of that mountain. So at the last minute some of them have their gear thrown in the boats. It was not a fine start. The boats had a long hard pull to the shore because the seas came up rougher than we thought they wd. We made land at 9 of the clock.

At this point, 2 big parties of Maoris appeared on the cliff tops. They were armed with a few muskets but they did not seem ready to make war. 2 men came down the cliff seeming not afraid. The 1 in front was Oaoiti.

He called out to us. The woman is with me.

The men in the boats looked at one another as if they were asking themselves what he meant.

What have you done to her you black devil? I shouted.

Lambert was in the boat alongside of us. Be quiet Guard he called.

There is no harm done to her. She and the girl are well.

Battersby interpreted this though there was no need on my account for I knew what he had said.

Where is my son?

He is not here.

Where is he?

I cannot tell you that.

Bring my wife to me I said. I did not care what Lambert thought.

I will see if she wants to come said Oaoiti.

What do you mean? She wd not stay with you not for a King's ransom.

At that he bared his teeth in a smile or a snarl.

But the men were looking at 1 another and I saw what they were thinking. Oaoiti approached the edge of the water.

Well what about a ransom he said mocking us. We heard we wd get a ransom for her.

Lambert's boat pulled alongside of ours. There was no ransom he said. Never in 100 years or 200 will we give you anything for someone who rightfully belongs with us.

All the same I wanted my wife back so I said to Lambert perhaps we could give them something, a little trifle of some kind.

I am under orders Guard Lambert said as if I was simple. To the Governor. There will be no ransom. You knew that from the beginning.

Let me see Betty I said to the chief.

Let me see the ransom Haari he said and laughed. I saw the way he stood proud as if he didn't give a damn for what was in my head.

Captain I said real quiet this man is a rogue. He is playing us all along. Let us take him captive and see what he has to say then.

For I saw the way it was — neither Lambert nor Oaoiti wd give way.

Right said Lambert in this I am in agreement with you Guard.

In less than a minute the order was given and passed along to Johnstone who ordered 4 of the redcoats into action. Oaoiti had got too sure of himself and waded out towards us. They grabbed him 1 on each of his hands and legs and flung him into my boat. He was at my feet. Another man took a boy perhaps a servant who was in the company of Oaoiti.

Lambert gave the order to push out to sea.

I leant over Oaoiti and said now it is me that has got you my friend and I pointed my musket at his head. I had not decided if

I wd kill him before Charley pushed my weapon away. Do not swing for him brother he said. But in a flash Oaoiti was over the side and in the water. I turned and fired and his red blood was in the sea and I laughed, the first time I have had a good laugh in many a day.

By now my men were on to it, they are my comrades in arms. They went after him. He dived under the boat and swam beneath the surface of the sea but he had to come up for air and we beat him on the head with the paddles and someone stuck a bayonet through his chest and then several more times and we got the bastard back in the boat. I thought he wd be dead but that was not to be. He wriggled like a fish and it was only by holding the ring in his ear and twisting it we were able to lash him to a thwart.

All this time Barrett Marshall is wringing his hands in the next boat and wailing at the top of his voice for us to stop. I was thinking if he did not shut it soon I might just put a bayonet in his arse if I could get near enough to Lambert's boat. Oaoiti saved us any more trouble by falling down in a faint so we could throw him on board the *Alligator*. Barrett Marshall went with him and we were put under orders to stay there until he had finished looking at our captive as Lambert pulled away.

I was all for leaving Barrett Marshall behind but now at least I knew the Captain was on my side I did not want to cause him offence and so we waited.

Barrett Marshall came back on our boat. He had put on a black cape edged with gold and sat down looking pleased with himself holding his sword upright between his knees. Over the water came music from the cooks. They were playing Onward Christian Soldiers.

At my suggestion said Barrett Marshall.

I see I said. Does that mean our fellow is dead?

No it means he is alive.

Then we headed back to the shore to join the landing party. Barrett Marshall rattled on about how his duty was back on board the ship. I said whose side are you on. I left England to get away from people like you.

Not a bit of it he said. We sent people like you to Botany Bay so that we did not have to live with heathens.

And what if my wife and child need a surgeon's touch? Will you not give them that?

Of course I will he said, it is my job to save any life, that is what a doctor does.

Even mine I asked as we neared the shore.

Even yours he said pious as ever.

I said nothing then. Besides we were watching out for our enemy as we pulled up on the shore again.

We made our way up to the pa. All was strange and quiet. I thought there must be some hidden trap. But there was nobody except 1 pig all on its own. The Maoris had gone leaving their potatoes cooking in their jackets.

We turned back to the beach and there I saw the trick they had in mind. They were ransacking the boats. The sailors left in charge were firing their weapons to keep them off.

So now what do you suggest Guard said Johnstone of the 50th.

I reckon the birds have flown.

That is very clear he said his voice dry as kindling wood.

But I said they have been taken by surprise and they may not have gone very far. We should search for them. We have fresh meat and warm beds here and we can put up for a day or 2 which with respect sir is what I thought you had in mind.

True he agreed.

That night the fires roared and the smell of cooking pig was in every man's nostrils.

I took a walk around the pa looking at the grass whares. I came to a house with a door made as Europeans wd build it, with leather thong hinges swinging on the empty room. I saw the remains of a blue dress, an end of soap and some infant's swaddling clothes.

I saw a bed of grass and fern covered with a mat, the hollow where bodies had lain.

30 September

A day passed. Then today Battersby and Barrett Marshall, myself and some soldiers came across a Maori party scouting in the bush. They came at us with pistols in their hands but saw they were outnumbered. They had come to tell us that a war party was on its way to do us in for having killed Oaoiti.

But he is alive said Barrett Marshall.

No they said. Obstinate like. He is dead. You have murdered him.

I tell you no. For once I am pleased to have Barrett Marshall on hand.

But they doubt what he has said. 1 said I do not believe you. Last night his spirit passed over us in a falling star and we know he is gone.

His companion said all of our tribes are coming together to fight you. We will take back Te Namu and fight you back to the sea.

Battersby said shall I bounce them?

What do you mean? said Barrett Marshall with his usual solemn manner.

I mean said Battersby shall I tell them a lie?

Certainly not. But pray what lie did you propose to tell them?

Why that if they won't promise to deliver up Guard's family we shall set fire to Te Namu.

I thought that a good idea but Barrett Marshall was having none of it.

At any rate we did burn it down. Johnstone thought it a capital idea that wd give the Maoris something to think about. We set fire in every house and pulled the stockades down and added it to the flames.

Back at the ship Oaoiti looked in good health. Barrett Marshall was full o' beans over this.

I wished him dead. I wish it still.

Lambert said never mind Guard, he is something to bargain with.

I took a cup of rum. There was not enough room aboard the *Alligator* for my bro. and the other crew members who had been taken on board at Moturoa. They had been put aboard the *Isabella*.

I am pleased about that. I have no wish to make conversation with Charley.

Chapter 32

Parramatta's five wide streets are built in a grid. The main street runs from Government House — the second Government House, but much grander than the one in Sydney — to the Parramatta River. Another ends in a plaza containing the newly built town hall. Shops and churches fill the other streets.

'So orderly, so pretty,' Adie Malcolm says. Her eyes sweep Government House with longing. The Parramatta residence stands in a park, with a lodge at its gates and, though the oak trees within its domain have been planted less than half a century, already they provide shade on the green lawns. Adie's hand rests on a wrought iron gate.

'Well,' she says, 'I don't suppose I'll be going to the Governor's residence again, here or in Sydney.'

'I'm sorry, Adie,' Betty says. 'I've brought a lot of troubles on you.'

Betty has never been to Government House in either place, though an invitation did come after her return from the New Zealand expedition. 'I was afraid of being stared at,' she tells

Adie, 'although I would like to have gone.'

The two women have slept as if drugged, which perhaps they were, for the cook had placed a carafe of wine on their tray the night before. Both had fallen into instant, deep and dreamless slumber. In the morning they had woken to the realisation of how little time remained until the lieutenant's return.

Betty has said several times that she will leave, but Adie will not countenance this. Instead, she has suggested a walk. The farm road into town is a distance of some two miles. They have started early in the morning to avoid the heat.

'Soon it will be over,' Adie says, 'one way or another. We might as well make the most of this time.' In town, she buys Betty a bracelet set with faceted beryl stones that gleam with pale green fire in the morning sunlight.

'You shouldn't,' says Betty. 'You can't afford it.'

'Fiddlesticks,' says Adie. 'It's bad manners to question the price of a gift.'

'But why?' asks Betty. 'I have more jewellery than you.' She suspects that this is the last money Adie has in the world that is not in her brother's and Maude's hands.

'Then,' says Adie, 'this will be a special piece, for it will remind you of me, long after we have parted company. In the same way that you will take out the earring you were given in New Zealand, in moments when you're alone, and remember what happened to you. Well,' she smiles, 'perhaps not in quite the same way.'

'That is best forgotten.'

'Still, it happened, and some day you might want to remember it. When I was a child and in pain, with a bad tooth or a cut, my father used to give me a ball of marble to hold which he said was magic and would take away the pain. I don't know that it did, but I believed it and the pain vanished. I adored my father. I wish Percy had seen him in the same light as I did. Anyway, you've given me several gifts.'

'Nothing like this.' Betty holds out her hand for Adie to do up the clasp of the new bracelet. 'I'll remember you anyway, but it's beautiful.'

'You still haven't told me how you left the pa.'

'Ah,' says Betty. 'That.'

When we were back at her brother's property at Malcolm Downs I did take up my story again, for it was almost over and I did not want to deny the governess the end to that which she had heard so patiently.

On nights when I found myself alone at the pa, not often I'm bound to say, there was a stillness that was never truly quiet.

How to explain the difference? There was the constant rustle of rats nearby, which made me draw Louisa's sleeping form close, and the screech of the night owl that sounds like *more pork* echoing through the palisades. And there were fleas that meant sleep was often fitful; if I had had fifty fingers it would not have been enough to keep the wretched things at bay. But in a way I welcomed this lightness of sleep for it kept me free of dreams.

The night before I had seen the ships on the horizon, I had been on my own for some time. I remember those last hours when Oaoiti was beside me. He was in a more serious mood than usual. He spoke of my beauty. I am not really beautiful, I said, feeling shy. You should see my mother and my Auntie Charlotte.

He said he would not want my mother or my aunt, however pretty they might look. He had seen only a few seen white-skinned people, and never a woman before he met me. When he looked at white men he couldn't imagine their women. He thought they might have beards, or skinny ribs like goblins with pointed ears and thin hair. But I was not like that and, he said, I had a smile like light on water. He wanted to know if I was happy.

Yes, I said, for I was not unhappy. I didn't tell him about the dreams when he wasn't there, or the sense of loss I could not shake. As I had never fallen in love before, the way I had with Oaoiti, I couldn't compare my feelings. But I guessed that it might be the same for all who fell in love — after all, I had seen enough of the way my mother carried on — that at the beginning everything is perfect. And then you begin to see that the world hasn't changed, only you. That the same ordinary things still have to be attended to. You start picking holes in your happiness.

Why can't John live with us? I asked.

He sighed then. That might happen some day, he said. Only, first I had to understand that John was to be a chief, and would grow to be an important man who would change the fortune of the tribe. He would be the white rangatira. I have told you all this before Peti, he said. Once you have accepted that, you will come to be honoured as his mother. As he spoke, his fingers traced my belly, bare and flat in the moonlight, and rested there, forming a little basket with his fingertips. I knew at once what he was suggesting: one is taken away but another will come.

Yes, I said, turning to him in drowsy anticipation. Straight away the idea had taken hold of me. The only surprising thing was that it hadn't happened already, but perhaps it had been too soon after Louisa. I knew my body was ready now.

But it didn't happen that night. Possibly he believed it done, though I knew otherwise. It's odd the way you know. He stood up, overtaken with restlessness, as if he had heard something. Soon after that he left.

I lay straining my ears in the darkness. Was it the change in the weather he heard? My ear had become attuned to shifts in the wind. But in fact the breeze that had played round the cliff all evening had dropped, and the air become still. Far below, the water lapped on the shoreline but very softly as it slid back and forth over the black rocks. And I heard something. Like the creak of a mast. The sound of a fiddle, a yearning note from afar. I thought, this is madness, I am losing my mind.

Eventually, I dropped into an uneasy sleep full of dreams and faces of the past. I told myself everything would be all right, that I had a purpose.

Morning dawned, and, as I think I've mentioned, it began to rain, delaying work in the gardens.

And then I saw the ships.

After one frightened glance, I turned and fled from the cliff top.

A woman called Mihingi came to my whare, sent by Ruiha. She was young and strongly built, handsome, with hair as thick as rope. But her face was tight with worry. They have come for you, she said. When I nodded my head, she said, I thought they had left you here for good.

They will have guns, I said. For of course I had seen that these were no whaling ships. Perhaps they're not for me, I said, for these are warships and my husband has only whaling ships. But I knew this was a false hope, for the men-o'-war were bearing towards us.

The ships, with their giant white rigging, were standing off the shore, their long and tapered spars extending every sail to the wind. Dark clouds tumbled towards the sea, the surf running hard. A whaleboat was lowered over the side of the *Alligator*.

Oaoiti came to the door. Quickly, he said, be prepared to leave.

I am not going with them, I cried in a piteous voice. They will kill me.

I do not think so.

I do not want to go.

Peti, are you sure of this?

It is you they will kill, I said.

It will not come to that, he said, without fear. But if you are sure you want to stay, you must keep out of sight. Don't let anyone see you, not even our people. Do exactly what you are told. Mihingi has been chosen to watch over you, for she will not be noticed as Ruiha is known to be your friend.

What will you tell the men on the boat?

I will decide that when the time comes.

What if my husband comes after you?

I will not see Haari unless I must. But I will not be afraid of him either.

The whaleboat came close in shore, and Oaoiti stood on the beach and spoke with the men. My husband was on the boat, and he and Oaoiti exchanged some words.

I told him you were at Waimate, Oaoiti said, later that night. He had come hurriedly to the whare, and spoke to me quietly. I asked for a ransom, he said, just to keep him guessing.

Then he left again.

The boats didn't land at Te Namu. From Mihingi I heard that a boat had landed in heavy seas, further along the coast, and two men had come ashore and been left on their own. Then the tall ships disappeared from the horizon and nobody knew where they'd gone.

Nor did anyone know who the two men were. But word travelled, as news does along that coast, that the crew of the *Harriet* had been set free at Moturoa. Scouts from our pa went into the bush to stop the strangers reaching us. I was relieved to learn that neither of them was Jacky.

A silence had fallen over Te Namu, as the men prepared themselves at the palisades for the arrival of an enemy.

The third night brought more news of the two white men. They told a scout party they spoke Maori but they could hardly make themselves understood. They had been left on shore to negotiate for my and the children's release. Their names were Battersby and Miller and, from the account I heard, two sorrier creatures were hard to imagine. They spent two nights in the bush, screaming and pleading for deliverance. The watchers in the trees shook with silent laughter at their antics. In the morning they showed themselves to the interpreters again. The men now told them they were to be waiting there when the ships returned. They promised their tormentors a great ransom in return for our safe passage.

The people will want the ransom, I said to Oaoiti. He had called at the whare, even though it was broad daylight and I could see that he was worried.

Yes, he said, there will be some who do.

Does that mean I must go with them? For still I did not want to leave.

I am sure your people will not hurt you. They will be pleased to have you back. But I saw he was becoming doubtful, that indecision had crept into his manner. If you are not here, he said, there is no point in them killing anyone. Dress Louisa warmly, put on the cloaks my sisters gave you, and go.

Where?

To Waimate, of course. I have spoken to Waiariari and he will take you.

I'm frightened of Waiariari, I said.

You have no need to be. He is a brother to me, Oaoiti said. I had never heard him speak of a brother, only sisters, but his words were meant to reassure me.

I am not ready to leave, I said.

I saw he was loathe to let me go, to vanish into the bush.

I am going down to the beach, he said. I will speak with the pakea.

They will not listen to you.

They will if I tell them we just want our ransom. That is what Haari said he would bring long ago.

But when they give it to you, then I will have to go with them.

Then it is for you to decide. If you change your mind, you can come down to the beach. I will pick up their ransom and walk back here, and you will go to them if that is what you decide. You will be gone, as if you had never been. I will divorce you in my heart. But if you decide you want to stay, Waiariari will take you south with him and I will see you again. Very soon.

His mind was made up. But I thought it was a bad plan, and that it could go wrong.

Already he had begun to approach the palisades, and behind him gathered the people of the tribe. They set up a war chant. The rain was easing and a watery sun broke through the clouds as the tribe stamped their feet in the haka, challenging the oncoming boat.

I couldn't help myself. I was drawn to follow.

Now Oaoiti descended the cliff. The sun touched his copper skin so that he glinted as he climbed. He carried no weapons. At the last moment, one of his servants, a boy called Tia, ran down after him. He is my chief, he said, as he peeled away from the warriors above. He joined Oaoiti and I saw them walking steadily towards the beach. On the clifftop, the crowd fell silent.

The first boat brought Jacky, grown more portly than when I last saw him. I knew the men with him: my brother-in-law Charley Guard, Daniel Harris, John Francis, John MacDonald and others. They were kitted out in spanking-new clothes; they could have passed for blue jackets, so smart was their appearance.

Oaoiti walked forward. Some conversation passed between them. Jacky looked up once or twice. I drew myself behind a whare, though I didn't believe he would recognise me as I was then. Still Oaoiti walked towards the boat, ankle deep in the water. I wanted to shout to him to turn back. I believe he might have been planning to greet the men, perhaps hongi with Jacky, press his nose to his. Another boat was close by, within hailing distance. A man in a cocked hat sat in the bow. He and Jacky called to each other.

And then, quick as a knife thrust, men jumped on the beach and Oaoiti was flicked into the boat. Jacky raised his bayonet. His comrades splashed in the water as they pushed back to sea.

I was surrounded by a cry like the heavens splitting. Behind me, Mihingi tried to pull me down, but I wouldn't let her hold me.

Oaoiti leapt from the boat and began to swim. On the whaleboat, muskets were raised and a shot rang out. Blood foamed on the crest of the wave. Oaoiti's body was picked from the sea by a grappling hook and thrown back into the boat. The men from the *Harriet* raised their bayonets, stabbed them down, up and down again, as the boat pulled back to the ships. A tidal wave of sobbing mounted beside me, and I fell weeping to the ground.

Many boats from the ship now headed towards the shore,

filled with red jackets and blue jackets, like a horde of parakeets flying the morning.

Among the crowd, word had gone out. Everyone was leaving Te Namu. Except me. I tried to stand but Mihingi pulled me down by the hair. Are you satisfied now? she said, or words that meant much the same, and kicked me in the stomach. She let me go, striding away from me, without a backward glance. I lay there long minutes, unable to move.

Behind me, I heard Louisa's cry. I picked myself up and ran back to the whare. When I picked her up, she touched my face with her little baby paws.

Outside, the crowd had melted away, spiriting themselves down the far cliffside towards the bush.

In a few minutes the place was empty. Louisa and I appeared to be alone. I would flee too, in whatever direction my feet would take me, as far away as I could go. I didn't know where to hide from the soldiers. I took some flax rope, lashed Louisa to my back and covered her with my cloaks.

As I prepared to leave, Waiariari and another man appeared in the doorway, each carrying a musket in one hand and a spear in the other, searching for those who might need help leaving the pa, like the old ones. The man with Waiariari raised his musket when he saw me, taking aim. Waiariari pushed it away with an impatient gesture, as if I wasn't worth the ammunition.

What are you doing here? he asked.

They would not take me.

He looked at me as if to say he didn't blame them. Come with me, he said.

Where are you taking me?

To Waimate, he said, which is where you were supposed to be all along.

I do not want to go.

You have said that once too often was his reply, and with that he poked me in the ribs with his spear. I backed away from him, Louisa on my back with her fingers clutching my hair, until I came to the edge of the hill, where a gate had been opened. It was not the precipice but still it was steep, and when I stepped out, space opened up before me. Louisa and I tumbled down the hill, with Waiariari in pursuit.

Now will you come with me, he asked.

I followed him, humbly, for my life was in his hands. By now I was used to walking through bush though, if left alone, I would easily be swallowed in its green depths. Waiariari gave me no quarter as we glided through the trees, faster than I had ever made the journey. Before long, we came to Waimate.

Chapter 33

I didn't know whether the people of Ngati Ruanui would give me up, or kill me, now that Oaoiti was dead. It was not clear why I had been brought here. Perhaps in the rush to get me away from Te Namu, nobody had had a chance to decide my fate. Or perhaps they thought I carried the seed of Oaoiti, and it must be saved. In which case, my days were numbered, because this was not true. My body was due to discharge its monthly cargo of blood.

Oaoiti's sisters were nowhere to be seen. I didn't dare ask after them, for I thought they would hate me now. I asked Waiariari if I might see John, but he shook his head. I thought he must be at Orangituapeka, beyond my reach. They would have known that I would want to find him. Later in the afternoon, Mihingi appeared at the pa. Wherever I went, she seemed close beside me watching me.

That night a fiery glow illuminated the sky to the north. People looked at each other uneasily. Why is it sunset so early? they asked one another. Heavy smoke drifted towards us, acrid and heavy with cinders. Word came that the soldiers had gone to

Te Namu and ransacked the pa. People from Te Namu, who had hidden in the bush for a night and day before fleeing, began arriving at Waimate seeking shelter, looking tired and desolate.

The men talked long into the night, each one getting up to make speeches, full of plans as to how they would kill the white men if they tried to land again.

Mihingi said to me: What will you do if the soldiers come here?

I want to stay, I said. For what else could I do? I couldn't leave John behind me. You're not wanted here, Mihingi said.

By now I had bled. People began to speak in hard, indifferent voices. Oaoiti was dead and I was his empty container. Soon, at best, I would become a slave.

But sooner or later the ships would go away, and they might let me see John again. He was only a little boy. Some day he would need me, even if he didn't think so now, and I would be gone. It passed through my mind, seeing the ships, that white men would come to live here, too, as they had at the whaling stations. And then John's life would change. When I thought of him, I saw in him his father Jacky Guard. There was the same shape to his head, the same way he stood as if ready to take on the world. And it was as if something that had been sleeping in me for months had awoken. When I closed my eyes, I could see my husband's face clearly for the first time since we had parted on the beach.

I was in the midst of great confusion. On the one hand, my old life beckoned. But if I was captured by the soldiers, I would have to give an account of myself. And there were no words to explain what had happened, certainly not to my husband. It would be better, I thought, to live as a slave than to face Jacky's unforgiving stare. I remembered the silence at Te Awaiti when Charley and I had talked together. It all came back, how I feared his silences, worse than blows. Yet all around me, I saw suspicious eyes. No longer Winter Woman, but the Woman Who Had Brought Trouble.

And more trouble soon came. At noon one day, the ships reappeared on the horizon. Within an hour, they lowered the boats. As they came towards us, hundreds of warriors from Waimate and Orangituapeka, and those who had come from Te Namu, now banded together at the top of the fortress, commencing a haka.

Waiariari came to me. Now you must decide whether you are for us or against us, he said.

What am I to do?

The women will go down to the shore and invite the men ashore. We know the white man, he is easily enticed by a woman. And you will go with them, with your daughter, and tell them it is safe.

And if I do not?

He shrugged. Who knows? Perhaps our spears will kill you as you wade through the water to the boats. Or you might die in the boats as we rain down fire upon the soldiers.

What if they will not come?

At least you will have tried.

But I am not needed here any more.

You are still worth a ransom. The people of Te Namu have lost everything, thanks to you.

I said that I would do it. I went down with Louisa to the throng of women on the beach, who began to dance and sing songs of welcome. The boats drew near, and I saw Jacky standing in the prow of a whaleboat. He looked directly at me, his face collected up in a pouch of anger. I saw no trace of gladness.

It's hard to recall the next part. As I had been instructed, I called out: Why don't you come ashore? We're all waiting for you.

But in the next moment, I began waving my arms, pointing the boats away from the beach. Go away, go away, I shouted, at the top of my voice. These words have come to haunt me. Some say they believed I was warning the soldiers to keep clear of the trap, others think I was letting them know I did not want to leave.

At that moment, I had no idea what I wanted. Though I didn't want to meet Jacky's stony stare, neither did I want to see him with a bullet through his heart.

The boats drew away. The men descended from the cliff. I couldn't tell what would happen next. There appeared to be a plan, the way the boats came and went, but it was impossible to follow. Something different would happen at the last moment of their approach. Perhaps it was just the weather.

Nobody paid me any attention now, except to throw occasional glances of scorn in my direction. An hour or more passed. A solitary boat approached. As it was clear this boat was not bent on war, the tribe held their fire. A man I later learnt was the surgeon helped a young man over the side.

It was Tia, the servant of Oaoiti.

He swam ashore, and the boat left. When the people recognised Tia, a cheer went up. He was embraced on every side, and inspected for wounds, but it was clear he was well.

When his welcome subsided, he told us that Oaoiti was alive and well on board the ship. At first, nobody believed him. But he described in detail the way the surgeon had tended Oaoiti's wounds and nursed him back to good health.

Turning to me, he said that if I would go back to the ship, Oaoiti would be sent ashore. Another boat was coming soon to fetch me.

That didn't happen that evening as the breakers rolled fiercely on the rocks. The boat drew away, and another night passed. For the moment I was safe from the tribe. But I knew I couldn't stay. That I would have to leave John behind. Either way, I was lost. When I heard that Oaoiti was alive I felt passionate joy, but I knew that, unless I first went out to the ship, he could not come ashore. We were to be exchanged, one for the other. We were each other's price.

The fires were stoked. The mountain gleamed with far-off reflected light. The debate raged on, speakers asking what should be done with me, while the rest sat listening in a circle. Some said Oaoiti would want me to stay, while others saw, as I did, that he would not be allowed to leave the ship until I left the pa.

When dawn was near, Waiariari turned to the people, asking if they agreed to my release. In one voice they shouted: Let the woman go. Let the woman go.

In the morning, I was cast out.

The boats came again. Dark clouds crawled down the sky to meet the sea.

The first boat carried Oaoiti, dressed in European clothes. I had some time to observe him, for he stood in the thwarts and addressed the people of Ngati Ruanui, ranged along the beach. His words mostly washed over me, because I couldn't take my eyes off his appearance. A Scots cap was tilted over one eye and it might have looked rakish and appealing, were it not for the rest. Next to his skin, he wore his customary blanket. Over that was drawn a white shirt, the cuffs turned back at the wrists, and on top of that bulged an army jacket worn back to front, with all the buttons done up. I knew someone had done this to him, for he couldn't have buttoned the jacket like that without help. And I knew that, behind him, would be two shiploads of sniggering soldiers and sailors. Already, I could hear the sneers in their voices, as they persuaded him that this was the way to dress for style.

I tried to hear his words. I have been well treated on the ship, he was saying. I have gifts for you. If you put down your weapons I can come ashore.

The weapons were lowered and he was able to pass free. I don't think he saw me, until he was almost upon me. Then he looked startled, as if he hadn't expected to see me, or had overlooked the reason he was taken hostage. I can't believe he had forgotten us. He had been possessed by me.

And now, I suppose, he was not.

I will never know, for Louisa and I were pushed roughly into a canoe which began paddling towards the *Alligator*, not waiting for the whaleboat.

I didn't look at Oaoiti again. As we passed each other, I averted my eyes. I remember this with shame. I could not acknowledge this man in his ridiculous costume.

As the canoe approached the ship, I heard the sound of fiddles playing a dance tune; I think it was a quadrille. I sensed an air of gaiety about the proceedings. Men lined the sides of the ship, watching my approach. The *Isabella* was hove to close by and ringing cheers and shouts of encouragement accompanied my progress from the men lining her decks as well. When I boarded the *Alligator*, a stampede like a haka rang on the decks, accompanied by whistling and clapping. I felt the men draw close to me and I realised that as Oaoiti's appearance would excite the tribe, I too was a novelty here, wearing my two cloaks and the long greenstone earring. Jacky walked towards me. It's hard to say what I expected — perhaps an embrace, or a hand to steady my arm, some smile of welcome.

He acknowledged me, as of course he must, in front of all those men. But there was dark rage seated behind his eyes. I understood, even before he had spoken, that already he was humiliated, first by the man who had left the ship, and then by my own wild appearance. I pushed my loose mane of hair behind my shoulder, and waited for him to speak.

Where is the boy? he said.

They wouldn't allow him to leave. They wouldn't let me have him.

The captain, whose name was Lambert, approached me, and shook me ceremoniously by the hand. My dear Mrs Guard, he said, welcome aboard. We are so very pleased to have you with us. You will find everyone on board anxious to make you comfortable, after so much suffering. You have had such terrible times. We have suffered for you.

Thank you, I said. I am well enough.

I saw him wince slightly. But you were attacked and injured.

I have been treated kindly, I said.

He shook his head in puzzlement. I wasn't sure what was expected of me.

Jacky was watching me. I thought, I cannot speak well of the clown they have just put ashore. He is already the subject of mirth.

I am sorry for the trouble I have caused you all, I said, choosing my words with care. I looked down at Louisa who was clinging to me like a little wretched monkey. My daughter has suffered a great deal. And then, as if to add substance to my words, I said, We look to God in times like this in order to gain strength.

I saw the look of relief in the captain's eyes. Dear Mrs Guard, he said, we must let you go below and recover yourself.

Jacky said, Some women's clothes were sent for you, in case you'd lost your own. You'll find them in the cabin below. With that, he turned away, leaving a young rating to show me the way.

I laid Louisa down in the bunk. Her cough had flared up again but she fell asleep straight away. I found three sets of clothes I usually stored in Sydney set out in the cabin drawers. I shook as I let the cloaks slide from my shoulders and stood naked in the room. I ran my hands down over my thighs, and, turning, saw myself full length in a mirror on the cabin door. I stared in astonishment.

You might not look at yourself in this manner, Adie. It is not done for women to take too great an interest in what lies beneath their stays. But now I was different and I lingered for a moment, before beginning my transformation back into a respectable woman. I touched myself everywhere, placing my hands beneath my breasts and feeling their weight in my hands, and then the dark secret place where pleasure hides. I cried out, once, and only once. If my husband had walked through the door then, all might have been well. But I had set the catch firmly in its place, and there were no footsteps in the passage.

I took up a petticoat and a brown woollen dress, which no longer fitted well, for I had lost weight in some places and filled out in others. I covered my shoulders with a cream-coloured shawl. I wound my hair up in a knot and pushed in a comb to keep it in place. In the mirror, I saw a woman quite different from the one who had stood there before. A light had gone out in her eyes.

I didn't know what to do next. I might have stayed there, but I heard the sound of cannon fire, and the ship lurched in grinding jolts. I ran along the passage and made my way to the top deck. Another boat had been sent out to fetch John but had returned empty-handed.

This had taken place while I was changing. Baskets of gifts had been taken to the shore, but they had been accepted without John being given in exchange. I could have told them that. The interpreter, a man called Battersby, who I was yet to meet, had told Lambert the tribe were a treacherous bunch. Soon afterwards, a musket had been fired from the shore.

They will not find him, I said to a man who stood beside me. This was the surgeon, Mr Barrett Marshall, who would become such an eager friend in the following days.

Really, he said, his eyes glowing moistly behind his spectacles. Do explain, Mrs Guard, I am so anxious to learn your opinion of these matters. Nobody can have such first-hand experience of the natives and their way of thinking as you. Why, yours is a truly remarkable experience.

Indeed, I said, casting my eyes down.

You will be relieved to be free of your captivity.

Yes, I said, in the same humble tone. How could I tell him that in captivity I had thought myself free, and that in freedom I already felt myself captive again.

Jacky walked over to me, ignoring the surgeon. I could see they were not friends. They would not hand him over, he said. The traitorous bastards, we have given up their chief.

I tried to explain. The chief you gave back is not the one who has taken John for his son, I said.

What more do they want, Jacky shouted.

I said again, they have given up Oaoiti in exchange for me, not John.

Then perhaps I should send you back, and they will send John.

I held my tongue. I could see there was no point in arguing with him, or trying to tell him that if it was an eye for an eye, they had got the wrong one. Barrett Marshall was looking embarrassed and eager to make his escape, but the captain joined us.

It looks as if it has been a fruitless expedition, Guard, he said. As far as the boy is concerned. I'm sorry it's come to this.

It was for the boy that we came, said Jacky.

Lambert looked sideways at me. He was certainly an important part of our mission, he said.

Are you going to let them get away with this? Jacky yelled, his eyes bulging. You came to protect British citizens, and one is still held. You cannot pick and choose one over the other. You can't say that having rescued my wife and daughter — for which I am properly grateful — you've finished the job. What did your instructions say? I've seen them too, you know. He paused in his tirade, and when Lambert did not answer him, he said, You were to stop the natives from making trouble with the white man. You were to teach them a lesson.

Without loss of life, said Lambert. If possible.

You haven't even frightened them, Jacky said, his voice thick with contempt.

You have, I said. You burnt their pa at Te Namu. They are full of grief for that.

Lambert brightened at this. Well, he said, I am pleased of that. We can certainly frighten them more. You should go below now, Mrs Guard, for there will be some action soon.

But of course, I didn't go below. For now a drum beat to quarters, and both vessels edged towards the shore until they touched bottom. The first cannons had only been an opening salvo. Now hundreds began to be unleashed above me, directed at the two pa.

For nearly three hours, and with more than three hundred cannon balls fired, the furious assault took place. The canoes that floated in the river between Waimate and Orangituapeka were the first to go, then the roofs of the two pa. When a few shots had been landed, a white flag was run up above Waimate. I wondered if it was some remnant of Louisa's clothing. Then it was taken down, and raised again, as if, within the pa, someone had told them the signal for a truce. I guessed this was something Oaoiti had learned on the ship.

I ran looking for Lambert, but he was out of bounds from me now, as the siege continued. I found Jacky, and grabbed his arm, which he seemed to raise like a shield against me. Please stop them, I implored him. Do something.

Do something? What should I tell them? What did you do, make a present of our son to your friends?

That is not fair, I cried. Our son may well be killed at this rate.

Well, it's too late for tears now, Jacky said. You don't seem to know how to get him back. To hell with them, I say.

As I walked away, I saw Mr Barrett Marshall being sick over the side of the ship.

I heard men's crazy laughter as they loaded more cannon. I remembered convict men run amok, and knew that when work like this began, it was a sport that can't be stopped until it's run its course. Long before it was over, I went below, crouching on the floor of the cabin with pillows over my ears. But nothing kept the sound at bay, the shudder of each blast.

Eventually, they left off, and we ran for anchor further south, where we would stay for several days, until the weather allowed for a new attempt.

Chapter 34

At sea, 4 October 1834

I do not like the way my wife and Barrett Marshall have their heads together as if they are friends. Whenever I go to talk to her she is speaking to him. There is something strange in her manner that makes me think the worst. And it is more than that for when I speak about the rescue of our son she seems almost indifferent. As if she no longer thinks of herself as his mother. Tonight I went to the cabin where she sleeps with our daughter. I am very tired Jacky she said.

I caught her by the wrist and backed her against the cabin drawers and pushed her a bit. Do not do that to me Jacky she said in a voice I did not know.

He is our son I said. You are not helping.

He belongs to Ngati Ruanui she said.

He does not belong to anybody but me.

They will not give him up.

You could have fought for him.

At that she laughed in a mad way and spat at my face. I dropped her wrist and smacked her hard about the arm. Fight she said. You think I did not fight.

I do not know what you have done Betty I said. Our son does not belong to a Maori tribe is all I know.

Don't be so certain she said. He is going to be their white chief. You might have to fight him 1 day.

I walked out without another word. As if I wd give up on John whatever crazy things she says to me. Thanks be neither wd the Captain. He can see he has the Maoris on the run.

6 October

At daylight we set forth again to Waimate. At 11 the gig was made ready and officers of the regiment headed ashore to demand John's release. The Maoris said they would not let him go.

They came back to the ship. Another 2 hours off they went again. The Maoris came down to the beach with my son. He was held up by an old man. So at least I could see he was alive. The old man put him on his shoulders. You see that I said to nobody in particular, they act like they own him. John waved to the soldiers. But when they asked for him again they were refused.

Who is that man I said to Betty. She was standing near the rails.

That is Mapiki she said.

7 October

The boats went back this morning. This time a message was delivered to say Mapiki was willing to bring John on board the ship if first some officers went ashore and waited while he was delivered.

It is because he wants presents Battersby said. The scoundrels are still humbugging us.

I have said no rewards, no ransom money, said Lambert.

You gave Oaoiti presents Betty said. I did not like the note in her voice. Nor do I like the way she has so much to say for herself to everyone but me. And I did not like the way the men hung upon her every word.

He was injured Lambert says rather quick. That is different. I felt some rebuke in what he said for there have been grumbles — Barrett Marshall, of course — as to how my men had stuck the bayonet in. At any rate he said I am not risking men's lives.

They will be out for revenge said Battersby, you mark my words.

And so we sailed away again and I was more low in spirits than at any time on this expedition for it seemed to me that after all Lambert had made the decision to give up. So I went to him and said sir listen to me. We have been going to these people where they can see us and flaunt themselves before us not to mention my boy. But what we need is stealth.

I saw interest dawning in his face. What exactly do you mean Guard?

I reckon we should land men further south where they cannot be seen as we did with the interpreters. Only this time I mean the regiment. All the soldiers. Then, while the ships are standing off in their usual position they will think the soldiers are aboard but all the time they will be stealing up from behind. Not for nothing had I watched Te Rauparaha at his tricks.

That is a clever idea he said. Tomorrow we will put that plan into action.

6 officers, 112 men and my men from the *Harriet* were landed. Charley was pleased to see me again. He and the men were cooped up aboard the *Isabella* where they had not been treated well, short of rations and worked hard as deckhands to earn their keep. The master had taken against the crew. Now we were out for action I was pleased enough to see him too. We landed a 6-pounder carronade 2 boxes of ammunition and a quantity of round shot as well as 3 days' provisions and 2 days' spirits.

I was in the last boat to come ashore. Some soldiers were already part way up the cliff before the Ngati Ruanui knew we were coming. The face of the cliff is almost perpendicular but 2 plaited ropes hung from stakes driven in the crevices. When

Ngati Ruanui saw the soldiers almost upon them a cry of terror went up.

Charley and me and the crew were still upon the beach as well as some sailors. Word came that John wd be brought to us. There wd be no more trouble. The troops above were ordered to withdraw to the edge of the cliff.

Mapiki walked towards us. He wore a white feather on his head and a mat across his back. Astride his shoulders sat my son also dressed in a mat with feathers in his hair. Behind them followed the scoundrel Oaoiti. And all along the beach, the warriors followed on.

Before I could reach them a sailor by the name of Ruff who was captain of the fo'c's'le on the *Alligator* had seized John. He was held to Mapiki's back by a string.

Ruff's knife flashed in the sun as he cut the cord. John fell on the ground. Ruff took John and thrust him at me as I ran towards them. Then he turned his musket on Mapiki with his free hand. He took aim at close range and shot him in the back.

From up above the soldiers had heard the shot. They thought the Maoris had begun to shoot and so they began to fire their weapons at the line of them who had followed Mapiki. Panic and confusion broke out as they hurried this way and that. But they had nowhere to run and hide. I heard officers above call for the soldiers to hold their fire but blood was raining all about and running on the sand and bodies falling.

I made my way towards the pinnace. All about me I heard the whimpering of the dying and hands reached out and fell. A voice called help me Haari but I do not know whose. My son screamed out in my arms Mapiki come and save me but the old man was but a scraggy bundle of feathers and straw mat face downwards in the seaweed. I pressed John's face against my shoulder so he wd not see. The sky seemed to turn green in colour. Dark cloud chased shadows over the beach. My nostrils were full of the stinging smell of gunpowder. I looked above. The soldiers standing shoulder to shoulder made a red ribbon band across the top of the cliff. Still voices were shouting do not shoot, you must not shoot. It was the officers but nobody paid them any heed. Soldiers be soldiers and they had spent many a long week on that coastline and were spoiling for a fight.

The pinnace was bobbing on its mooring, pulling away from the beach. I had to wade towards it all the time the boy wriggling to get free from my arms. The crewmen who had come with me started clubbing Maoris like seals upon the rocks. Their blood seeped over the beach. The breakers caught it and spread it out to sea. The stain floated around the boat. Come I cried out be done with it. For now my only wish was to take my boy to safety and the line of fire had turned our way.

They came then ducking and weaving between the musket fire blood on their hands. We rowed off out to sea towards the ships. Some scores of men and women lay dead behind us upon the beach. The Maoris who were in the pa took up their muskets and a gun battle broke out on the cliff. But it was too late. Soon the tribe left the pa climbing down their ladders and vanishing into the bush. Later it was told that Waiariari who ruled over the 2 pa was the last to leave. They wd tell how he left slowly taking one long last look over the ruins of what was once his village. The musket balls were flying all about and knocking the dirt around him. I think it was the surgeon who said this. But he is a great 1 for a good story.

As we pulled away I had trouble in my heart. But also in my arms I had the son I loved.

The boats had all returned to the ships. It began raining fast. A shroud of mist fell across the sea between us and Waimate and everything was blotted out.

So the *Alligator* and the *Isabella* headed away and left the soldiers and sailors on land. For an instant the fog parted. We saw the Royal Standard flying above one of the pa but it was as nothing to me. I am a whaler not a soldier and now it was over I wanted nothing more of war.

When I went on board the *Alligator* I saw Betty on the deck.

Here I said here is your son.

Did Mapiki give him to you?

I shrugged and turned away.

He is dead is he not she whispered.

He is a rascal I said.

For another 3 days we stood off until it was safe to land. Each night the sky was lit by fires as the pa were destroyed by the soldiers. The blazing ruins were so bright you wd think they could be seen as far as Sydney town. In the end it was safe to bring the men back on board. They spoke as if it had been a great adventure and a merry one at that. I had put a sign on the chief's house and called it Government House. Another they called the Pig and Praties for that is what they enjoyed for their tea each night. Some other wretch's hut they had made a barber's pole to place above and called it a shop for Fashionable Haircutting. They brought with them the head of a Maori. It was dented through being kicked from man to man on the beach.

Betty went white and shuddered. It is the head of Mapiki she said.

Betty

As we drew away from the Taranaki coastline, that last night, I watched the pyramids of fire rolling and boiling in the sky, the reflection of those ferocious flames cast upon the waters below. I smelled burning manuka wood, sweet and spicy like cooking fires.

Later, much later, someone came to fetch me, and I was taken to eat dinner at the captain's table. A midshipman had been sent to watch my sleeping children. In the days since he had come back to me, John was by turn angry and defiant, kicking his heels against the floor, at other times, lying still and hunched on his bunk.

The messroom looked very pretty with flags and lights. The cooks, now their work was done and dinner served, played a mazurka, as chirpy as birds at daybreak. My dear, Lambert said, over the brace of roast pigeons they had cooked, and some fine claret, now it is over, you can tell us all about your adventures.

When I said nothing, he said, perhaps it is all too distressing?

I have witnessed terrible things, I said. I saw my brother killed before my eyes. For a moment I was overcome. I didn't want to tell of David but I felt I must.

We will do all we can to put right the wrongs against you, said the captain.

I took a deep breath. I wish to put the matter behind me as quickly as I can, sir. My husband and I, and here I looked at Jacky as winningly as I could, wish only to be a united family again.

I turned to the surgeon then and said, I would be obliged, Mr Barrett Marshall, if you could spare some time to examine my daughter, for our life among the savages has left her weak and unwell.

Upon hearing this, the men around the table, even Jacky, nodded in sympathy. Captain Lambert raised his glass. To Mrs Guard, he said, a brave and plucky little woman.

I would not have described myself as little but enough of that.

JOURNAL OF JOHN GUARD

At sea, 13 October 1834

We sailed for Kapiti and landed to take on water. Te Rauparaha saluted me when he heard what we had done. Why did you not bring me some of my enemy to eat, he said.

Lambert put out a proclamation then to be handed out round the settlement. He showed me a copy that I have in front of me. Written from HMS *Alligator* at Entree Island, the English name for Kapiti, it is dated 11 October 1834. It begins by telling of the arrival of the 2 ships of war belonging to His Majesty King William the 4th in consequence of the horrid murder of the crew of the *Harriet*. The rest were made slaves it says by the people of

Mataroa, Nummo, Taranachee and Wyamati. The proclamation tells then of the severe punishment inflicted on the tribes and says that the King of England however much he might want to be friends with the New Zealanders wd not countenance what they had done to my family. If it happened again it wd be treated with equal severity.

It is about this time I noticed that my wife no longer had any words at all for me.

Part 8

What is Past

Chapter 35

At sea, October 1834

From Kapiti we made sail for the Bay of Islands where Busby the British Resident waited on the report of Captain Lambert. Busby was rather sour and as full of God as ever. I have heard of this expedition he said in his prissy English way. It was taken without consulting me.

Good God man said Lambert. Did you expect us to ask your permission while a white woman and her children were at the mercy of savages? You are here to protect such unfortunate people.

I am here also said Busby to prevent outrages against the Maori people. I wd like an account of what has taken place Captain Lambert.

I have made a proclamation said Lambert. He handed over a copy.

Busby stood and looked at it. So you have made an example of Ngati Ruanui he said.

Yes said Lambert. You could say that.

You do realise sir said Busby that this is the first time armed warships have engaged against the New Zealanders. We have been at war with the Maoris.

Yes said Lambert and if the natives interfere with the King of England's subjects I wd do it again.

The *Harriet* crew and me and my wife and children were put ashore while the ship stocked up for the run to Sydney. My family and I stayed near the pa of a chief I had had dealings with in the past. We took a place near the beach in a hut with a plank roof. This was a come down after life on board the ship. Yet I was more than fed up with that. I had had enough of the soldiers and their airs and jokes that did not make me laugh. I liked well hearing rain on the roof above us in the night and the sound of land birds again. Our children slept in rough cribs beside us. John was the same as ever to me but my wife seemed troubled about taking him back as if he no longer belonged to her. I think he is a boy who likes the company of men.

I said to Betty I have put myself out on your account and I will have some good cheer from you. But she turned her head away, and did not favour me with a word.

Well then. 2 can play at that game.

I asked her. What did you get up to with that man.

Cambridge Street, the Rocks, March 1835

I do not know where my wife is. Jezebel. Nothing will please the woman. You are cold Jacky she says and there is tears everywhere. What am I to do.

She is full of grief said her mother Harriott Deaves with deep reproach. She has lost her daughter. She was your girl as well Jacky Guard.

I know that I said. I have tried to give her comfort.

Then her mother looked at Charlotte. I do not know what has passed between these 2.

Mostly I have not wanted to lay my poker in my wife since

we came back from New Zealand but neither does she fancy me. Months have passed and it has all got worse. The night we laid Louisa to rest I took her to me. She did not like it well. I said we best mend things but she acted like a hellcat. She has too much of her grandmother in her. I have heard a story or 2 about Granny Pugh that would curl a man's hair. Well it seems I have landed myself the same. But I cannot say I did not want her when I took her.

Now she is gone and I do not know where. It is said she took a ferry up the Parramatta some 4 days back and I will have to go cap in hand to get the baggage back.

Perhaps she will not come Charlotte said hopeful like. So now I have 2 problems on my hands, 1 likes me too well and the other not enough.

Betty has not spoken with me unless spoken to since we left the Bay of Islands. True I was hard on her. But I reckon it was what she deserved. All the same I think back often to that night and wish some things different.

Chapter 36

15 March 1835

Dear Captain Guard

Your wife, Mrs Betty Guard, has been residing at my property this past week or so, keeping company with my sister Miss Adeline Malcolm. My sister is a kind-hearted woman who has befriended your wife in what I understand to be a time of great distress. They have spent many hours talking and comparing their fortunes, and it is pleasing to see a younger woman offering such respect to someone in middle years.

I have no complaint about such a *flowering* of friendship. Yet I must implore you to come and take your wife home where she belongs, for my establishment is sorely stretched by her presence. Our sons' nanny has had to rearrange her quarters in order to accommodate the visitors.

You would do me a great favour if you could come immediately, for others do not view the matter with the same sympathetic eyes. Indeed, my wife, a woman of normally strong constitution, has been laid low by the situation, and it requires an early resolution. A Lieutenant Roddick has also intervened, for want of a better word, on behalf of my sister, who has been part of his establishment in Sydney for the past two years. The Lieutenant finds the presence of Mrs Guard very disturbing and fears that she may not be a good influence on the reputation of Miss Malcolm.

I would not wish you to think I have anything but the best opinion of Mrs Guard who, by all accounts, is a woman of great valour and virtue, but you know how things begin, and idle words lead to grief.

Sir, it is in the interests of everyone if your good lady were to leave as expeditiously as possible.

I am having this letter delivered by my man, in the carriage, who will be happy to bring you here to my residence, to collect your wife.

Yours faithfully
Perceval Malcolm

The dew is still settled on the dahlias when Gerald Roddick arrives at Malcolm Downs. The blue gums shift and settle their leaves and at last there is a breeze. Pink light shimmers near the eucalypts; some attribute this to reflections of light from the leaf tips while others say it's the essence of the gum tree itself. The carriageway, at this otherwise quiet hour, is almost crowded with the number of people making their way towards the farm.

Roddick is on horseback, accompanied by his brother-in-law Sebastian Stenson, who arrived from England on a visit, the week before. Stenson has made the journey to see whether he might persuade the lieutenant to leave Australia and take the Roddick children to England, now that he is nearing retirement.

'I am sure it is what Emmeline would have wanted,' Stenson has said, with increasing firmness. He has not travelled well and it has taken him some days to recover. 'She would have wanted them to grow up near her family, to know her aunts and uncles and all her cousins.' Stenson has eight children, all thin and pale, as Roddick remembers them from his last visit to England. He sees no reason why anyone would want to know such a crawling nest of white mice. Sometimes he harbours the bleak thought that his son Austen is more of Stenson stock than his own, something he would prefer his uncle not to see.

But Stenson has reminded Roddick of a bitter truth. His wife did indeed express the wish, as she lay dying, that the children return to England, whereas he, Gerald, cannot imagine life beyond these shores.

All this has given a sense of urgency to his mission to retrieve Adie Malcolm. He needs to demonstrate to his brother-in-law that the children are well suited to their circumstances. And it has occurred to him that if he should turn up with this emissary from England, she will understand how serious the situation is, how imminent the departure of his children should she not return.

Sebastian is not pleased to be roused at five in the morning but Roddick says they must travel before the heat.

'I'm puzzled as to why you're at such odds over a governess and a convict's wife. Are they worth it?' He has asked this more than once, for Roddick has been evasive over the details of his pursuit.

'It's a matter of honour,' Roddick says for what seems like the tenth time.

They are overtaking a carriage carrying a single person, the servant who delivered a letter to Captain Guard the evening before. Guard declined his offer to accompany him.

When I fetch my wife, that is, if I do, I will not be driven there by a lackey. I will find my own way. The servant spent much of the night in the Currency Lass, before wending his way back to Parramatta.

And, as the two men put their horses to the gallop, they come across another carriage, in which three people are travelling. These are Jacky Guard himself, Ivy Kentish and her husband, Robert. Anyone observing this trio would notice that the two men look strained and anxious, though the woman seems indifferent to all but the passing delights of the landscape.

Roddick reins in his horse for just the few moments it takes to register the identities of these travellers. Then he sets out at a hard gallop, with Stenson following more sedately, on his unfamiliar mount. They are the first to arrive at Malcolm Downs. Percy approaches them, looking awkward and apprehensive as he crosses the lawn.

'I have told you, I'm not a fighting man,' he says. His wife stands close behind his shoulder and gives a small snort of disgust, as if she had hoped for better but was not expecting more. His sister walks through the trees from the path that leads to the cottage, accompanied by Betty Guard.

'What is it to be?' asks Stenson, willing to take part now that the action is at hand. He is a fair man with what passed for a withering stare in his days in the army. 'Is it a duel?'

Roddick twitches uncomfortably. 'I think you've misunderstood. That would be beyond the pale.'

'Which of these ladies is the subject of the quarrel?' Stenson asks, his gaze settling on Betty. 'Well, I need not ask.'

'It's not as simple as that,' the governess begins, as Percy tries to effect some introductions. But they are interrupted by the arrival of the following carriage. Roddick's gaze has fallen on Betty Guard.

'Well,' says Stenson, 'I understand there is honour at stake.' He turns to Roddick for an explanation but his brother-in-law looks as if he is having difficulty remembering why he is here.

'You're mistaken, sir,' Betty says, addressing Stenson. 'It's not my honour that's at stake, I am only the cause of another's disgrace.'

'I am quite confused,' says Stenson.

The carriage draws up, and Jacky Guard steps down, leaving Kentish to help his wife. Ivy is wearing a sprigged pink muslin dress with small appliqué roses on the skirt and a green hat with a rolled-back brim.

'Now *there* is a lady,' says Stenson, his eyes wide with admiration, and after the second round of introductions he says; 'Well then, Mr Kentish, perhaps you will be kind enough to act as a second for Mr Malcolm, for it seems the gentlemen are preparing to fight.'

'No, they are not,' says Adie, flinging her arms around her brother.

Jacky walks over to his wife and takes her by the arm. 'I've come to take you home,' he says. Ivy stands behind him, her hands clasped in the air, while her husband looks red-cheeked and alarmed.

'I have no home,' Betty says, flinging Jacky's hand away.

'Sir,' Roddick says, remembering himself and addressing Percy, 'you must order the woman to leave.'

'I have asked her to go. That is why I have invited the lady's husband to come and collect her. What more can I do?'

Although the morning is still cool, there are beads of sweat on Roddick's moustache. He raises his fists and advances on Percy, who backs towards the roses. 'You don't know what's at stake, man.'

'Come on Percy,' Maude says, 'why don't you just get it over and done with.'

'What kind of man are you?' Roddick says, still bearing down on his victim.

Adie's scream fills the morning. Percy has fainted clean away and lies collapsed at his wife's feet.

I walk back down the path and into the cottage. Inside, is a wash bench that serves us for our toilette, holding cakes of soap, two clean towels and the pitcher and bowl. I put the jug to one side so I can vomit in the bowl. Behind me, I hear Adie arrive, and turn to see her looking as scared as a cornered opossum.

'It is all right, Betty,' she says, 'they've gone. Everything is all right.'

I place a towel across the bowl. 'It's nothing,' I say, wanting to push past her and get rid of the contents.

'You mustn't be frightened like that.'

'Frightened?' I want to laugh in her owlish earnest face. 'It is you who has had the fright.'

'Yes,' she says, sitting down suddenly and heavily. She shades her face with a trembling hand, and I am very sorry for her. 'But you're ill.'

'For the moment, but it will pass,' I say, fatigue washing over me. 'What happened out there was play-acting. I doubt that anyone would have got hurt, even if there had been a fight. You learn to tell the real thing when you see it. As you'll have gathered.'

At least I suppose that she has understood. One evening earlier in the week she said to me, you must write all of this down, what has happened to you. I'd laughed when she said that, for it is easier for me to talk than to read and write. What I took her to mean was that she hadn't heard everything I'd told her. I'd seen her short upper lip twitching between her gentle snores. And yet she really wants to know, as if I hold the key to life's mysteries. As I watch her, I feel sad, knowing she is in love, or thinks she is, and that it will not come easily to her, being with a man. How much more simple it would have been if Percy could have remained her companion and friend, if he had not married Maude.

When it comes down to it, I don't know how much I have told her, and how much I merely think I have. In the nights spent here among the trees, with the moon slanting between the shades, I have talked to myself at length, trying to make sense of what had gone before.

'We must seem silly to you,' she says at last. 'Inconsequential.'

I want to agree, and say that yes, it was like a tableau at the Royale where only my husband seemed like a real person, and even he had an air of menace like the man who lurks at the edge of the stage, about to disappear behind a curtain. But I hold my tongue on the subject of her family, for she has been hospitable to me, and I have made life intolerable for her.

'It's nothing,' I say again, 'you haven't made me sick, I am simply with child again.'

When I have made my escape with the bowl, and cleaned my face and straightened my clothes, I ask Adie what has happened. My hair is combed and arranged, held up in a knot with some of her hairpins.

'Lieutenant Roddick and his odious brother-in-law have left,' says Adie.

'I'm so sorry,' I tell her.

'It was never possible,' says Adie. 'Besides he's too stubborn a man for my taste.' She smiles wanly. 'Not that I've ever had a taste for a man before.'

'Too many Greek gods in temples,' I say, and for a moment she almost laughs, pleased with her protégée. 'But what of my husband?'

'Captain Guard and the Kentishes have gone down to take refreshments at the Ramparts,' says Adie. 'They said they'd be back, but they looked very grave.'

'I can't believe my husband would bring those people with him.'

'He thought Mrs Kentish might talk you round, but it seems she is more delighted with the novelty of the situation than in making a serious effort to converse with you.'

'She was always a silly woman,' I say.

Adie looks even more worried than usual. 'I thought the matter was solely to do with my brother's embarrassment, or rather Maude's fury at having us here. But there is more to it than that. From what I overheard pass between Lieutenant Roddick and your husband, there's talk of a court of inquiry into the rescue of the *Harriet*'s passengers and crew.'

'I see,' I say, and straight away I do see that someone might raise questions. 'It will be Mr Barrett Marshall.'

'I should think so. I'm sure I told you that I met that young man at Government House some months ago. He was on his way to England, set to write a book about what he described as "the incident".'

'In that case, I suppose I will have to go and find Jacky,' I say. 'This baby?'

I look at her, trying to work out what was going through her head.

'Is this the one that the gossip is about?'

'Adie,' I say, with some astonishment, 'Do I look like someone who is five months gone?'

'Forgive me,' she says, going her old familiar shade of crimson, 'I'm no expert in these matters. But I can't help wondering, if that is the case, whether it isn't time to put the past behind you. Surely your husband tried to do his best for you, even if he's rough in his ways.'

'He's been with another woman,' I say. 'He thinks I don't know. Why do you think he brought the Kentishes?'

'Because the Kentishes are familiar with the ways of the Governor, and how the colony is administered.'

'That is not the reason. It is because my own family is not willing to look at me straight. I see the way Charlotte's hungry eyes follow him around the kitchen.'

'Charlotte?'

'Well, of course.'

'But you'd been distant with your husband before you returned to Sydney. You told me so yourself.'

So, I think to myself, she has heard more than I have given her credit for.

When had this baby happened? The night Louisa was buried, I suppose, though I was in such a torment of sorrow I scarcely remember what passed between me and my husband. I know he had his hands upon my wrists, and that he shouted at me. He said, You will not let me near you and it is killing me, Betty.

I do remember saying, Shouldn't you have thought about that?

The long day passes, and still nobody comes. I cannot keep still in the tiny cottage. I want to get out of here and walk on my own. But where? The place seems surrounded, as hostile as Maori territory when there are scouts in the bush. Towards evening the serving girl comes with another tray and we are both very famished. 'We have been sent to Coventry this time,' Adie said at some stage, but I don't know where Coventry is; I only know I'm stuck here, and soon I will have to leave.

At dusk, the cook sends us barley soup, which Adie would have turned her nose up at were she not so hungry, and slices of cold mutton, full of gristle. There is no dessert. When the serving girl comes to fetch the tray she tells us she has heard in the kitchen that my husband and 'his party', as she describes it, have retired for the evening to a Parramatta inn.

'Adie,' I say, when we are alone again, 'whatever happens, this will be the last night we spend together.' She nods her head in agreement, for we both know that things cannot continue in this way any longer. 'There is nobody else I would tell. But I will tell you — I am in some agreement with what Mr Barrett Marshall thinks.'

'I thought as much,' she says. 'That does make things difficult.'

'I don't want to be cross-examined any more than I have already been by the newspapers,' I say. 'For if I show sympathy to what befell my friends at Taranaki, it will be taken as an admission of wrongdoing committed against the Maoris. If you know of Captain Lambert's proclamation, you will see that I am setting myself against him and the official story.'

'You haven't told your husband?'

'How could I?'

'Oaoiti?' Adie ventures.

'You've heard how they dressed him up like a laughing stock and sent him ashore. My husband's a jealous man at best.'

'But he doesn't know what happened?'

'I haven't told him anything of what passed between Oaoiti

and me. Though he has asked me. Because of this, we have nothing to say to each other.'

The moon has come up, one of those big hanging moons like I used to watch in Taranaki. I want to tell her everything that happened. But that will surely turn her against my husband once and for all, and that is not what I have set out to do. Somewhere in the space of this peculiar day, I have realised I would like peace between him and me, even if we go our separate ways.

'Tell me,' she says. 'I have a need to know.' She does not say a right, and I like her all the better for that.

So I do tell her. How in the morning at the Bay of Islands, after our first night alone, Jacky had bid me rise and wash my face. I complained that I had long been without rest and this morning there was surely no need to hurry. He had pushed his face close to mine. I have business for you, he said.

What business? I asked, afraid of him.

You will find out. Now see to your children for I am going out.

He did not return till near evening. I held Louisa on my hip and skipped stones with John on the calm waters of the bay, as I had learnt to do in Charley's company. He complained that he wanted to go with his father. We tried to catch a fish and failed. After awhile he settled in my company. There was flour and other victuals at the hut, and I made some damper but by late afternoon we were hungry.

On his return Jacky stood at the door and looked through me as if I wasn't there. He carried bread and oranges, for the missionaries had planted orchards and there was much fruit to be had around there.

He placed these on the bench, and spoke with his back to me. We are poor, he said, we have nothing left. I have no ships, and no way back to our home. You can do a bit of trade for me.

I was filled with foreboding.

There is gunpowder at the pa next door, he said, looking at me at last. His eyes were mean. One of the chief's sons has heard you are rather nice to men. He would like you as a wife for a night.

You would not do this, I said, backing away into a corner.

Six canisters of gunpowder. That would be very useful. A gift for Mr Campbell to whom I owe some favours. Like the loss of two ships.

It is not I who lost the ships, I said.

No, but I have been at sea looking for you some six months now when I could have been restoring my fortunes and repaying Campbell.

You have your son, I said, my voice full of stones.

It is time you earnt your keep, Betty.

I looked at him with contempt. I knew he was waiting for me to refuse, to protest my virtue. Very well, I said. I will go.

When I returned to him next morning, the gunpowder was handed over. I hear you were not worth the price, he said. I thought he took a grim pleasure in that.

Probably not, I answered.

You didn't have to do it.

Perhaps, I said. But you want someone to pay for all that has happened. You can't have it both ways, Jacky.

I saw how bitter he was with himself, and sorry for what he'd done.

When the *Alligator* arrived in Port Jackson, there were bands playing and flags flying. A flotilla of small boats came out to meet us and sailed with us the last part of the way. I looked over the rails at the crowd gathered. There must have been two hundred at least, men and women, and children being held up to get a better look. A military guard stood to attention in honour of the returning soldiers.

I wonder what is happening, I said to Mr Barrett Marshall, standing beside me. Some big event must be taking place. Or someone important is coming to town. You don't think the King is paying Australia a visit, do you?

My dear Mrs Guard, he said, I think you will find that it is you the people are greeting.

And he was right. When I stepped off the boat a cheer went up. I found out afterwards that a whaling ship had left the Bay of Islands the day before us, and already the whole town knew about the rescue.

As I disembarked onto the dock, my shawl drawn up around my throat and my bonnet tied firmly beneath my chin, a man pushed his way to the front of the crowd. Mrs Guard, he cried. I am so happy to meet you. He wore a hairy brown coat, a red waistcoat and a yellow cravat. My name is Ralph Wallace.

She has nothing to say to you, Wallace, said Jacky close behind me.

Who is he?

Nobody you need to know.

Sydney Morning Herald, said my new friend as I tried to make my way towards my mother and half-brothers who were among the crowd. At the sight of my mother I began to cry. Mama, I said, we should never have taken David with us. I am so sorry Mama. He loved you to the end.

I could see how people around me were affected. The cheering quietened down as my mother stepped forward and embraced me. Oh Betty, she kept saying, and squeezing the children and me. At least we have you. Women in the crowd had taken out their handkerchiefs, and I saw men put their sleeves to their cheeks.

Mr Wallace stood at a respectful distance. Forgive me, Madam. When you are able, I would be grateful for a word.

I have told you, said Jacky, leave her alone. Clear off.

No, it is all right, I said. I will tell you my story. We have suffered the most terrible ordeal. I am eternally grateful to everyone who helped to rescue me and my children, and brought us to safety.

I can see the trials you've been through written on your face, Mr Wallace said.

Yes, I said. I have suffered.

Beside me, I felt Jacky relax, almost heard his gulp of relief.

But my mind was made up. I did not want him as a husband any more.

'I can hardly blame you,' says Adie, her face pallid in the moonlight.

'But now I'm having another baby. In my misery after Louisa died, I couldn't think clearly, wasn't sure where this baby had come from. But it's his, not due for many months, towards the end of the year.'

'Does he know?'

'I haven't told him. There's nothing to hold me now, except our son. Perhaps it would be better to let him go. I did that once when I had no choice. If I am ever to make my own way, now's the time.'

'You haven't got long to decide,' says Adie.

'I know that,' I say. I can hardly keep my eyes open. It's usually Adie who falls asleep the minute her head touches the pillow, and I who stay awake much of the night. But this time I'm drowning in sleep before I lie down. I feel Adie ease the buttons of my dress and take off my shoes.

Chapter 37

Parramatta, March 1835

This morning I took a room in a small hotel in this town. This place is different from any I am used to. It does not make me comfortable in myself. I fed the black swans that swim on the river as a boy wd when he has nothing else to do. They cackled and arched their necks at me and squawked when I ran out of food. As evening fell they tucked their heads beneath their wings and I think that even they have turned their backs on me.

Mr Kentish and his lady wife have stayed overnight. I believe they have an engagement with the Governor tomorrow night. I do not wish to see them. I am sick through and through. The lamps still shine across the park from Government House but 1 by 1 the lights go out. Even the taverns grow dim.

I thought I should eat at the tavern but when it came to it I did not want the food and pushed away the plate. I had some rum and left. What is there to do but sit here and think about the morning. Betty is going to take her leave of me. I saw it in her face as plain as I saw the look she has when she is with child.

That is something she cannot hide from me.

In my mind I see the girl who long ago I took to collect oysters.

I have been reading the book my father gave me as a boy. I have not read it in a long time, though I keep it with me.

Does a man beset by worry have the leisure to sleep? This is what the book says. 'If the good Man of the House had known what hour the Thief would come, he would have watched, and not suffered his house to be broken up.' It comes to me then, that I am the thief in my own house.

Betty

Adie touches my shoulder, some time around dawn. At once, I am fully awake and clear-eyed.

'You must decide,' she says.

'What would you do?' I say, though in my head I know already.

'There's a saying. Even God cannot change the past.'

'Adie, don't talk to me in riddles,' I say. 'I'm not so keen on the Bible, as you know.'

'It is not in the Bible,' she says with some irritation.

'Your Greeks?' I say, smiling.

'Well, yes,' she admits. 'A man called Agathon. But I think of it as true.'

On an impulse, I go over, put my arms around her and drop a kiss by her ear. 'I would have died without you,' I say. The bracelet she gave me glints on my arm.

'Nonsense,' she murmurs. 'After all you've been through. You'd have survived.' But her arms tighten around me, and for a moment we hold each other before I step back.

She is pink and I see a hint of tears in her eyes. 'Thank you,' I say.

She begins packing her few possessions into a portmanteau. 'What will you do now?' I ask.

She takes a deep breath. 'I promised Emmeline I would look after her children,' she says. 'I can't think how I forgot about that. Poor little Austen, he'll be beside himself without me there.'

She does not seem surprised when I tell her that I am going for a walk.

JOURNAL OF JOHN GUARD

Parramatta, March 1835

I thought I had not slept at all but I must have dozed because Betty's knock woke me from a slumber in which I saw her dying. I woke with a shout startled by the rattle of the door handle. Her voice outside said let me in Jacky. It is me Betty. When I opened it I wanted to seize her in my arms so relieved was I to see that she was alive.

She stepped aside from my embrace and closed the door behind her.

Betty I said. I heard myself croaking, not able to bring out the words I wanted to say.

What do you want of me Jacky she said.

I want you to love me I said helpless as a woman.

She looked puzzled. But I have always done that.

You cannot love 2 people at once.

Yes it is possible.

It is not possible for me I said. She gave me a look then which told me she knew of Charlotte. At that moment I thought no woman could know me like Betty does.

I shook my head. It was not like that. I have no love for your aunt.

Doesn't that make it worse she said.

I thought she was trying to make a fool out of me as if our trouble was all to do with me. What surprised me was that she was not in tears. Once she wd have wept and begun to plead with me. But something in her had changed. For a moment I thought I saw the eyes of Granny Pugh looking at me. That frightened me.

You wd have chosen him I said as rough as I could. That clown.

Why did you dress him up like that she asked her eyes hot.

I did not. It surprised me that she wd think that of me. It was Charley I said.

She was silent. She knew what I said was true. And she was surprised Charley hated the chief enough for that.

At last she said I never had a chance to choose anyone. I do not expect you to understand what happened between Oaoiti and me. But it had nothing to do with what I have felt for you. We are different.

I wanted to ask her in what way but I did not. Of course we are different her and me. Still I said you loved him.

Yes she said. I did and now I do not. But I am forever changed by it.

I saw there was no shaking her over this nor could there be any taking back the things that had been said.

Betty I said. I want you to forgive me for what I did to you at the Bay of Islands.

She looked at me in a blank way, as if she did not know what I was talking about then gave a short hard laugh which I did not understand.

Betty

The son of the chief I was to lie with couldn't have been a lot younger than me, but he had a boy's narrow chest and weedy arms. He was dressed in European clothes as if in honour of the occasion, though he had taken off his jacket when I arrived and sat nervously unbuttoning his shirt buttons. I could see that he was frightened.

I greeted him and he nodded in return with downcast eyes.

Was this the first time he had been with a woman? Had I been his father's idea, or was any of it their idea? I thought it more likely that Jacky had offered me.

I put my hand out and touched the young man's skin. He flinched as if my whiteness might be catching. I let my hand rest on his and he appeared calmer. I turned his hand over and saw dark stains like ink on it. I breathed deeply and closed my eyes for a moment, and I smelled again the familiar scents of Te Namu — the brush mattress, the ti-tree walls, food cooking near by. I was so hungry I felt faint, and a longing stirred inside me. It would not have been difficult to fondle and excite him, to trade my body for gunpowder.

I opened my eyes to see the boy unbuckling his belt. I said, Do you work for the missionaries?

He said he was one of Henry Williams's printers, something I had guessed from the ink.

What would the Reverend Williams make of this? Your father paying for a woman like me?

He wouldn't like it.

No, of course not.

Would you tell him? he asked, with alarm.

Well I might, I said. It depends on whether I see him or not. This was hardly likely, but I didn't tell him that.

All of a sudden, he pulled his clothes together and fled from the room. Soon afterwards, his father appeared in the doorway.

You'll be in big trouble with your husband, he said to me in Maori.

Yes, I said. My hands were shaking. But what is to be gained from me making love to a young man who would rather not? Besides, he has a good employer in the missionaries and I don't think they would like this.

At this he nodded and withdrew from the room. After that, a woman came and said that I could stay the night if I wished.

I was given food, offered with kindness. In the morning I walked back to the hut where we were staying. On the way I met

Edward Markham, an English adventurer who Jacky knows, and does not like, as I recall. He had a smile playing around his lips, but not his eyes. He raised his hat. Nice morning, Mrs Guard, he said and tipped me a wink.

Six cases of gunpowder had already been delivered at our door. The next day, the *Alligator* sailed, our booty stored on board.

What I did not know was that Markham had joined the ship, for he was leaving New Zealand, and the Captain had given him a berth to Sydney. I kept below decks as much as I could in order to avoid him. When the children and I did venture forth I saw that Barrett Marshall had taken up with Markham. I raised my chin, and thought that is where it will stay when I touch land in Australia.

Did it make it easier to forgive because I had not done what Jacky asked of me?

I suppose it must, because forgiving is what I have chosen to do. My husband could not have known that, in offering me up in rage, he gave me the first true choice of my life. I will not explain or defend myself. I know what happened. He will have to decide for himself.

Now a second choice has been delivered to me. I will take you back, I said.

The secret of that night stays with me.

Chapter 38

Governor Bourke gives his dinner party this evening at the Parramatta residence. Jacky and I are his extra guests. Earlier in the day, Ivy Kentish and I have been shopping, as if we are old friends.

The shops are far better here than in Sydney, announced Ivy gaily, as we floated from one establishment to another, several boxes in our arms.

I don't know what I'll use for money, I said as we set out. Besides I have fancy dresses at home.

Well, you haven't got time to go and get them today, and besides, you want to be up with the times when you step out this evening, Ivy said.

She assured me that the money was all taken care of; she had smiled charmingly at Percy Malcolm as she and her husband took their leave after a late breakfast. Breakfast had been an elaborate affair, taken on the Malcolms' lawn under umbrellas, all of us — Percy and Maude, and their sons Herbert and Nathaniel, who seemed pleased to be the centre of their mother's attention for once; Adie; Lieutenant Roddick who had ridden forth again in the early morning; Jacky and me, and the Kentishes.

Percy slipped me an envelope, Ivy said. He said it was for you and me.

Really? But what for?

Why, because he knows how badly his wife has behaved. It is for treats, he said when he gave it to me, meaning not a word to a soul about what has happened here. He knew you wouldn't take it.

It is Adie to whom he should be giving envelopes, I said hotly.

Oh, I think somehow she will get a large envelope. Wouldn't you say? His own sister.

Jacky had wanted to leave right away, after I had agreed to go back to the Rocks, but I wanted to go back to Malcolm Downs once more, to take proper leave of Adie. And from there, one invitation flowed into another, and it seemed that if we did not stay to breakfast it would be considered rude, just when things were being mended all round. Besides, I was feeling, if not exactly carefree, at least as if I might enjoy my life again.

Why is the Governor inviting us to dinner this evening? I ask Ivy, as we retire to the inn to unload our boxes. (Ivy has some of her own, though she had brought a portmanteau the previous day, for since the wreck of the *Waterloo* she never travels anywhere without a complete change of clothes.)

Well, says Ivy, smoothing the pleats in her day dress. It's true, there is to be a court of inquiry in England, about the *Harriet* affair.

Is that what they're calling it?

Indeed. The inquiry may not be convened straight away but I think Governor Bourke will want you to be seen in the very best light.

You mean he will not want to have sent two ships to war on account of a currency lass with no manners?

Ivy is only momentarily abashed. I've always thought of you as rather clever, she says.

But not clever enough for the Governor?

You have a big heart, Betty. Look what you did for Robert and me in New Zealand. Don't give it a thought.

My Granny would call it making a silk purse out of a sow's ear, I say.

All the same, when I enter the dining room, it is not the first time I have had all eyes upon me, only now I feel more at ease than when I stepped aboard the *Alligator*. Looking around, I see familiar faces. I am wearing a dark blue dress with a wasp waist and a huge skirt, leg o'mutton sleeves, a ruched bodice and a wide neckline that skims the sleek tops of my breasts, where a gold chain nestles. Long and graceful waterfalls of rubies hang from my ears. My hair is piled high, exposing the length of my throat. I carry a fan. The Governor steps forward and offers me his arm.

'Mrs Guard, thank you *so* much for coming. I have placed you beside me at table this evening, and we will have a good talk about everything.'

We don't talk about everything, of course. I talk about the races that are on in town, and where the best fruit can be bought at the markets, and tell him a little about our house at Port Underwood in New Zealand, and how I had endeavoured to start a garden there. I sense that I am saying exactly what he wants to hear.

A Frenchman who says he is an artist attends the dinner too. He speaks rather loudly, and with enthusiasm for everything, with little pattered asides in the French language. I must paint you, he says, I really must, your silhouette is magnificent. His name is Thierry, and nothing will do but that I sit for him this week, as he leaves for Paris in a month. I look first to see whether the Governor is approving of this idea, and then at Jacky.

The Governor smacks his hand on the table and says: 'But you must Thierry, you cannot let such a charming inspiration go to waste.'

It is on the tip of my tongue to say that I will soon go to waist if Thierry does not attend to the matter, but I close my lips on such an indelicate comment. Glancing at Jacky, I see he is nodding his head, looking somewhat bewildered. I think, with a tingle of my old spite, that he should be getting used to me being the centre of attention.

So it is arranged that I will sit for Thierry the following day. I would like to leave some image in place of myself. I have nothing of Louisa but a lock of her hair. And if I am to have a picture done, it would be nice if it was while I still had a figure. I have yet to turn twenty-one and I am expecting my third child.

For a brief month or so, before my condition becomes apparent, I have a flurry of social life in Sydney. I am all the rage at fancy parties. I do want you to meet the delightful Mrs Guard, host-esses say. I have had more than one toast proposed to me. The picture that Thierry paints is much admired. On these rounds, I meet Gerald Roddick, but avoid him. I don't think it my business to enquire of him after my friend Adie Malcolm. I half expect to see her on these rounds, for now that I am in such favour, there is no reason for her to be dismissed from Sydney society.

Of course, this whirl cannot last, for Jacky and I have no money, and I am nothing more than a pretender from the Rocks. As I grow stout, I withdraw from these gatherings. I imagine people asking each other, have you seen that Mrs Guard lately? But soon they will get over it and move on to other wonders.

One or another of the sea captains obliges Jacky with work at sea, and he is away on and off for several months. When he leaves, I live again with my mother. It is not that I fall out with Charlotte. I simply don't want to live at Cambridge Street any more. There is only young John and me now, not enough to make much difference to my mother and John Deaves's living arrangements. My sister Sophia has gone into service at a large house at Vaucluse, which is flash territory indeed. She has a day off every week but she comes to visit only on the last of these each month. The three Deaves boys are growing up: the oldest one is already working as a carpenter; the others go to the Ragged School.

'You are thinking of going back to New Zealand, aren't you?' my mother asks me one morning. She seems gentler than in the past. For one thing, she dotes on young John, and he has taken to her well, though still there are moments when he does not listen to what I have to say to him. I have set myself the task of getting to know my mother better. I believe I understand her more than I did for, among other things, chosen or not, my life holds a wildness about it, as hers did when she was young.

We have spent the early morning toiling over the bubbling copper, boiling up the linen, rinsing and bluing it, ready for the clothesline. I have noticed how she takes a pride in clean clothes, even though it takes all of Monday to iron and press the laundry, and many blisters from the iron as she takes it from the stove. Harriott and John Deaves do not seem the happiest couple at the Rocks, for they have lost their spark, but on Sundays, when the family walks out, they are among the best dressed in the neighbourhood. Through this alone my mother has gained some authority as 'a good woman'. Now we have stopped to rest, or at least I have, for it is close to my time, and I have done as much as I can for the moment.

'I will have to see what Jacky thinks,' I say.

'You still have land over there?' she prods.

I tell her yes, for I have been turning over in my mind the land at Cloudy Bay, in particular shining little Kakapo Bay, where until just last year I had a home. There is nothing to be done until I give birth, but I have been wondering whether Jacky will consider a return. I expect to have word on whether it is safe to go back when he comes home from his travels.

Part 9

Kakapo Bay

Chapter 39

Jacky tells me there are great shifts occurring among the Taranaki Maoris. Hundreds are going to live in the Chatham Islands, which lie far beyond New Zealand. Many have already left. I do not ask about Oaoiti. It is best that I do not know. He tells me, too, of another bout of fighting around Cook Strait. But many more sealers and whalers have arrived, and it sounds as if the stakes are becoming more even. Te Rauparaha is said to have tired of war.

Meanwhile, the rules for the court of inquiry in Britain are being set. What will they want to know, I ask Jacky.

As he explains to me, they will ask whether Busby should have been consulted before the expedition set out (something he cannot answer), whether a ransom should have been offered for us and whether the interpreters had the skills to translate what was being said to them. ('Of course they did not,' Jacky said when he told me this). Then there is the question of whether the soldiers had the authority to burn the three pa.

But more important to us, the question is being asked

whether Jacky planned to murder Maoris, as the surgeon Barrett Marshall claimed when he returned to England.

This last is the one question that makes me truly anxious. Jacky has done many things but, so far as I can see, what he set out to do was get us back.

I think it better if we leave here, I said to Jacky. Sooner or later, the Governor's officials will come looking for you. Who knows, they may not all remain your friends.

That is what we have decided upon, to leave Sydney and return to Kakapo Bay. I told Jacky I would like us to farm our land some day.

At first he said I'd been spending too much time with fancy folk.

I've seen that land can produce a living, I told him. Then I confessed how I was not so keen on whaling.

But that is *my* living, he protested.

I told him of the nightmare that follows me, the cow whale separated from her calf. Supposing, I said to him, that the whale has two calves, and one goes in one direction and the other is taken by the tide in the opposite way?

He was quiet for a while. I don't blame you for what happened at Taranaki.

And that, I think, must be an end to it.

We could build a new house at Kakapo Bay, I say, further up the hill with a view to the sea, and a verandah, and rooms for each of our children, and a dining room that is set apart from the kitchen.

I received two strange proposals of marriage before I returned to New Zealand. The first was from Charley. He sat on the steps of my mother's house, one afternoon.

I will make you happier than Jacky ever can, he said when he was putting his case.

But I'm the wife of Jacky, I said, and you betray him by asking me this.

I don't think you are his wife, he said, not as far as the law is concerned.

It will happen, I said, though I am not sure myself.

I know what happened at Taranaki, he said. I was there, and it doesn't matter to me.

I will be all right, I told him. I remembered how much I had once liked Charley, but my views of him had changed. There was no point in raising the way he had made Oaoiti ridiculous in the eyes of other men, but it had told me something about the way he did things and I did not like it.

He will leave you, Charley said, if you do not have a wedding.

Oh I said, turning my ring on my finger, I think I am married enough. Jacky and I were married for life. No going back now.

Then there's nothing here for me, Charley said. I cannot bear to see you throw your life away on my brother.

When he told me that he was going back to England, I thought it for the best. Charley has never belonged here. He left while Jacky was at sea. I think we may never hear from him again.

The second proposal came after the birth of Thomas, my second son. He was born with an ease that surprised me, as if I was getting the knack of having babies. I didn't have a long lying in, and my figure shrank back to near its normal size in a matter of weeks.

I had been thinking for some time of going to see Adie, to check that all was well with her. So I swaddled Thomas up, and carried him through the Rocks and up town. Sydney was changing fast, with more buildings and shops taking the place of the markets.

When I arrived, I found the garden at Lieutenant Roddick's house overgrown and in disarray, as if nobody had tended it in a long time. I was looking at this in some surprise when the door was opened to my knock by Hettie, the cook I had always disliked.

She has gone, said Hettie, in a flat unfriendly voice.

But where?

Bound for England.

And where are the children?

With a great show of reluctance, the cook said, There is a letter here for you.

May I come in? I said, for the day was growing hot, and I had planned to stay awhile and rest within the shade of the house.

She sat me in the dusty parlour, and produced an envelope from behind the silverware, on a tea trolley. It was meant to be delivered to you a while ago, she said with indifference.

While she fetched me a glass of water, I opened the letter and read it.

Dear Elizabeth,

I recall how you once told me your name was Elizabeth Parker, the schoolgirl with the quick tongue. I never gave your name its due. Well, now you are Betty to the world, but I will remember you as that fiery girl with a mind and name of her own. I shall never forget the way you told me you were off to be married, all those years ago. What an adventuress I thought you. But what a friend you have become to me. I think of you with great fondness.

I do not know whether this will reach you before I leave Sydney, for a berth has been booked on board the *Maiden Miss* for the children and me. The ship sails on Thursday. I know that is close to your time. If you are able to come and farewell us that would make me very happy, but if it cannot be, I want you to know what a special place you will always hold in my heart.

Mr Stenson has persuaded Lieutenant Roddick that the children should go to England. He believes a sea voyage would do young Austen's health the world of good. I am not so certain about this, but I cannot deny that the children would be better placed if they were near their mother's family. I have agreed to accompany them on their voyage and, God willing, or the Stenson family (who, from the way that Mr Stenson talks, you would think to be one and the same), I may be allowed to stay on with them in England. The Lieutenant may join the family later.

I have been persuaded on another count that it is better to leave this place. You are the only person I can ever tell: dear Gerald and I did consider a union. I know that for his part it was on account of the children, and, to tell the truth, my own ardour had faded. Nevertheless it was proposed, and I considered it very seriously. In fact, I even accepted and for one whole night, I was engaged to be married. But, at about three o'clock in the morning, I sat bolt upright and thought that I was not in my right mind. I do not want to be indelicate, but I could not imagine the bed with two people in it. If you understand me.

I found that I could not surrender myself in a way that would be expected, either in body or soul. And yet, in my heart, I envy you. Your spirit has soared in captivity. Despite all you have endured, I would have given much to have lived a life as full as yours.

Now my dear, in case I do not see you before my departure, I take my leave of you.

Perhaps I will see the great temples of Greece again some day. I will take you with me in my heart. I do not believe I ever mentioned this, but the goddesses are as interesting as the gods.

Your affectionate friend
(Miss) Adeline Malcolm

I laid the letter down, and as I did, I heard a sound in the passage. I looked up to see Gerald Roddick standing in the doorway, dishevelled and bloodshot of eye. Mrs Guard, he cried, staggering forward. You have come for your letter at last.

Did you keep it here on purpose? I asked, as coolly as I could.

I could not think how else I might see you again.

On the chaise longue where I had laid him, Thomas had begun to cry. I gathered him up in his shawl and stood, ready to leave.

The lieutenant offered me his hand then, begging me to stay with him, offering me the world. But looking at his haggard face, and knowing the company he kept, I could not imagine a world I wanted less, even had his proposition not been so ridiculous. I thought then how strongly I wanted to leave Sydney, and how much of my life might still be fulfilled if I were to go to New Zealand again.

The night before we left, the family gathered for what I knew would be the last time at Cambridge Street. This house would now be Charlotte's, for which I was pleased enough, for few would buy a house among the sandstone Rocks of Sydney, and it was best that she had a roof over her head. My mother and John were there, and Sophia and the boys. We ate dinner together and sang some of the old songs we knew. My sister sang in a sweet voice I did not know she possessed:

> *I will give my love an apple without e'er a core*
> *I will give my love a house without e'er a door,*
> *I will give my love a palace where-in she may be,*
> *And she may lock it without any key.*

And that, too, sure and true, was the sound of Granny's voice as I first remember her. It helped me feel less afraid of the distance between us all and the place I had come to think of as my home.

Chapter 40

February 1836

Today we sail for New Zealand my wife and me and the 2 boys and the memory of the girl who is gone.

It is not for me to look into the future. That is for those with crystal balls and magic tricks in the market place and I will have none of that.

I said to Betty we will do as best we can.

This book of mine holds many secrets. I must decide what I will do with it. I do not know as how I want it handed on or not. Perhaps it will find a place in a rafter somewhere or perhaps I will throw it in the sea.

All of this will soon be forgot.

Betty

I walk late one evening at Kakapo Bay. The first part of our new house is built, and we have moved into the kitchen part and the main bedroom. I carry Thomas on my hip. John runs ahead.

He usually does these days, but now that are were home again, it is just childish energy. When we returned to New Zealand he came back to me, as if there had been nothing between us. He stumbles on something lying in the grass.

Mama, he calls, look what I've found. He picks up a large object and carries it like a shield before him, offering it up. His face shines with pleasure that he has something to give me.

There, glimmering green and milky white, is the dish I had thought lost forever. How such a large plate could have escaped notice, or being trampled, is one of the miracles of coming home.

It is June when we make this discovery. June is a wonderful month, the time of Matariki, which is the cluster of stars known as the Pleiades. These are the seven daughters of Atlas placed in heaven to form that group of stars, something I would not have known had I not been taught by Miss Adie Malcolm at the Ragged School in Sydney. Matariki means a plentiful time for food, the main bird-catching season when birds fat from ripe autumn berries are snared and preserved for the coming year. In Taranaki we ate berries too — miro, tawa and makomako. They are tart in taste, not like raspberries and strawberries, but they leave the mouth feeling clean and rinsed.

Here in Kakapo Bay, I can look at the stars every night of my life, at the sea and all the teeming life of this bay.

My bones will be laid in this soil.

Acknowledgements

I gratefully acknowledge the assistance of Creative New Zealand for providing a grant to help write *The Captive Wife*. It would have been impossible to undertake the required research and travel without it.

Nor could I have written the book without the help of Narelle and John Guard of Kakapo Bay, and Narelle's sister June Wilson. I thank the Guards for their hospitality, and their generosity in sharing information. Ian Kidman sowed the seeds of this story 45 years ago; he taught at the whaling station on Arapawa Island in the 1950s, and once nearly persuaded me to go there to live. Dr Vincent O'Malley, Dr Joanna Kidman, Dr George Davies, Jennifer Shennan, Robert Oliver and Oriana Tui are among the many who have helped me with research. Special thanks to those descendants of Taranaki tribes who have assisted with information.

I appreciate the very professional assistance of staff at Te Papa, in particular, Carolyn McGill; the Alexander Turnbull Library, Wellington; the Mitchell Library, NSW; Puke Ariki, New Plymouth; the Wanganui Regional Museum, the South Taranaki District Museum, Patea and the Opunake Public Library.

The quotation at the opening is by Geoffrey Scott, from his book, *Sydney's Highways of History*, published Georgian House 1958. Attempts to trace the author have been unsuccessful. Contact by the copyright holder would be welcome.

As ever, I cannot thank my editors, Anna Rogers and Harriet Allan, enough for their inspiration and skill.

Fiona Kidman